James Burks

Bird & Squirrel On Fire

graphix
An Imprint of
SCHOLASTIC

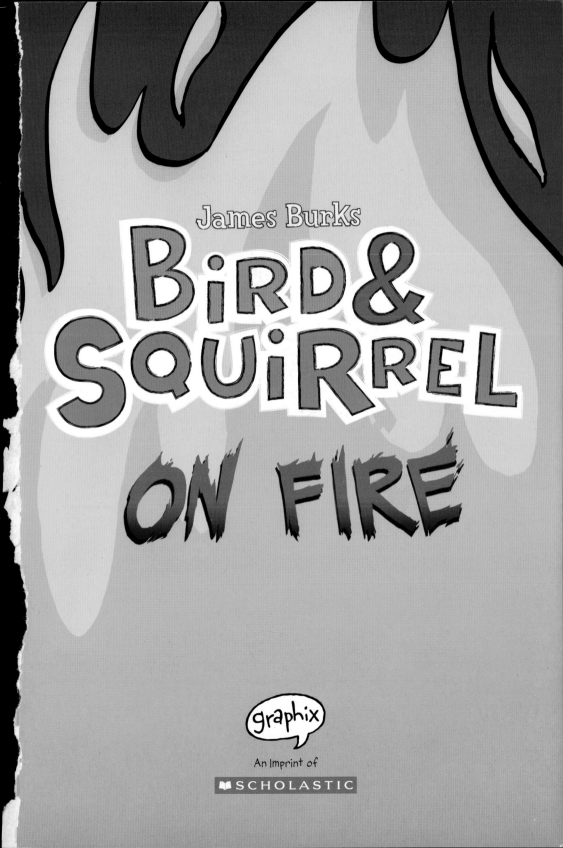

For Adam -- Here's to this and many more adventures to come. Thanks!

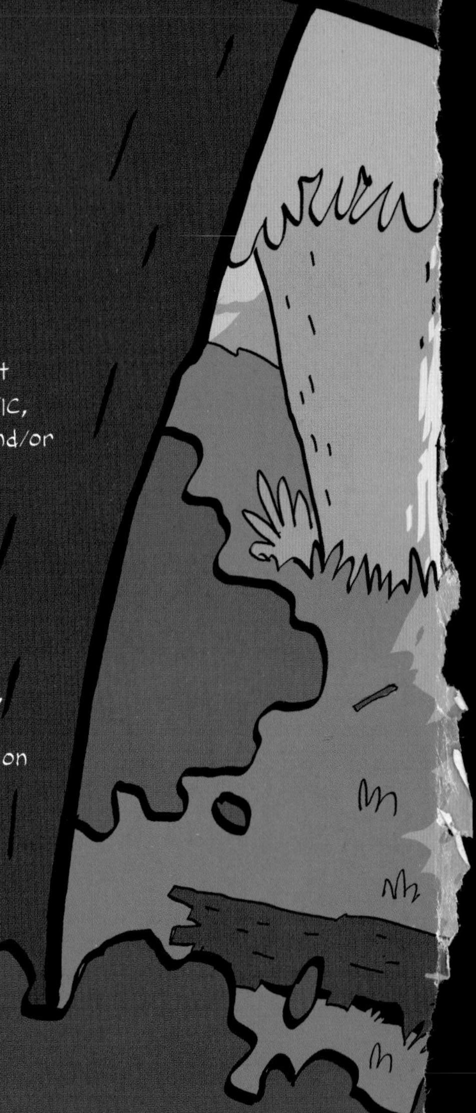

Library of Congress Control Number: 2016947440

ISBN 978-0-545-80429-5 (hardcover)
ISBN 978-0-545-80430-1 (paperback)

16 15 14 13 22 23
Printed in China 62

First edition, February 2017

Edited by Adam Rau
Book design by Phil Falco
Creative Director: David Saylor

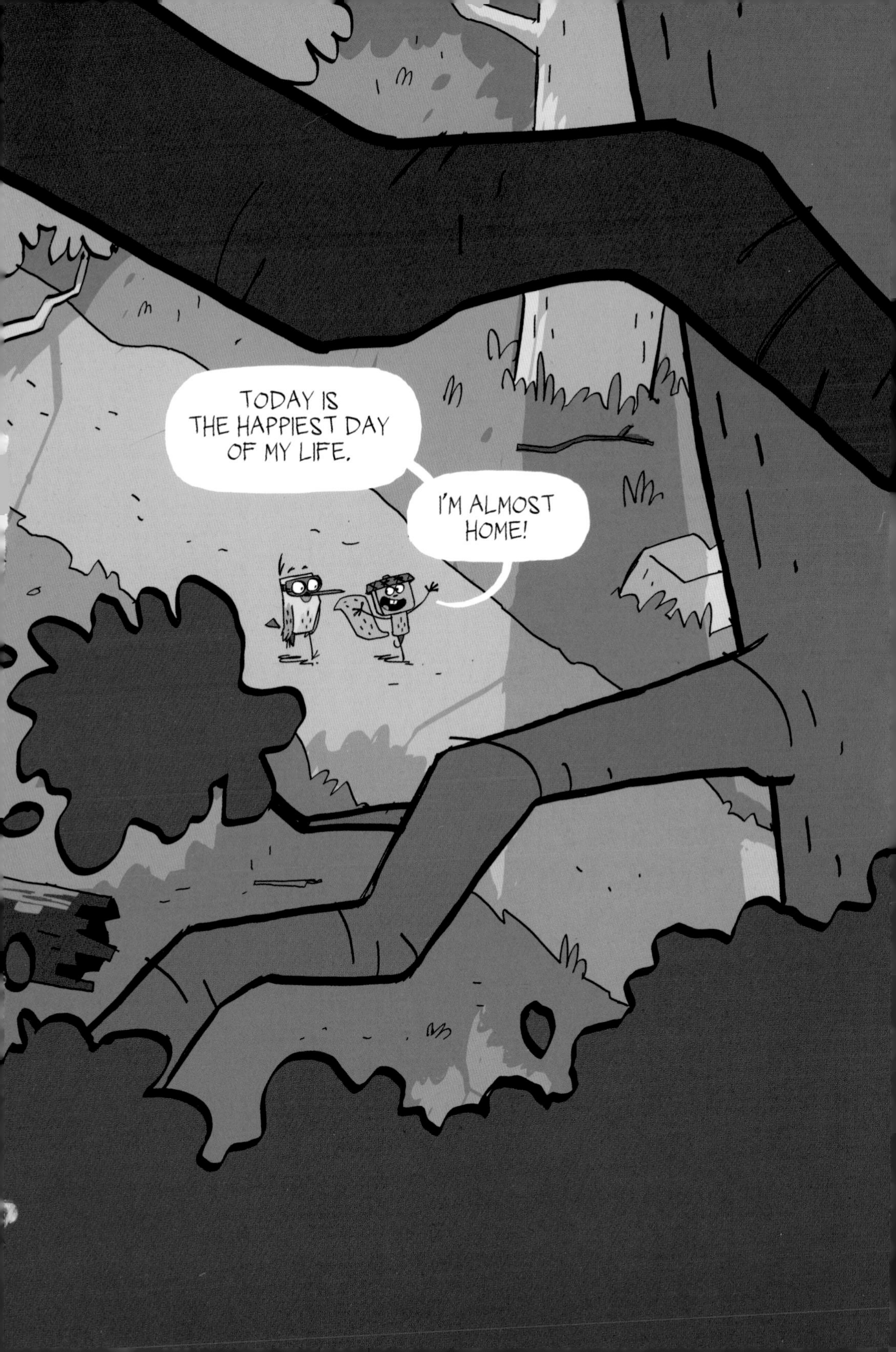
TODAY IS THE HAPPIEST DAY OF MY LIFE.
I'M ALMOST HOME!

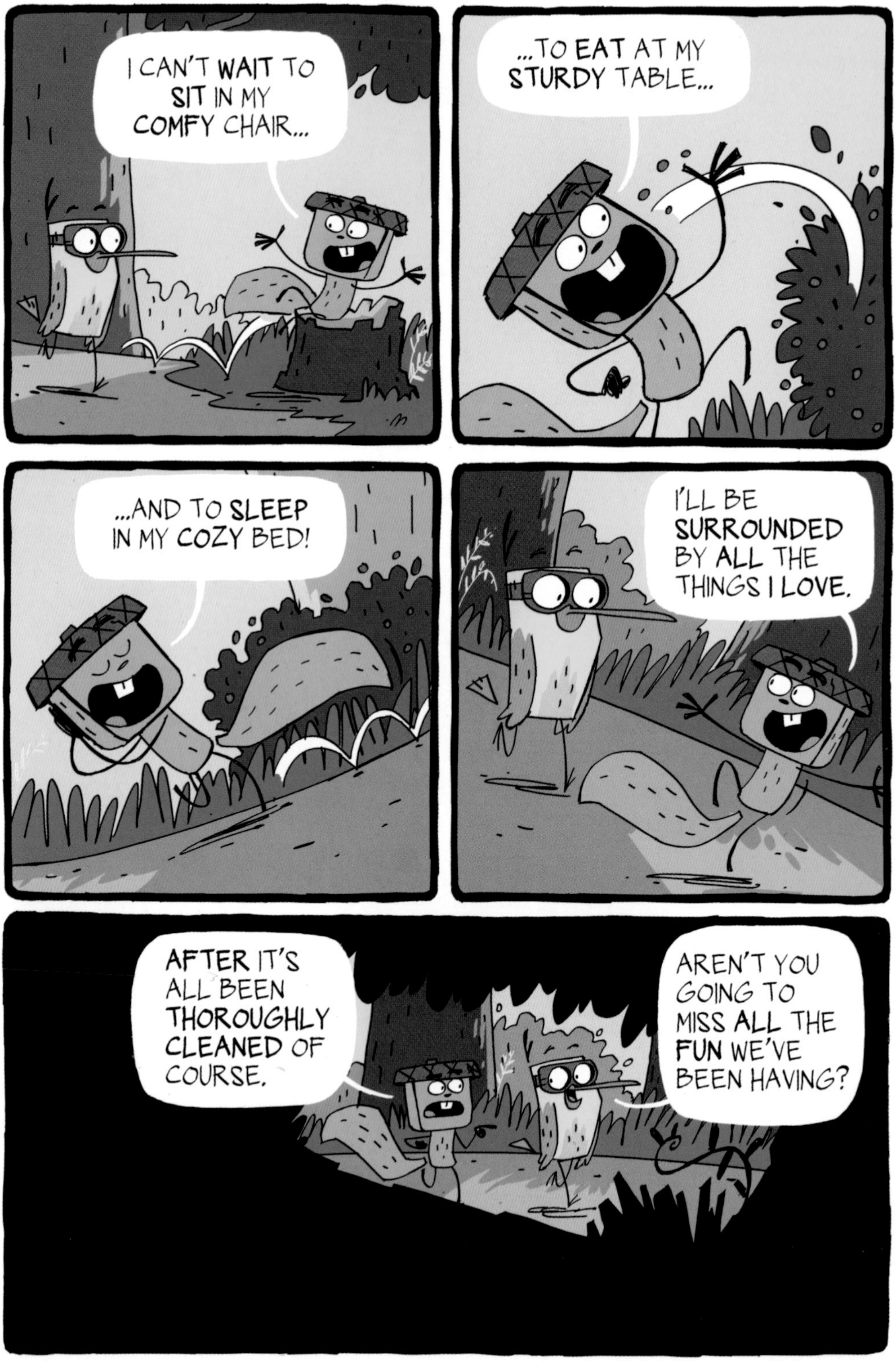
I CAN'T WAIT TO SIT IN MY COMFY CHAIR...
...TO EAT AT MY STURDY TABLE...
...AND TO SLEEP IN MY COZY BED!
I'LL BE SURROUNDED BY ALL THE THINGS I LOVE.
AFTER IT'S ALL BEEN THOROUGHLY CLEANED OF COURSE.
AREN'T YOU GOING TO MISS ALL THE FUN WE'VE BEEN HAVING?

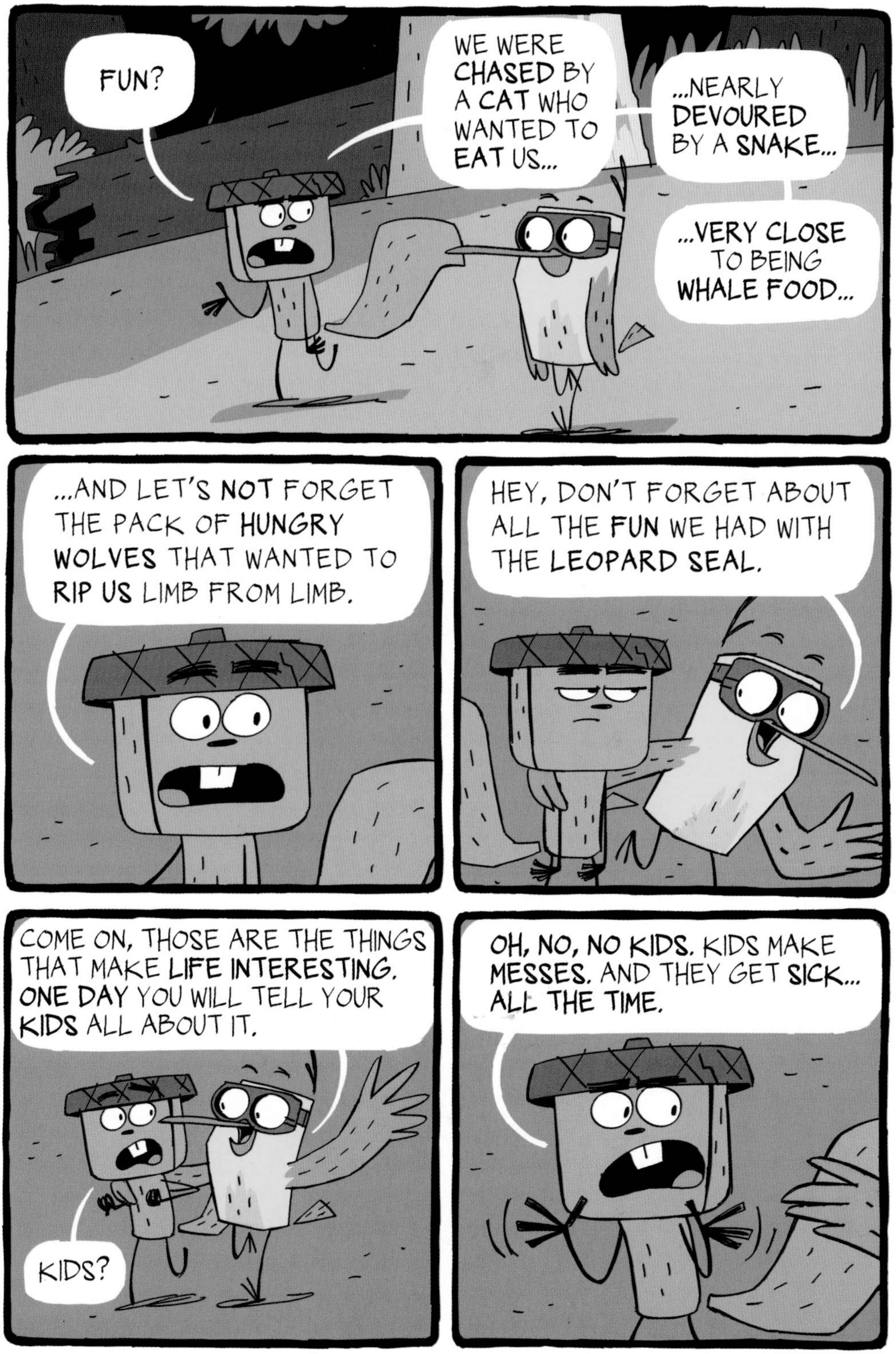
FUN?
WE WERE CHASED BY A CAT WHO WANTED TO EAT US...
...NEARLY DEVOURED BY A SNAKE...
...VERY CLOSE TO BEING WHALE FOOD...
...AND LET'S NOT FORGET THE PACK OF HUNGRY WOLVES THAT WANTED TO RIP US LIMB FROM LIMB.
HEY, DON'T FORGET ABOUT ALL THE FUN WE HAD WITH THE LEOPARD SEAL.
COME ON, THOSE ARE THE THINGS THAT MAKE LIFE INTERESTING. ONE DAY YOU WILL TELL YOUR KIDS ALL ABOUT IT.
KIDS?
OH, NO, NO KIDS. KIDS MAKE MESSES. AND THEY GET SICK... ALL THE TIME.

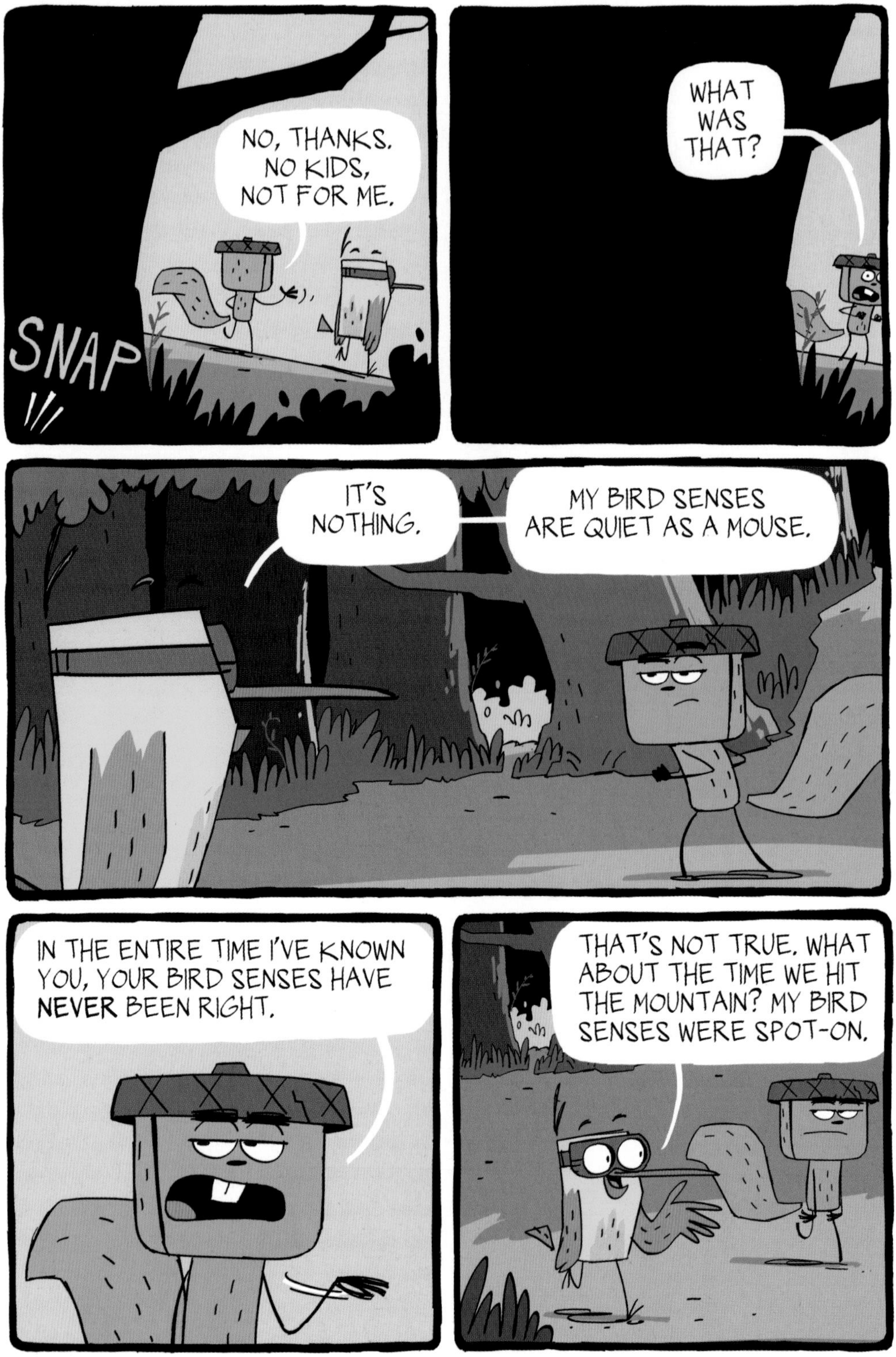
NO, THANKS. NO KIDS, NOT FOR ME.
SNAP
WHAT WAS THAT?
IT'S NOTHING.
MY BIRD SENSES ARE QUIET AS A MOUSE.
IN THE ENTIRE TIME I'VE KNOWN YOU, YOUR BIRD SENSES HAVE **NEVER** BEEN RIGHT.
THAT'S NOT TRUE. WHAT ABOUT THE TIME WE HIT THE MOUNTAIN? MY BIRD SENSES WERE SPOT-ON.

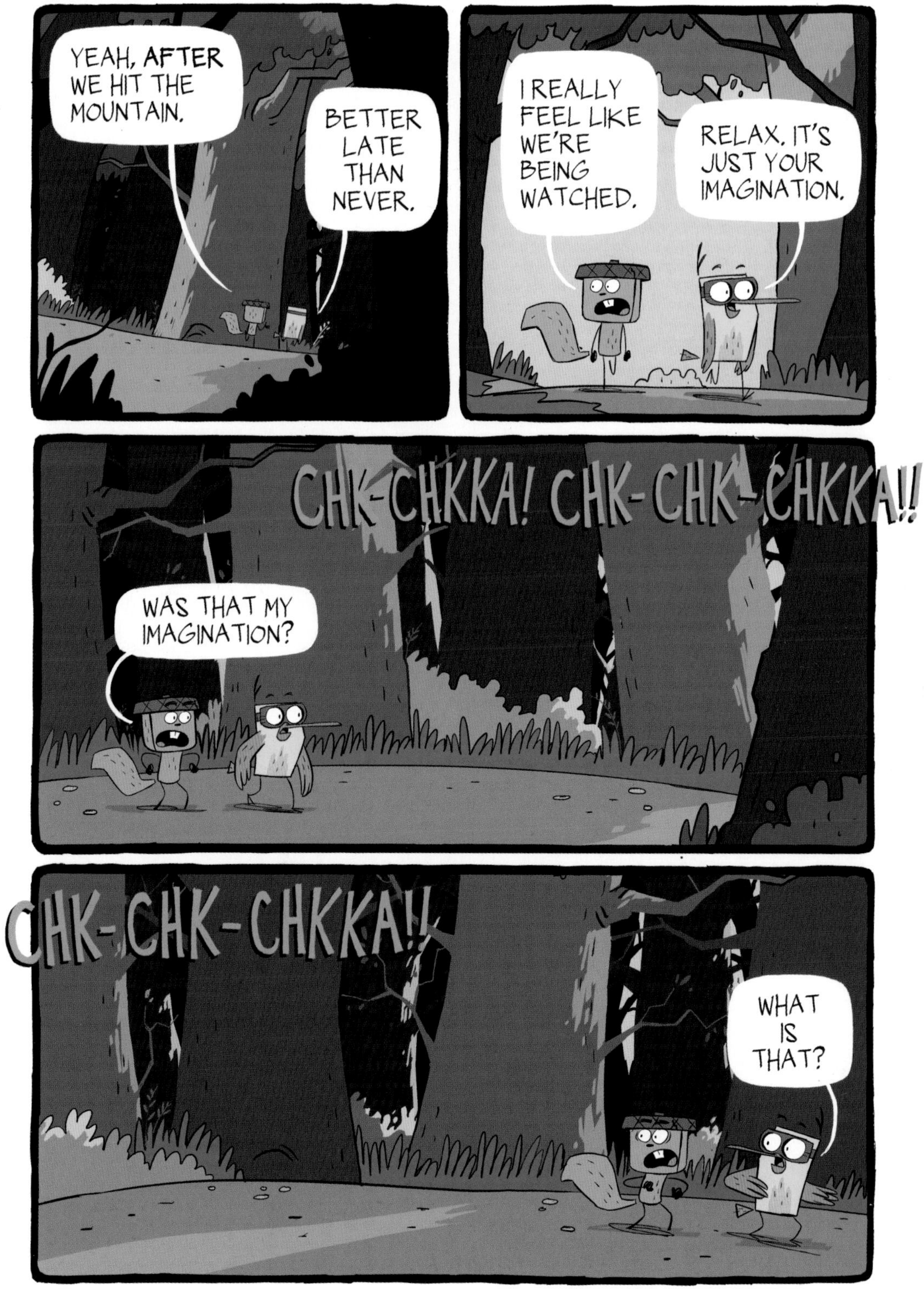
YEAH, **AFTER** WE HIT THE MOUNTAIN.
BETTER LATE THAN NEVER.
I REALLY FEEL LIKE WE'RE BEING WATCHED.
RELAX. IT'S JUST YOUR IMAGINATION.
CHK-CHKKA! CHK-CHK-CHKKA!!
WAS THAT MY IMAGINATION?
CHK-CHK-CHKKA!!
WHAT IS THAT?

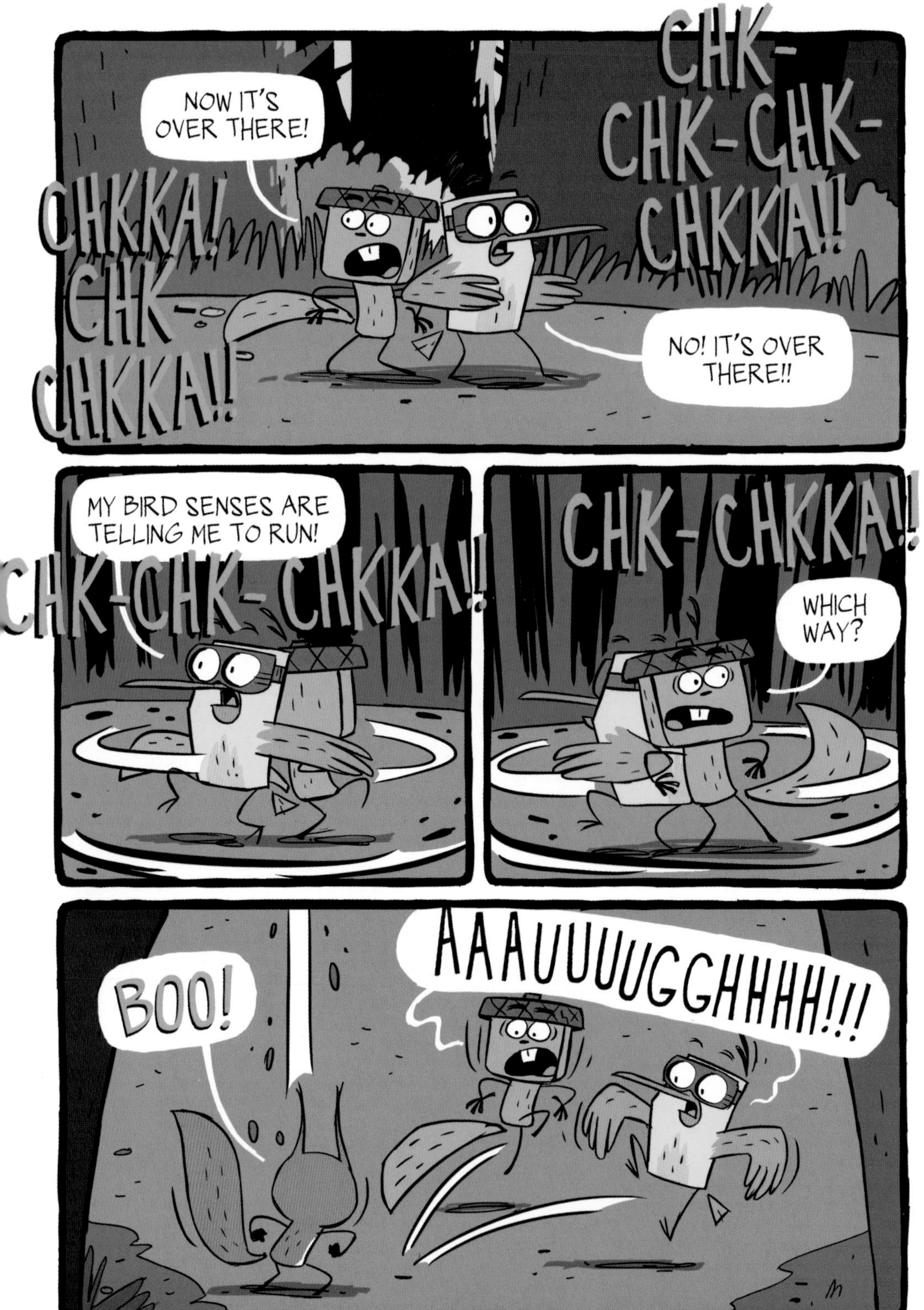
NOW IT'S OVER THERE!
CHKKA! CHK-CHKKA!!
CHK-CHK-CHK-CHKKA!!
NO! IT'S OVER THERE!!
MY BIRD SENSES ARE TELLING ME TO RUN!
CHK-CHK-CHKKA!!
CHK-CHKKA!!
WHICH WAY?
BOO!
AAAUUUUGGHHHH!!!

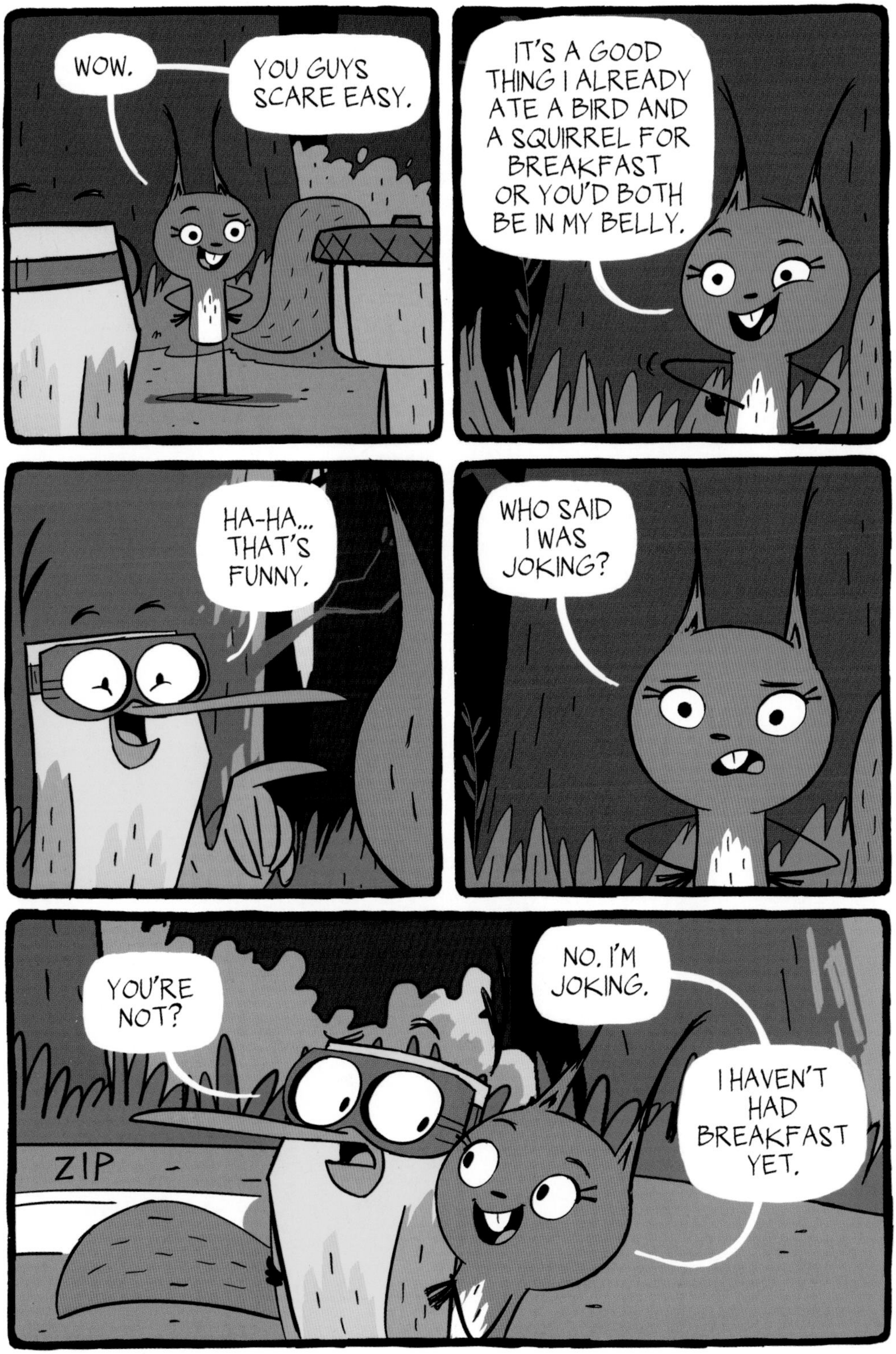
WOW.
YOU GUYS SCARE EASY.
IT'S A GOOD THING I ALREADY ATE A BIRD AND A SQUIRREL FOR BREAKFAST OR YOU'D BOTH BE IN MY BELLY.
HA-HA... THAT'S FUNNY.
WHO SAID I WAS JOKING?
YOU'RE NOT?
NO. I'M JOKING.
I HAVEN'T HAD BREAKFAST YET.
ZIP

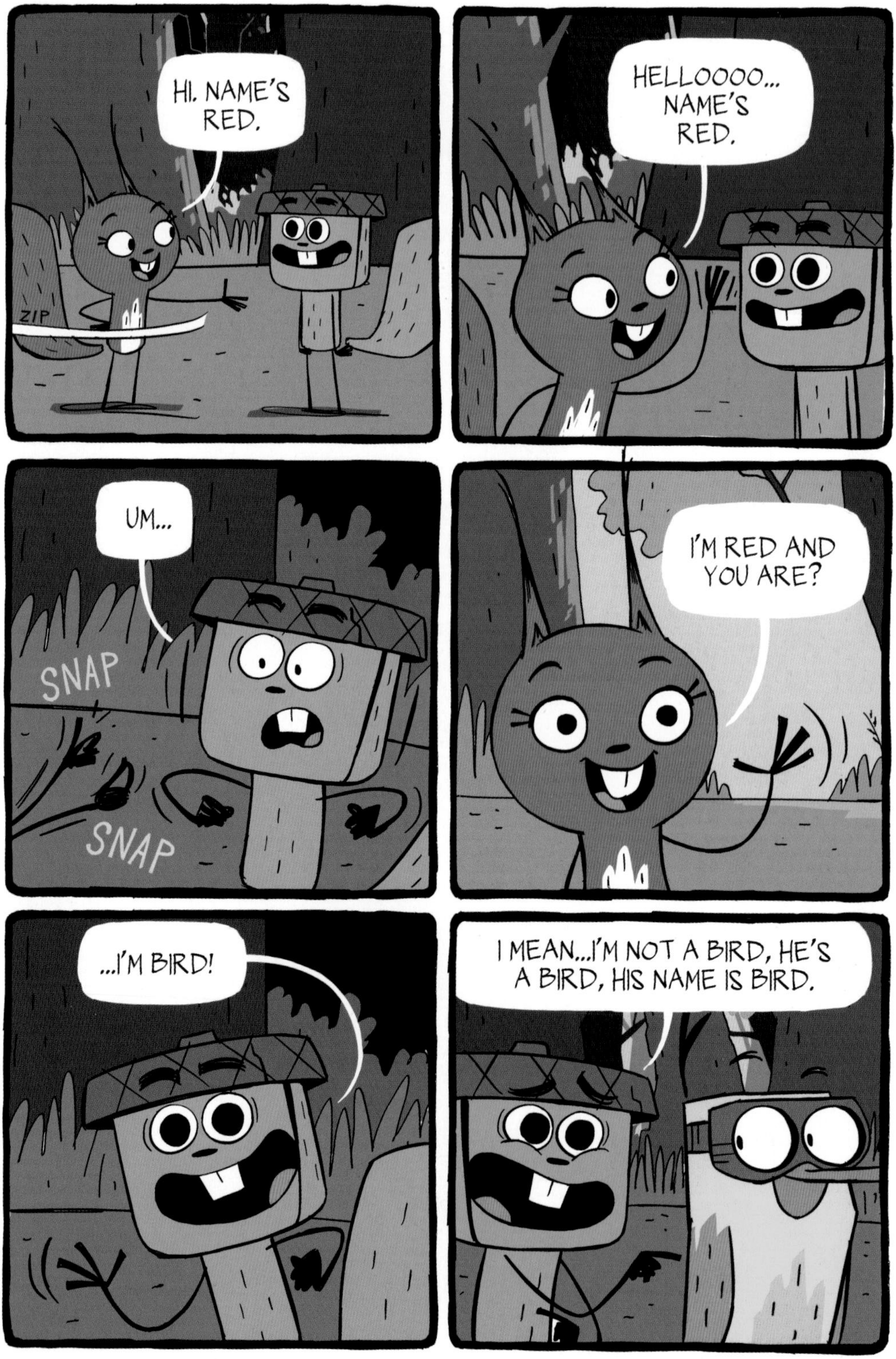
HI. NAME'S RED.
ZIP
HELLOOOO... NAME'S RED.
UM...
SNAP
SNAP
I'M RED AND YOU ARE?
...I'M BIRD!
I MEAN...I'M NOT A BIRD, HE'S A BIRD, HIS NAME IS BIRD.

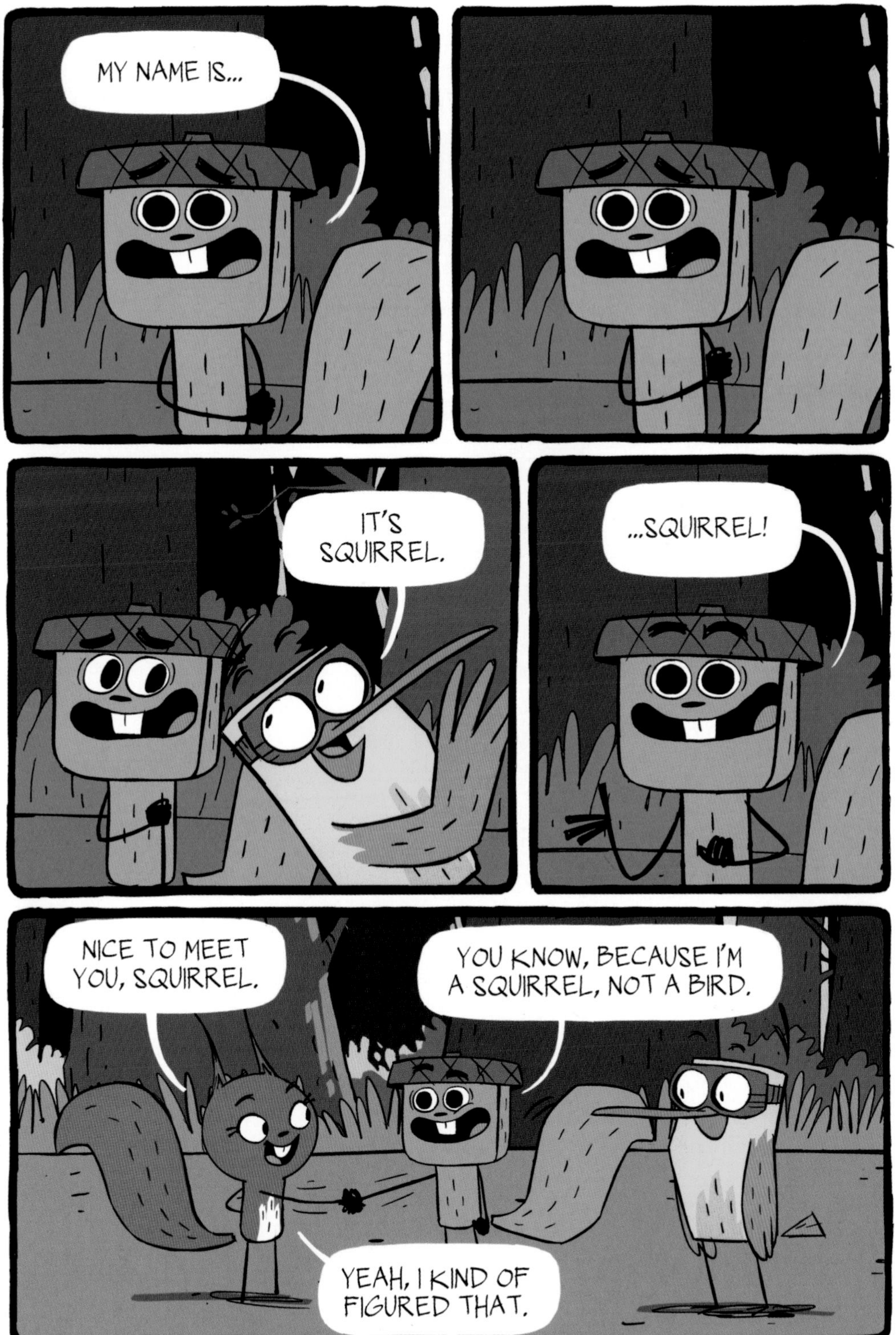
MY NAME IS...
IT'S SQUIRREL.
...SQUIRREL!
NICE TO MEET YOU, SQUIRREL.
YOU KNOW, BECAUSE I'M A SQUIRREL, NOT A BIRD.
YEAH, I KIND OF FIGURED THAT.

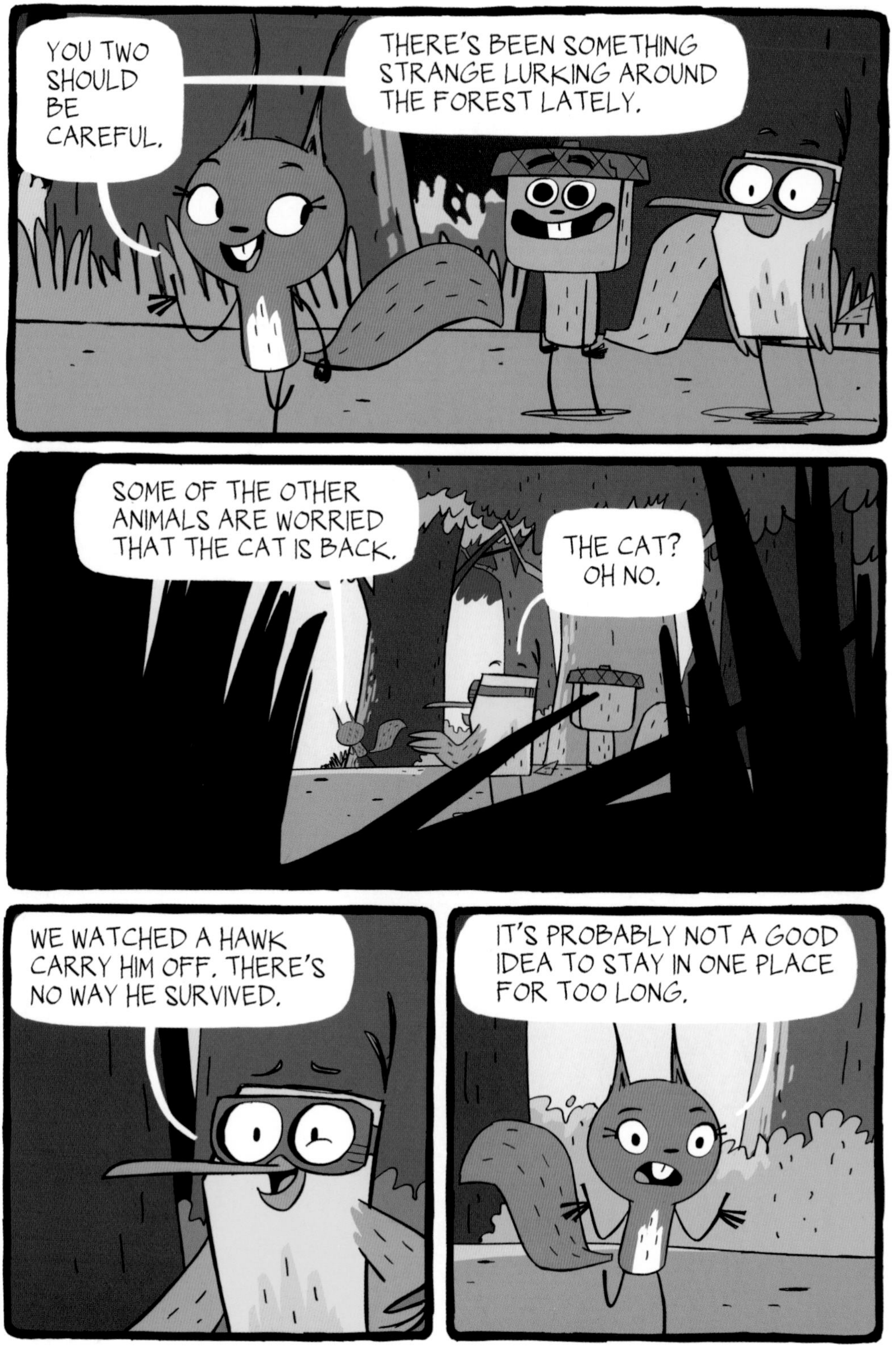
YOU TWO SHOULD BE CAREFUL.
THERE'S BEEN SOMETHING STRANGE LURKING AROUND THE FOREST LATELY.
SOME OF THE OTHER ANIMALS ARE WORRIED THAT THE CAT IS BACK.
THE CAT? OH NO.
WE WATCHED A HAWK CARRY HIM OFF. THERE'S NO WAY HE SURVIVED.
IT'S PROBABLY NOT A GOOD IDEA TO STAY IN ONE PLACE FOR TOO LONG.

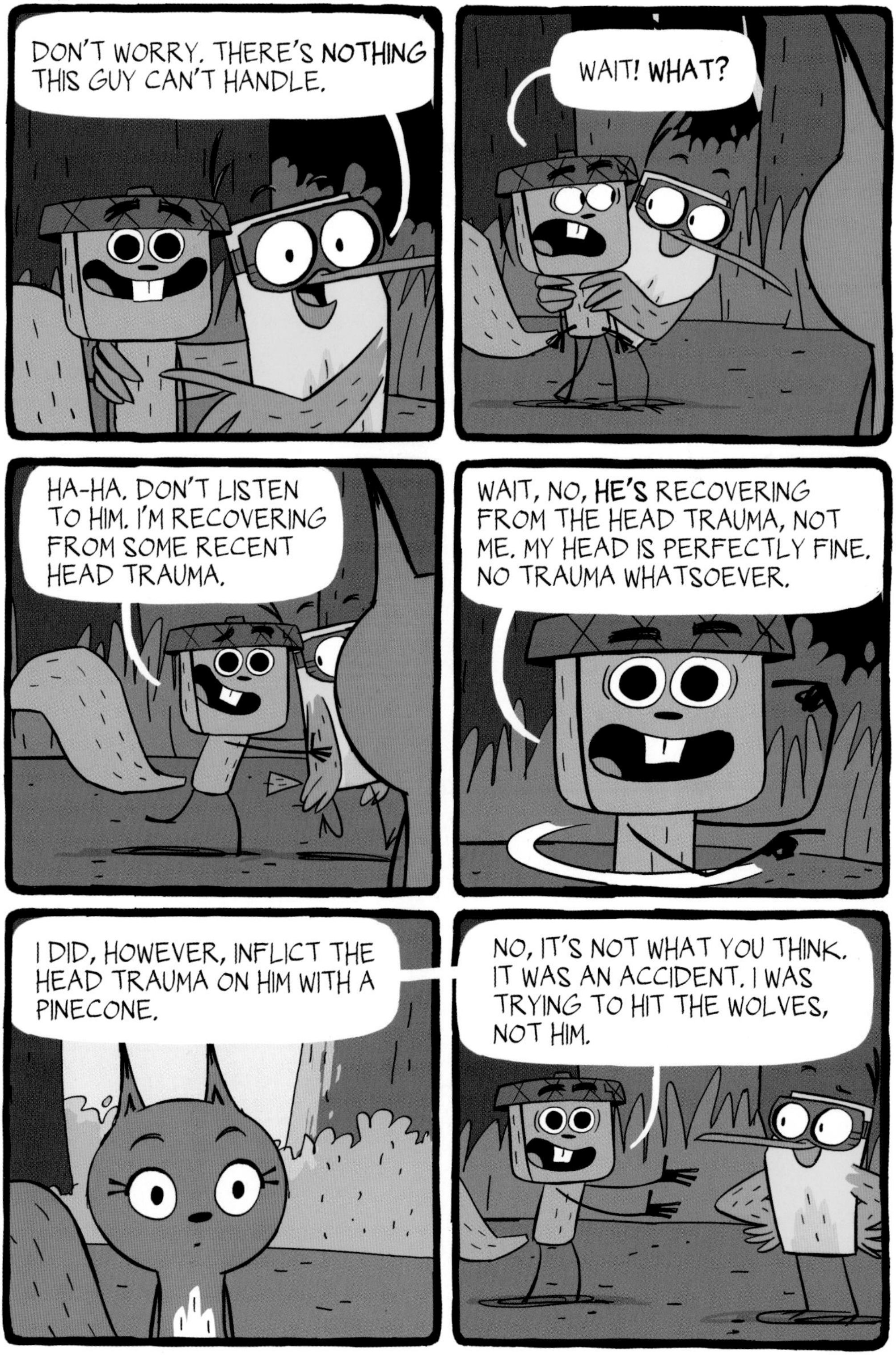
DON'T WORRY. THERE'S NOTHING THIS GUY CAN'T HANDLE.
WAIT! WHAT?
HA-HA. DON'T LISTEN TO HIM. I'M RECOVERING FROM SOME RECENT HEAD TRAUMA.
WAIT, NO, HE'S RECOVERING FROM THE HEAD TRAUMA, NOT ME. MY HEAD IS PERFECTLY FINE. NO TRAUMA WHATSOEVER.
I DID, HOWEVER, INFLICT THE HEAD TRAUMA ON HIM WITH A PINECONE.
NO, IT'S NOT WHAT YOU THINK. IT WAS AN ACCIDENT. I WAS TRYING TO HIT THE WOLVES, NOT HIM.

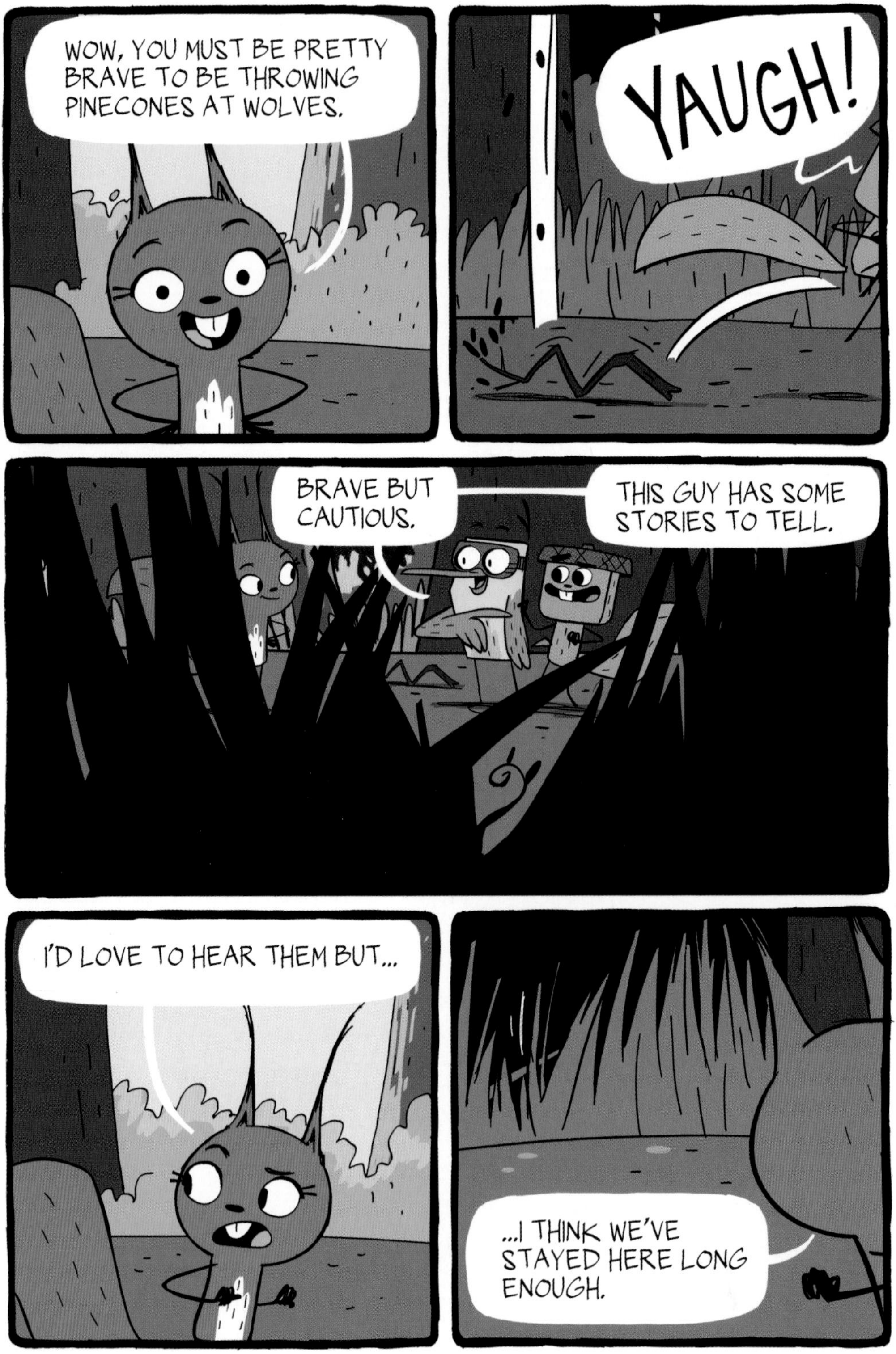
WOW, YOU MUST BE PRETTY BRAVE TO BE THROWING PINECONES AT WOLVES.
YAUGH!
BRAVE BUT CAUTIOUS.
THIS GUY HAS SOME STORIES TO TELL.
I'D LOVE TO HEAR THEM BUT...
...I THINK WE'VE STAYED HERE LONG ENOUGH.

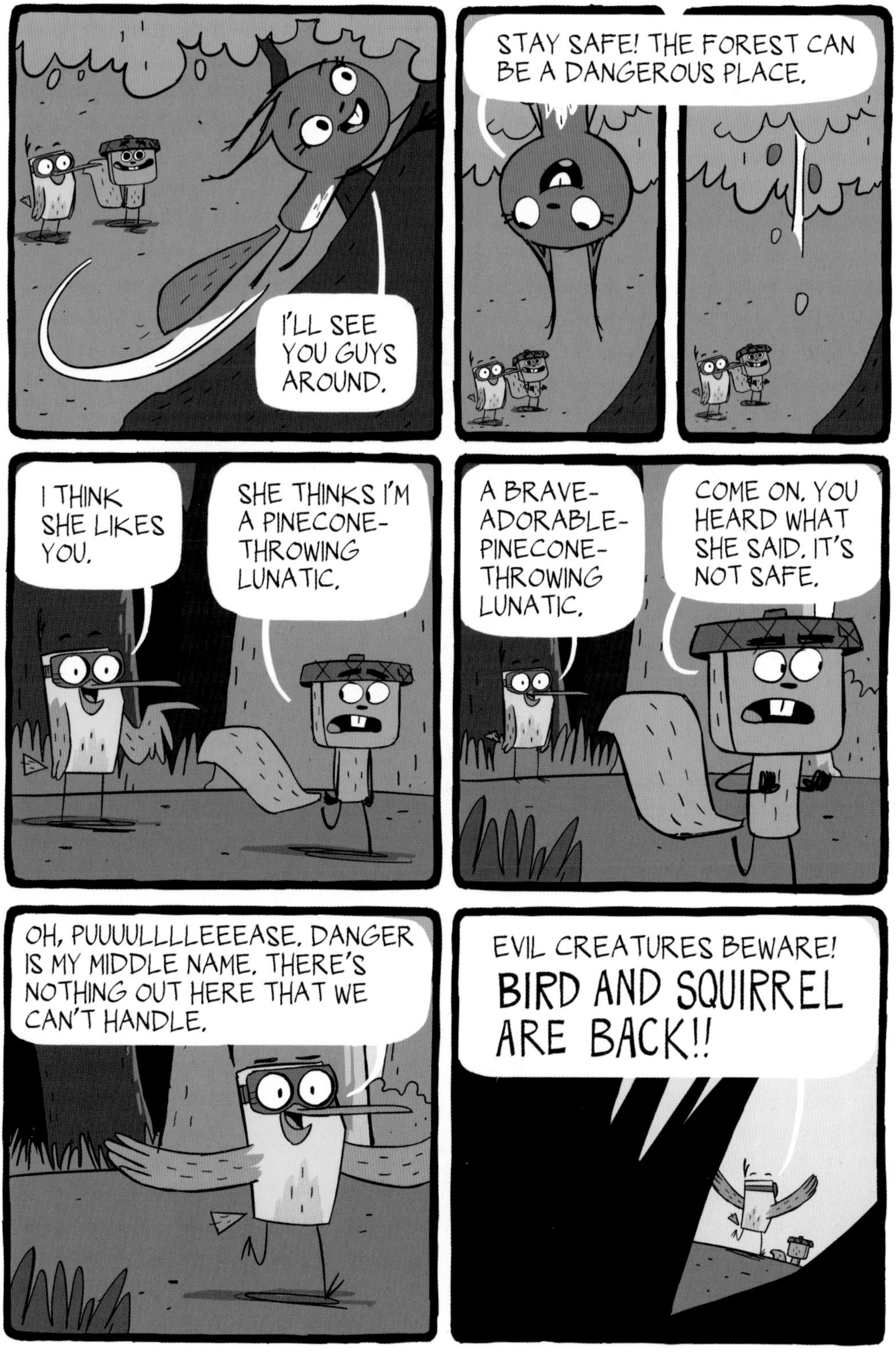
I'LL SEE YOU GUYS AROUND.
STAY SAFE! THE FOREST CAN BE A DANGEROUS PLACE.
I THINK SHE LIKES YOU.
SHE THINKS I'M A PINECONE-THROWING LUNATIC.
A BRAVE-ADORABLE-PINECONE-THROWING LUNATIC.
COME ON. YOU HEARD WHAT SHE SAID. IT'S NOT SAFE.
OH, PUUUULLLLEEEASE. DANGER IS MY MIDDLE NAME. THERE'S NOTHING OUT HERE THAT WE CAN'T HANDLE.
EVIL CREATURES BEWARE!
BIRD AND SQUIRREL ARE BACK!!

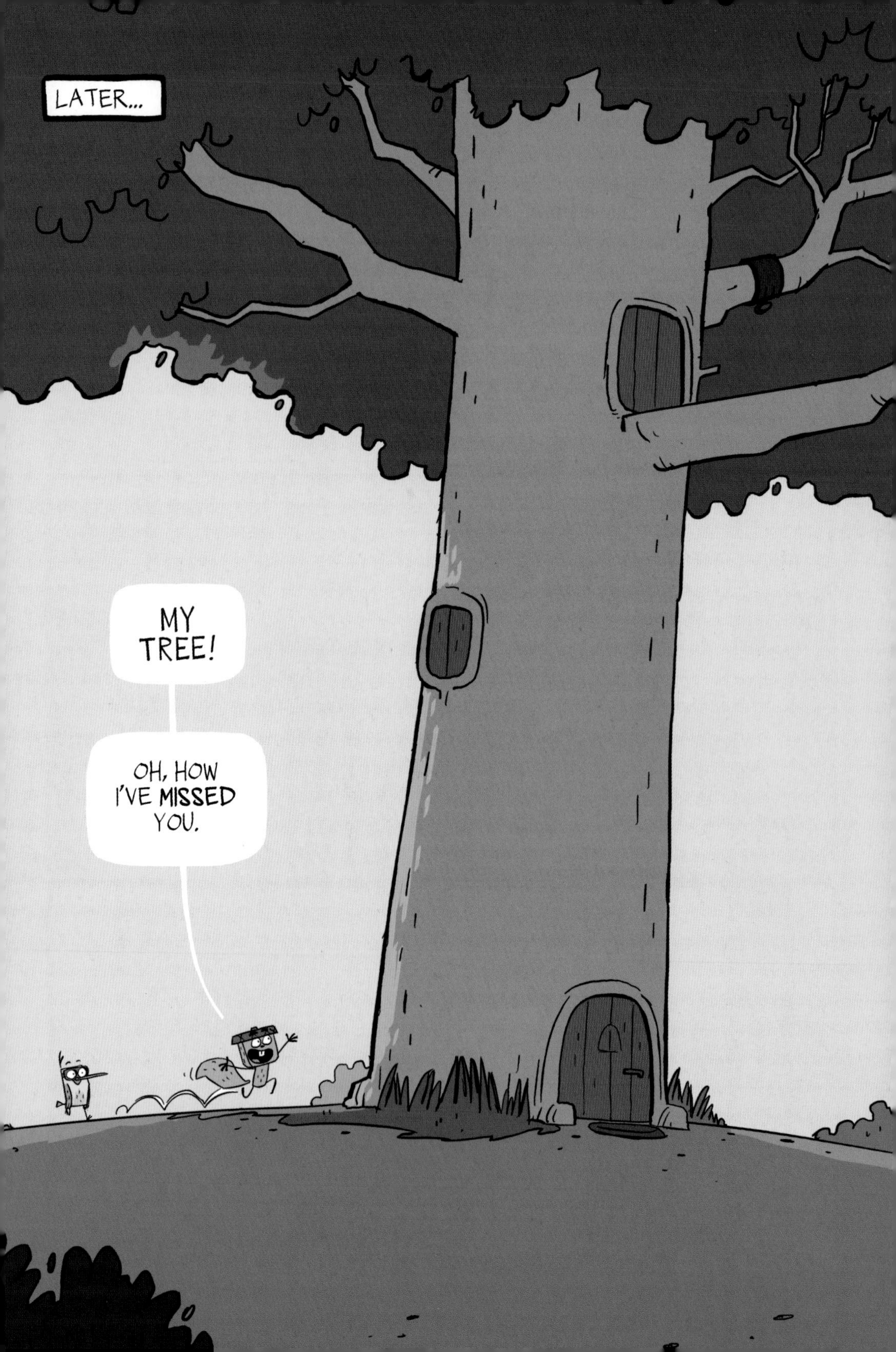
LATER...
MY TREE!
OH, HOW I'VE MISSED YOU.

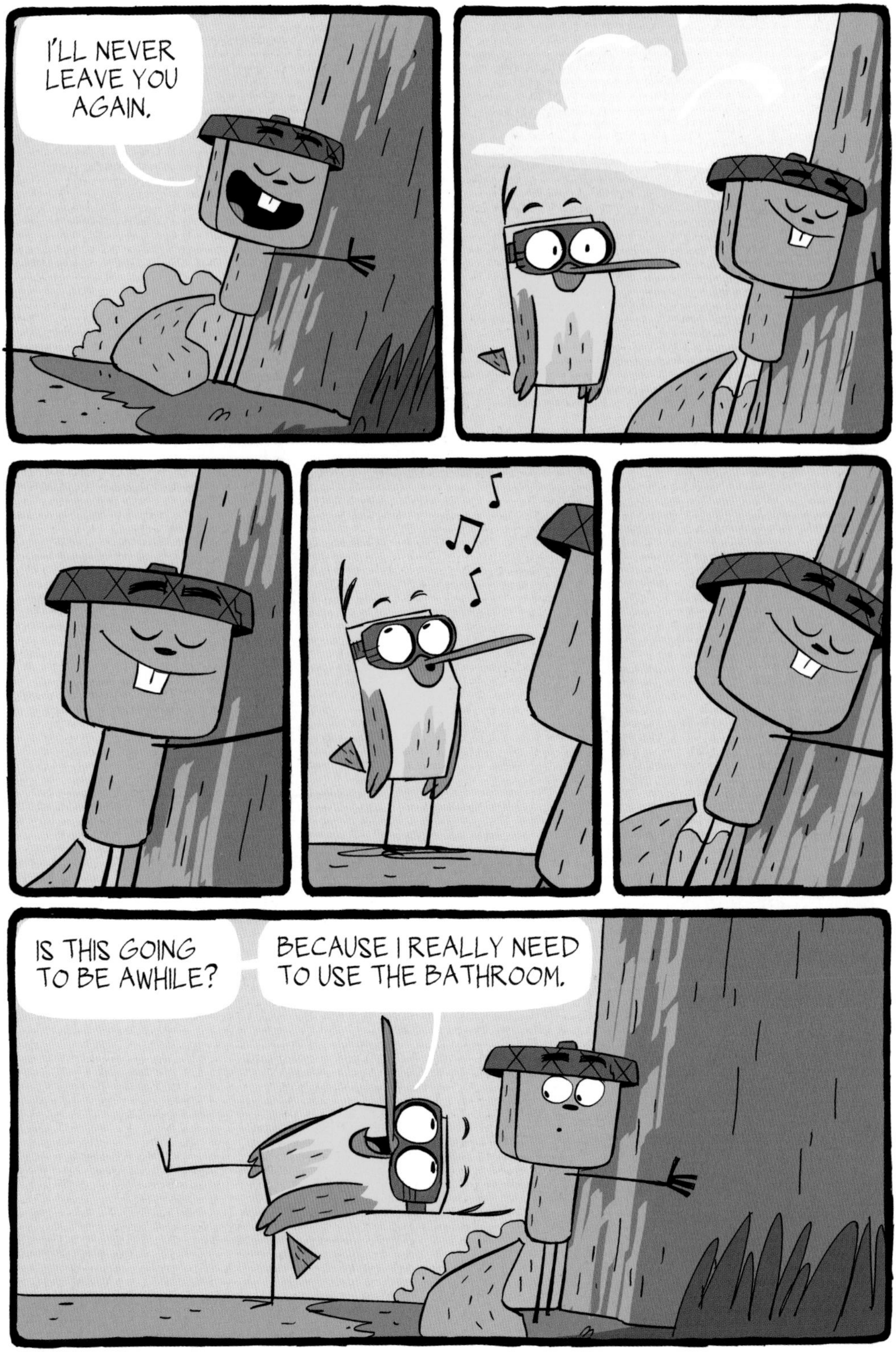
I'LL NEVER LEAVE YOU AGAIN.
IS THIS GOING TO BE AWHILE?
BECAUSE I REALLY NEED TO USE THE BATHROOM.

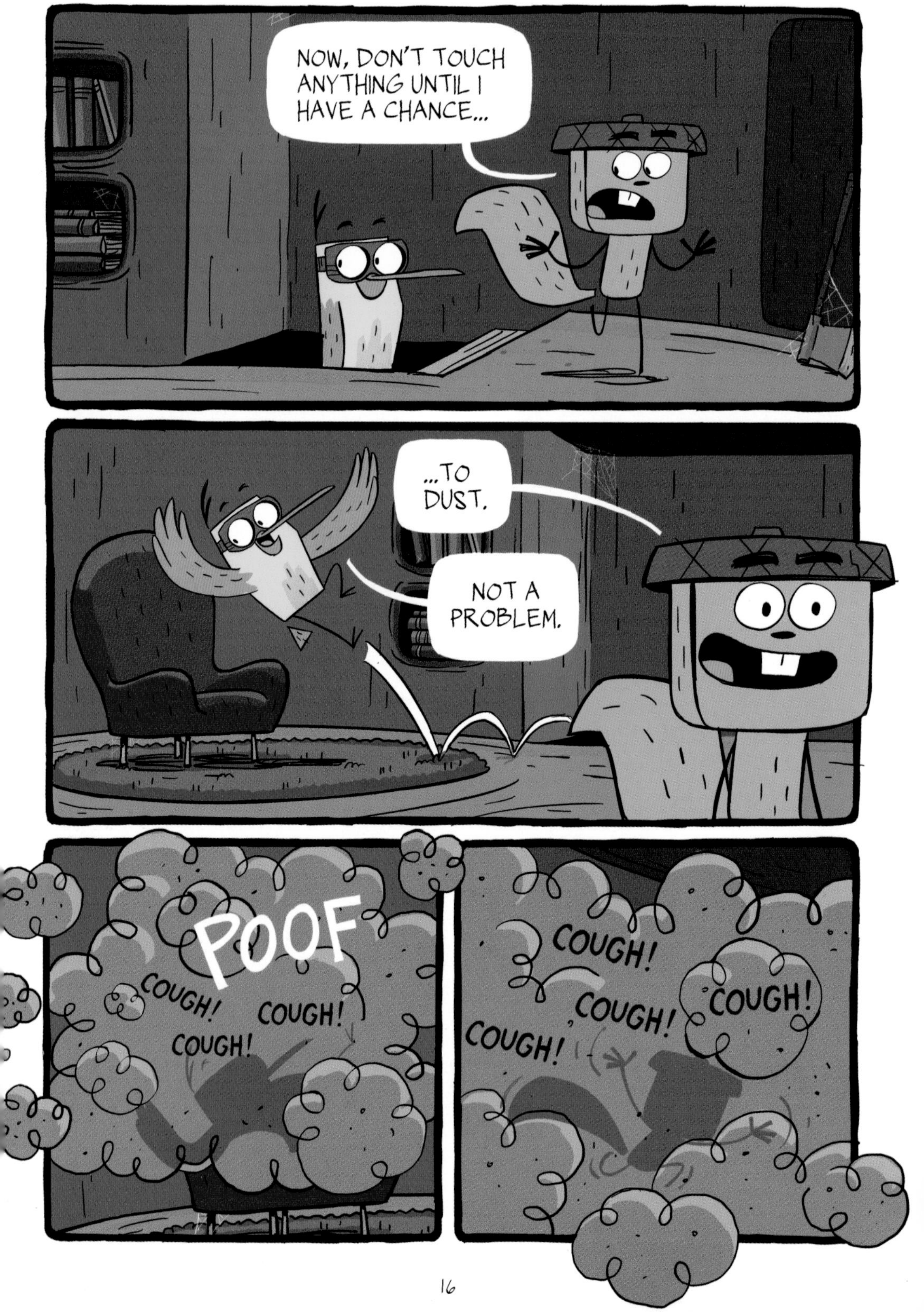
NOW, DON'T TOUCH ANYTHING UNTIL I HAVE A CHANCE...
...TO DUST.
NOT A PROBLEM.
POOF
COUGH! COUGH!
COUGH!
COUGH!
COUGH!
COUGH!
COUGH!

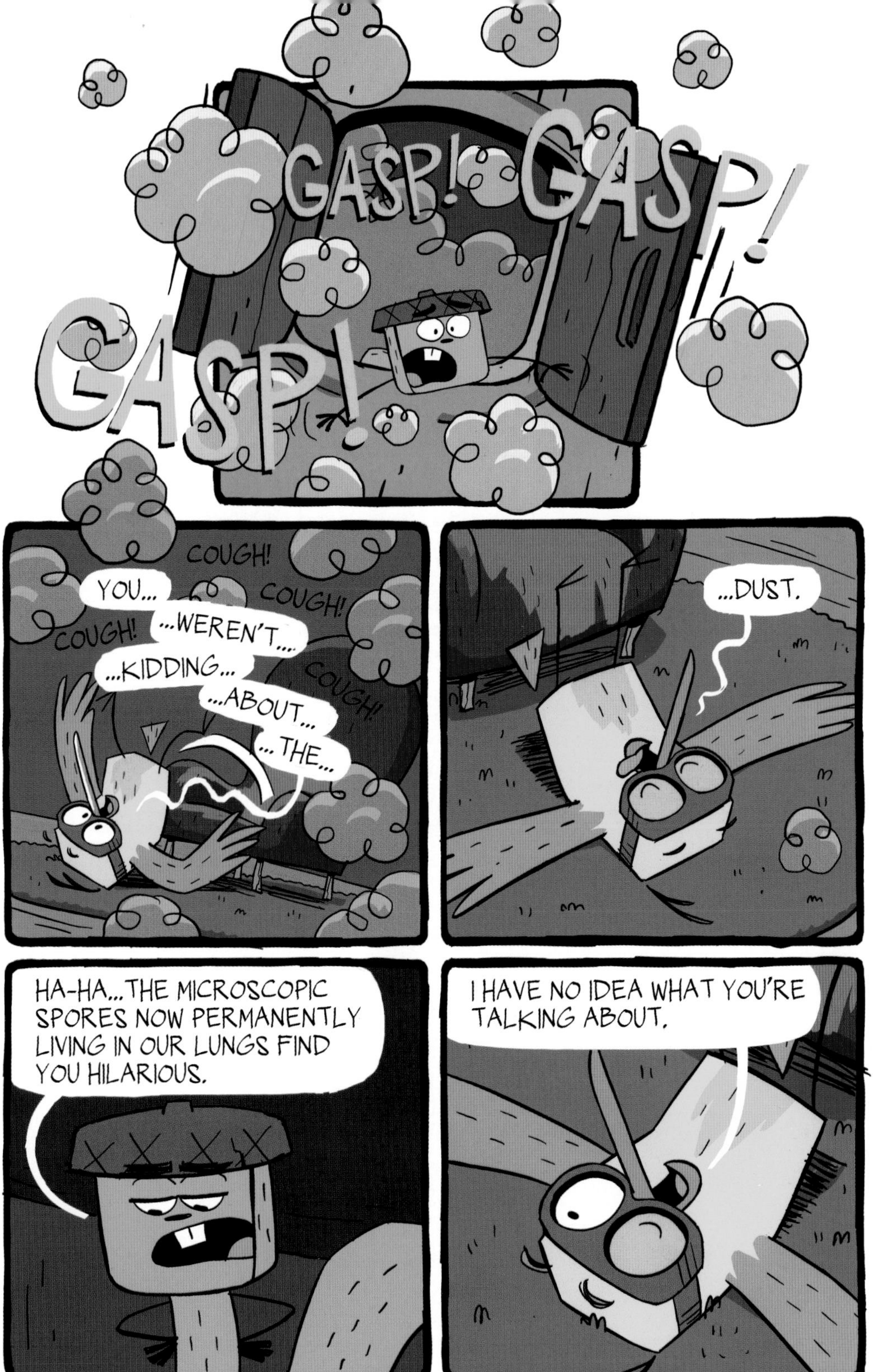
GASP! GASP!
GASP!
COUGH!
YOU...
COUGH!
COUGH!
...WEREN'T...
...KIDDING...
COUGH!
...ABOUT...
...THE...
...DUST.
HA-HA...THE MICROSCOPIC SPORES NOW PERMANENTLY LIVING IN OUR LUNGS FIND YOU HILARIOUS.
I HAVE NO IDEA WHAT YOU'RE TALKING ABOUT.

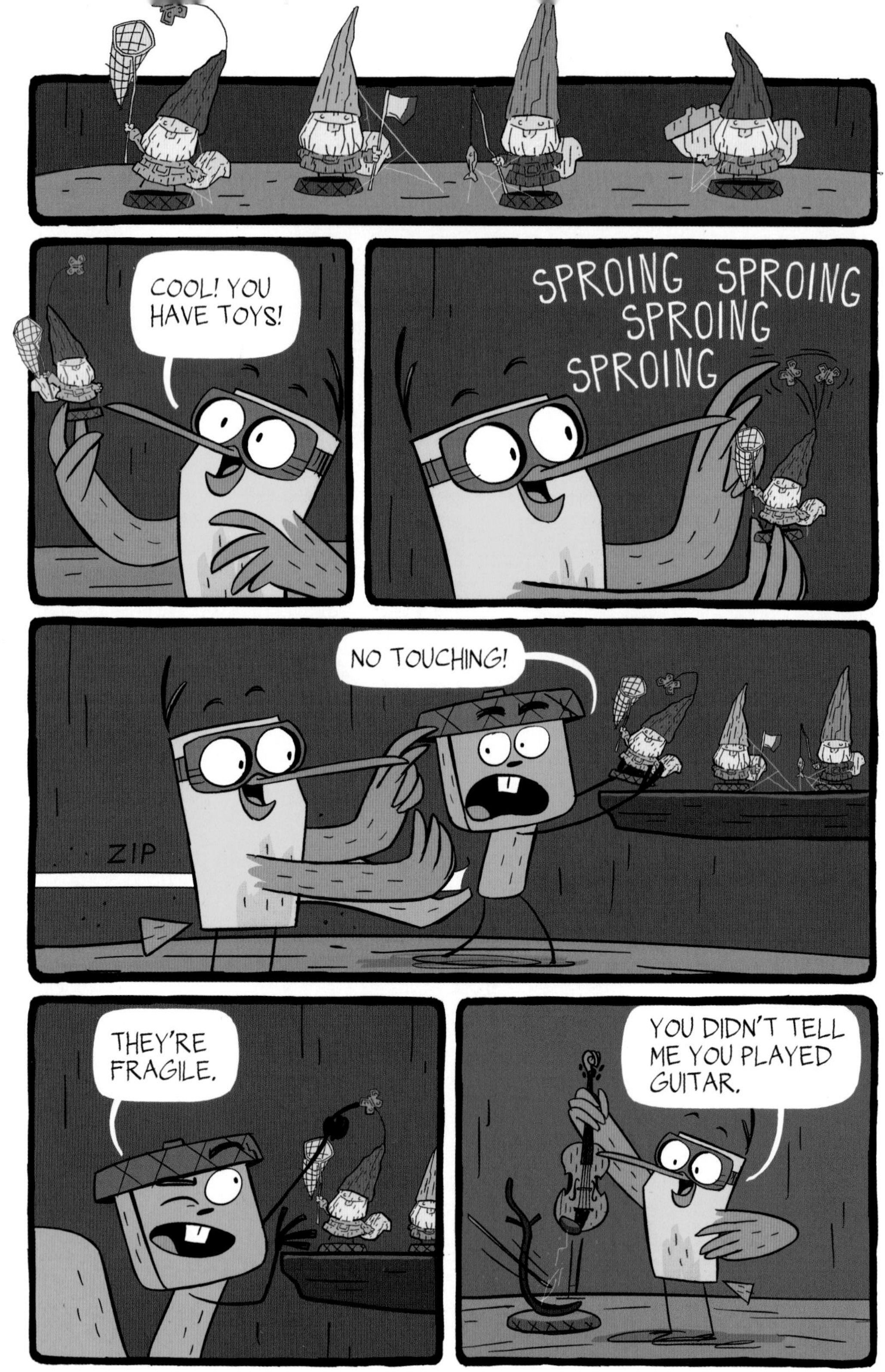
COOL! YOU HAVE TOYS!
SPROING SPROING
SPROING
SPROING
NO TOUCHING!
ZIP
THEY'RE FRAGILE.
YOU DIDN'T TELL ME YOU PLAYED GUITAR.

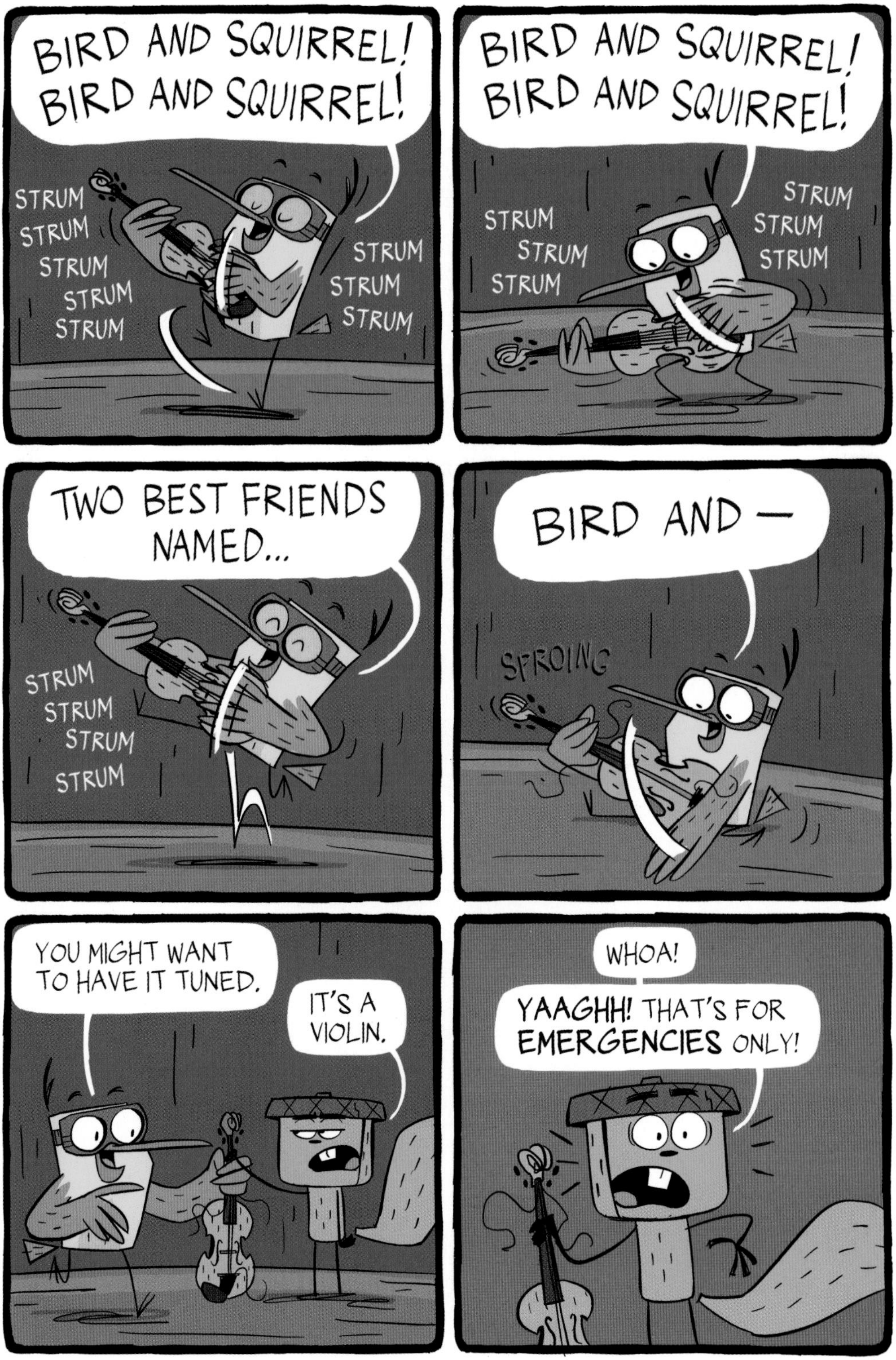
BIRD AND SQUIRREL! BIRD AND SQUIRREL!
STRUM STRUM STRUM STRUM STRUM
STRUM STRUM STRUM
BIRD AND SQUIRREL! BIRD AND SQUIRREL!
STRUM STRUM STRUM
STRUM STRUM STRUM
TWO BEST FRIENDS NAMED...
STRUM STRUM STRUM STRUM
BIRD AND —
SPROING
YOU MIGHT WANT TO HAVE IT TUNED.
IT'S A VIOLIN.
WHOA!
YAAGHH! THAT'S FOR EMERGENCIES ONLY!

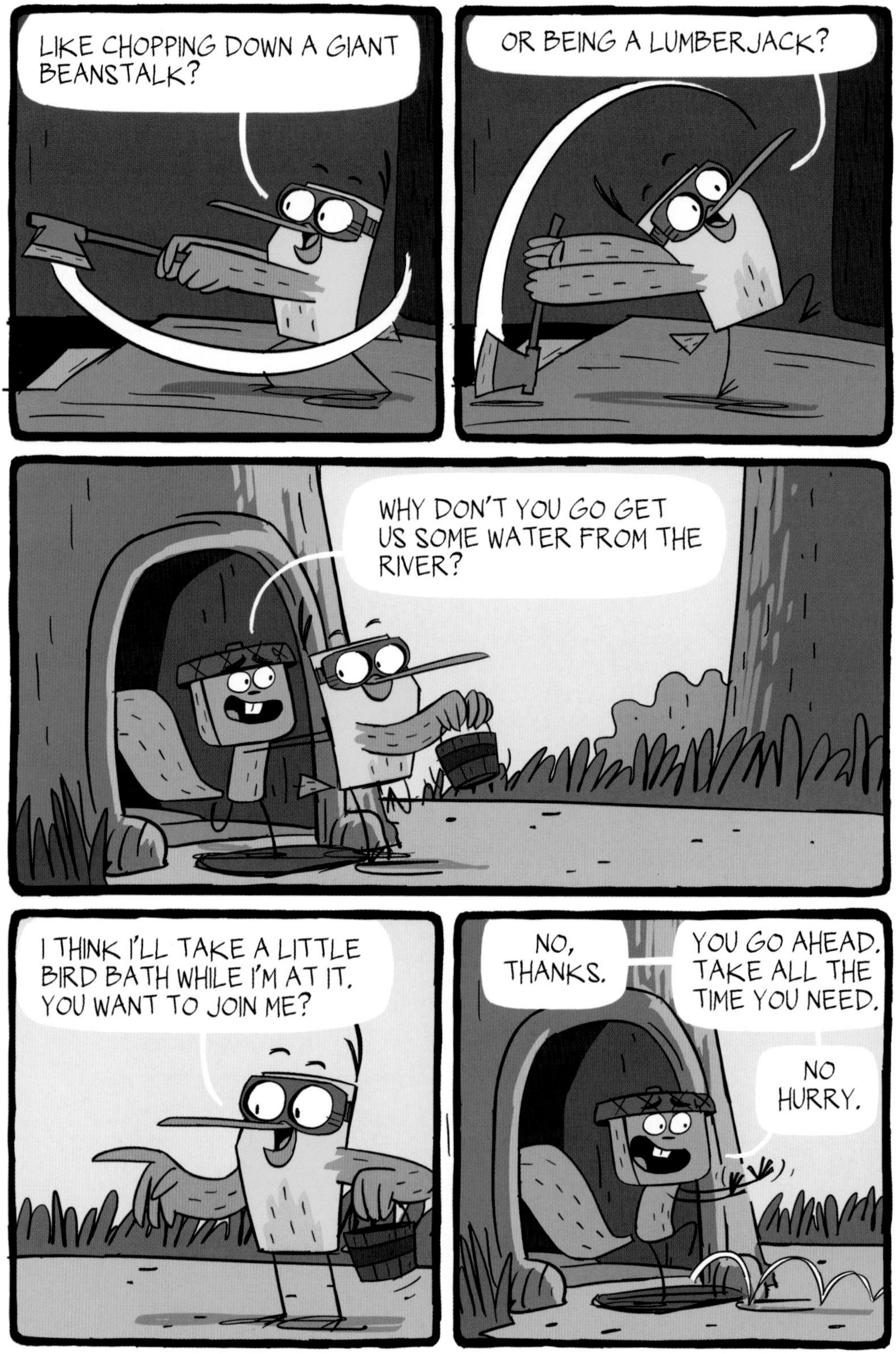
LIKE CHOPPING DOWN A GIANT BEANSTALK?
OR BEING A LUMBERJACK?
WHY DON'T YOU GO GET US SOME WATER FROM THE RIVER?
I THINK I'LL TAKE A LITTLE BIRD BATH WHILE I'M AT IT. YOU WANT TO JOIN ME?
NO, THANKS.
YOU GO AHEAD. TAKE ALL THE TIME YOU NEED.
NO HURRY.

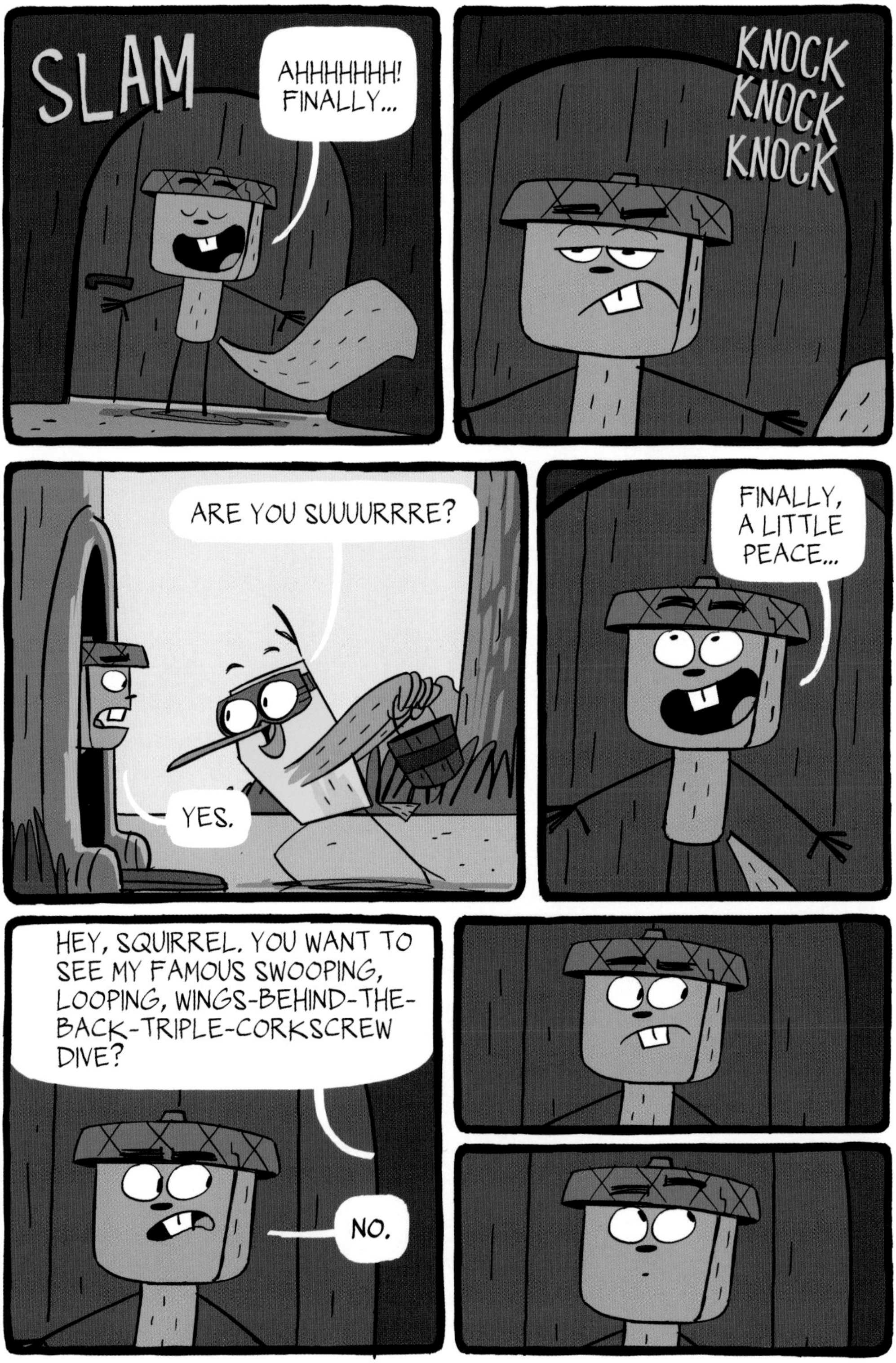
SLAM
AHHHHHHH! FINALLY...
KNOCK KNOCK KNOCK
ARE YOU SUUUURRRE?
YES.
FINALLY, A LITTLE PEACE...
HEY, SQUIRREL. YOU WANT TO SEE MY FAMOUS SWOOPING, LOOPING, WINGS-BEHIND-THE-BACK-TRIPLE-CORKSCREW DIVE?
NO.

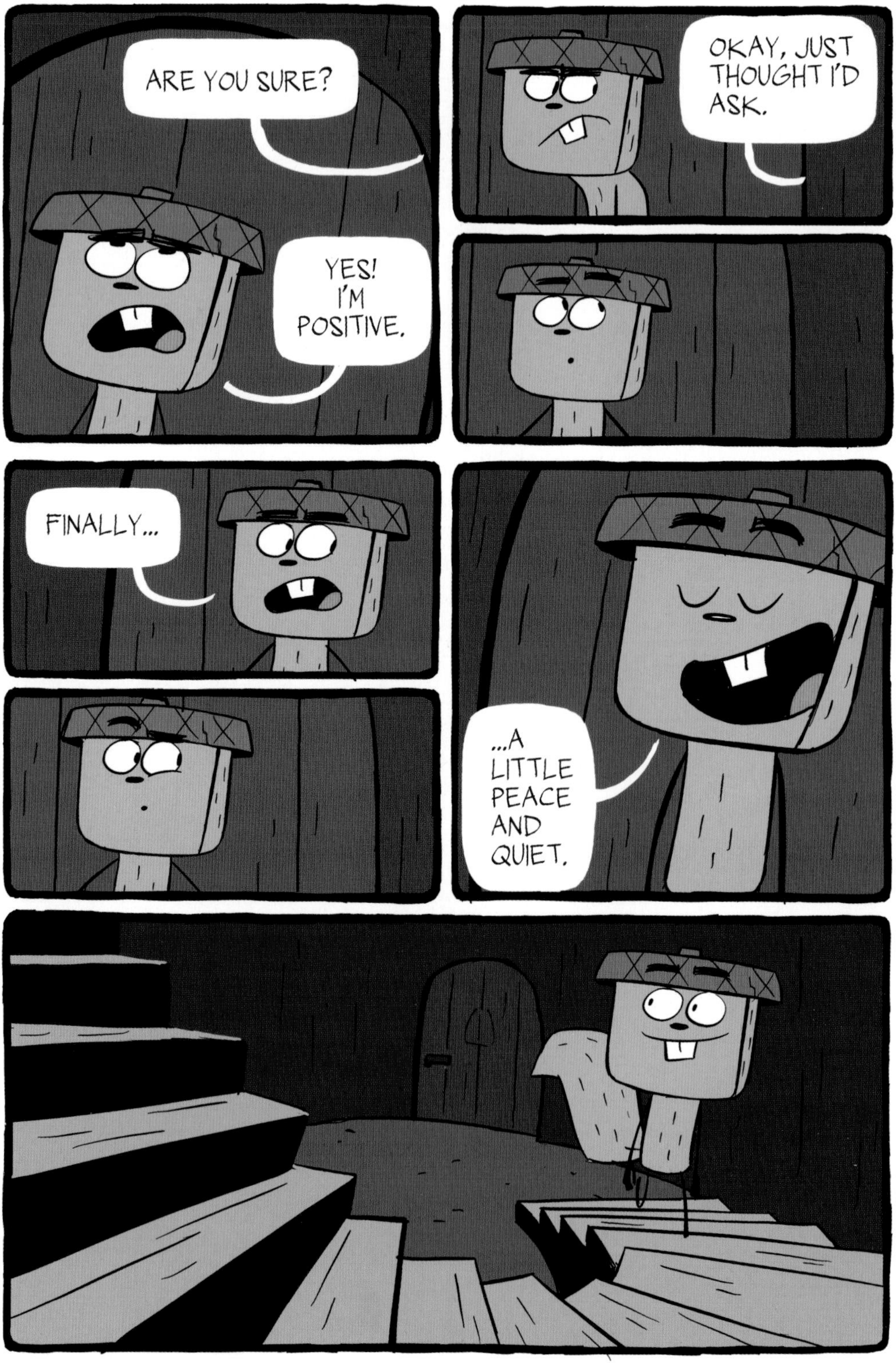
ARE YOU SURE?
YES! I'M POSITIVE.
OKAY, JUST THOUGHT I'D ASK.
FINALLY...
...A LITTLE PEACE AND QUIET.

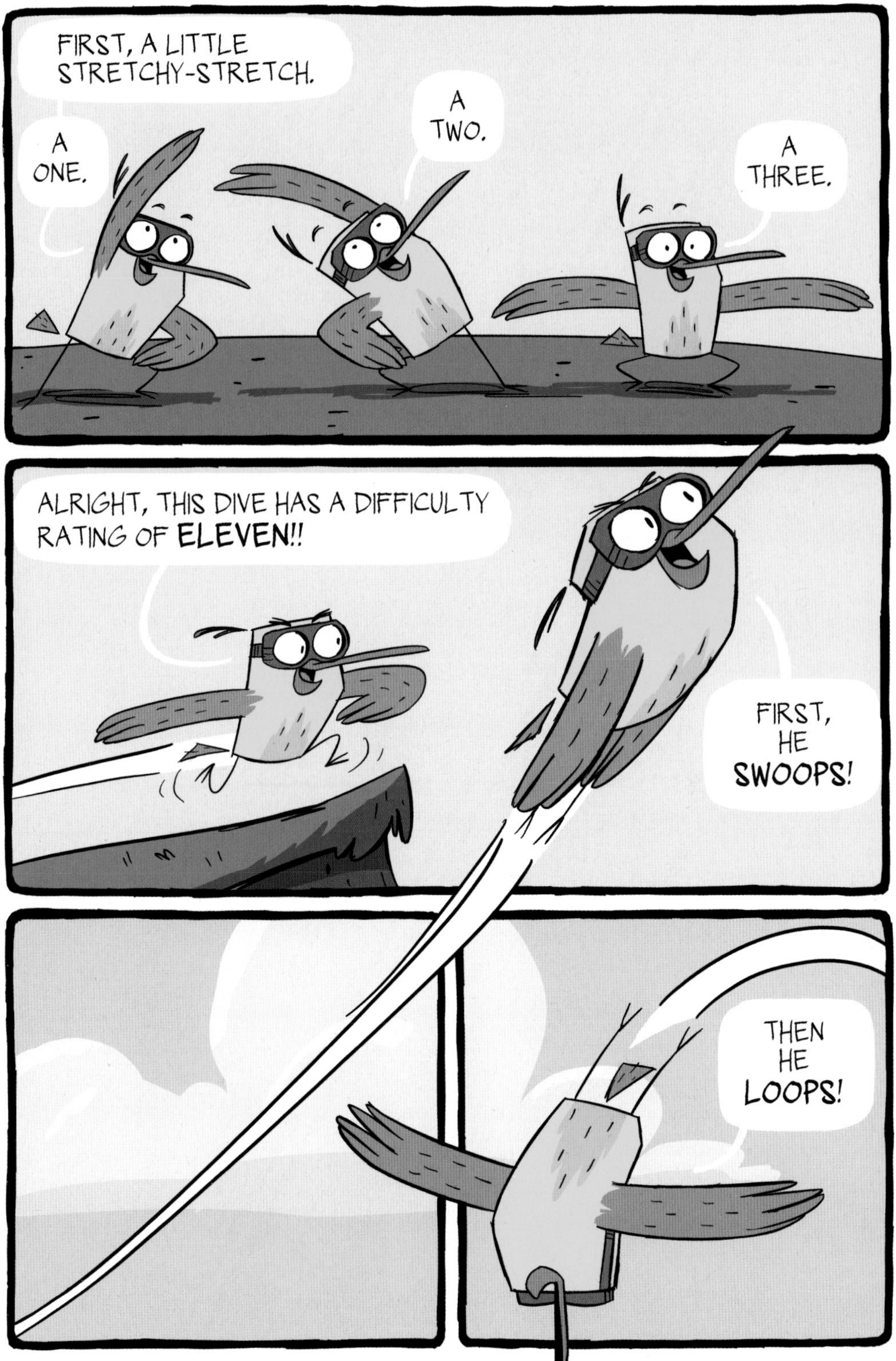
FIRST, A LITTLE STRETCHY-STRETCH.
A ONE.
A TWO.
A THREE.
ALRIGHT, THIS DIVE HAS A DIFFICULTY RATING OF ELEVEN!!
FIRST, HE SWOOPS!
THEN HE LOOPS!

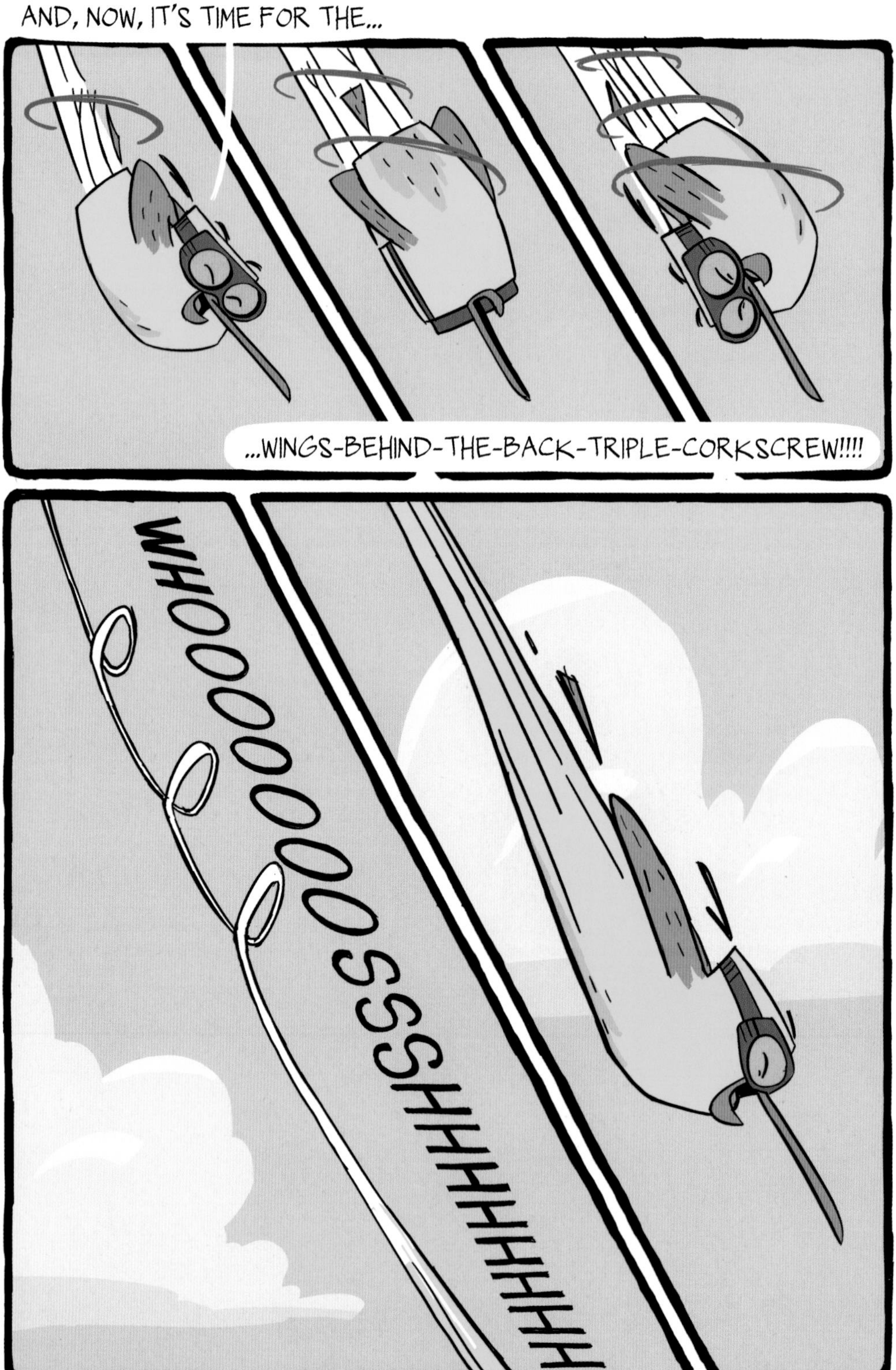
AND, NOW, IT'S TIME FOR THE...
...WINGS-BEHIND-THE-BACK-TRIPLE-CORKSCREW!!!!
WHOOOOOOOOSSSHHHHHHHHHH

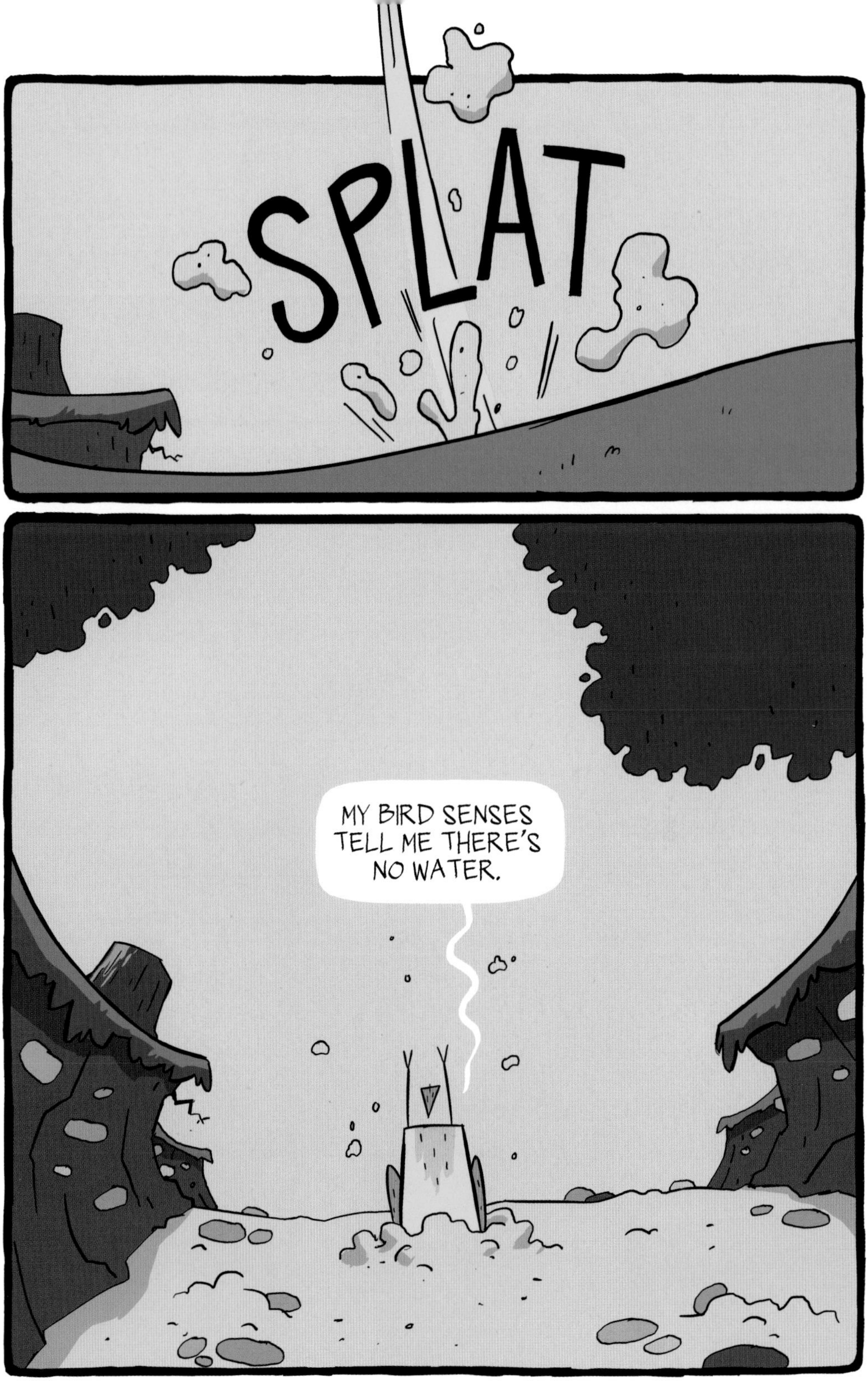
SPLAT
MY BIRD SENSES TELL ME THERE'S NO WATER.

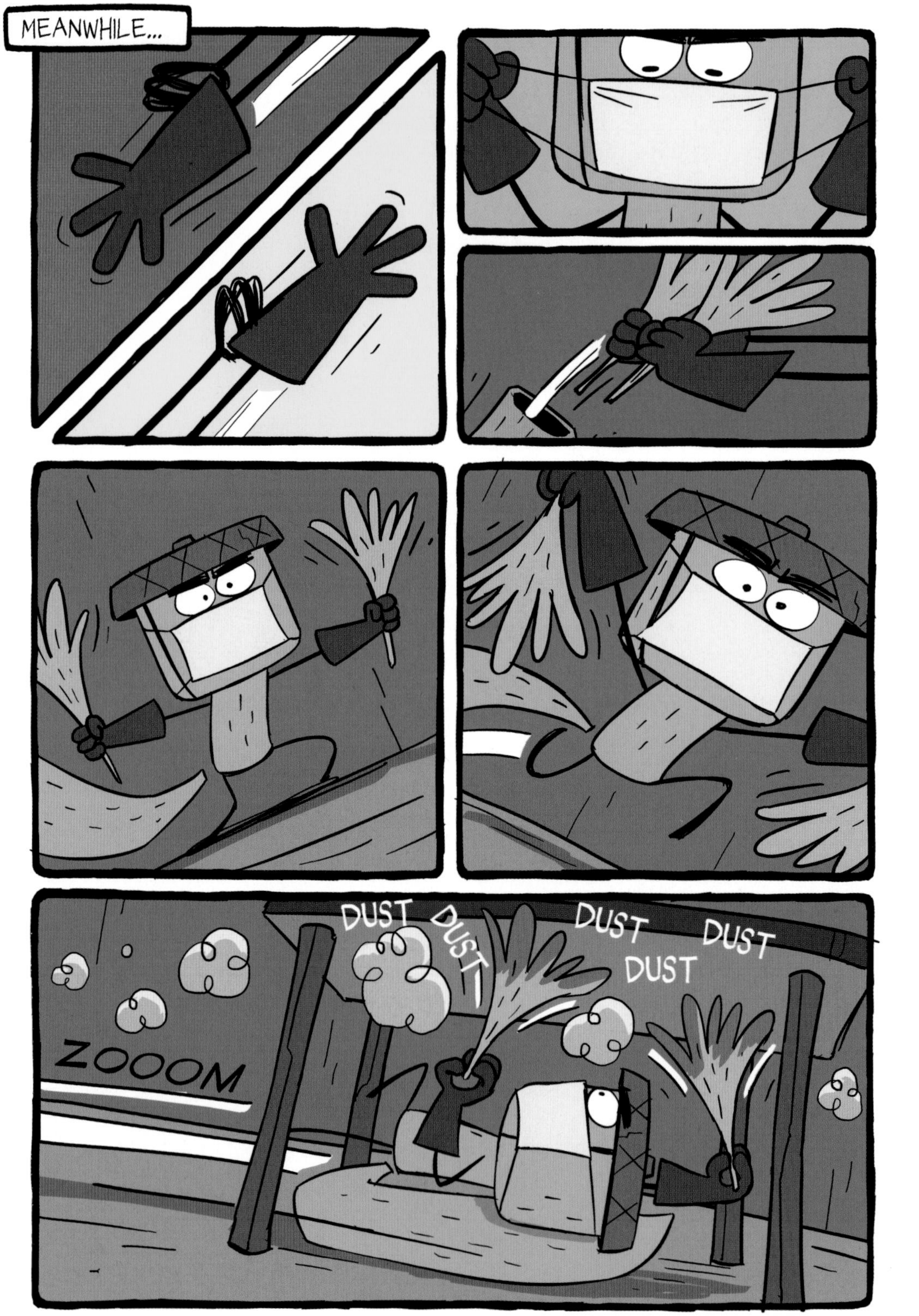
MEANWHILE...
DUST
DUST
DUST
DUST
DUST
ZOOOM

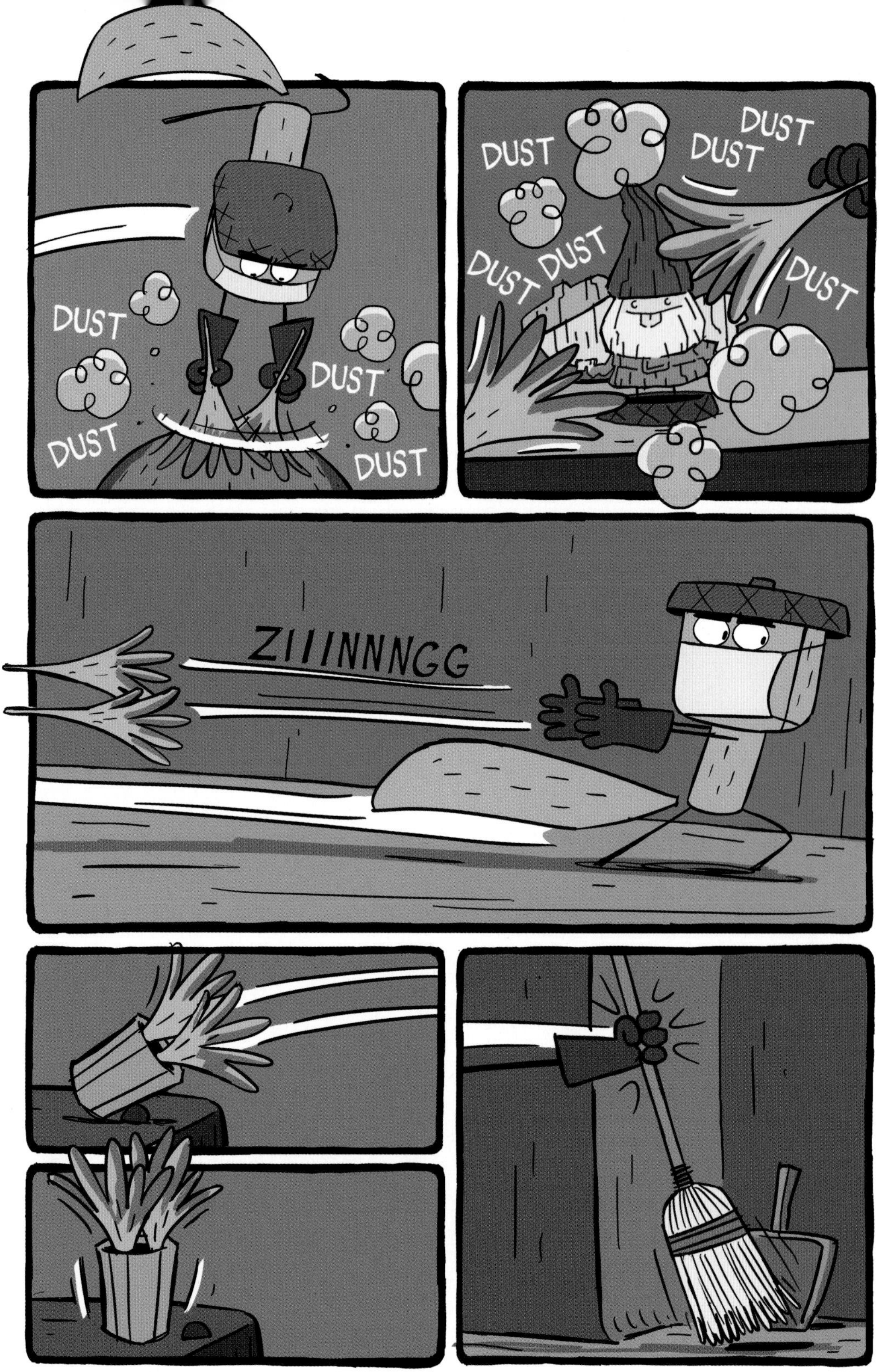
DUST
DUST
DUST
DUST
DUST
DUST
DUST
DUST
DUST
DUST
DUST
ZIIINNNGG

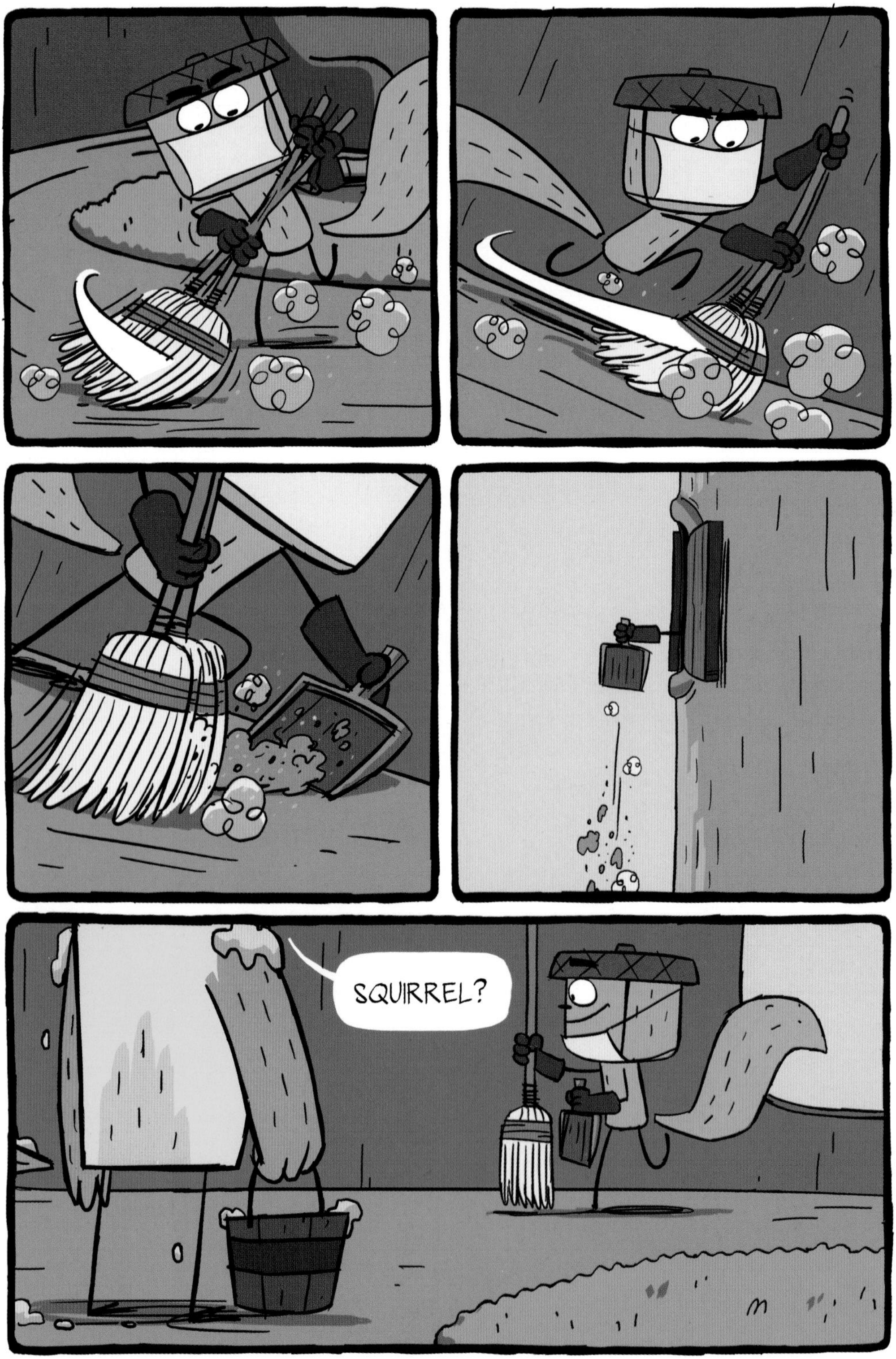
SQUIRREL?

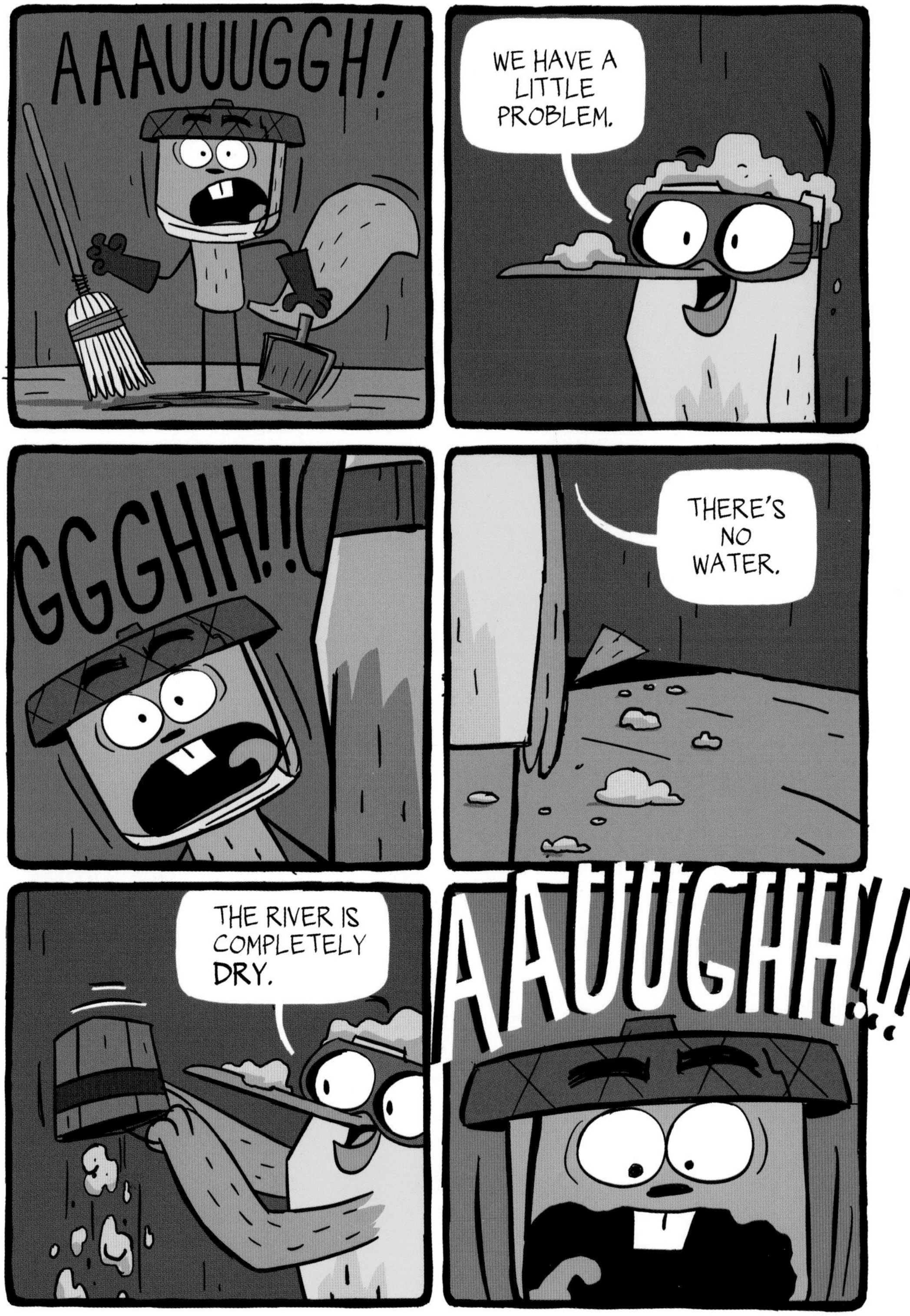
AAAUUUGGH!
WE HAVE A LITTLE PROBLEM.
GGGHH!!
THERE'S NO WATER.
THE RIVER IS COMPLETELY DRY.
AAUUGHH!!!

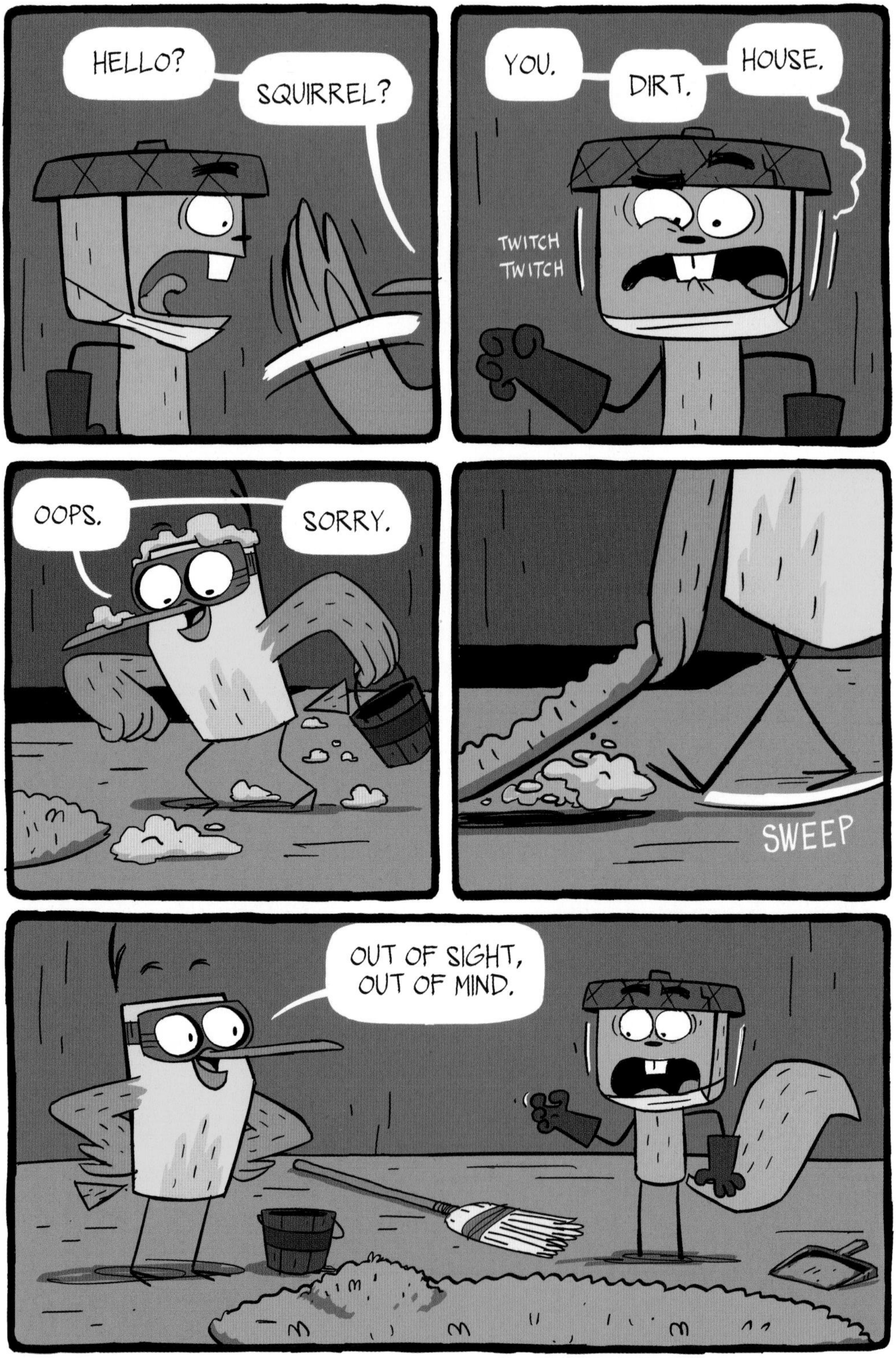
HELLO?
SQUIRREL?
YOU.
DIRT.
HOUSE.
TWITCH TWITCH
OOPS.
SORRY.
SWEEP
OUT OF SIGHT, OUT OF MIND.

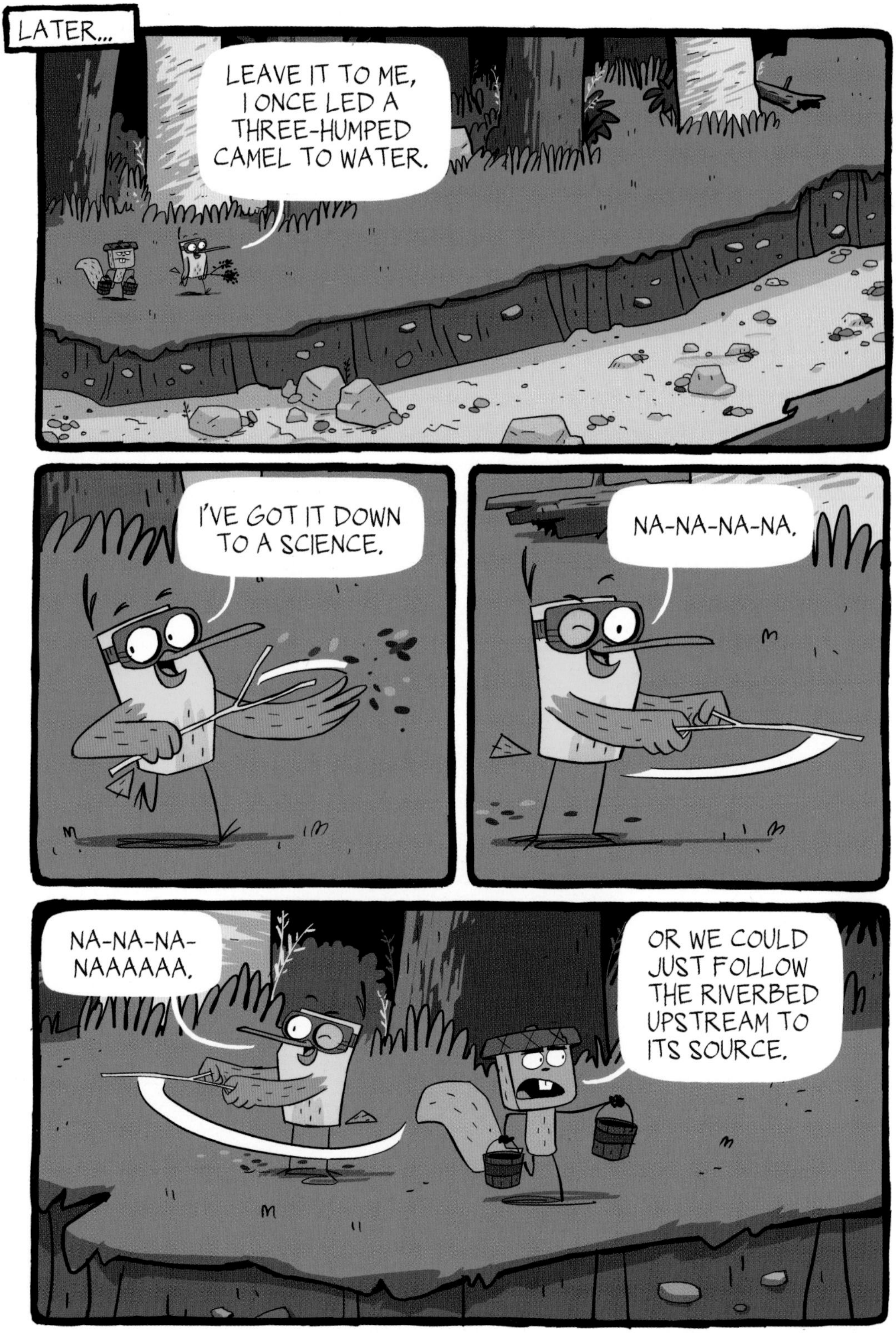
LATER...
LEAVE IT TO ME, I ONCE LED A THREE-HUMPED CAMEL TO WATER.
I'VE GOT IT DOWN TO A SCIENCE.
NA-NA-NA-NA.
NA-NA-NA-NAAAAAA.
OR WE COULD JUST FOLLOW THE RIVERBED UPSTREAM TO ITS SOURCE.

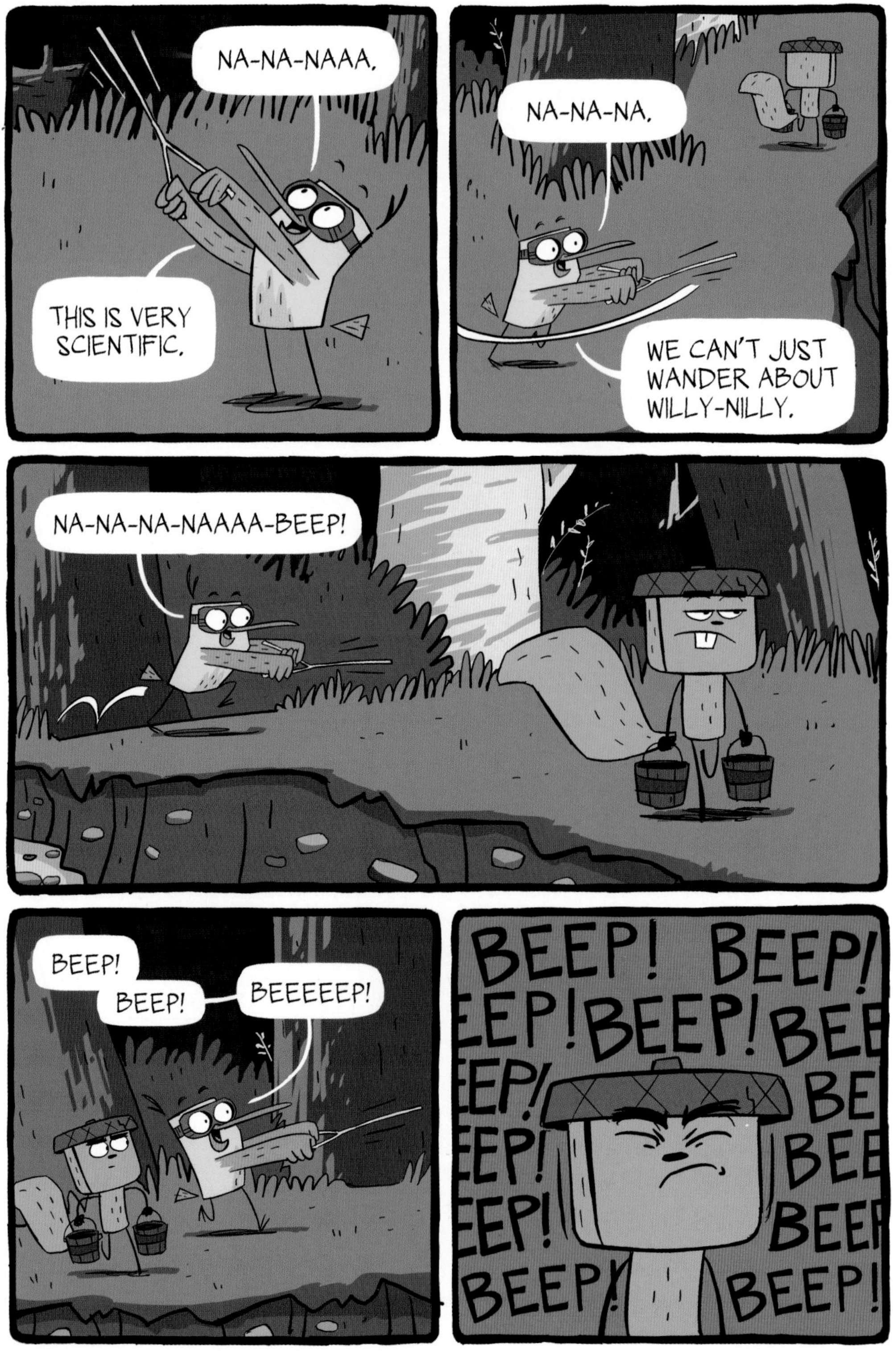
NA-NA-NAAA.
THIS IS VERY SCIENTIFIC.
NA-NA-NA.
WE CAN'T JUST WANDER ABOUT WILLY-NILLY.
NA-NA-NA-NAAAA-BEEP!
BEEP!
BEEP!
BEEEEEP!
BEEP! BEEP! BEEP! BEEP! BEEP!

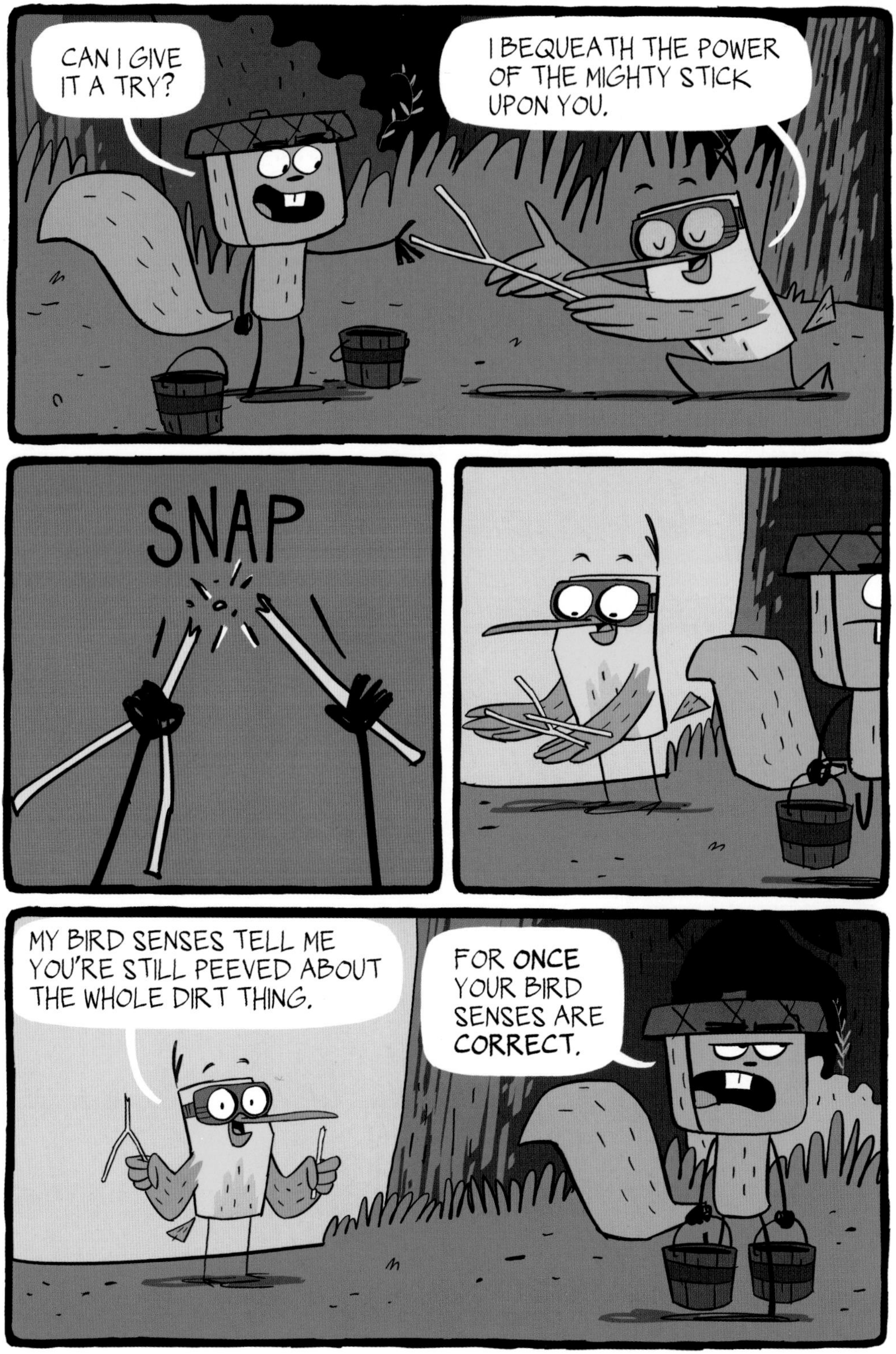
CAN I GIVE IT A TRY?
I BEQUEATH THE POWER OF THE MIGHTY STICK UPON YOU.
SNAP
MY BIRD SENSES TELL ME YOU'RE STILL PEEVED ABOUT THE WHOLE DIRT THING.
FOR ONCE YOUR BIRD SENSES ARE CORRECT.

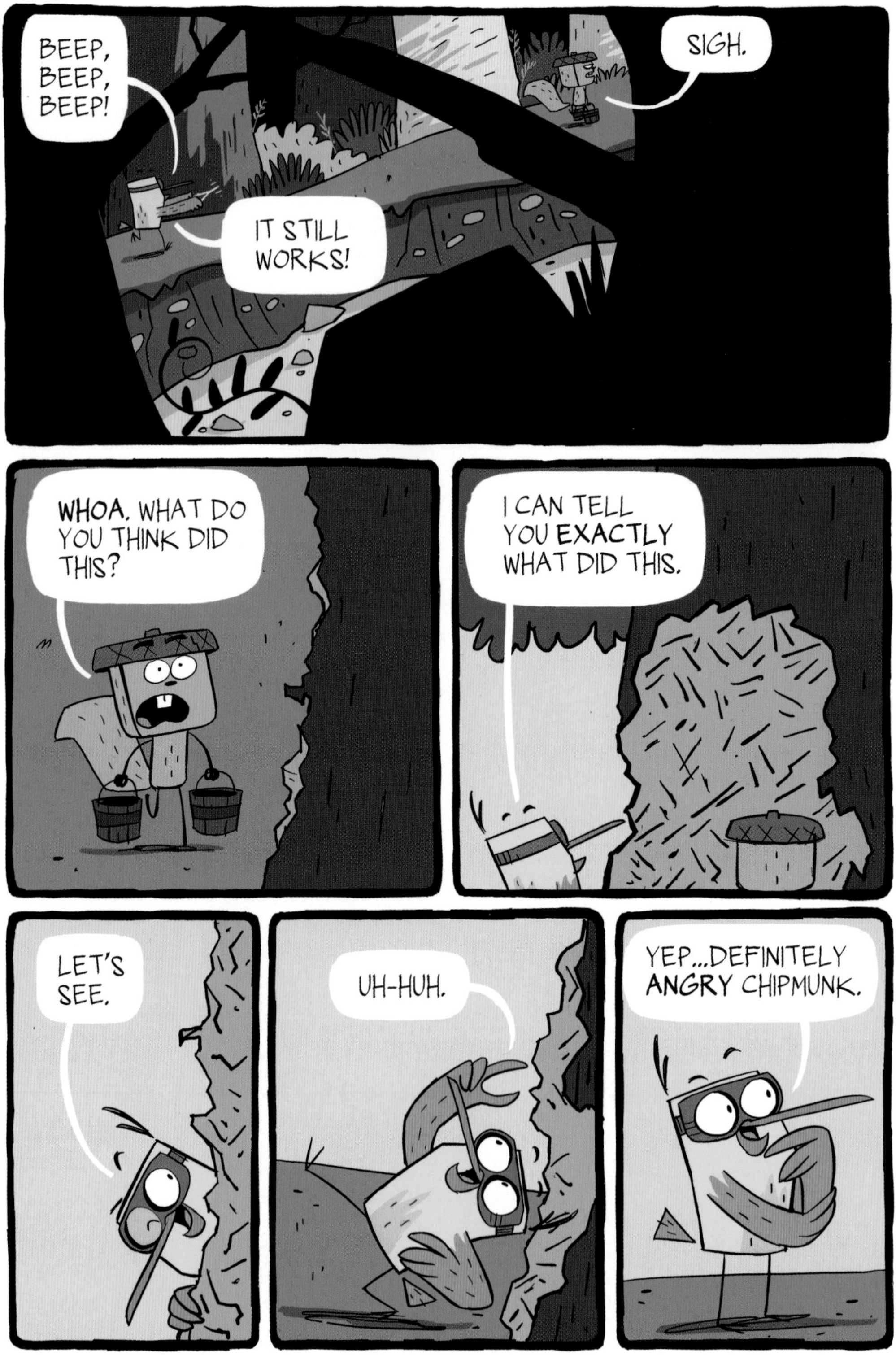
BEEP, BEEP, BEEP!
SIGH.
IT STILL WORKS!
WHOA. WHAT DO YOU THINK DID THIS?
I CAN TELL YOU **EXACTLY** WHAT DID THIS.
LET'S SEE.
UH-HUH.
YEP...DEFINITELY **ANGRY** CHIPMUNK.

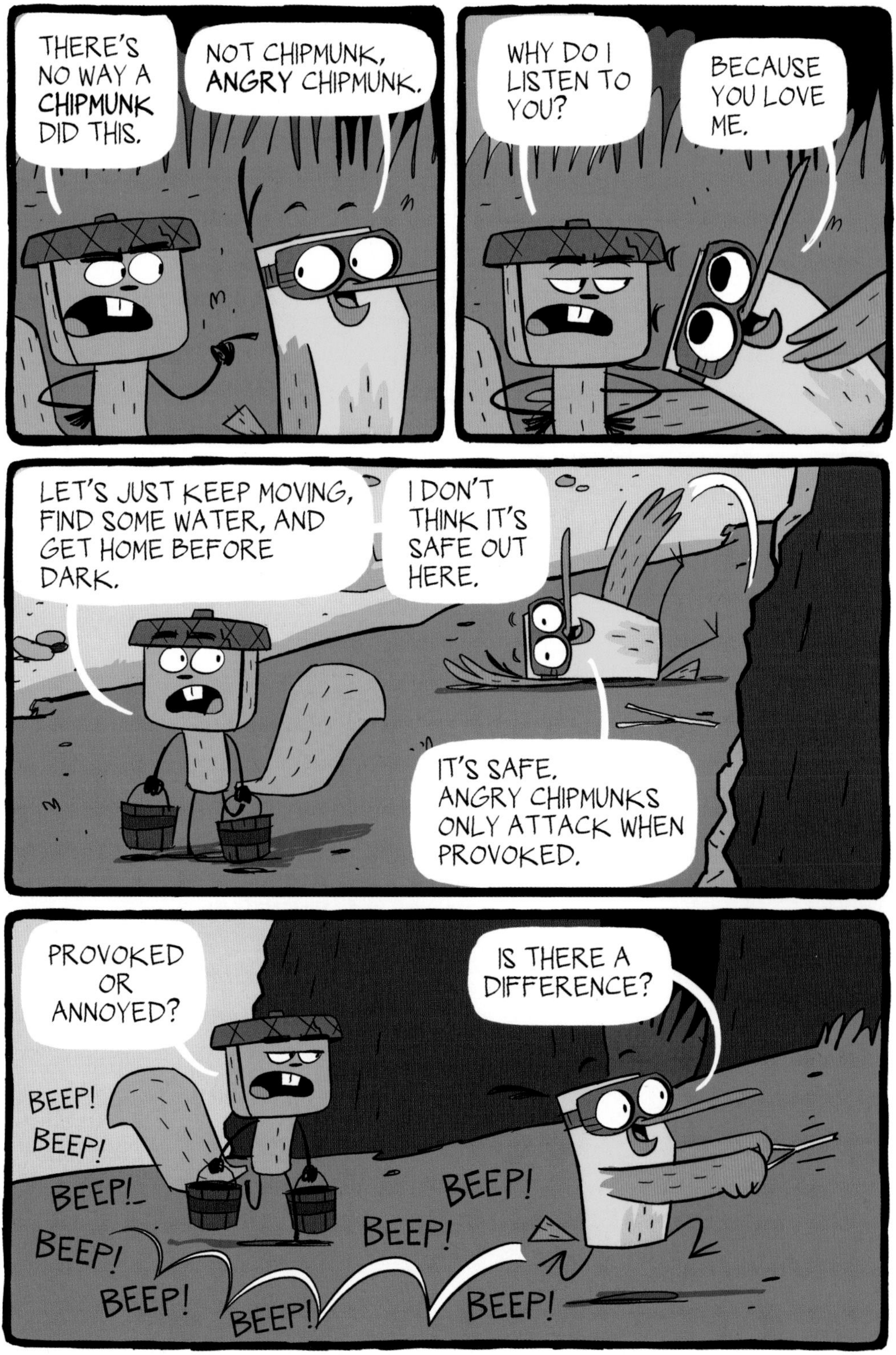
THERE'S NO WAY A **CHIPMUNK** DID THIS.
NOT CHIPMUNK, **ANGRY** CHIPMUNK.
WHY DO I LISTEN TO YOU?
BECAUSE YOU LOVE ME.
LET'S JUST KEEP MOVING, FIND SOME WATER, AND GET HOME BEFORE DARK.
I DON'T THINK IT'S SAFE OUT HERE.
IT'S SAFE. ANGRY CHIPMUNKS ONLY ATTACK WHEN PROVOKED.
PROVOKED OR ANNOYED?
IS THERE A DIFFERENCE?
BEEP!
BEEP!
BEEP!
BEEP!
BEEP!
BEEP!
BEEP!
BEEP!
BEEP!

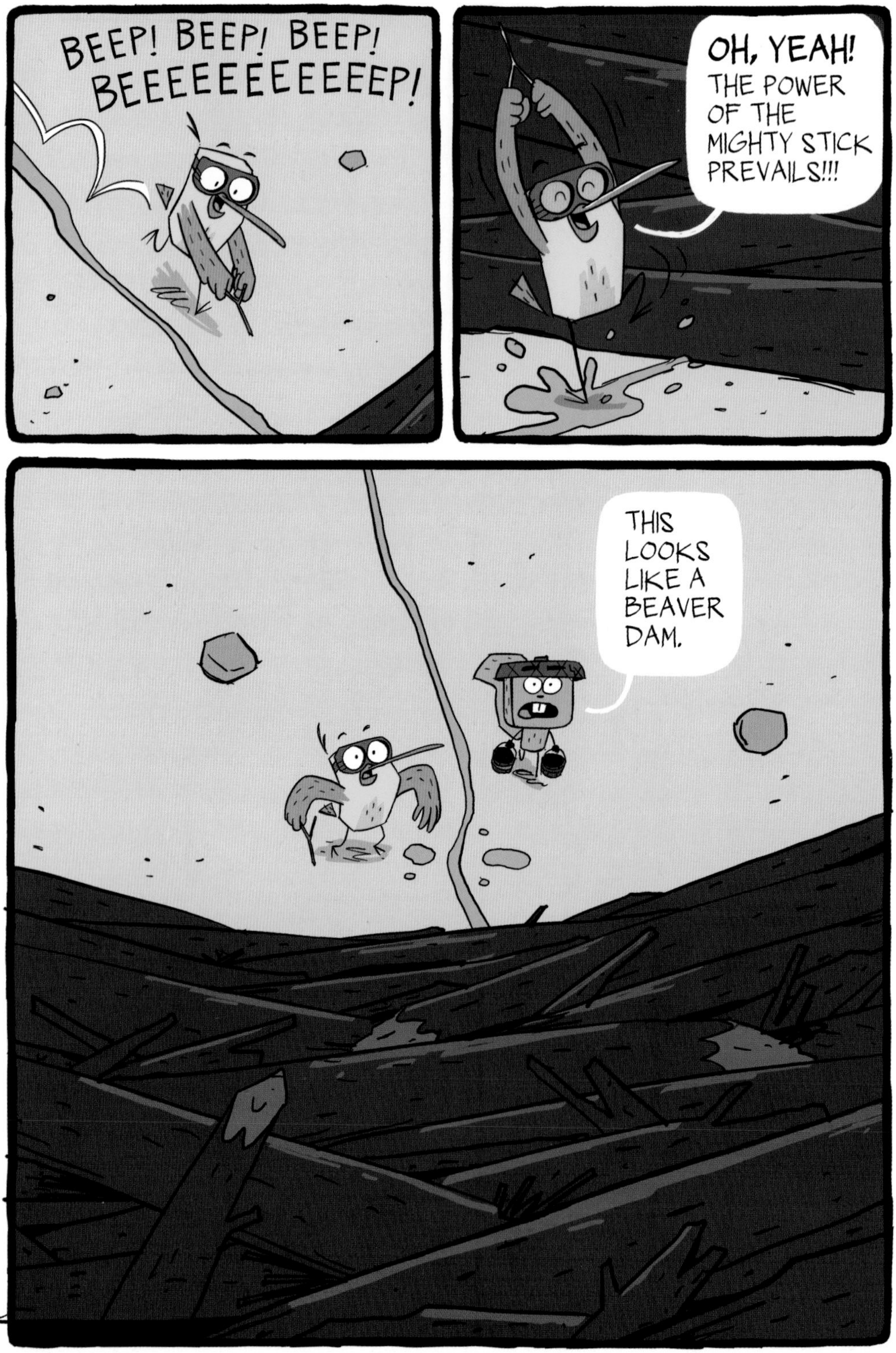
BEEP! BEEP! BEEP!
BEEEEEEEEEEEP!
OH, YEAH! THE POWER OF THE MIGHTY STICK PREVAILS!!!
THIS LOOKS LIKE A BEAVER DAM.

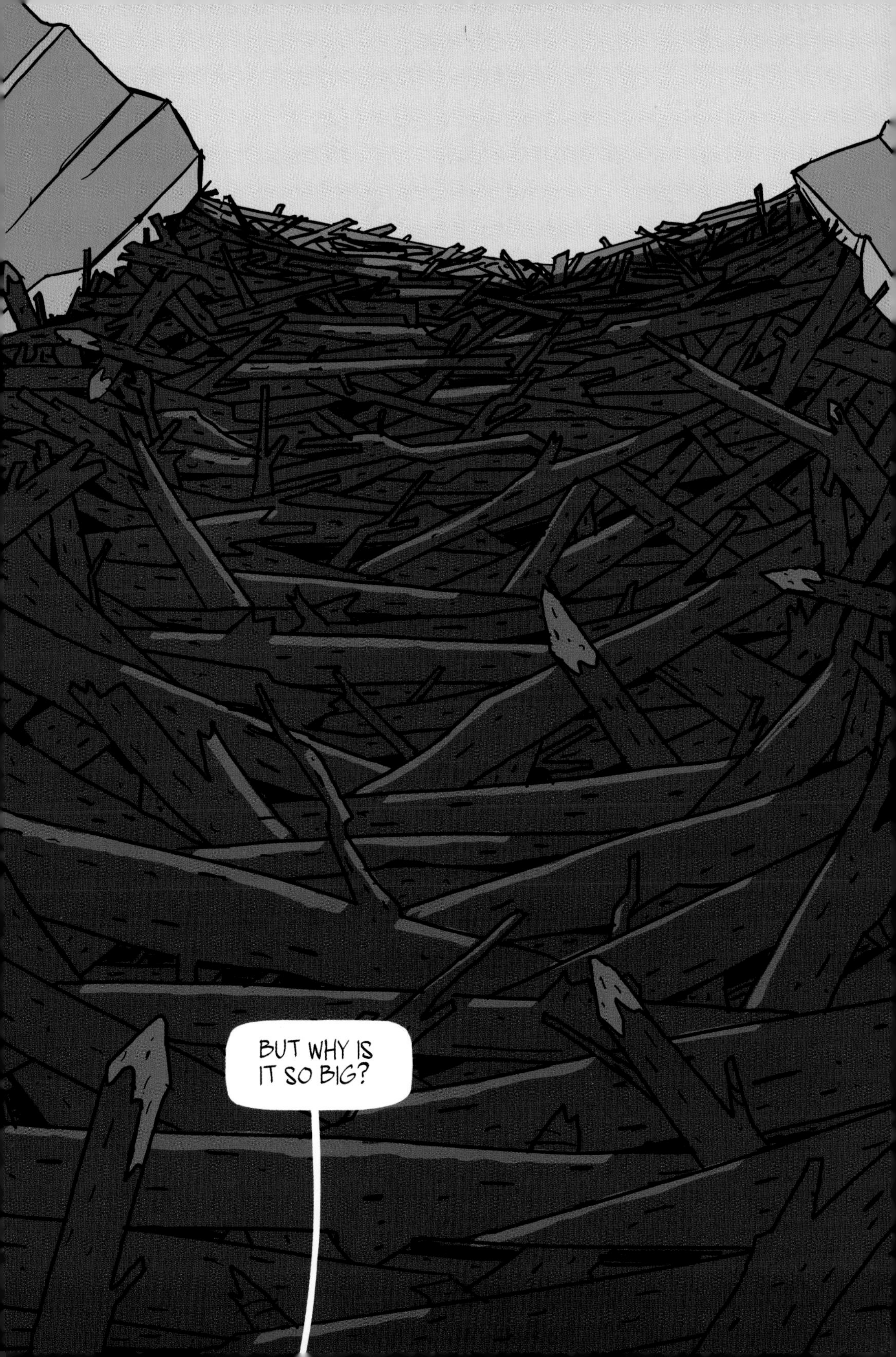
BUT WHY IS IT SO BIG?

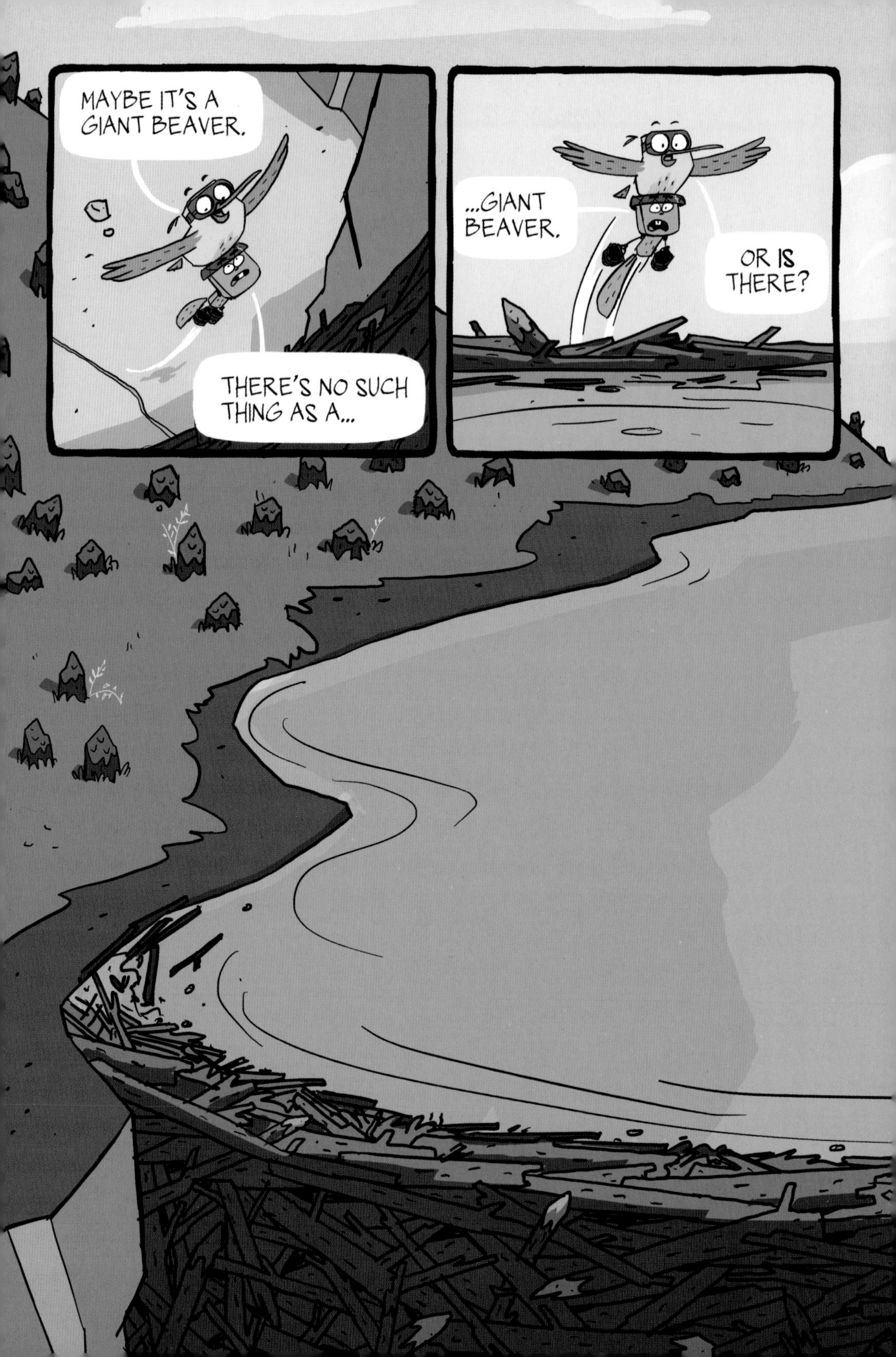
MAYBE IT'S A GIANT BEAVER.
THERE'S NO SUCH THING AS A...
...GIANT BEAVER.
OR IS THERE?

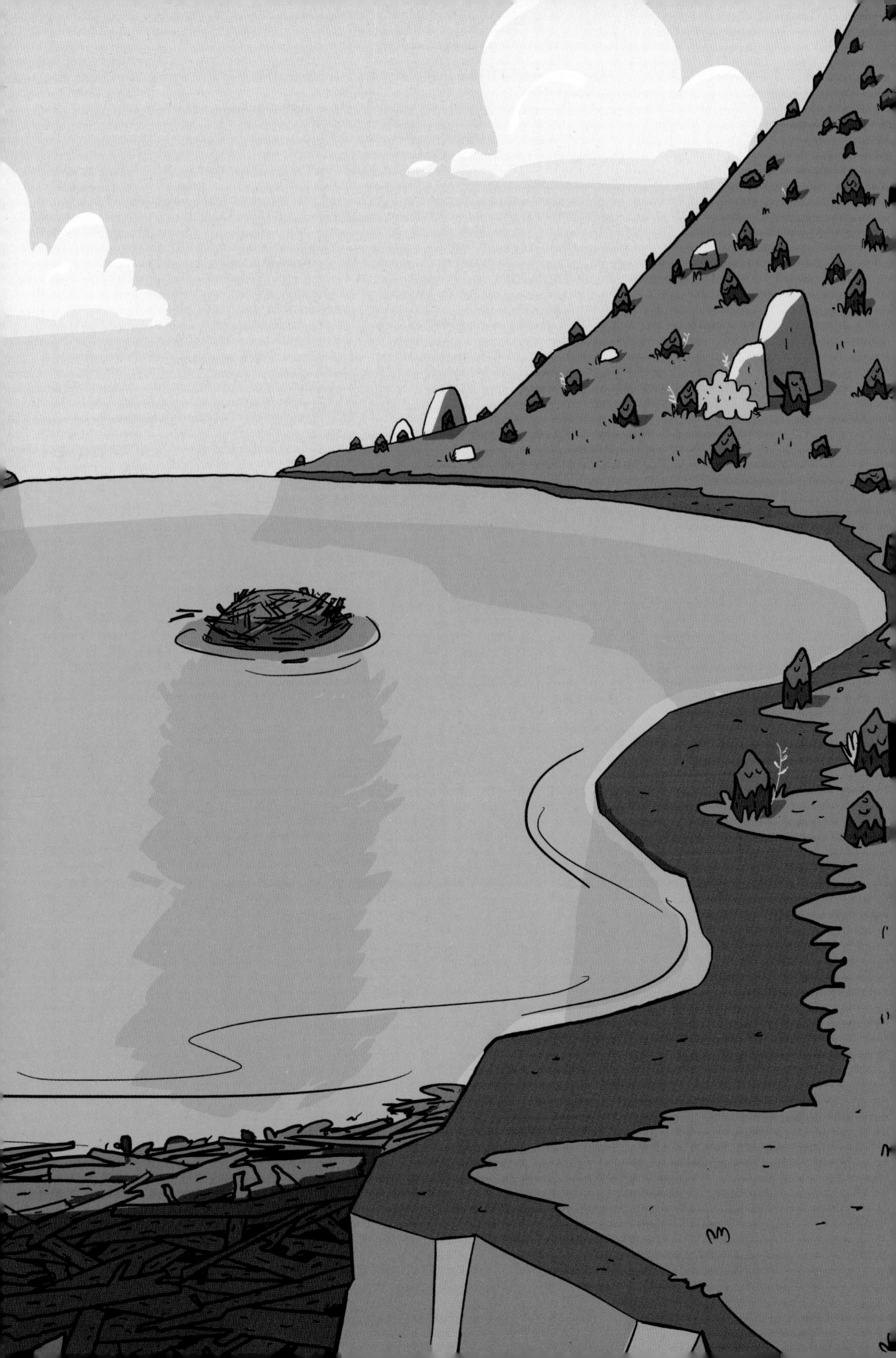

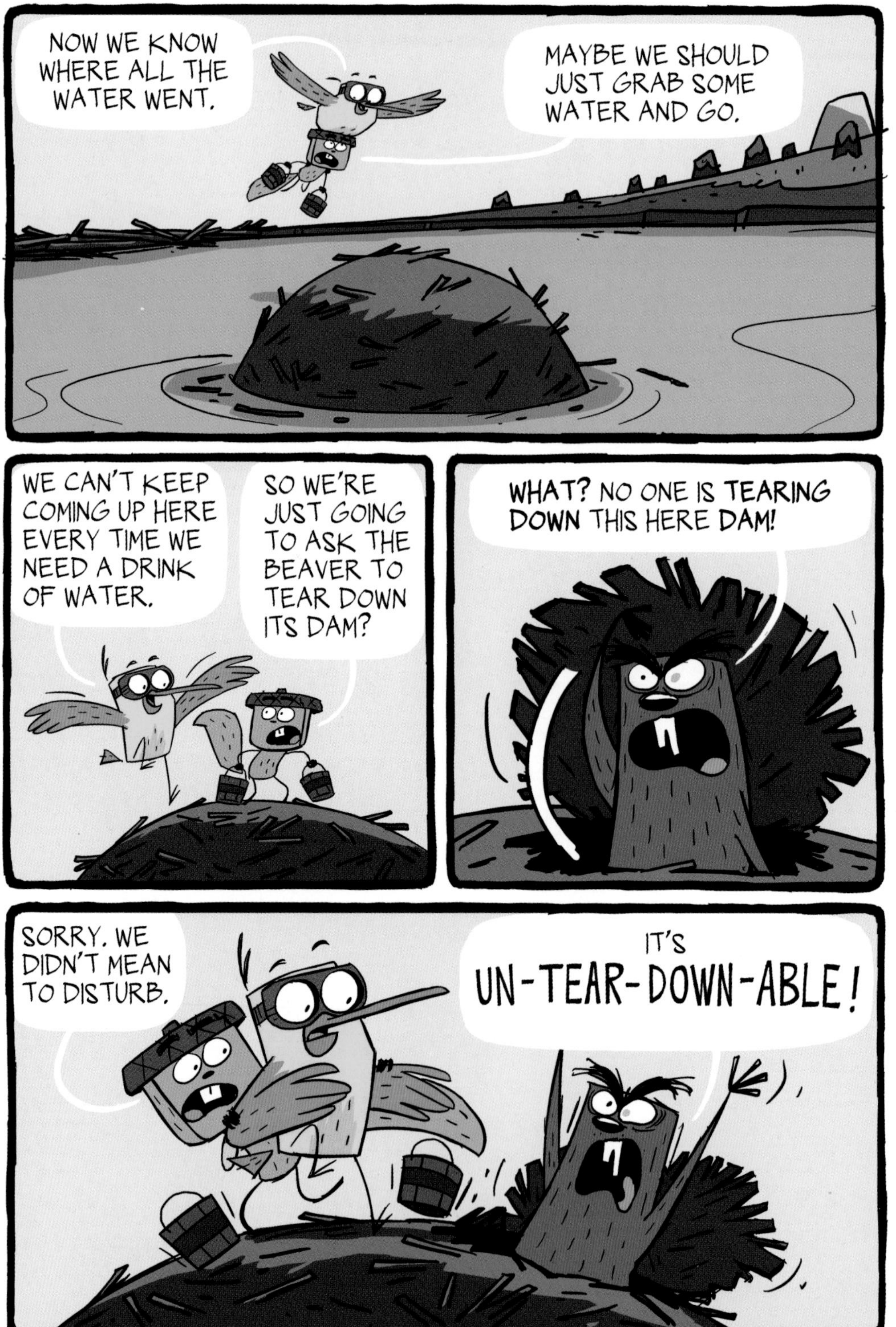
NOW WE KNOW WHERE ALL THE WATER WENT.
MAYBE WE SHOULD JUST GRAB SOME WATER AND GO.
WE CAN'T KEEP COMING UP HERE EVERY TIME WE NEED A DRINK OF WATER.
SO WE'RE JUST GOING TO ASK THE BEAVER TO TEAR DOWN ITS DAM?
WHAT? NO ONE IS TEARING DOWN THIS HERE DAM!
SORRY. WE DIDN'T MEAN TO DISTURB.
IT'S UN-TEAR-DOWN-ABLE!

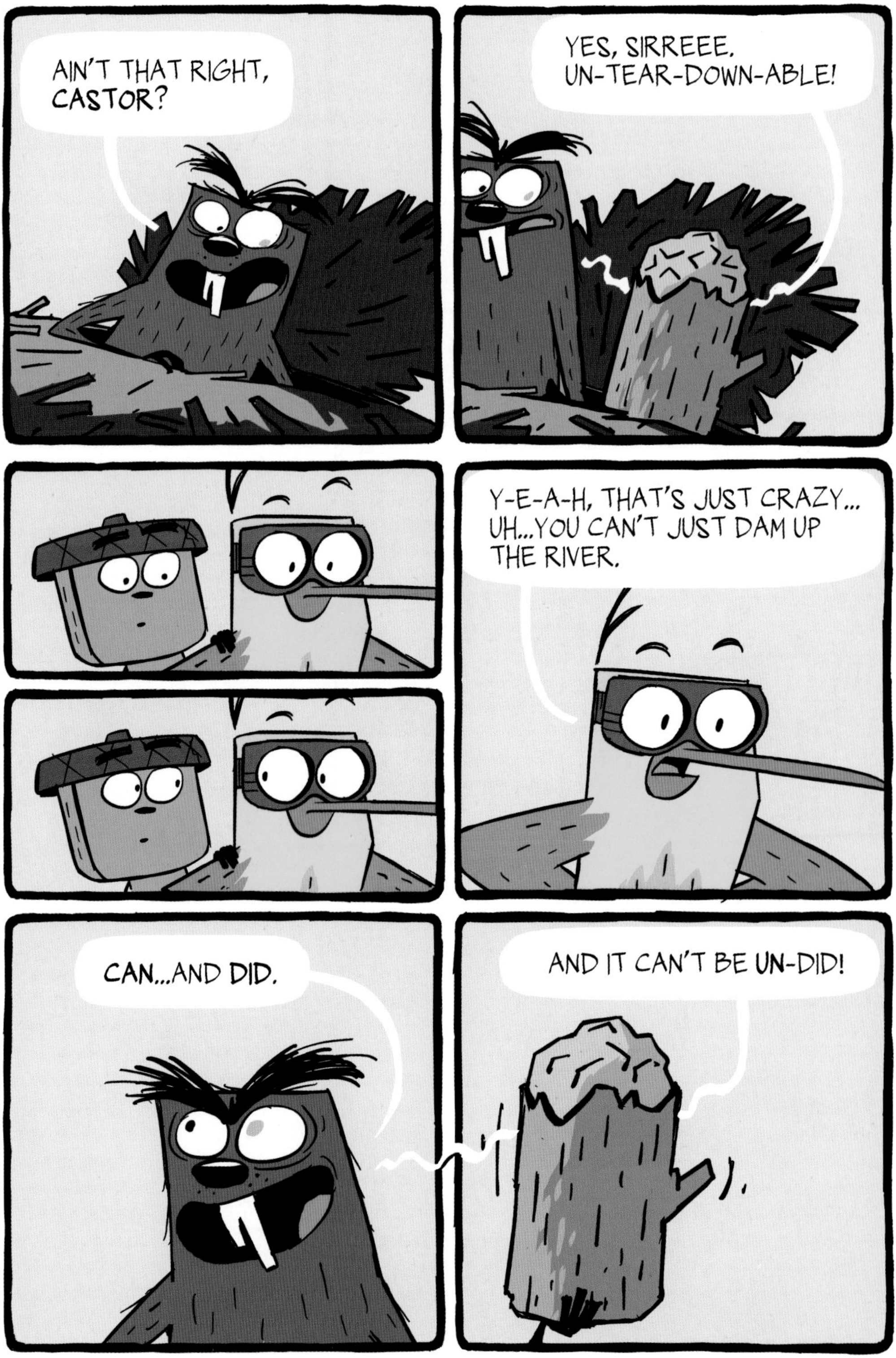
AIN'T THAT RIGHT, CASTOR?
YES, SIRREEE. UN-TEAR-DOWN-ABLE!
Y-E-A-H, THAT'S JUST CRAZY... UH...YOU CAN'T JUST DAM UP THE RIVER.
CAN...AND DID.
AND IT CAN'T BE UN-DID!

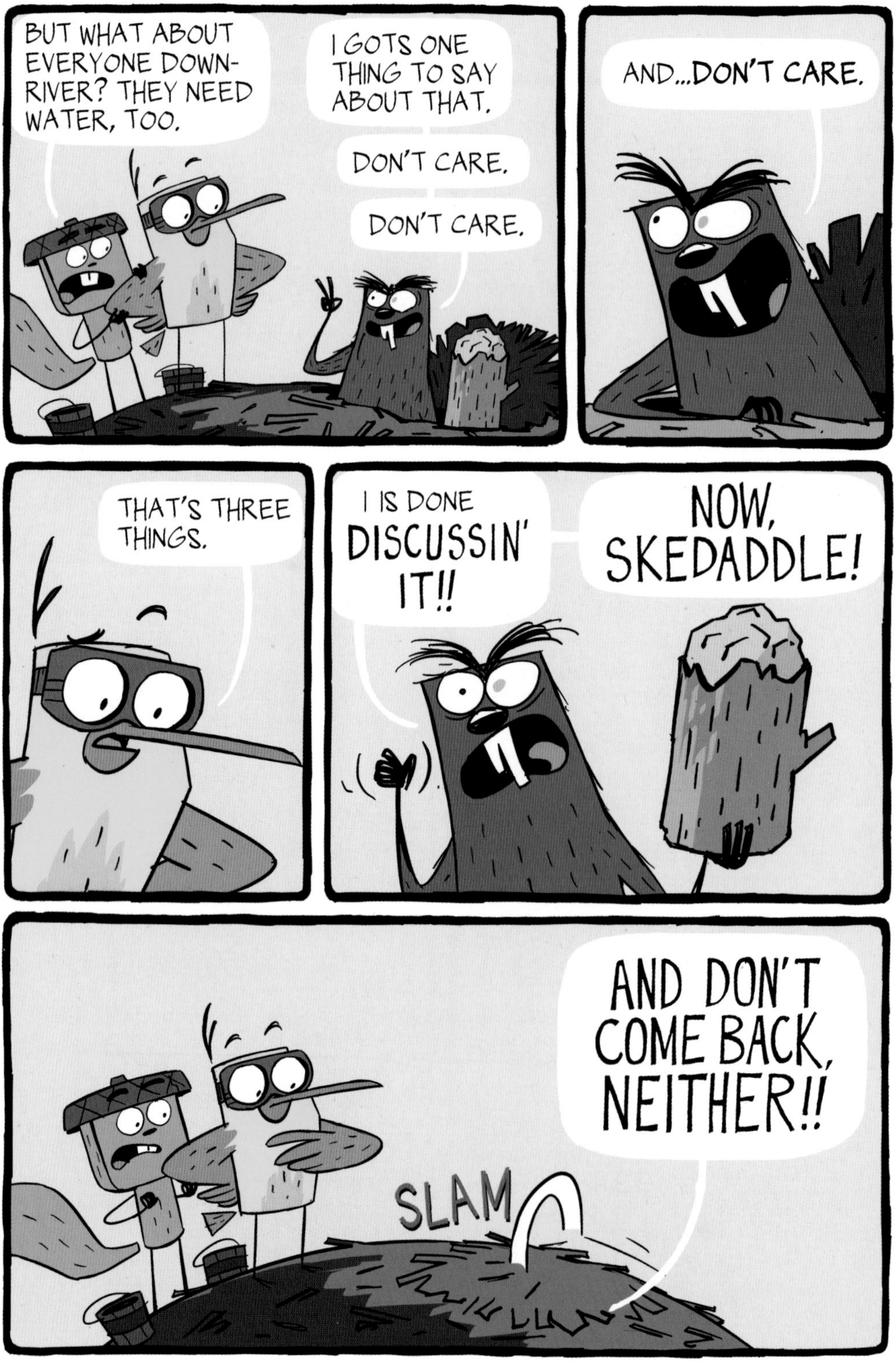
BUT WHAT ABOUT EVERYONE DOWN-RIVER? THEY NEED WATER, TOO.
I GOTS ONE THING TO SAY ABOUT THAT.
DON'T CARE.
DON'T CARE.
AND...DON'T CARE.
THAT'S THREE THINGS.
I IS DONE DISCUSSIN' IT!!
NOW, SKEDADDLE!
AND DON'T COME BACK, NEITHER!!
SLAM

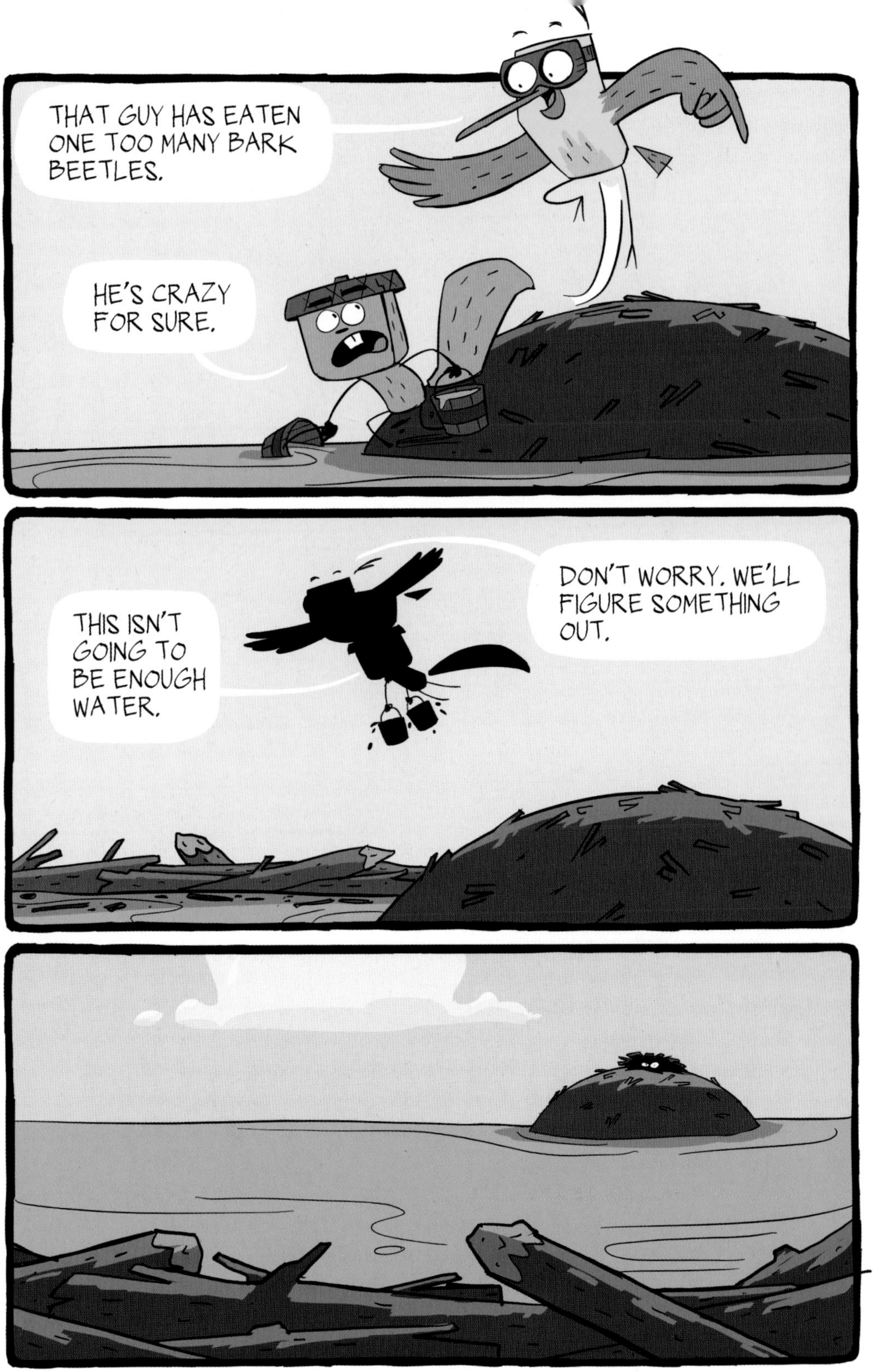
THAT GUY HAS EATEN ONE TOO MANY BARK BEETLES.
HE'S CRAZY FOR SURE.
THIS ISN'T GOING TO BE ENOUGH WATER.
DON'T WORRY. WE'LL FIGURE SOMETHING OUT.

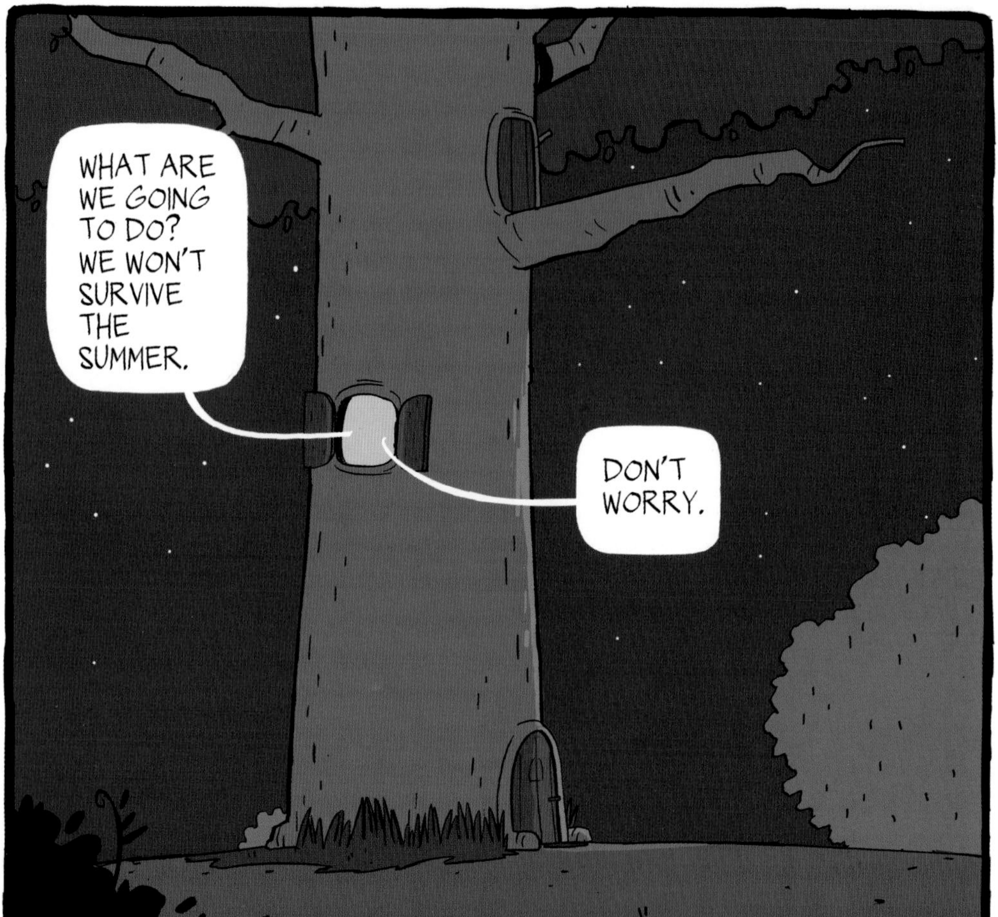
WHAT ARE WE GOING TO DO? WE WON'T SURVIVE THE SUMMER.
DON'T WORRY.

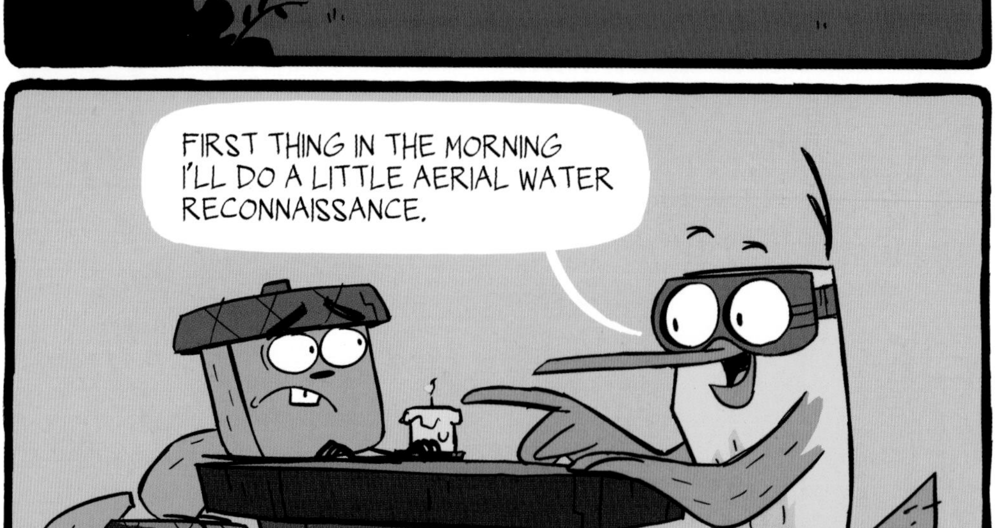
FIRST THING IN THE MORNING I'LL DO A LITTLE AERIAL WATER RECONNAISSANCE.

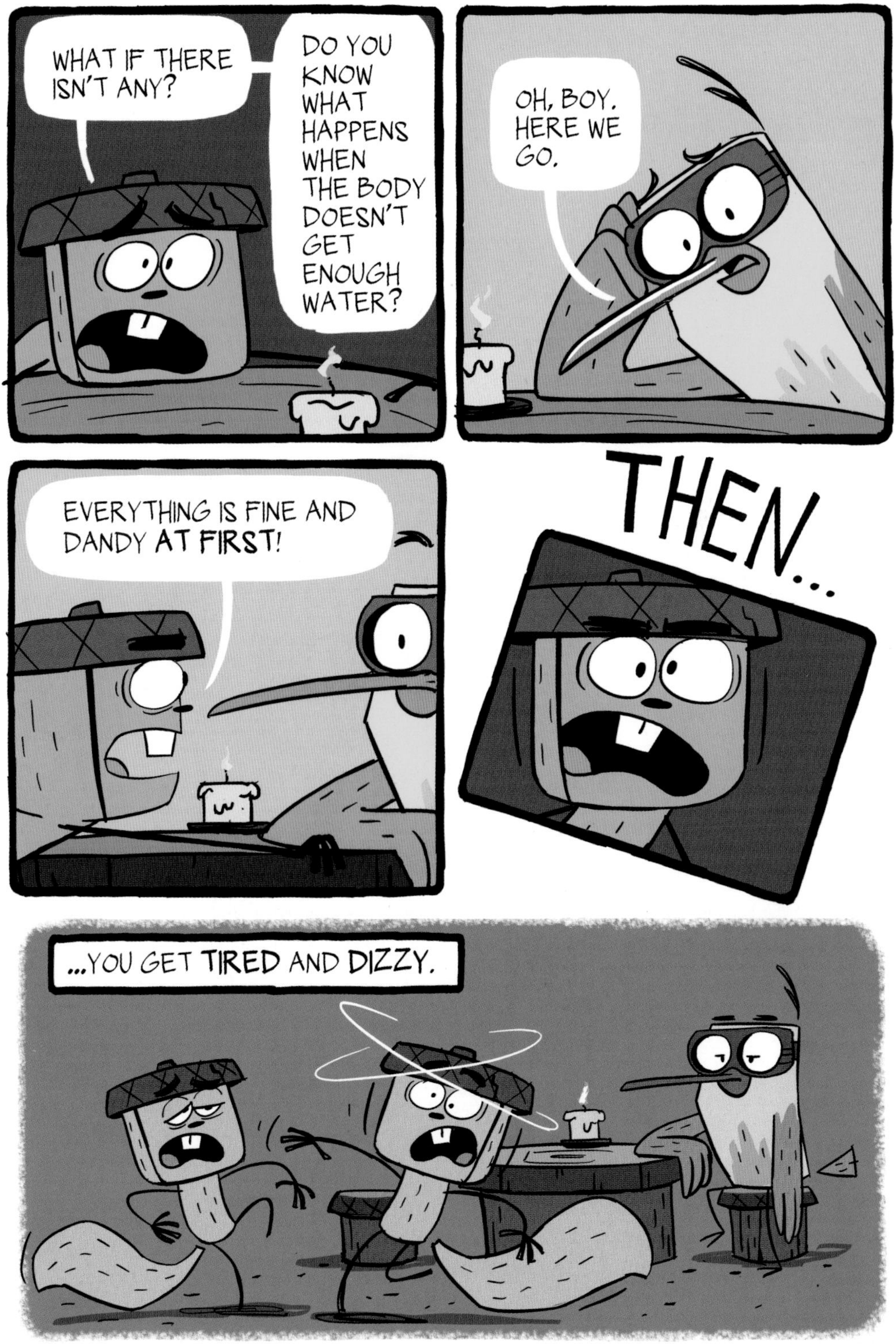

WHAT IF THERE ISN'T ANY?
DO YOU KNOW WHAT HAPPENS WHEN THE BODY DOESN'T GET ENOUGH WATER?
OH, BOY. HERE WE GO.
EVERYTHING IS FINE AND DANDY **AT FIRST**!
THEN...
...YOU GET **TIRED** AND **DIZZY**.

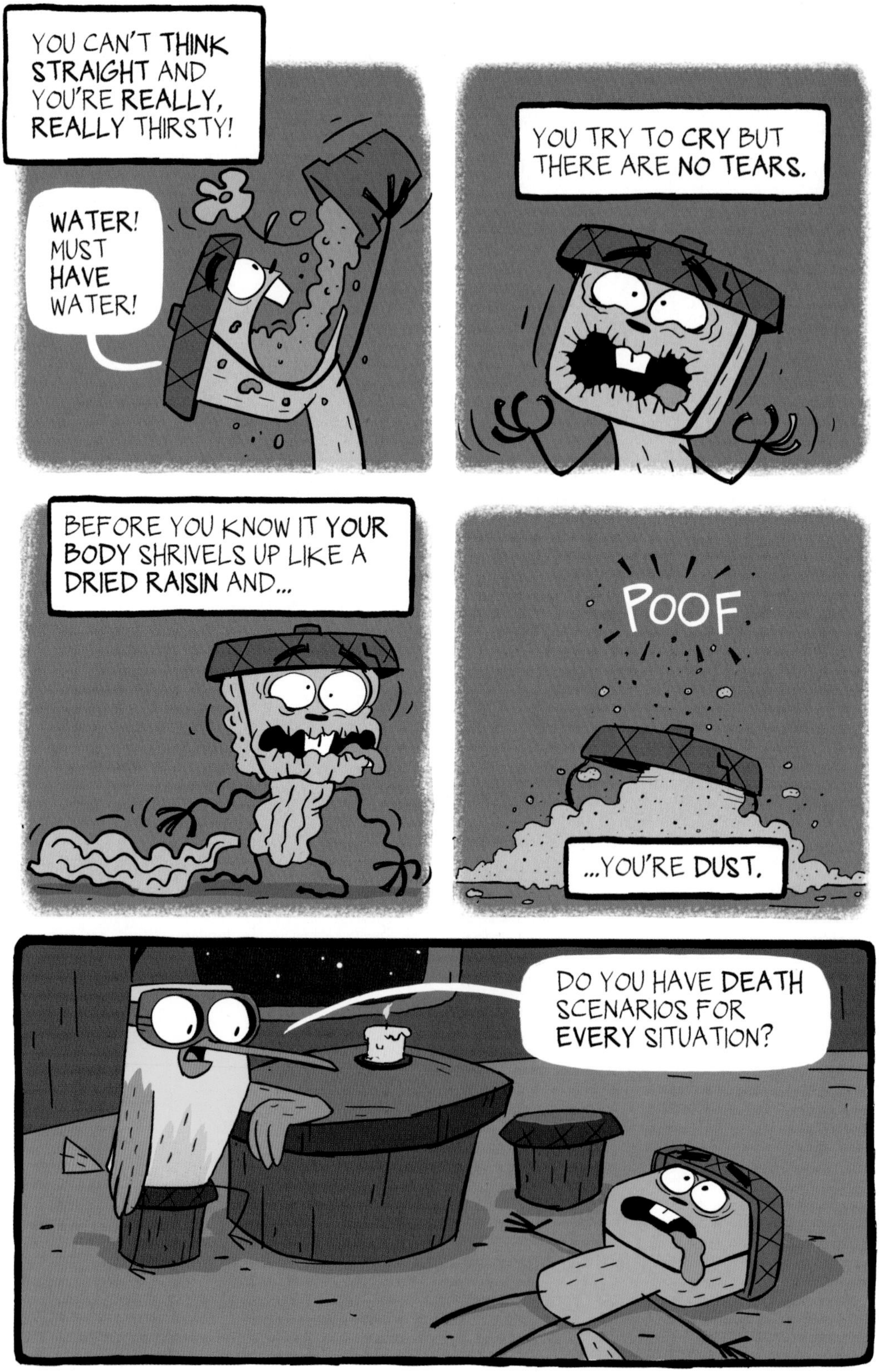

YOU CAN'T THINK STRAIGHT AND YOU'RE REALLY, REALLY THIRSTY!
WATER! MUST HAVE WATER!
YOU TRY TO CRY BUT THERE ARE NO TEARS.
BEFORE YOU KNOW IT YOUR BODY SHRIVELS UP LIKE A DRIED RAISIN AND...
POOF
...YOU'RE DUST.
DO YOU HAVE DEATH SCENARIOS FOR EVERY SITUATION?

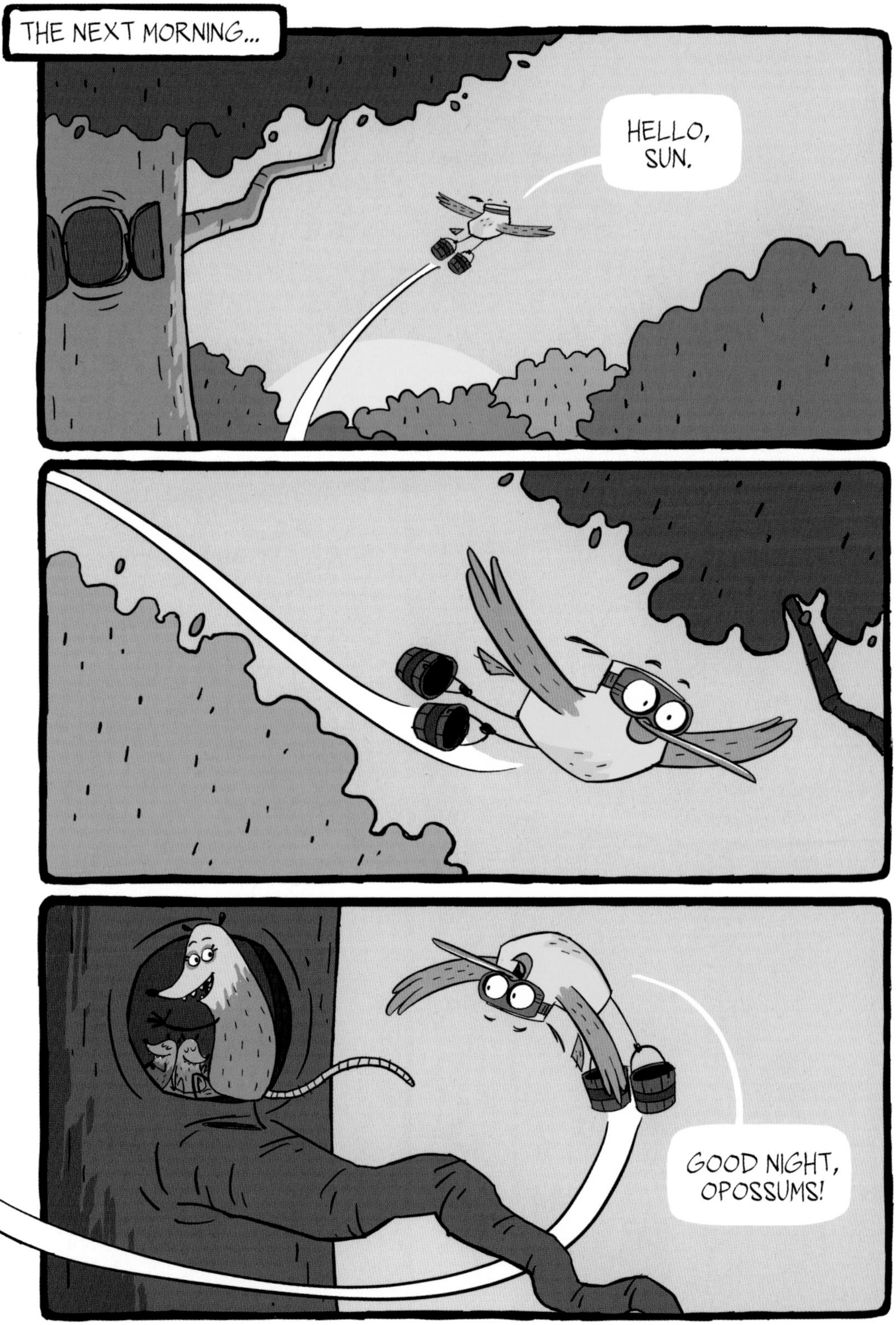
THE NEXT MORNING...
HELLO, SUN.
GOOD NIGHT, OPOSSUMS!

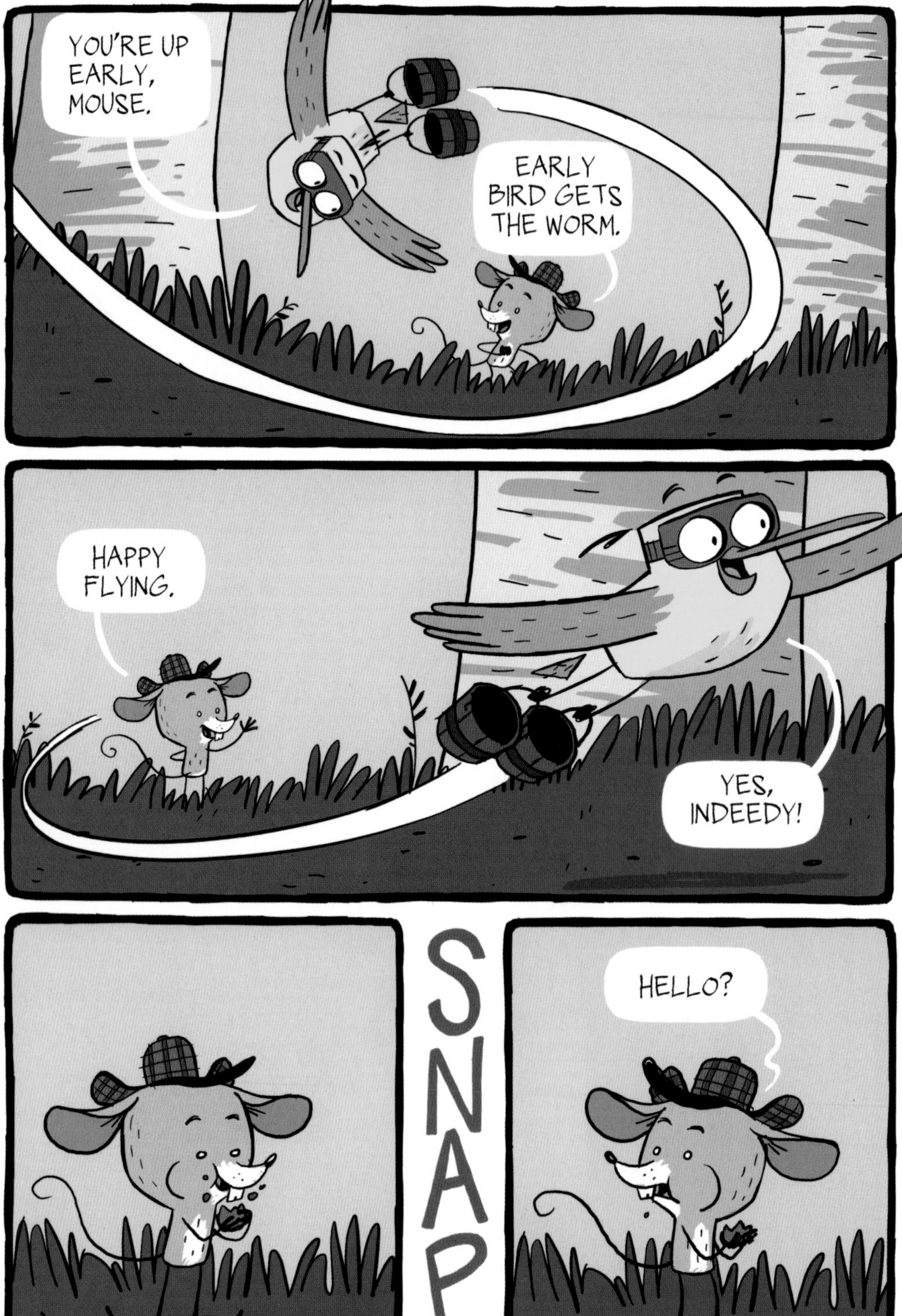

YOU'RE UP EARLY, MOUSE.
EARLY BIRD GETS THE WORM.
HAPPY FLYING.
YES, INDEEDY!
SNAP
HELLO?

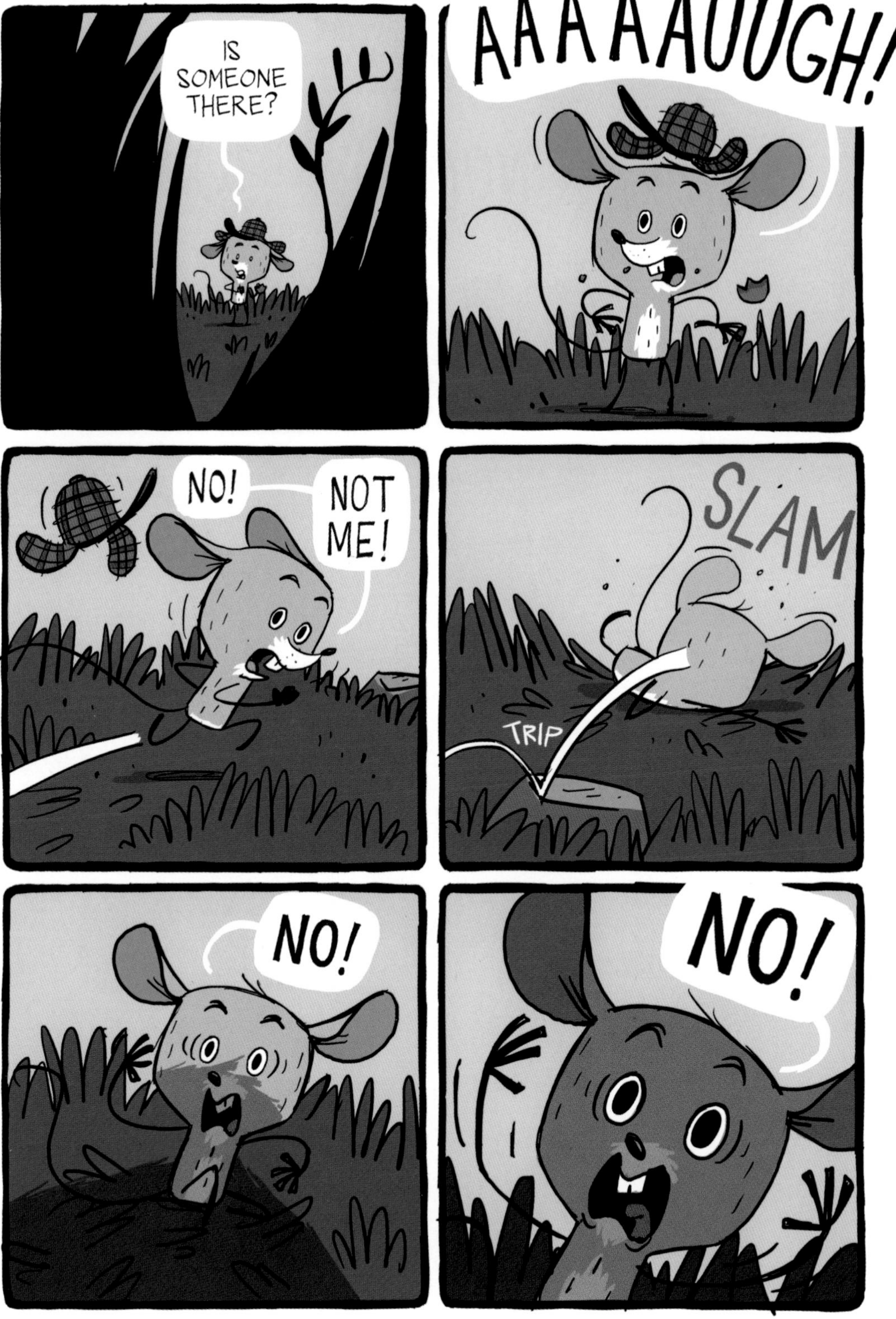
IS SOMEONE THERE?
AAAAAUUGH!
NO!
NOT ME!
SLAM
TRIP
NO!
NO!

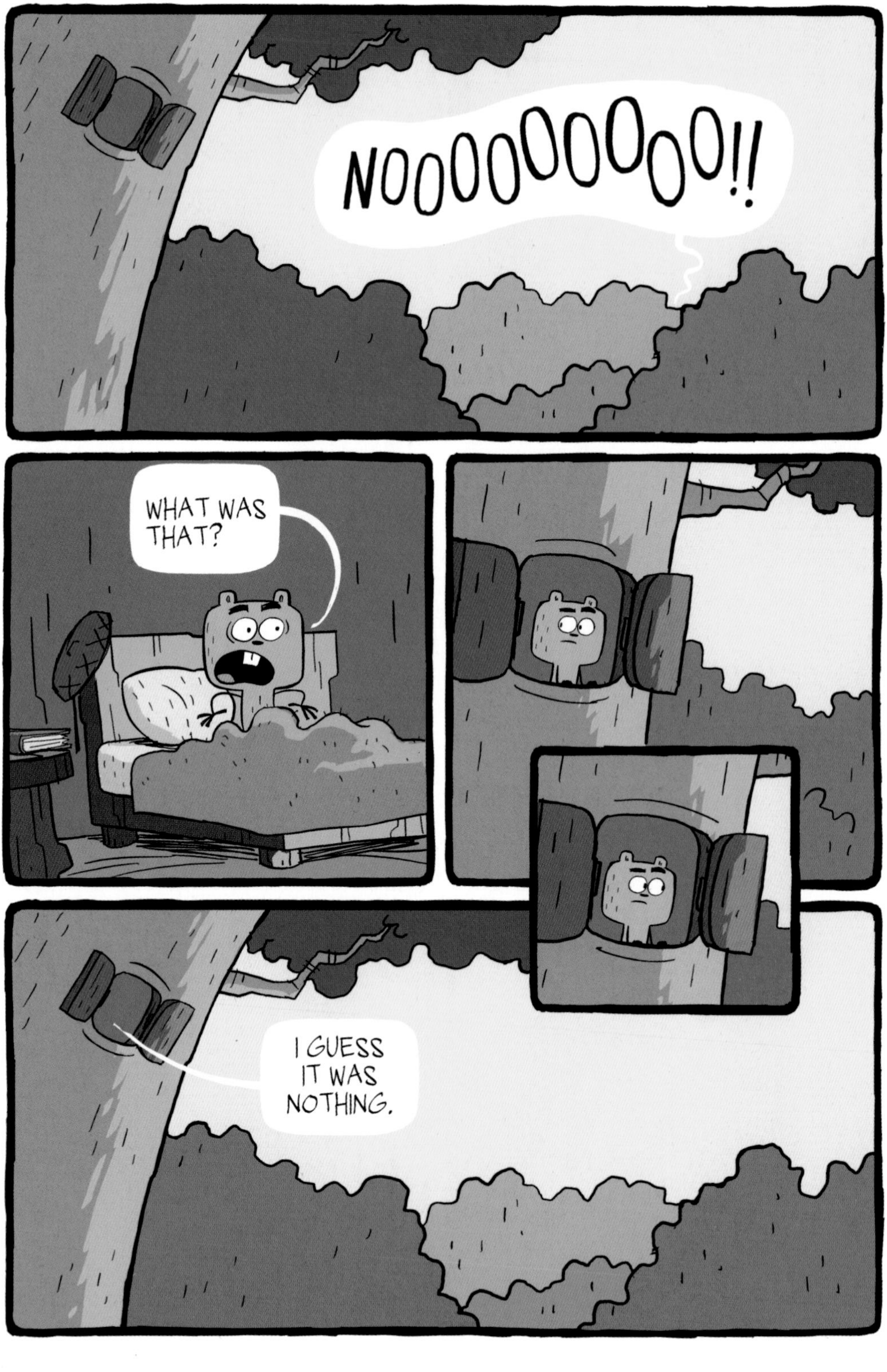
NOOOOOOOOOO!!
WHAT WAS THAT?
I GUESS IT WAS NOTHING.

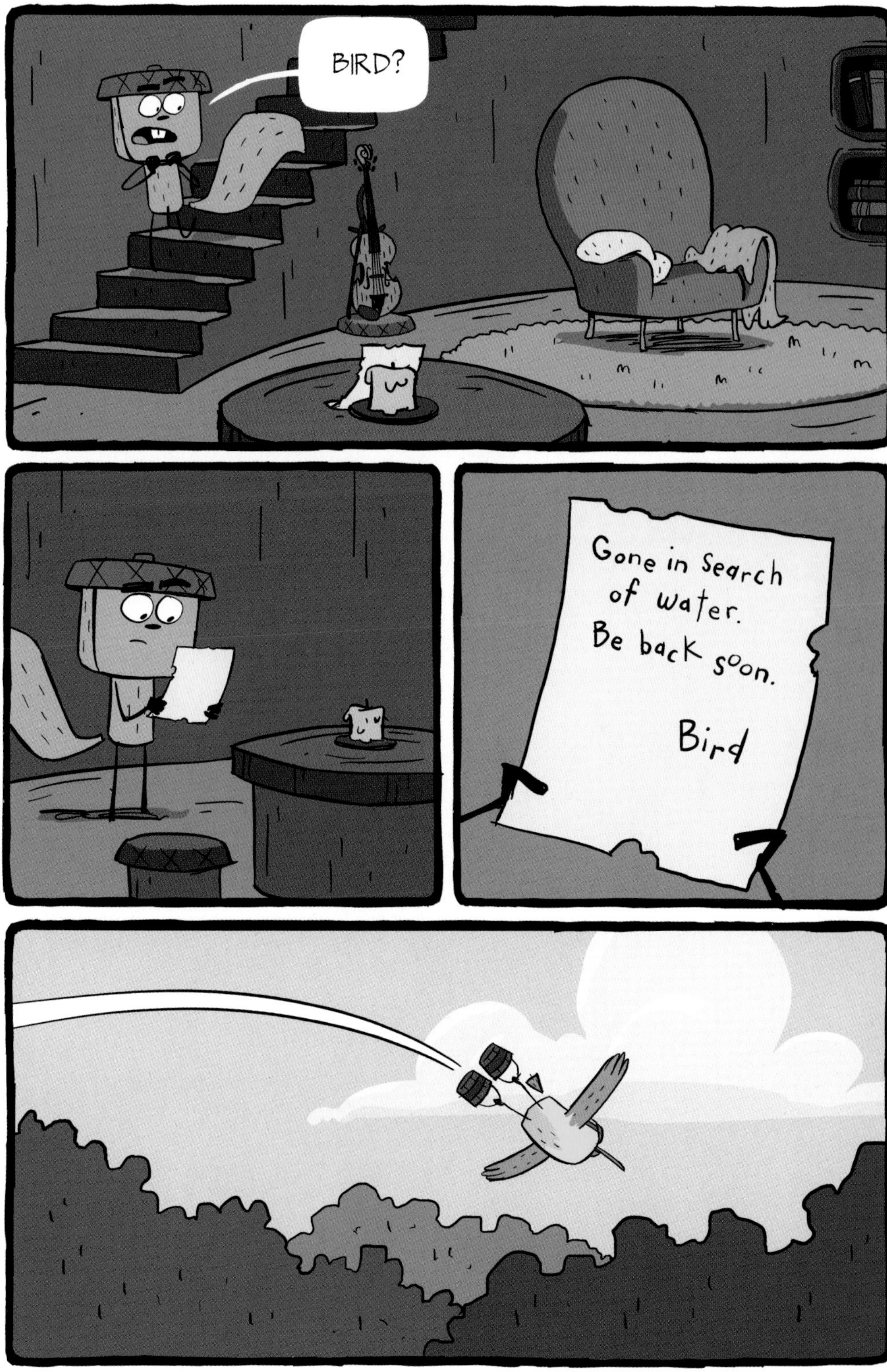
BIRD?
Gone in search of water. Be back soon.
Bird

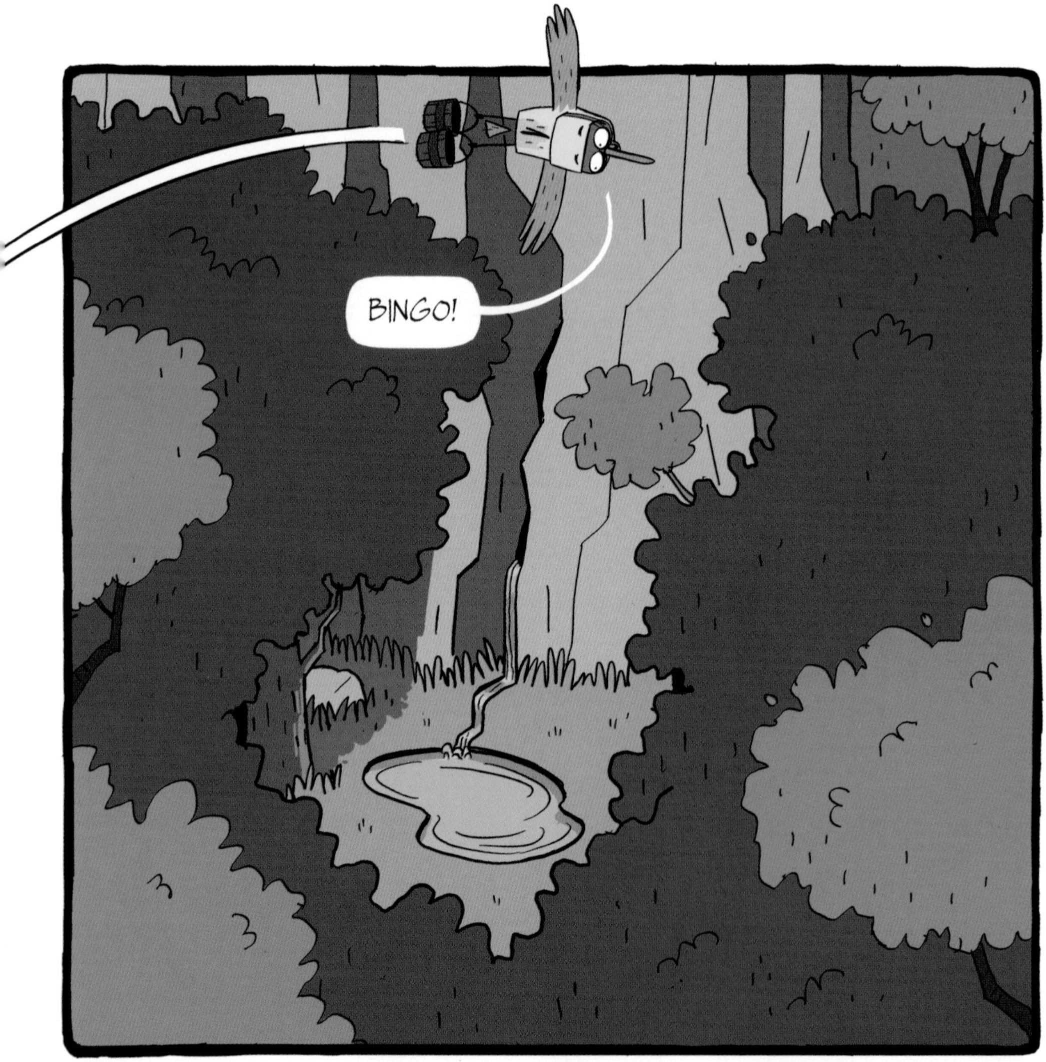
BINGO!

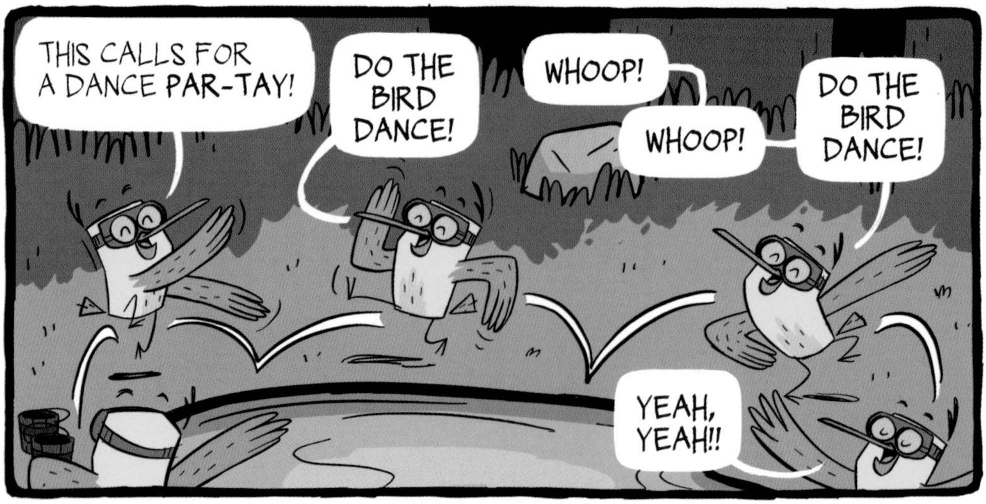
THIS CALLS FOR A DANCE PAR-TAY!
DO THE BIRD DANCE!
WHOOP!
WHOOP!
DO THE BIRD DANCE!
YEAH, YEAH!!

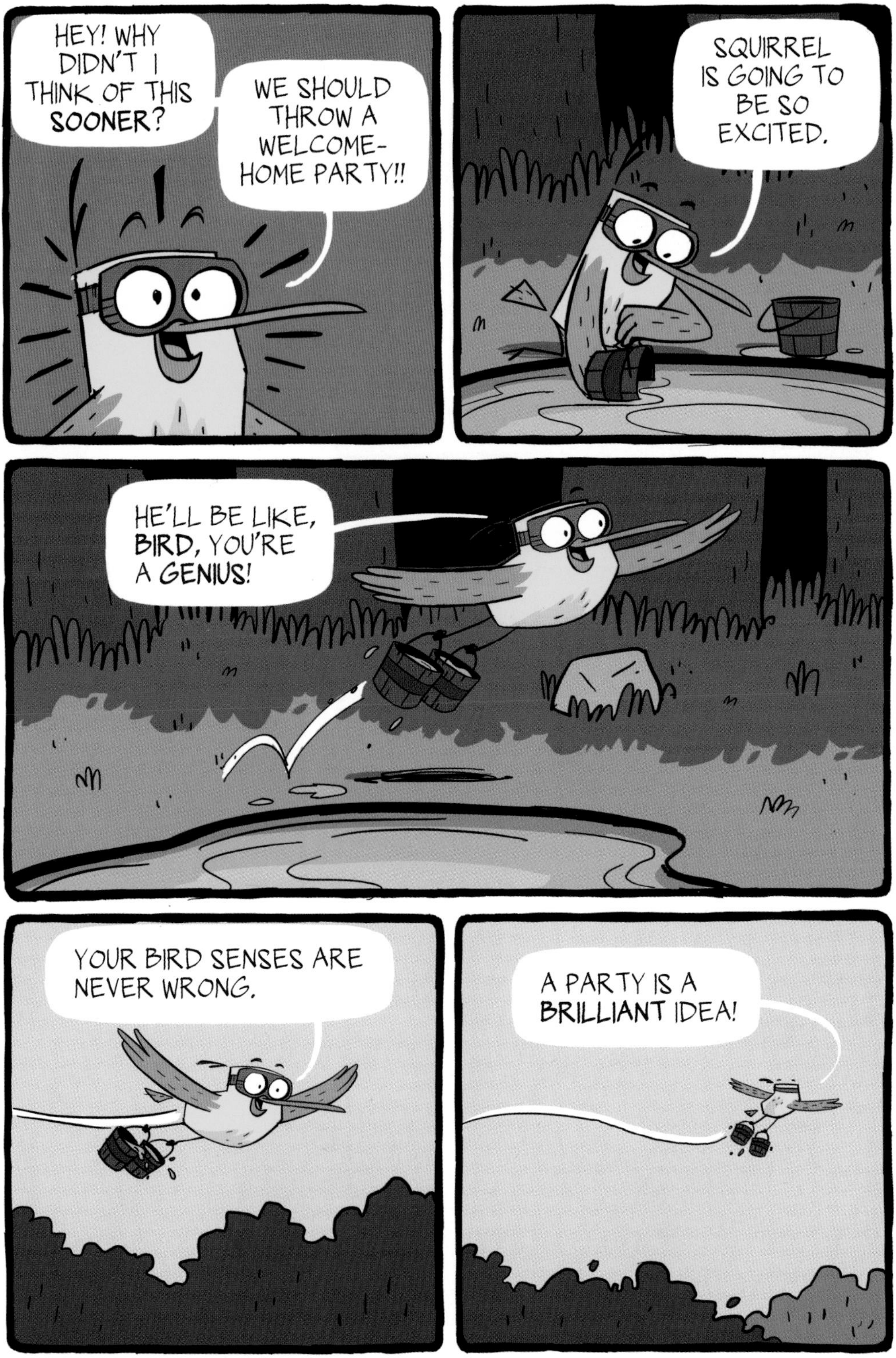
HEY! WHY DIDN'T I THINK OF THIS SOONER?
WE SHOULD THROW A WELCOME-HOME PARTY!!
SQUIRREL IS GOING TO BE SO EXCITED.
HE'LL BE LIKE, BIRD, YOU'RE A GENIUS!
YOUR BIRD SENSES ARE NEVER WRONG.
A PARTY IS A BRILLIANT IDEA!

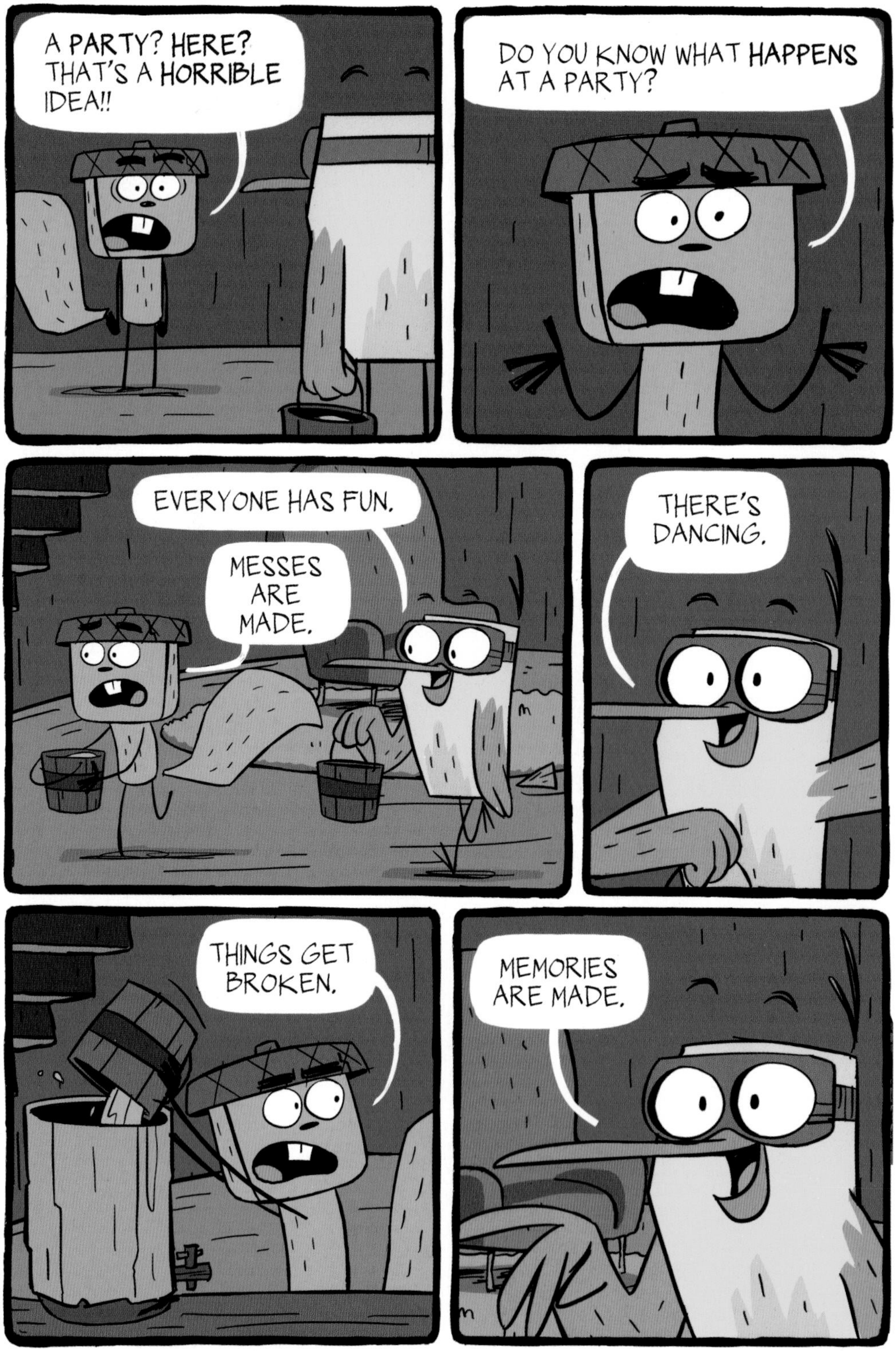
A PARTY? HERE? THAT'S A HORRIBLE IDEA!!
DO YOU KNOW WHAT HAPPENS AT A PARTY?
EVERYONE HAS FUN.
MESSES ARE MADE.
THERE'S DANCING.
THINGS GET BROKEN.
MEMORIES ARE MADE.

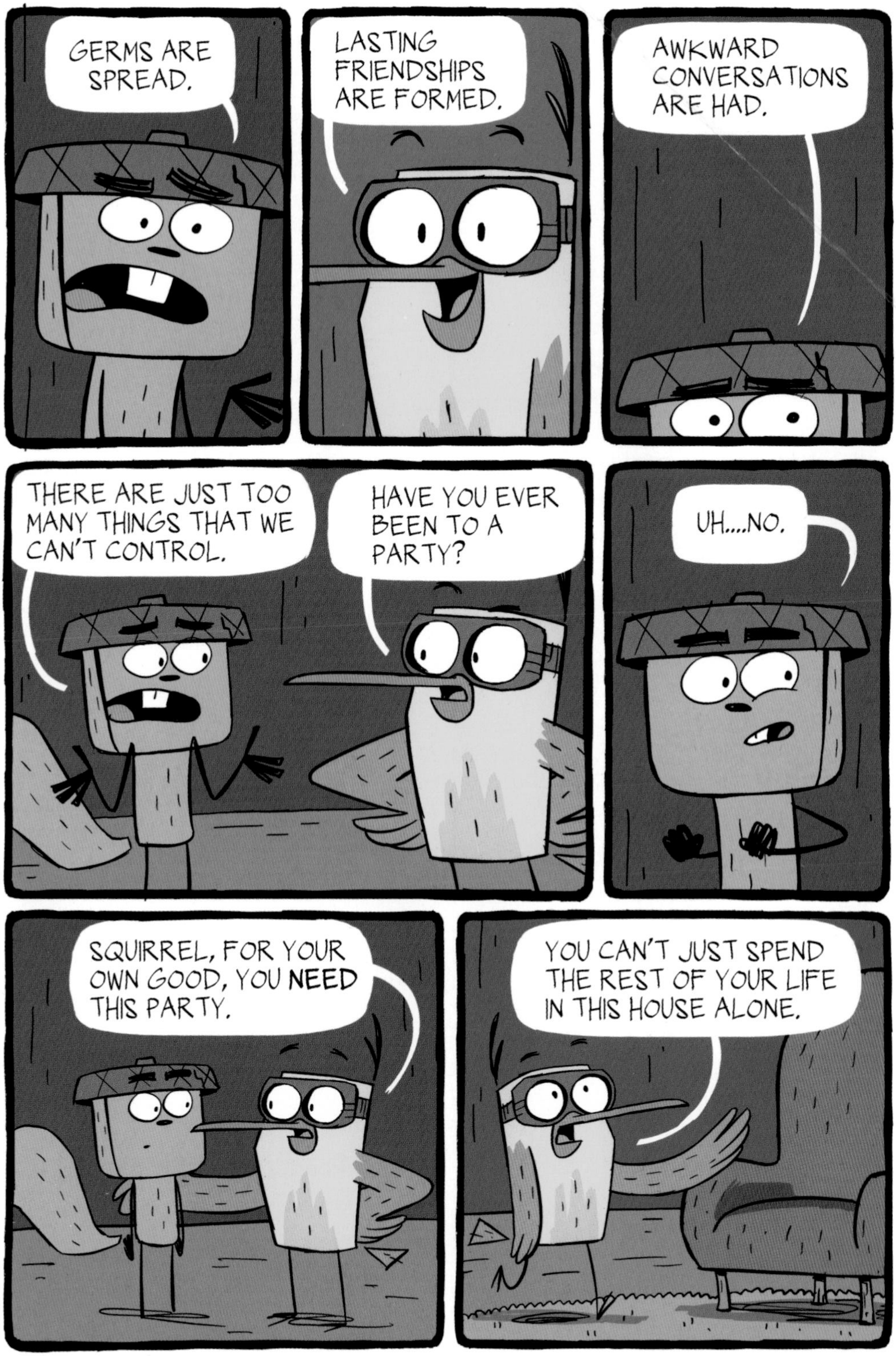
GERMS ARE SPREAD.
LASTING FRIENDSHIPS ARE FORMED.
AWKWARD CONVERSATIONS ARE HAD.
THERE ARE JUST TOO MANY THINGS THAT WE CAN'T CONTROL.
HAVE YOU EVER BEEN TO A PARTY?
UH....NO.
SQUIRREL, FOR YOUR OWN GOOD, YOU NEED THIS PARTY.
YOU CAN'T JUST SPEND THE REST OF YOUR LIFE IN THIS HOUSE ALONE.

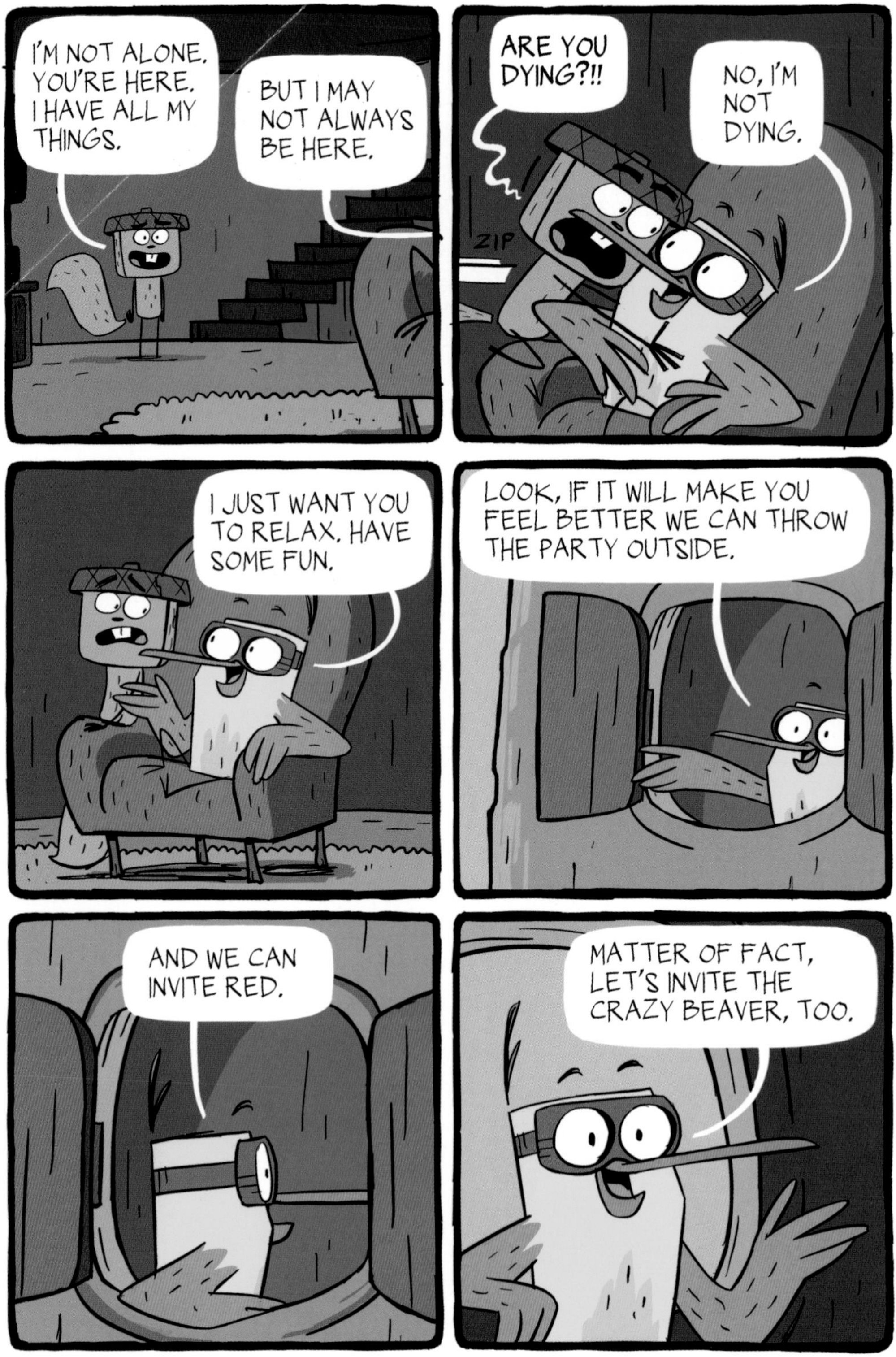
I'M NOT ALONE. YOU'RE HERE. I HAVE ALL MY THINGS.
BUT I MAY NOT ALWAYS BE HERE.
ARE YOU DYING?!!
ZIP
NO, I'M NOT DYING.
I JUST WANT YOU TO RELAX. HAVE SOME FUN.
LOOK, IF IT WILL MAKE YOU FEEL BETTER WE CAN THROW THE PARTY OUTSIDE.
AND WE CAN INVITE RED.
MATTER OF FACT, LET'S INVITE THE CRAZY BEAVER, TOO.

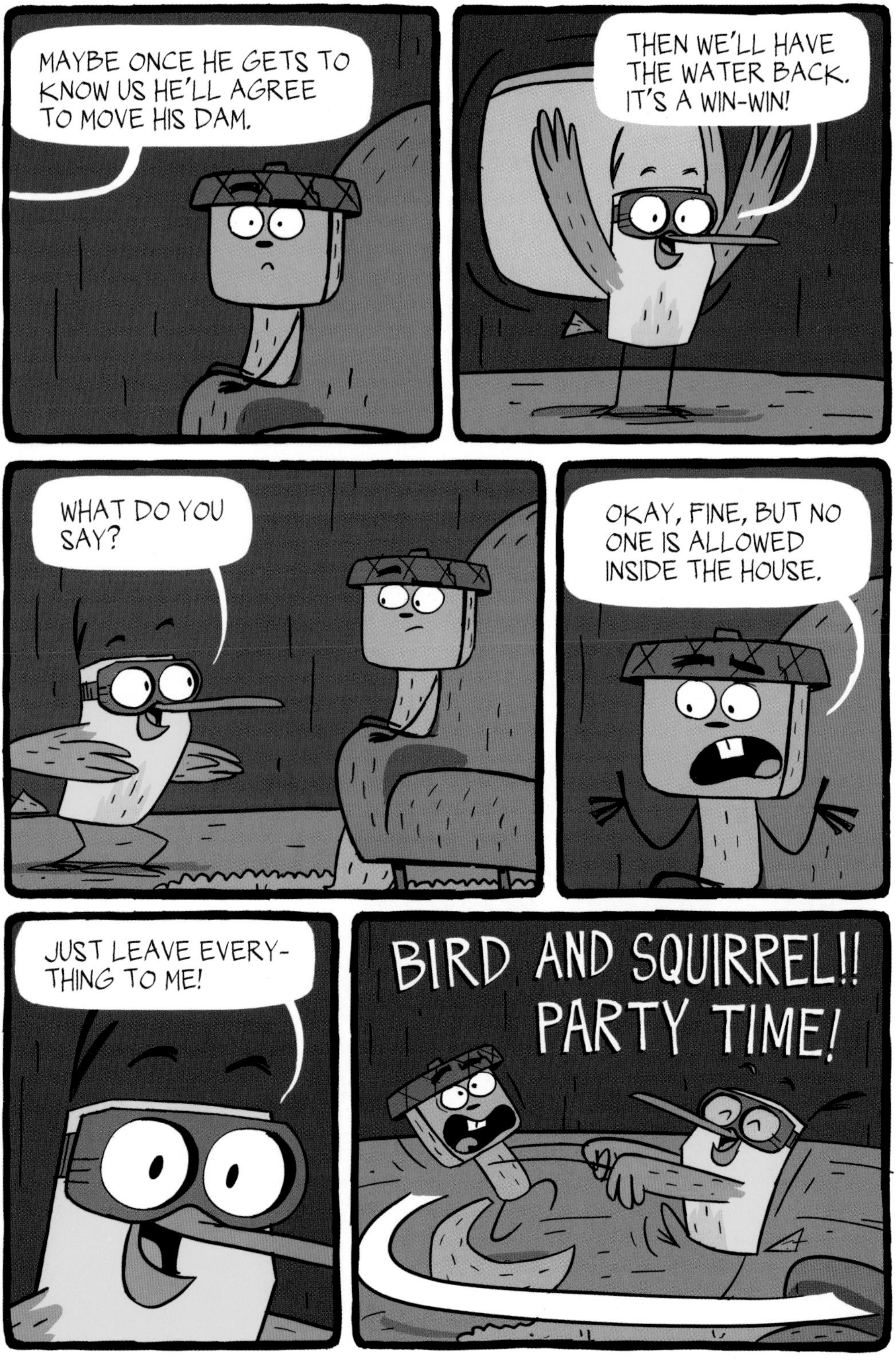

MAYBE ONCE HE GETS TO KNOW US HE'LL AGREE TO MOVE HIS DAM.
THEN WE'LL HAVE THE WATER BACK. IT'S A WIN-WIN!
WHAT DO YOU SAY?
OKAY, FINE, BUT NO ONE IS ALLOWED INSIDE THE HOUSE.
JUST LEAVE EVERY-THING TO ME!
BIRD AND SQUIRREL!! PARTY TIME!

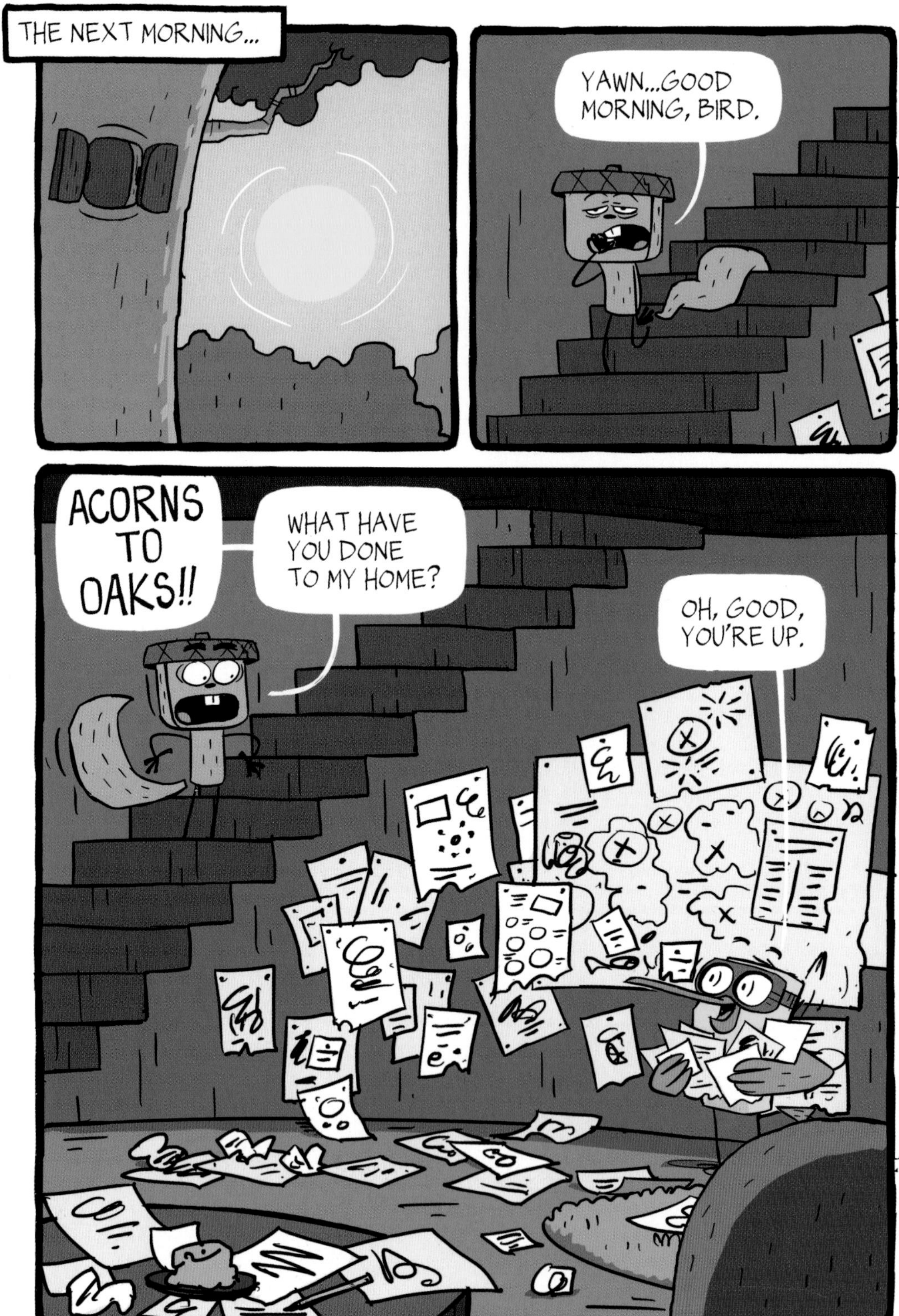
THE NEXT MORNING...
YAWN...GOOD MORNING, BIRD.
ACORNS TO OAKS!!
WHAT HAVE YOU DONE TO MY HOME?
OH, GOOD, YOU'RE UP.

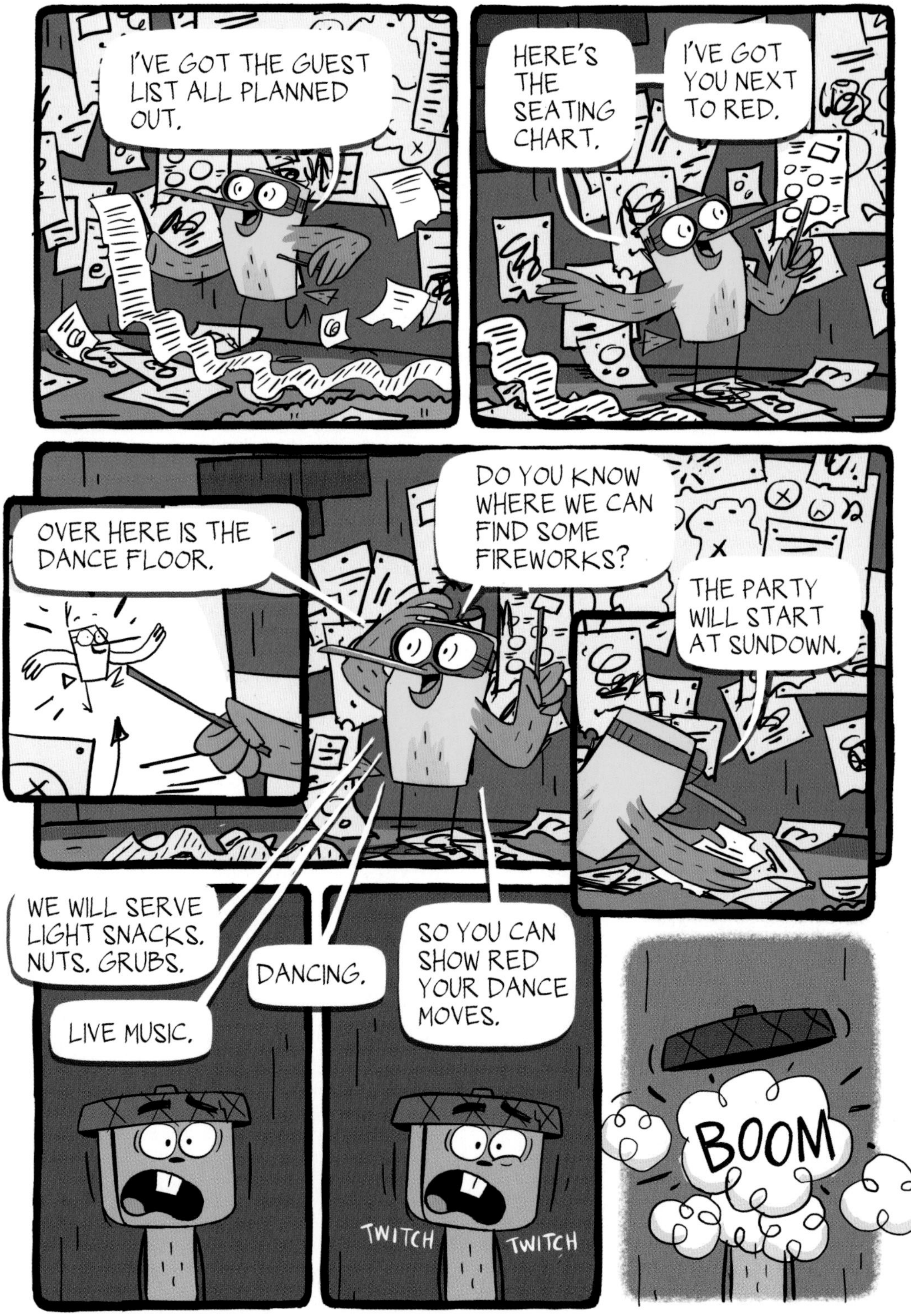
I'VE GOT THE GUEST LIST ALL PLANNED OUT.
HERE'S THE SEATING CHART.
I'VE GOT YOU NEXT TO RED.
OVER HERE IS THE DANCE FLOOR.
DO YOU KNOW WHERE WE CAN FIND SOME FIREWORKS?
THE PARTY WILL START AT SUNDOWN.
WE WILL SERVE LIGHT SNACKS. NUTS. GRUBS.
LIVE MUSIC.
DANCING.
SO YOU CAN SHOW RED YOUR DANCE MOVES.
TWITCH
TWITCH
BOOM

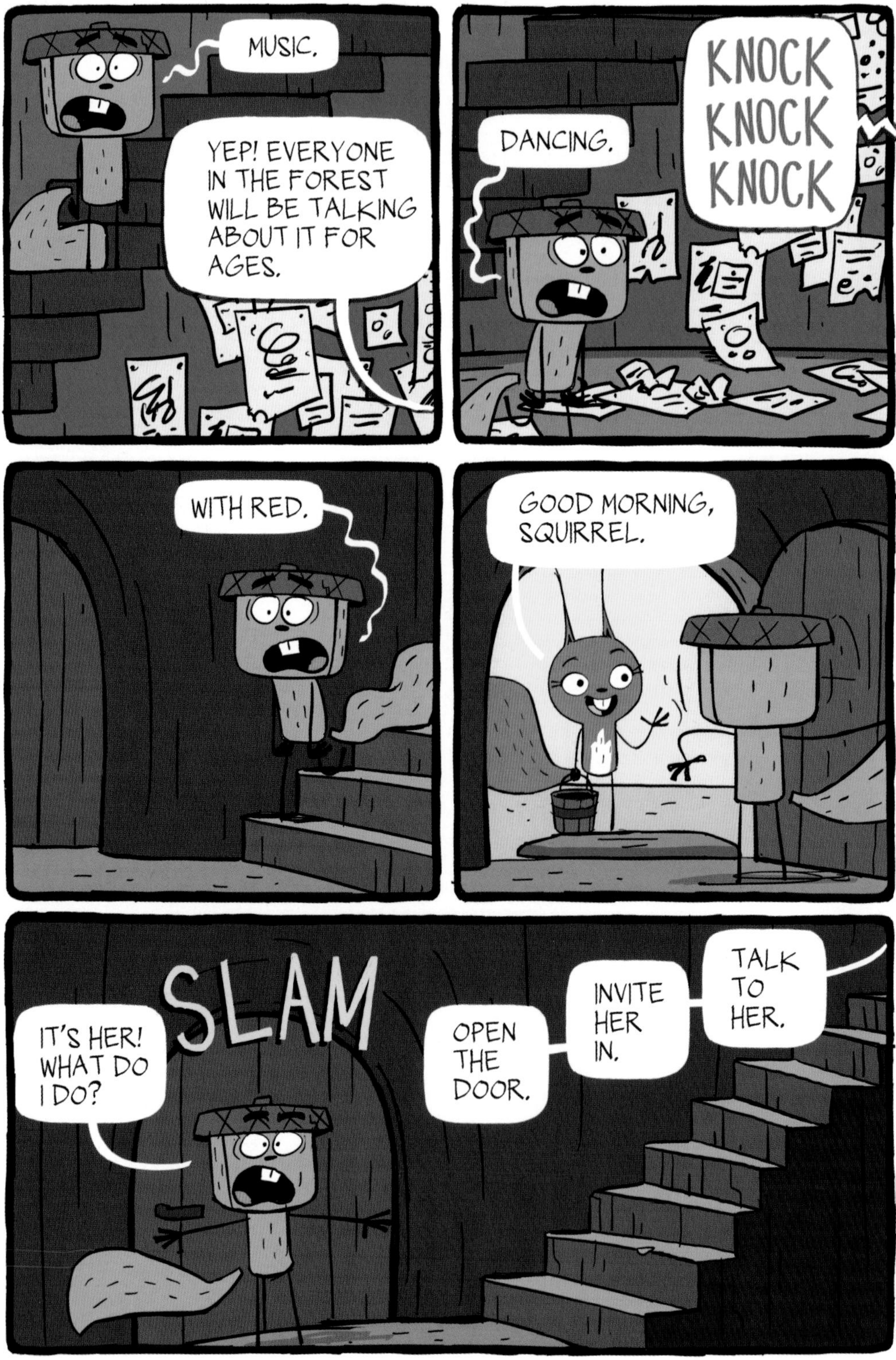
MUSIC.
YEP! EVERYONE IN THE FOREST WILL BE TALKING ABOUT IT FOR AGES.
DANCING.
KNOCK KNOCK KNOCK
WITH RED.
GOOD MORNING, SQUIRREL.
SLAM
IT'S HER! WHAT DO I DO?
OPEN THE DOOR.
INVITE HER IN.
TALK TO HER.

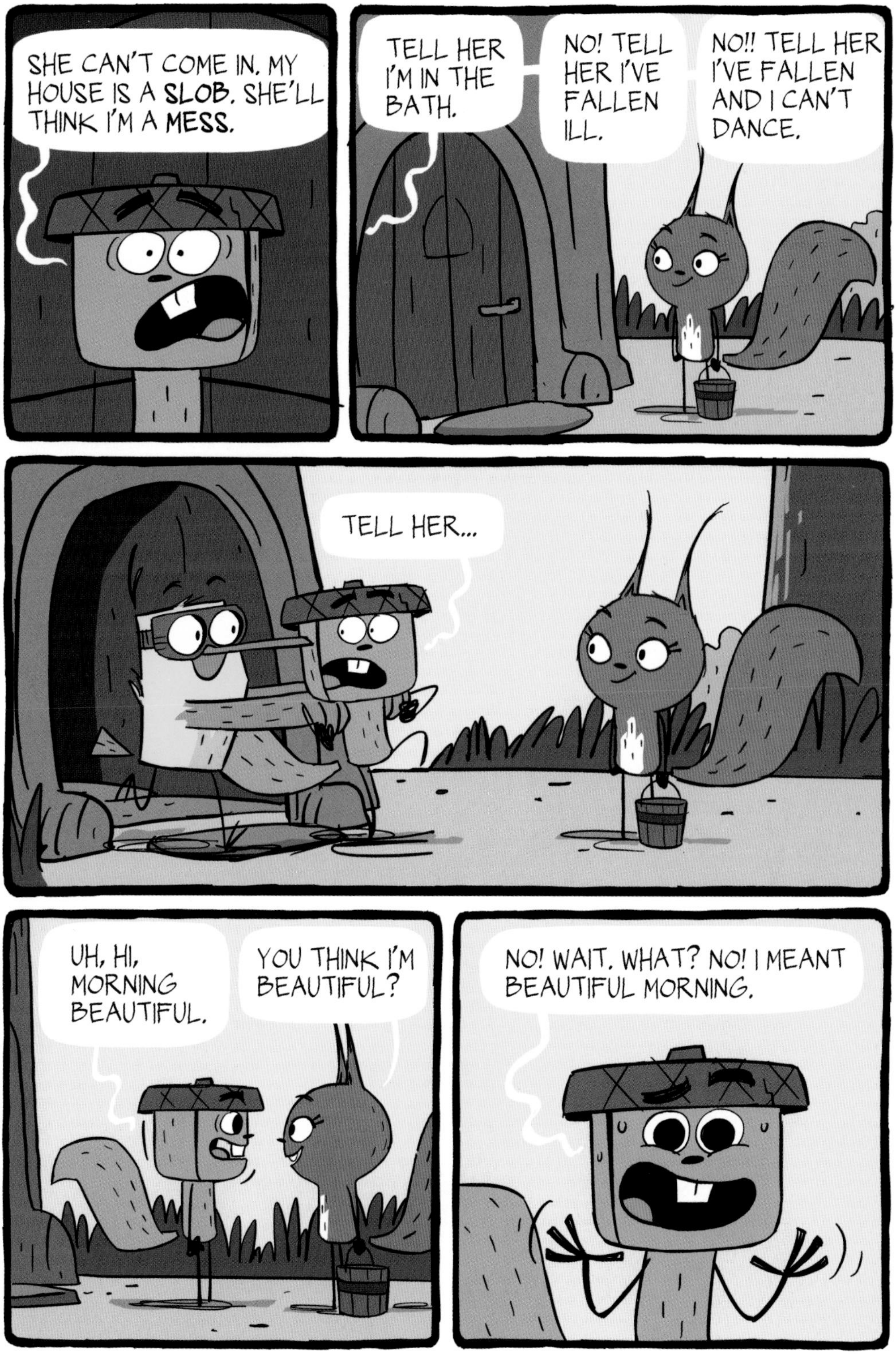
SHE CAN'T COME IN. MY HOUSE IS A SLOB. SHE'LL THINK I'M A MESS.
TELL HER I'M IN THE BATH.
NO! TELL HER I'VE FALLEN ILL.
NO!! TELL HER I'VE FALLEN AND I CAN'T DANCE.
TELL HER...
UH, HI, MORNING BEAUTIFUL.
YOU THINK I'M BEAUTIFUL?
NO! WAIT. WHAT? NO! I MEANT BEAUTIFUL MORNING.

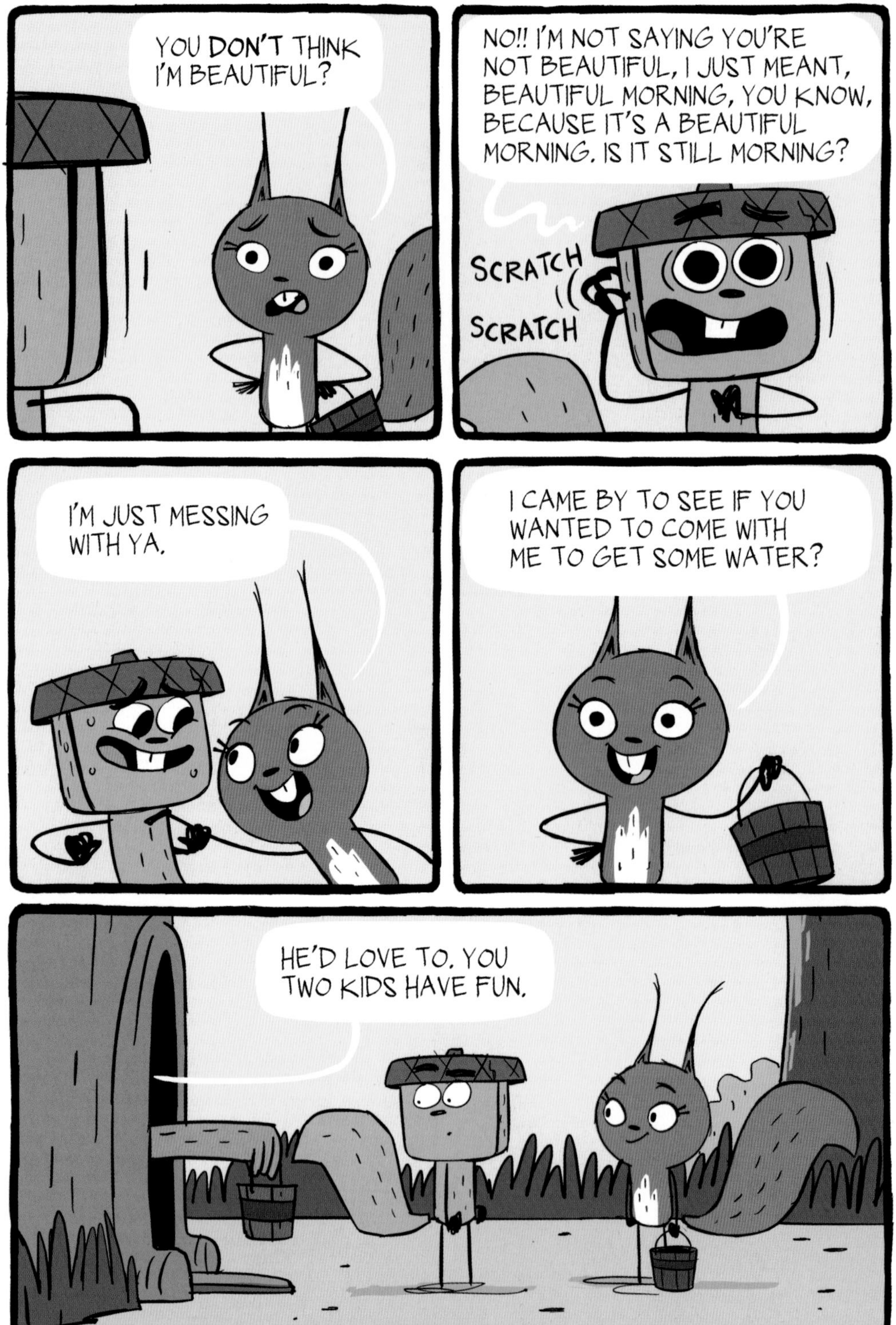
YOU DON'T THINK I'M BEAUTIFUL?
NO!! I'M NOT SAYING YOU'RE NOT BEAUTIFUL, I JUST MEANT, BEAUTIFUL MORNING, YOU KNOW, BECAUSE IT'S A BEAUTIFUL MORNING. IS IT STILL MORNING?
SCRATCH
SCRATCH
I'M JUST MESSING WITH YA.
I CAME BY TO SEE IF YOU WANTED TO COME WITH ME TO GET SOME WATER?
HE'D LOVE TO. YOU TWO KIDS HAVE FUN.

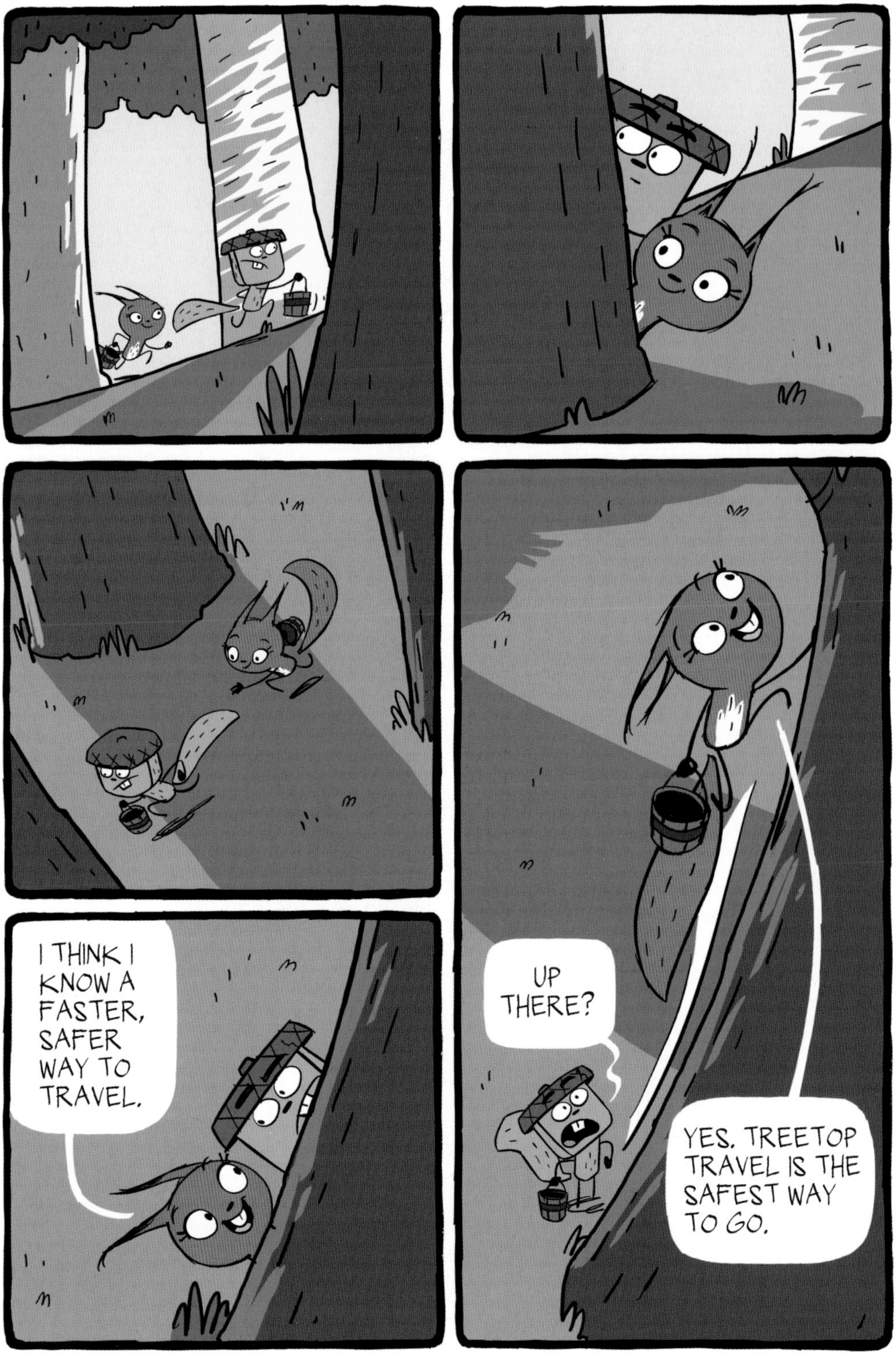
I THINK I KNOW A FASTER, SAFER WAY TO TRAVEL.
UP THERE?
YES. TREETOP TRAVEL IS THE SAFEST WAY TO GO.

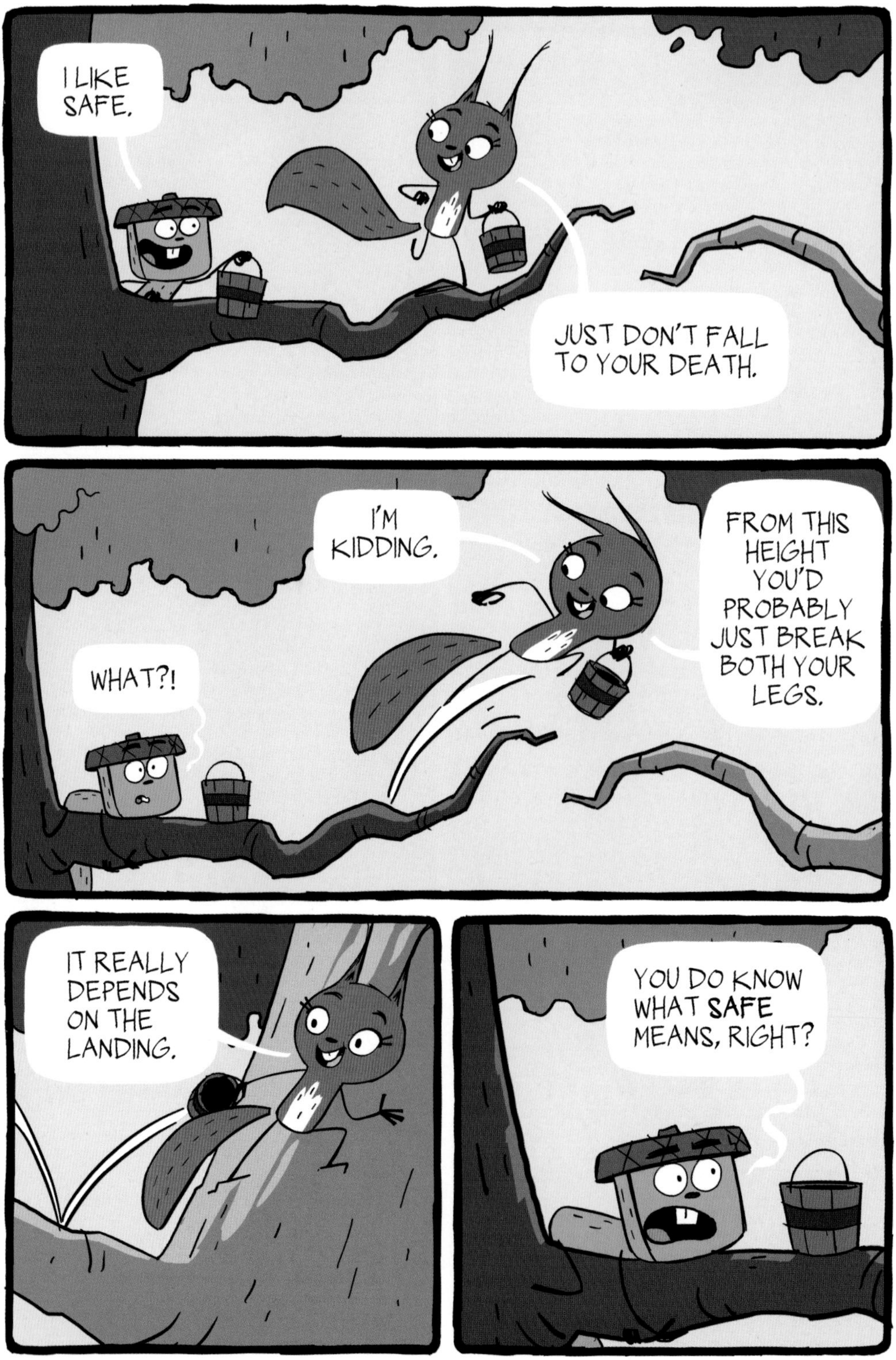
I LIKE SAFE.
JUST DON'T FALL TO YOUR DEATH.
I'M KIDDING.
FROM THIS HEIGHT YOU'D PROBABLY JUST BREAK BOTH YOUR LEGS.
WHAT?!
IT REALLY DEPENDS ON THE LANDING.
YOU DO KNOW WHAT **SAFE** MEANS, RIGHT?

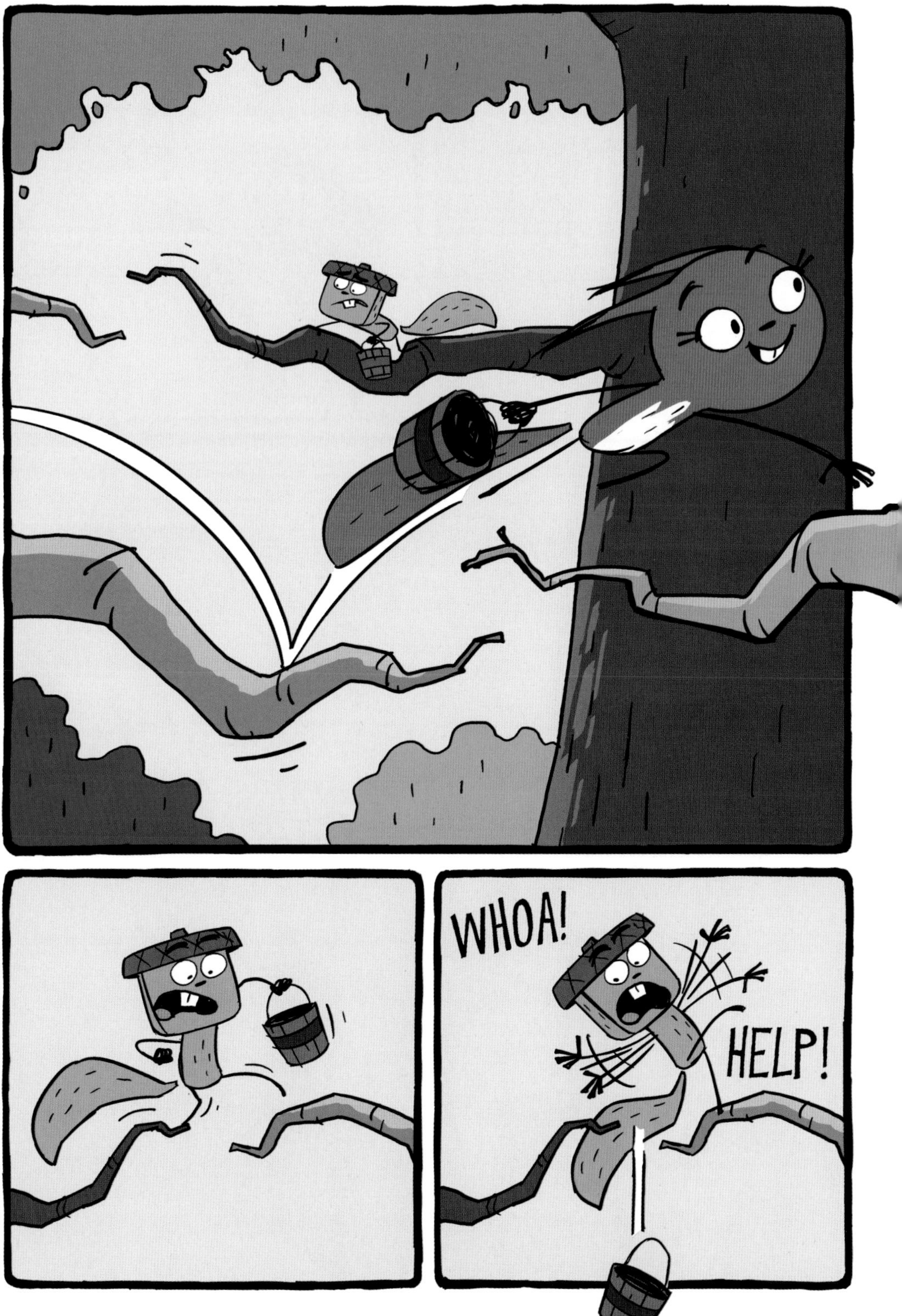
WHOA!
HELP!

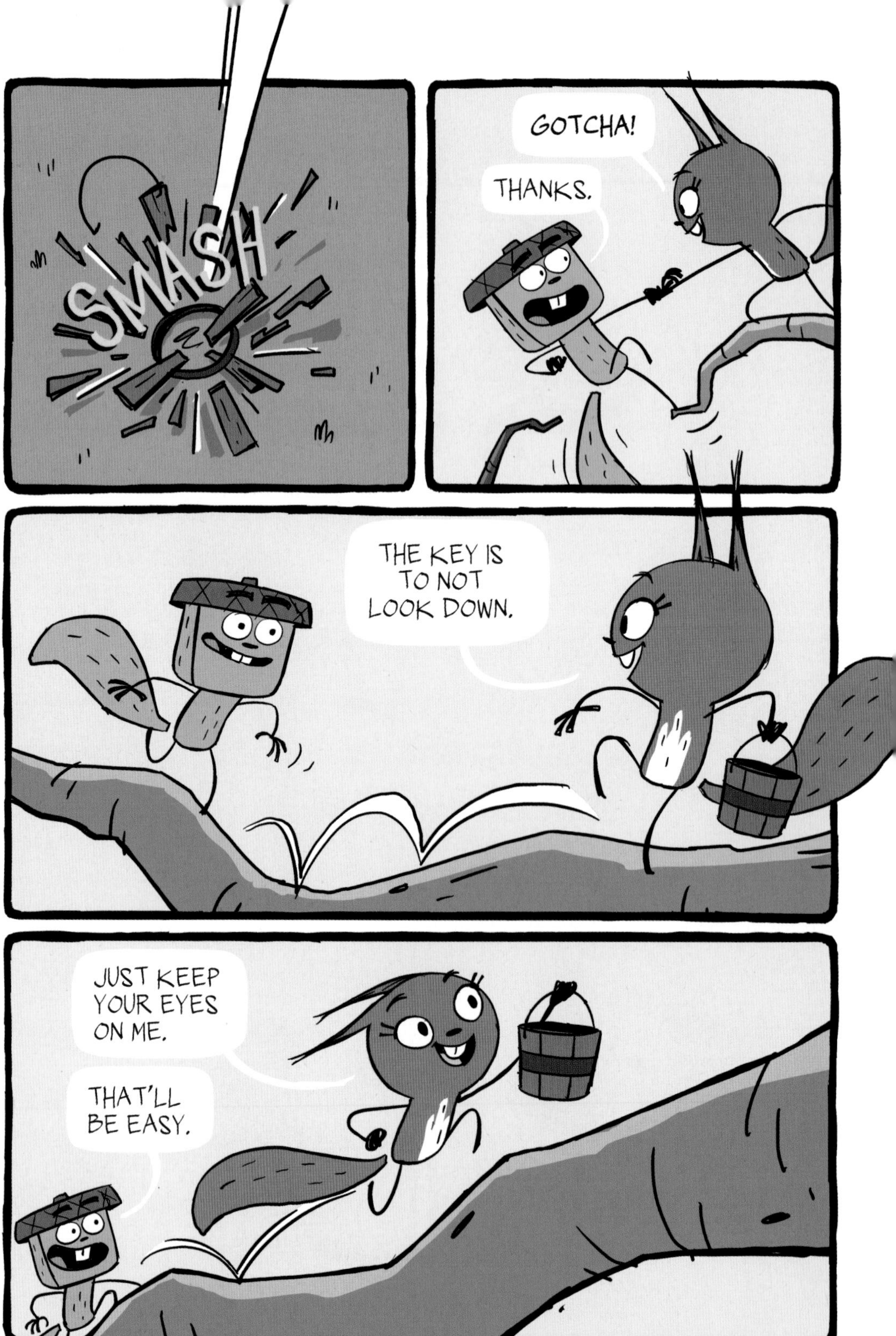
SMASH
GOTCHA!
THANKS.
THE KEY IS TO NOT LOOK DOWN.
JUST KEEP YOUR EYES ON ME.
THAT'LL BE EASY.

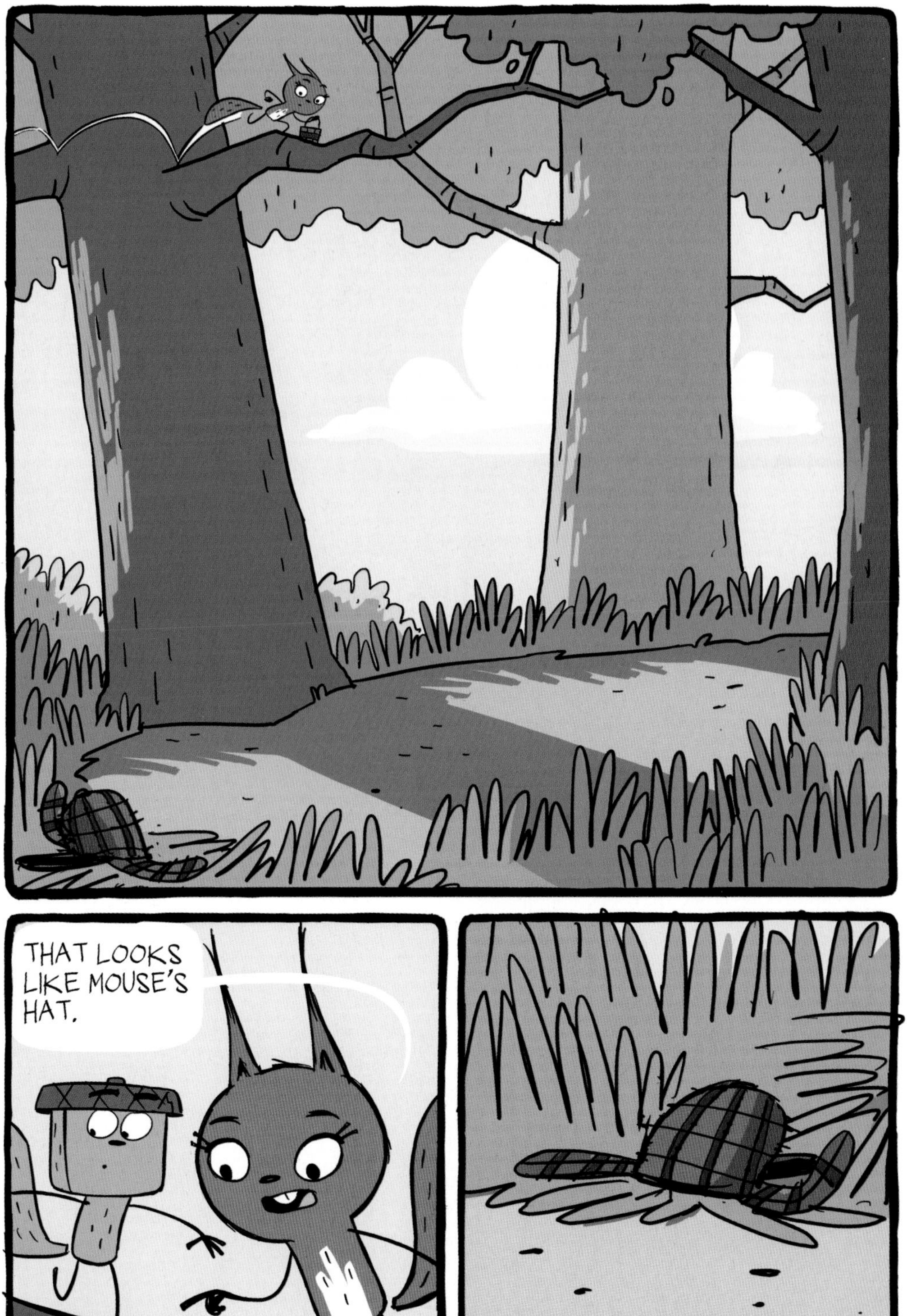
THAT LOOKS LIKE MOUSE'S HAT.

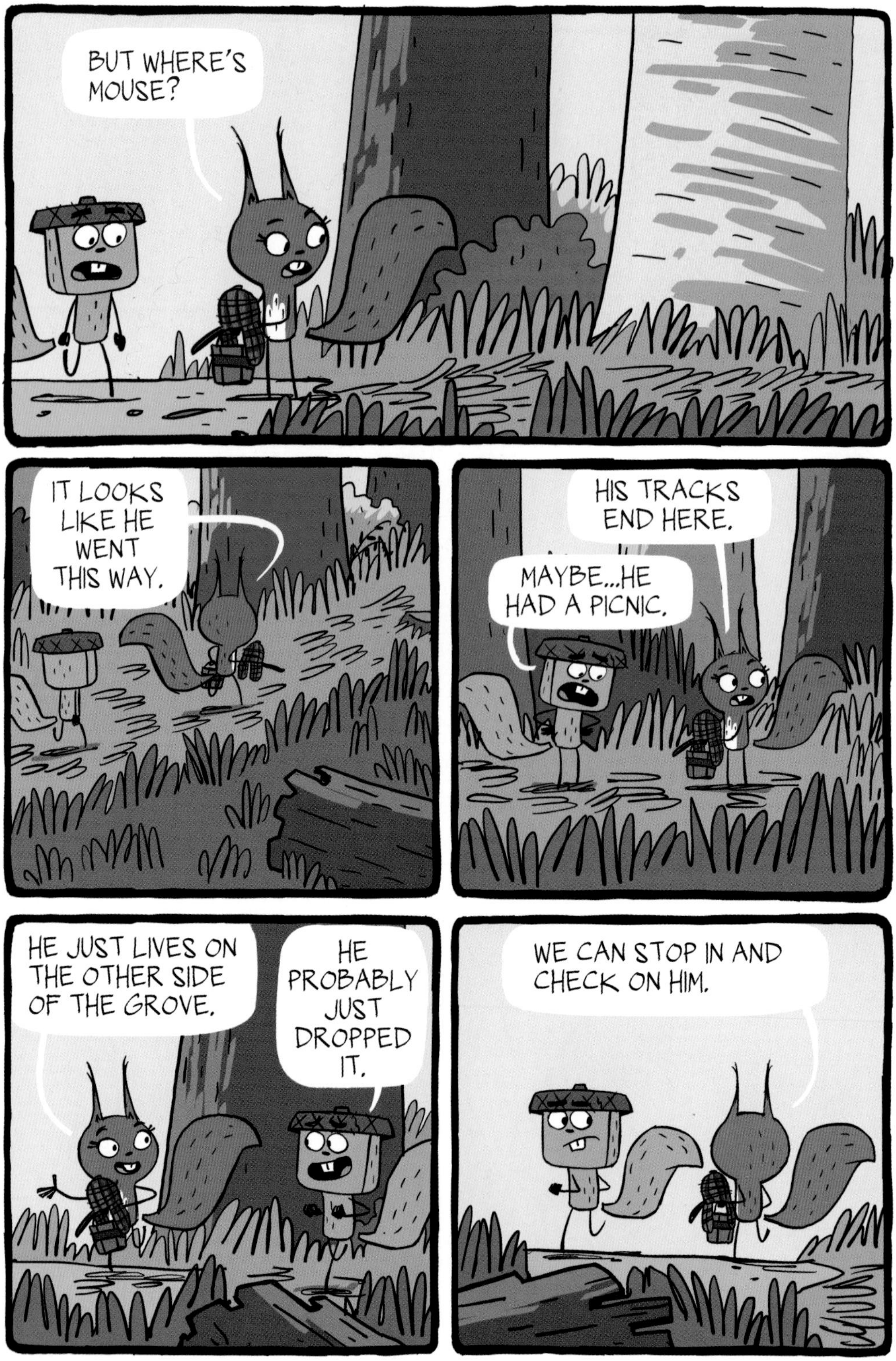
BUT WHERE'S MOUSE?
IT LOOKS LIKE HE WENT THIS WAY.
HIS TRACKS END HERE.
MAYBE...HE HAD A PICNIC.
HE JUST LIVES ON THE OTHER SIDE OF THE GROVE.
HE PROBABLY JUST DROPPED IT.
WE CAN STOP IN AND CHECK ON HIM.

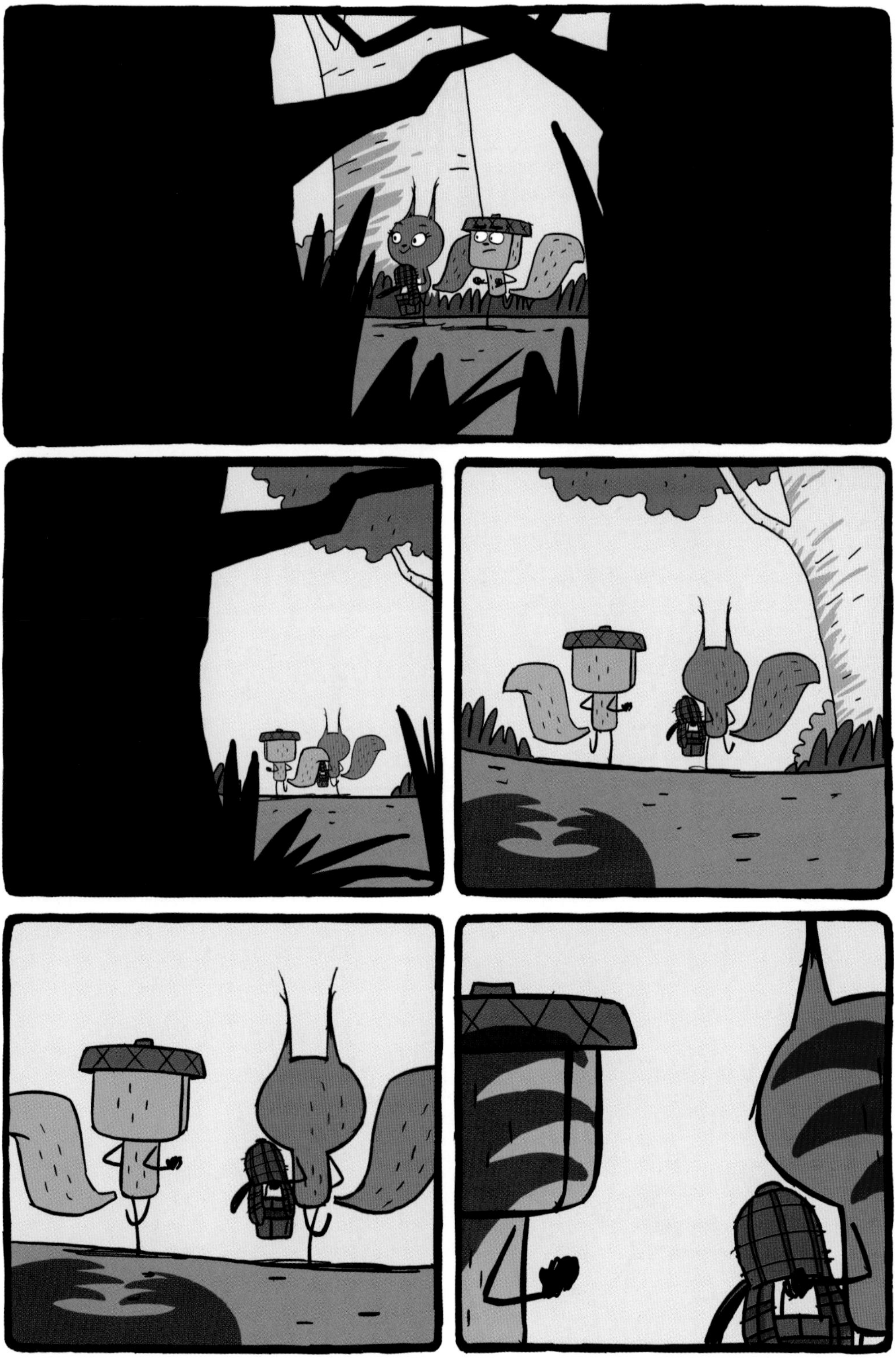

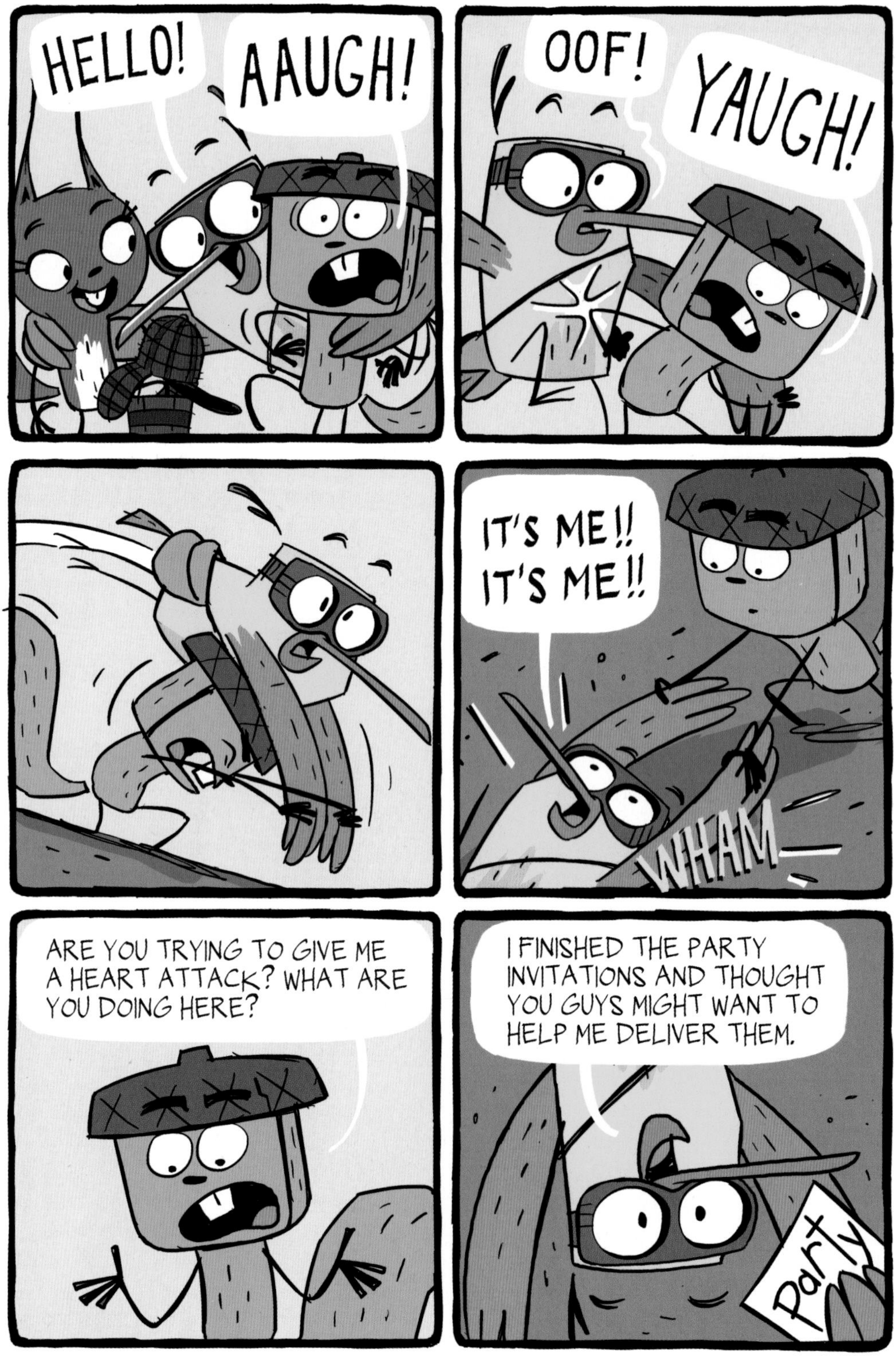
HELLO!
AAUGH!
OOF!
YAUGH!
IT'S ME!!
IT'S ME!!
WHAM
ARE YOU TRYING TO GIVE ME A HEART ATTACK? WHAT ARE YOU DOING HERE?
I FINISHED THE PARTY INVITATIONS AND THOUGHT YOU GUYS MIGHT WANT TO HELP ME DELIVER THEM.
Party

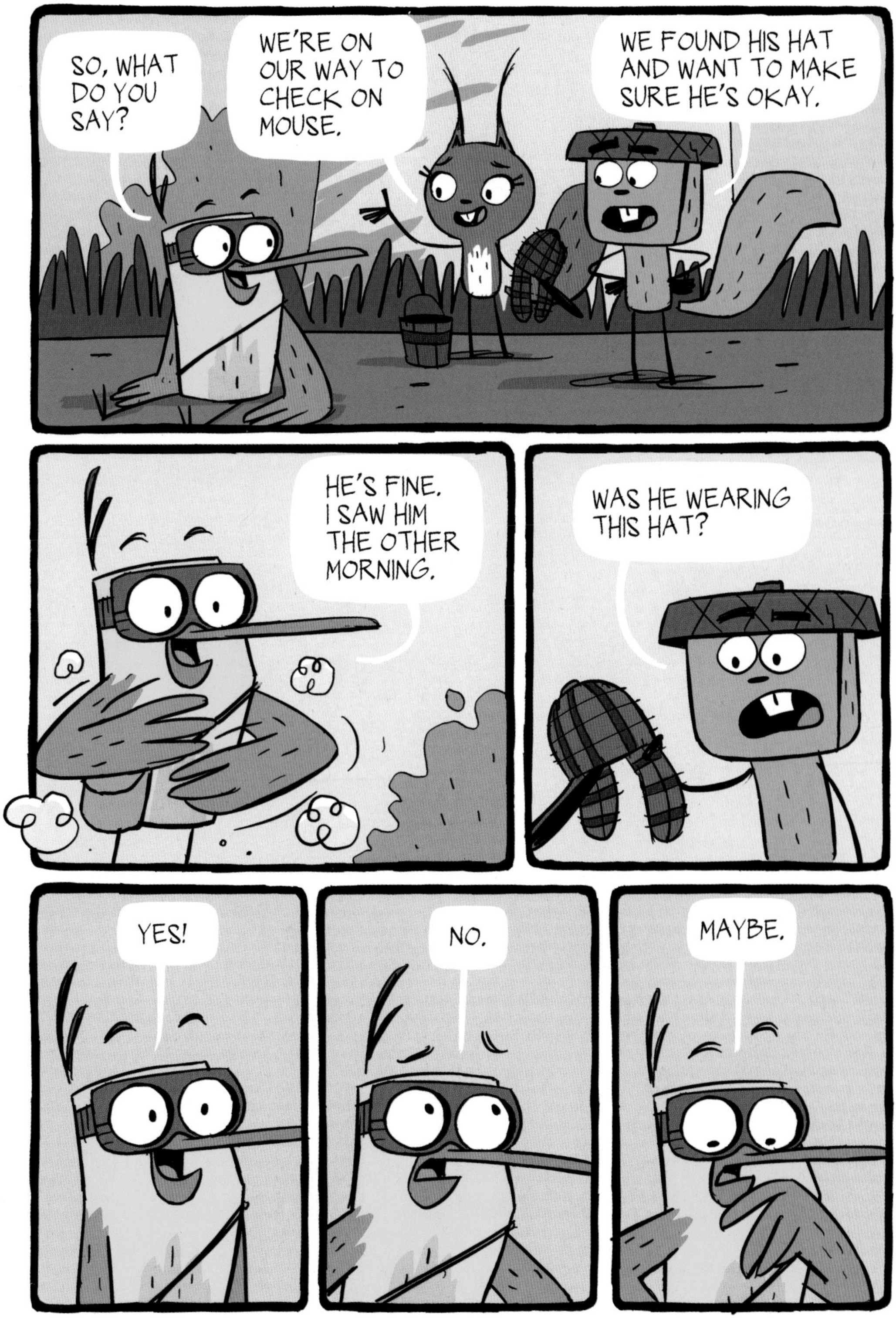
SO, WHAT DO YOU SAY?
WE'RE ON OUR WAY TO CHECK ON MOUSE.
WE FOUND HIS HAT AND WANT TO MAKE SURE HE'S OKAY.
HE'S FINE. I SAW HIM THE OTHER MORNING.
WAS HE WEARING THIS HAT?
YES!
NO.
MAYBE.

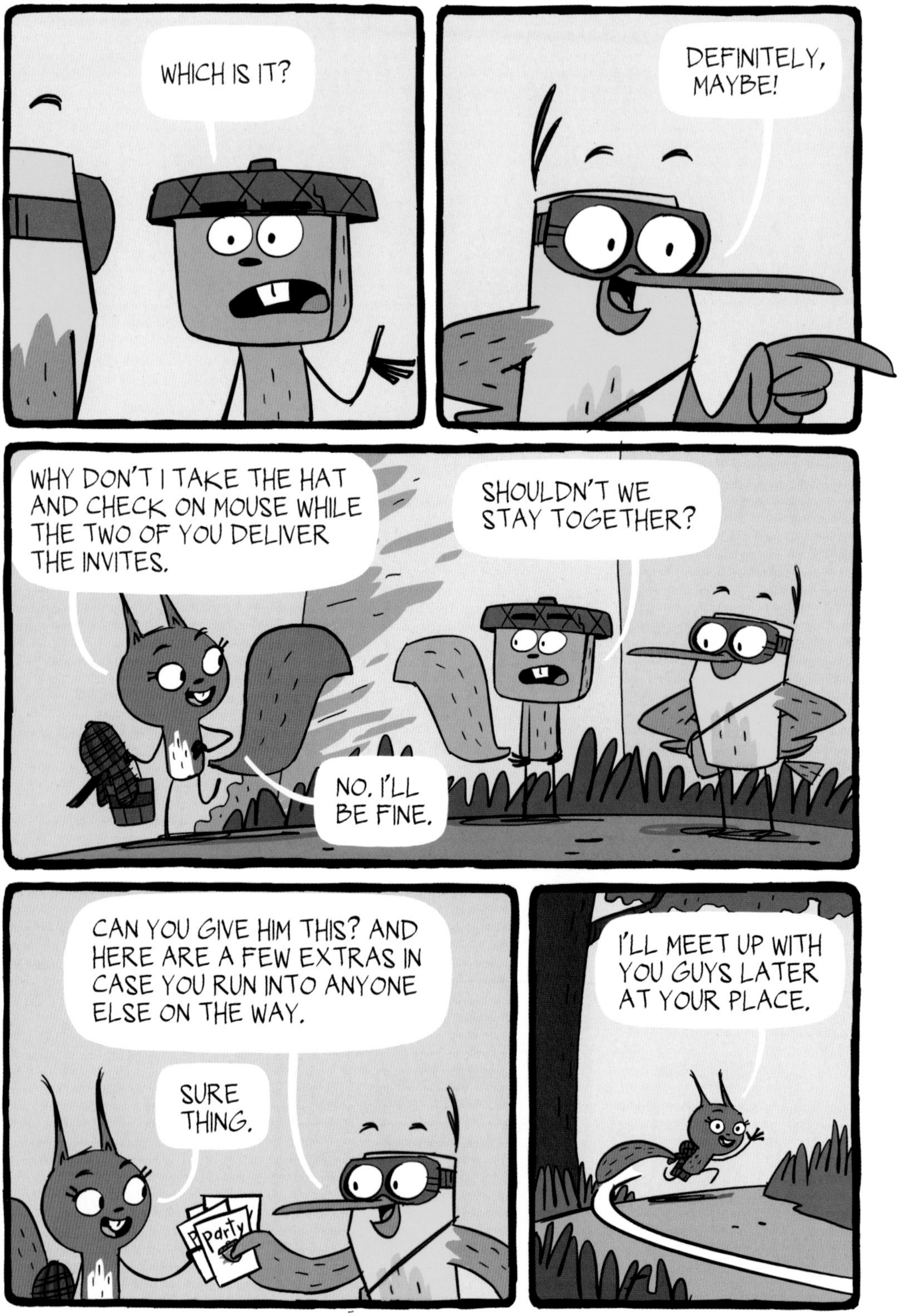
WHICH IS IT?
DEFINITELY, MAYBE!
WHY DON'T I TAKE THE HAT AND CHECK ON MOUSE WHILE THE TWO OF YOU DELIVER THE INVITES.
SHOULDN'T WE STAY TOGETHER?
NO. I'LL BE FINE.
CAN YOU GIVE HIM THIS? AND HERE ARE A FEW EXTRAS IN CASE YOU RUN INTO ANYONE ELSE ON THE WAY.
SURE THING.
Party
I'LL MEET UP WITH YOU GUYS LATER AT YOUR PLACE.

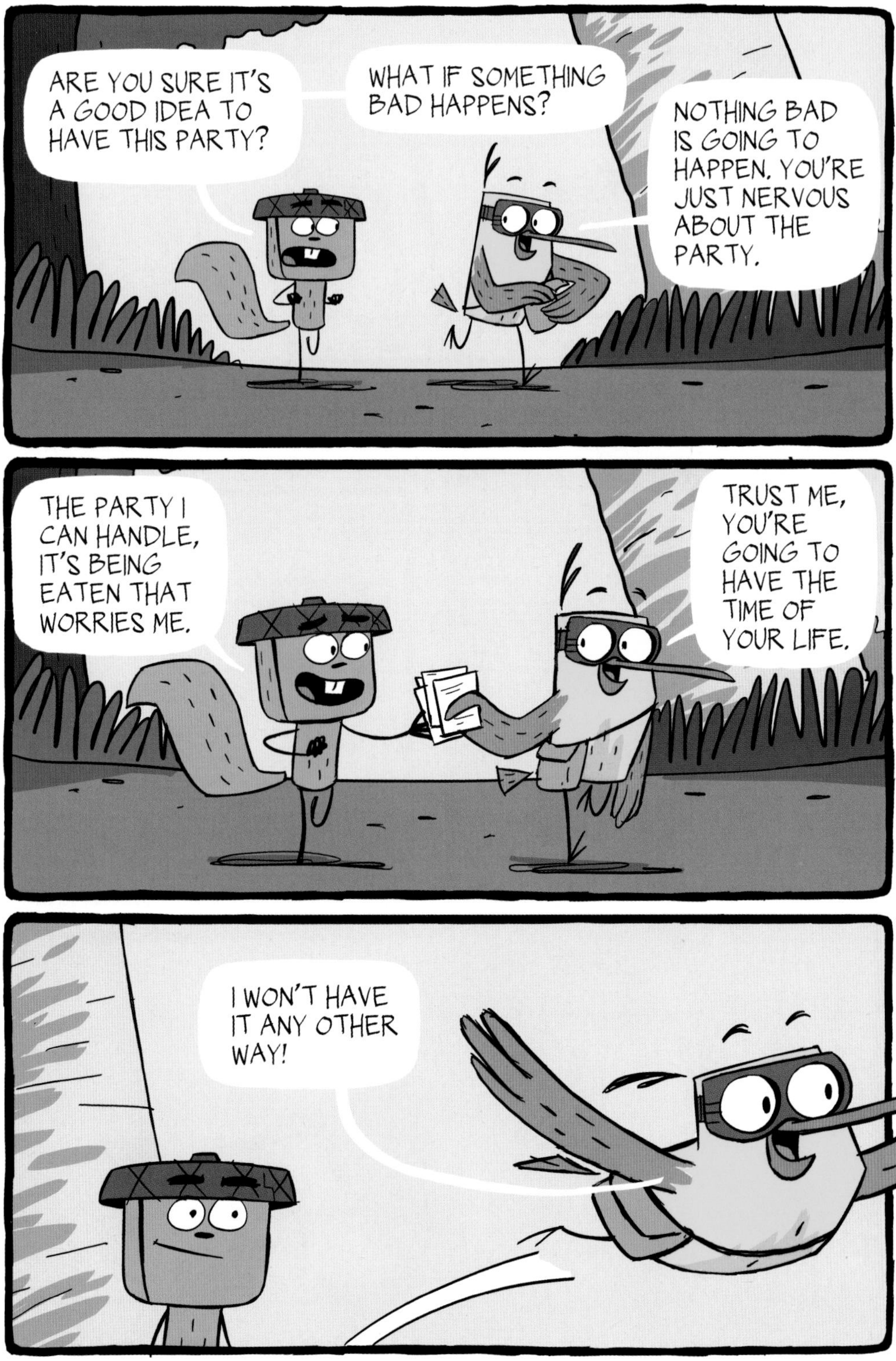
ARE YOU SURE IT'S A GOOD IDEA TO HAVE THIS PARTY?
WHAT IF SOMETHING BAD HAPPENS?
NOTHING BAD IS GOING TO HAPPEN. YOU'RE JUST NERVOUS ABOUT THE PARTY.
THE PARTY I CAN HANDLE, IT'S BEING EATEN THAT WORRIES ME.
TRUST ME, YOU'RE GOING TO HAVE THE TIME OF YOUR LIFE.
I WON'T HAVE IT ANY OTHER WAY!

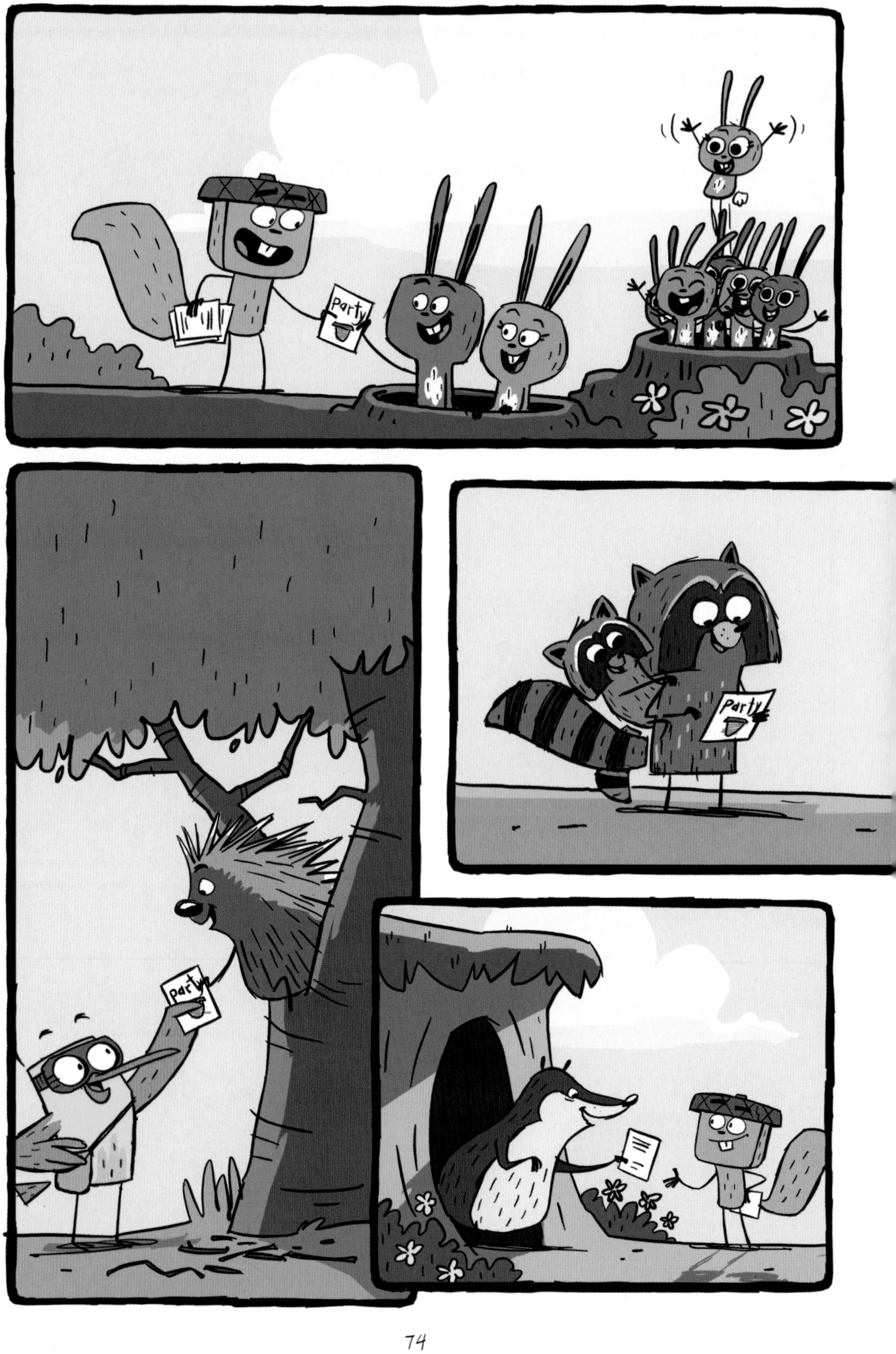
party
party
party

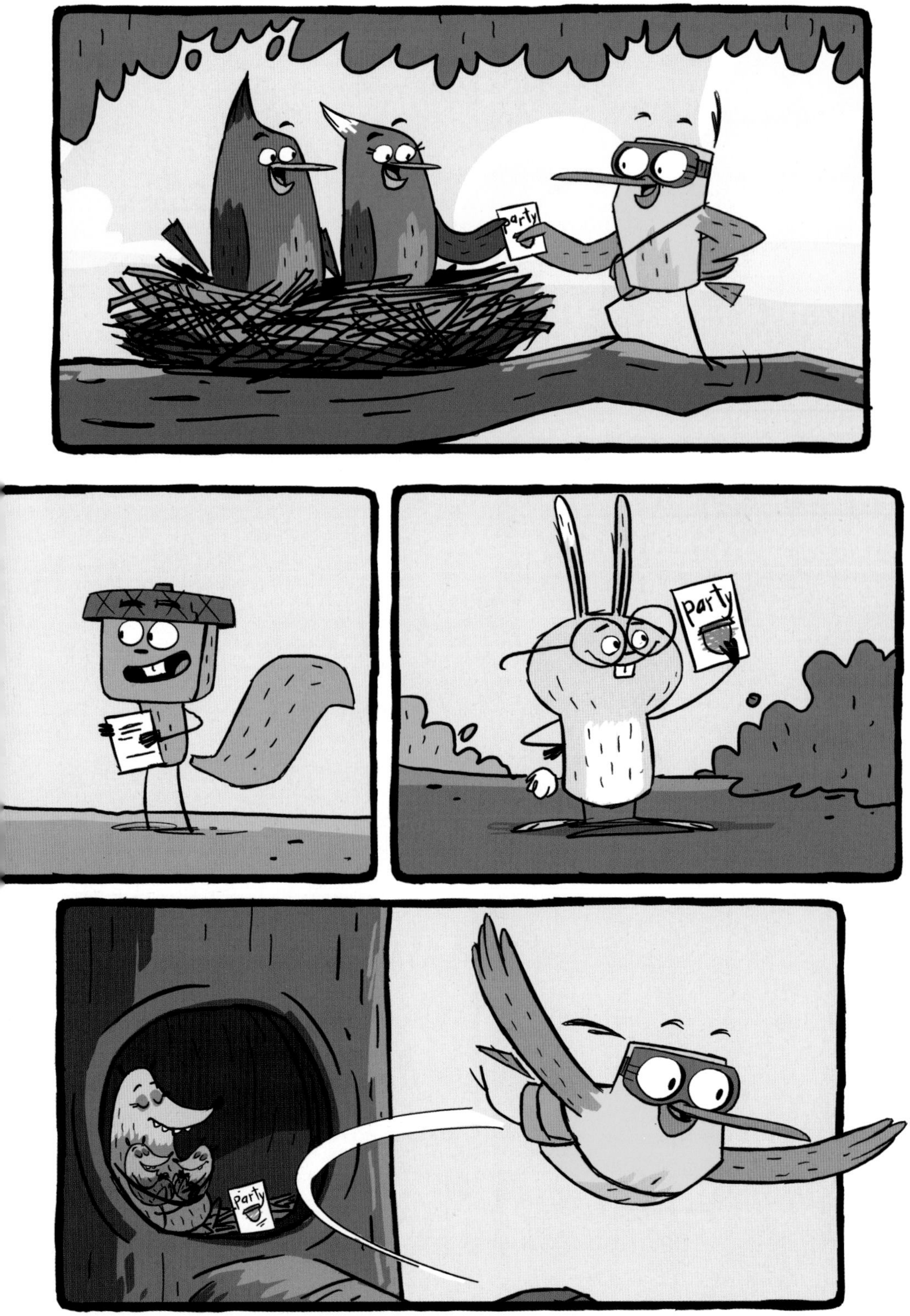
party
party
party

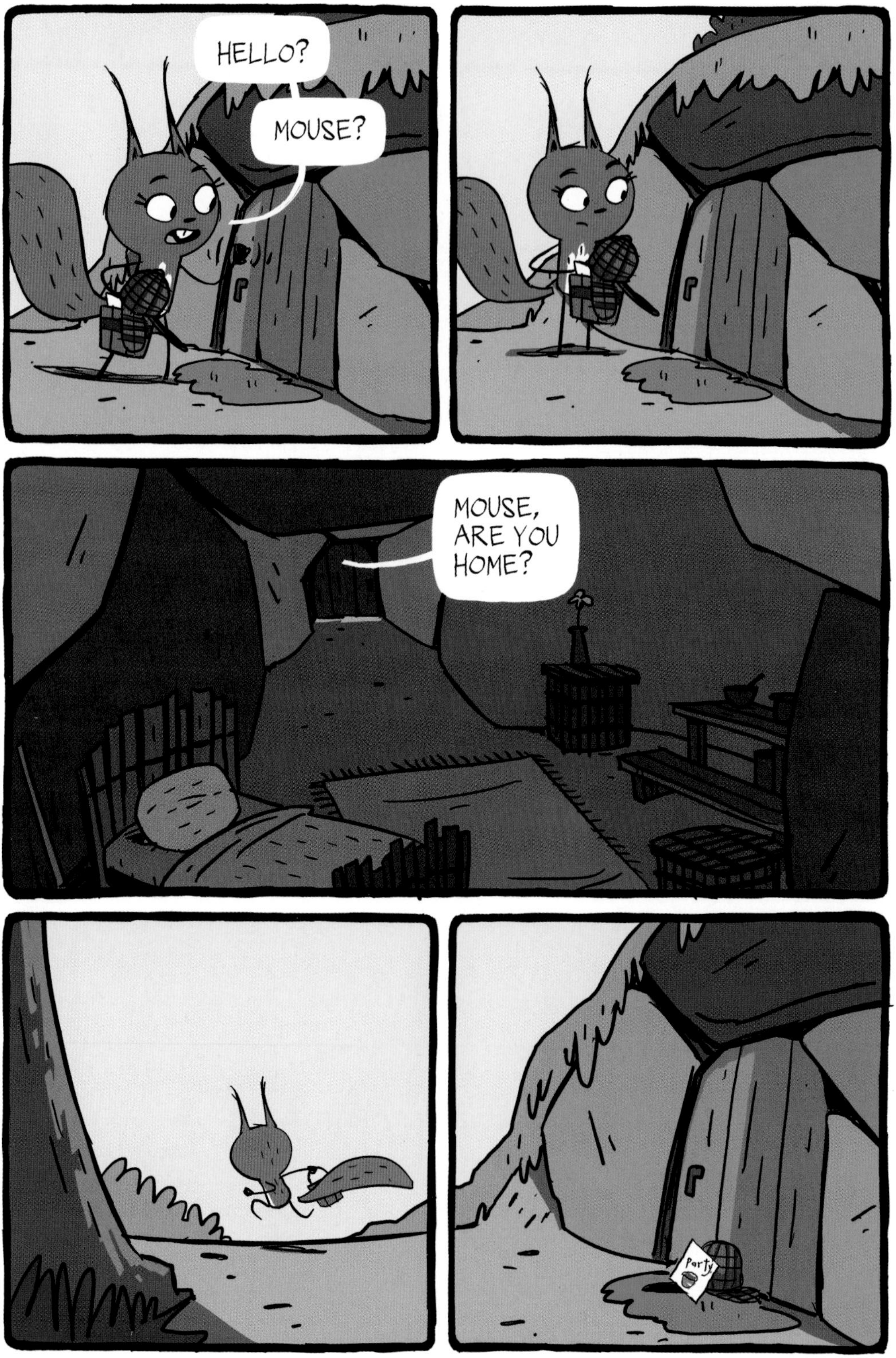
HELLO?
MOUSE?
MOUSE, ARE YOU HOME?
Party

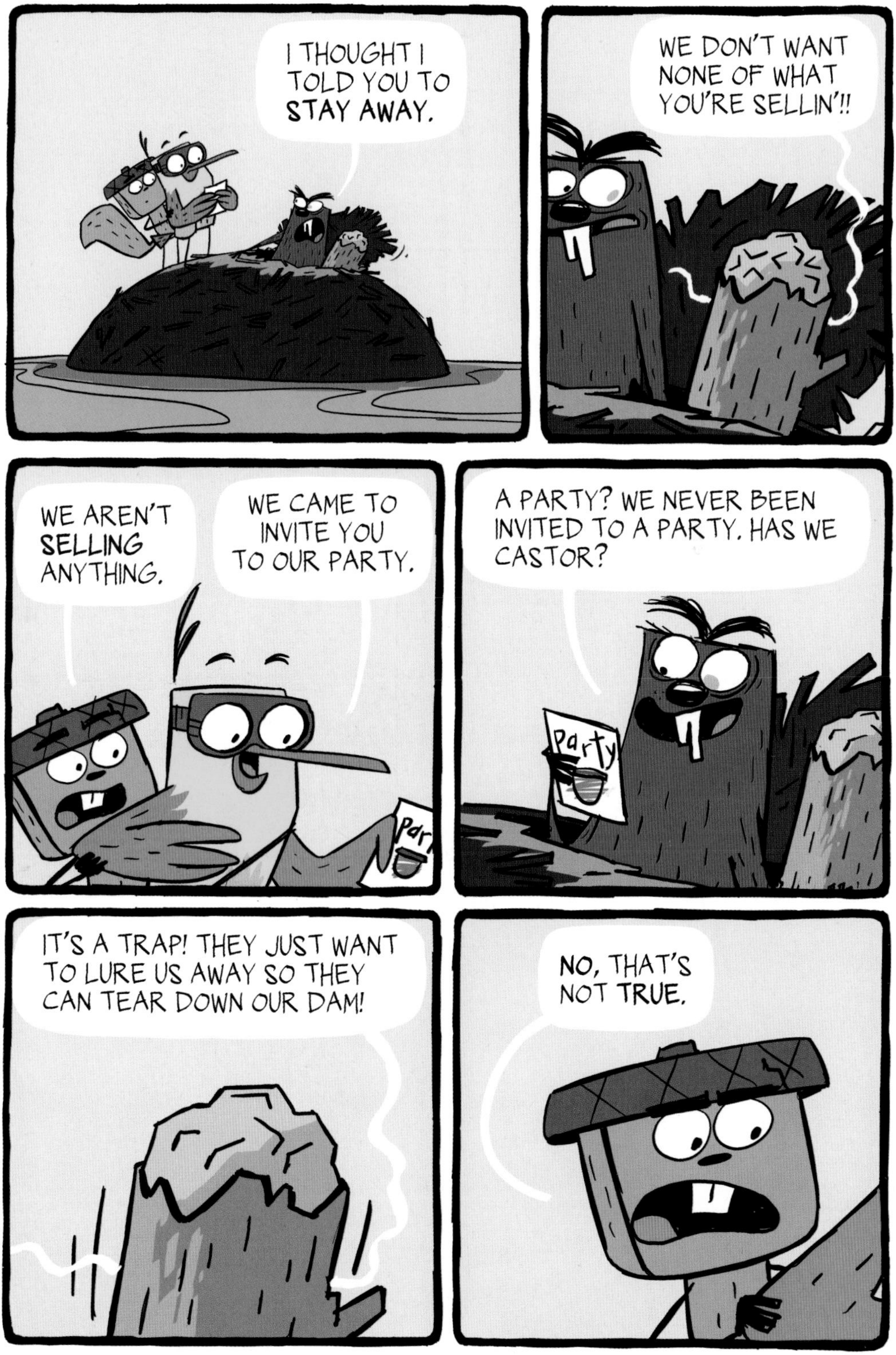
I THOUGHT I TOLD YOU TO STAY AWAY.
WE DON'T WANT NONE OF WHAT YOU'RE SELLIN'!!
WE AREN'T SELLING ANYTHING.
WE CAME TO INVITE YOU TO OUR PARTY.
Par
A PARTY? WE NEVER BEEN INVITED TO A PARTY. HAS WE CASTOR?
Party
IT'S A TRAP! THEY JUST WANT TO LURE US AWAY SO THEY CAN TEAR DOWN OUR DAM!
NO, THAT'S NOT TRUE.

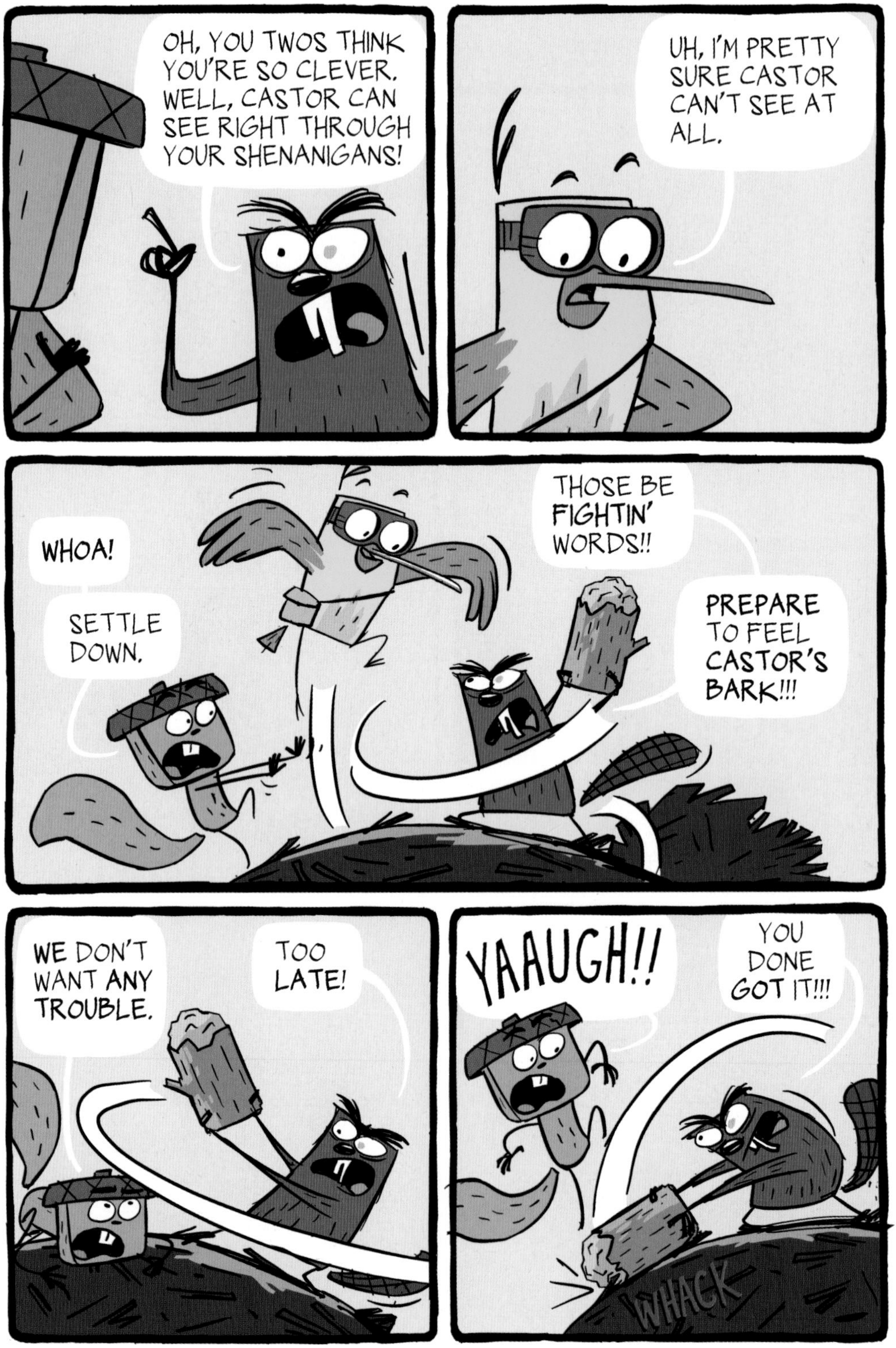
OH, YOU TWOS THINK YOU'RE SO CLEVER. WELL, CASTOR CAN SEE RIGHT THROUGH YOUR SHENANIGANS!
UH, I'M PRETTY SURE CASTOR CAN'T SEE AT ALL.
WHOA!
SETTLE DOWN.
THOSE BE FIGHTIN' WORDS!!
PREPARE TO FEEL CASTOR'S BARK!!!
WE DON'T WANT ANY TROUBLE.
TOO LATE!
YAAUGH!!
YOU DONE GOT IT!!!
WHACK

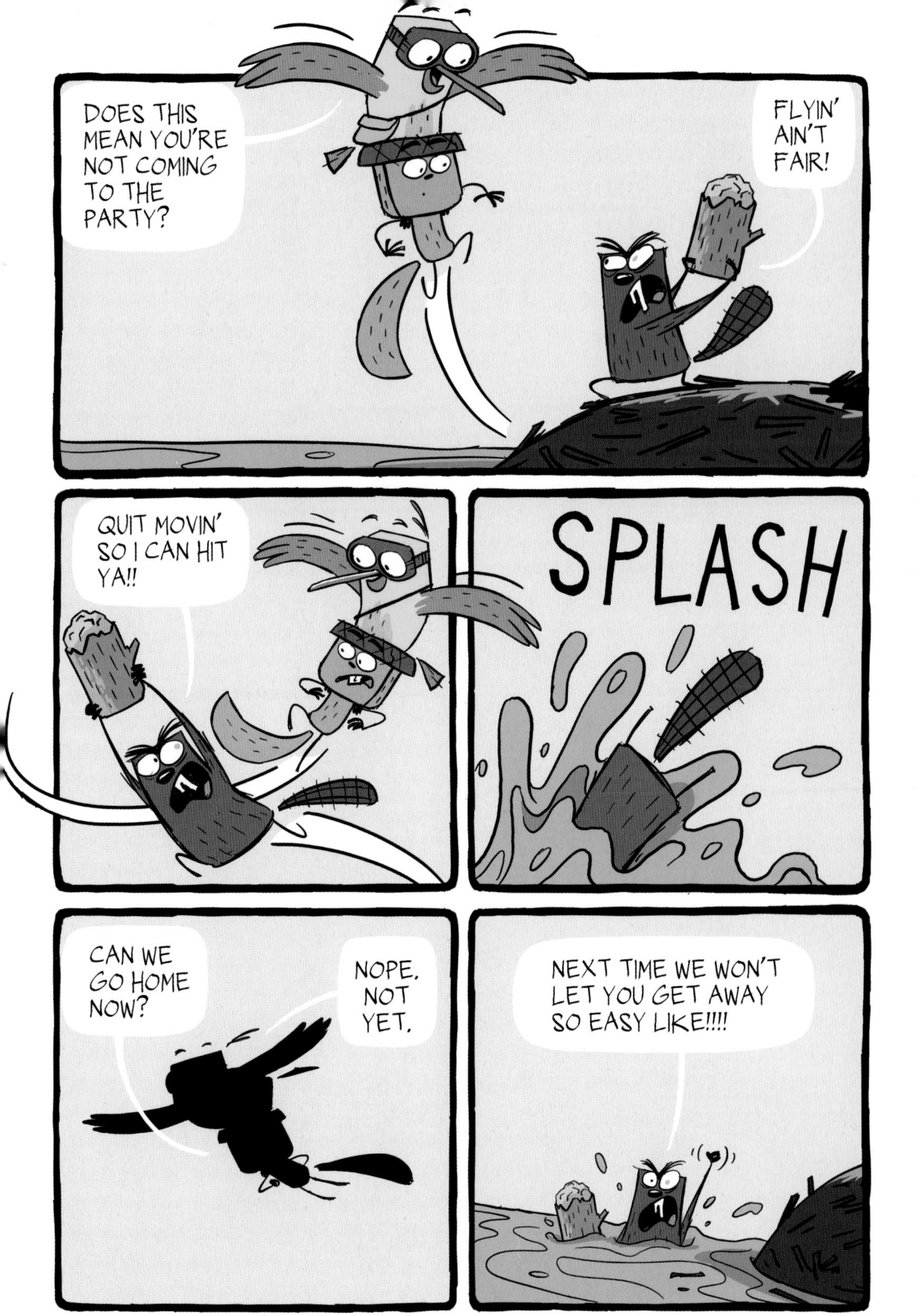
DOES THIS MEAN YOU'RE NOT COMING TO THE PARTY?
FLYIN' AIN'T FAIR!
QUIT MOVIN' SO I CAN HIT YA!!
SPLASH
CAN WE GO HOME NOW?
NOPE. NOT YET.
NEXT TIME WE WON'T LET YOU GET AWAY SO EASY LIKE!!!!

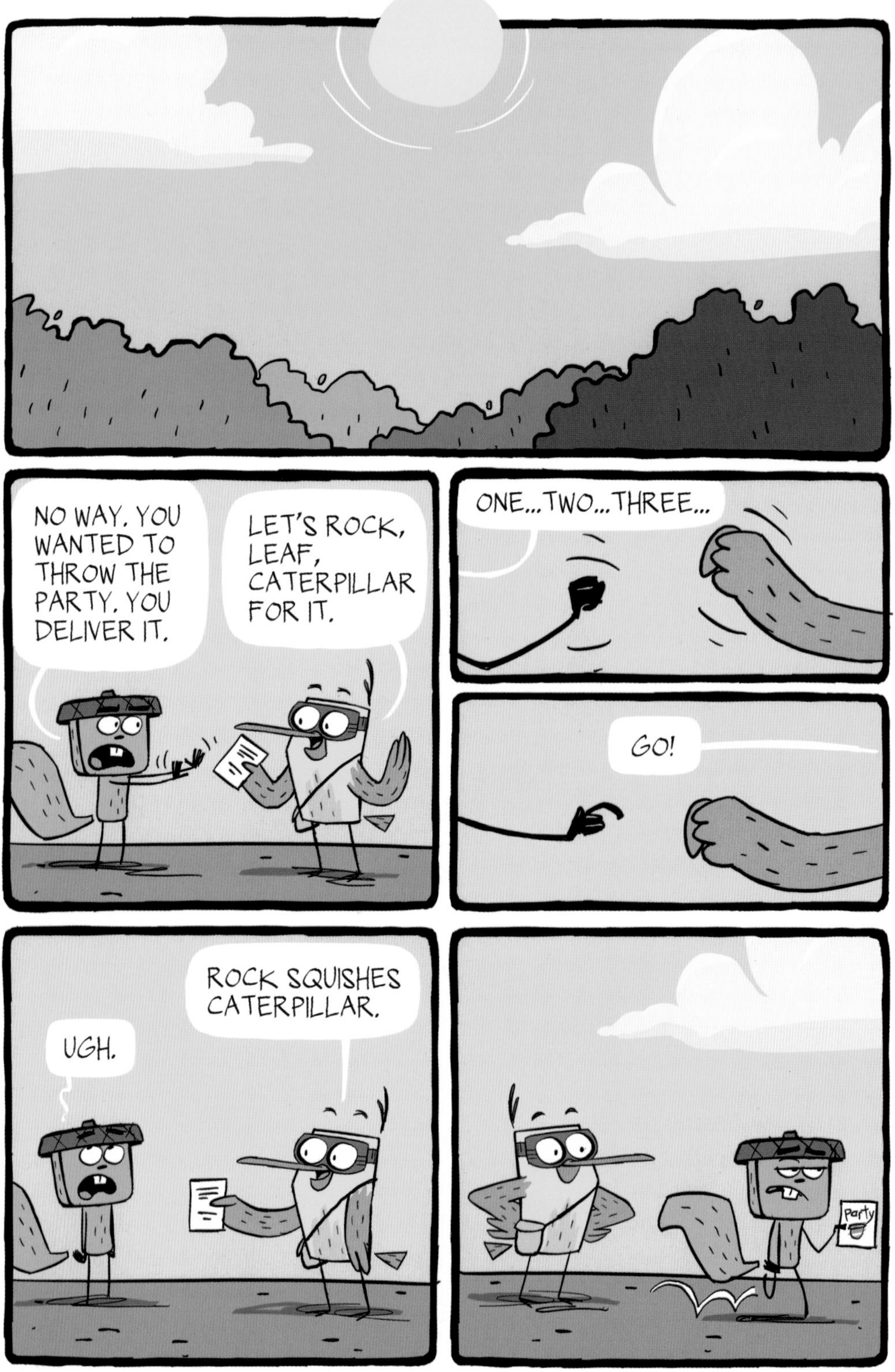
NO WAY. YOU WANTED TO THROW THE PARTY. YOU DELIVER IT.
LET'S ROCK, LEAF, CATERPILLAR FOR IT.
ONE... TWO... THREE...
GO!
UGH.
ROCK SQUISHES CATERPILLAR.
Party

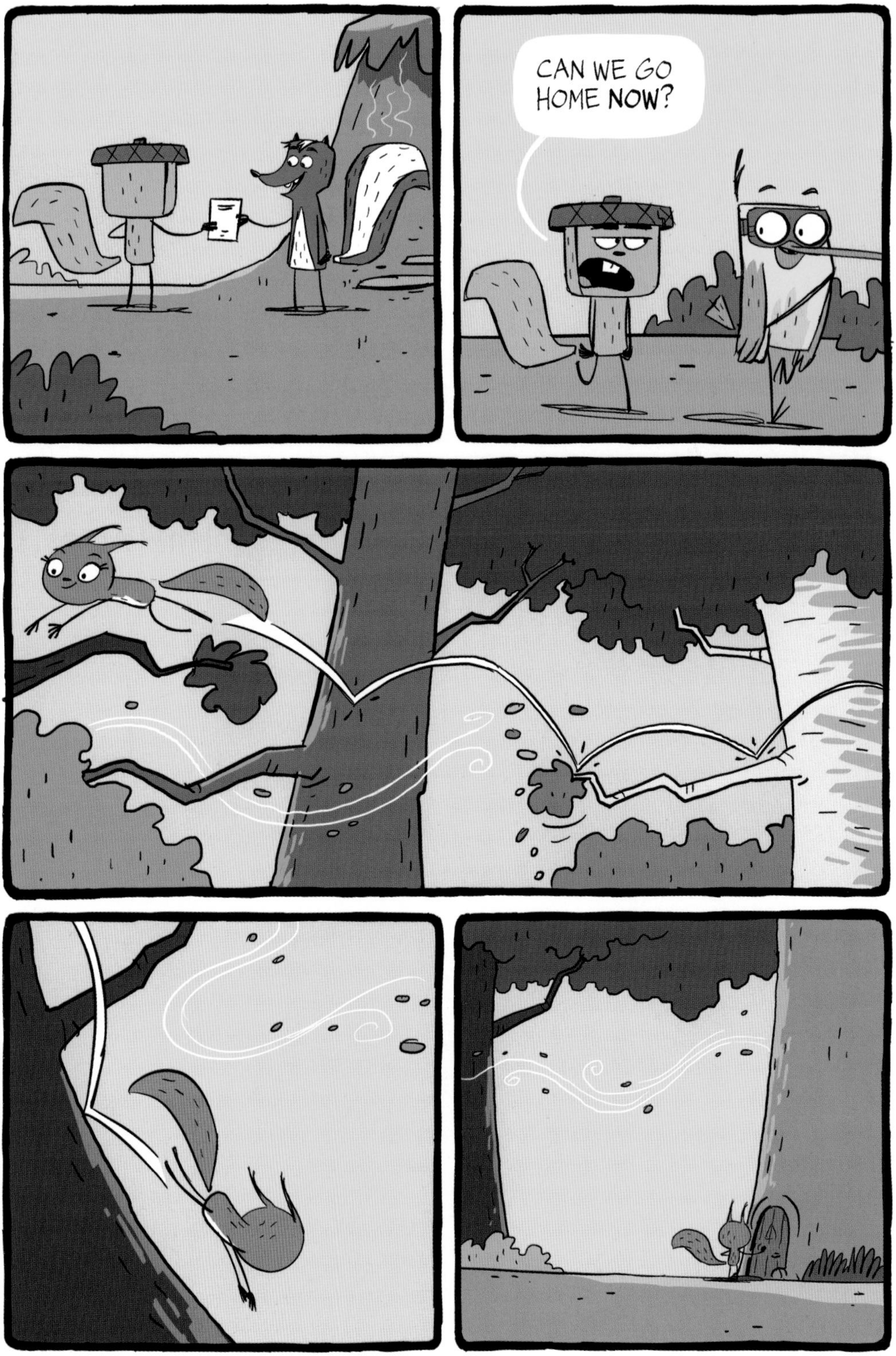
CAN WE GO
HOME NOW?

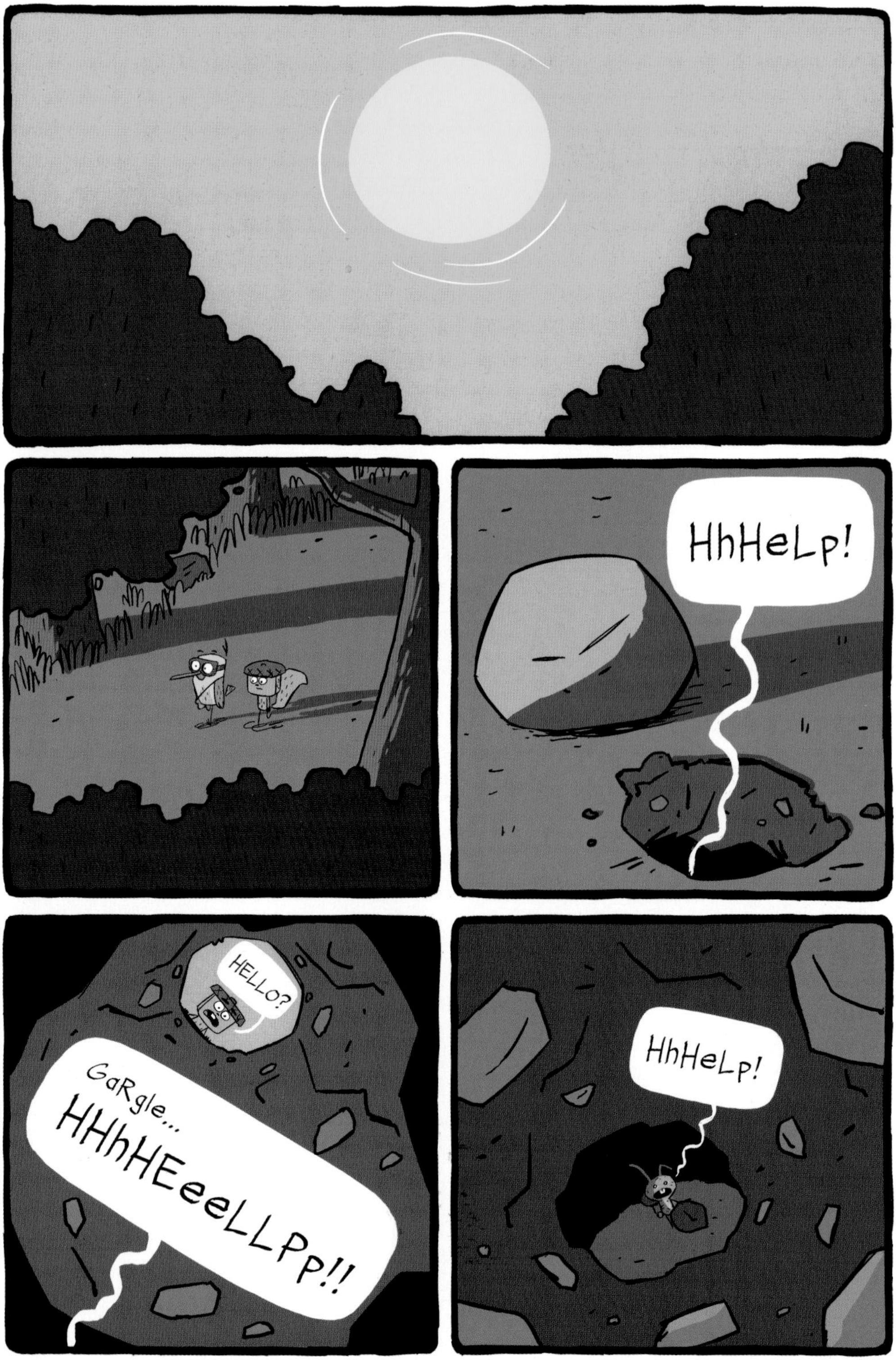
HhHeLp!
HELLO?
GaRgle...
HHhHEeeLLPp!!
HhHeLp!

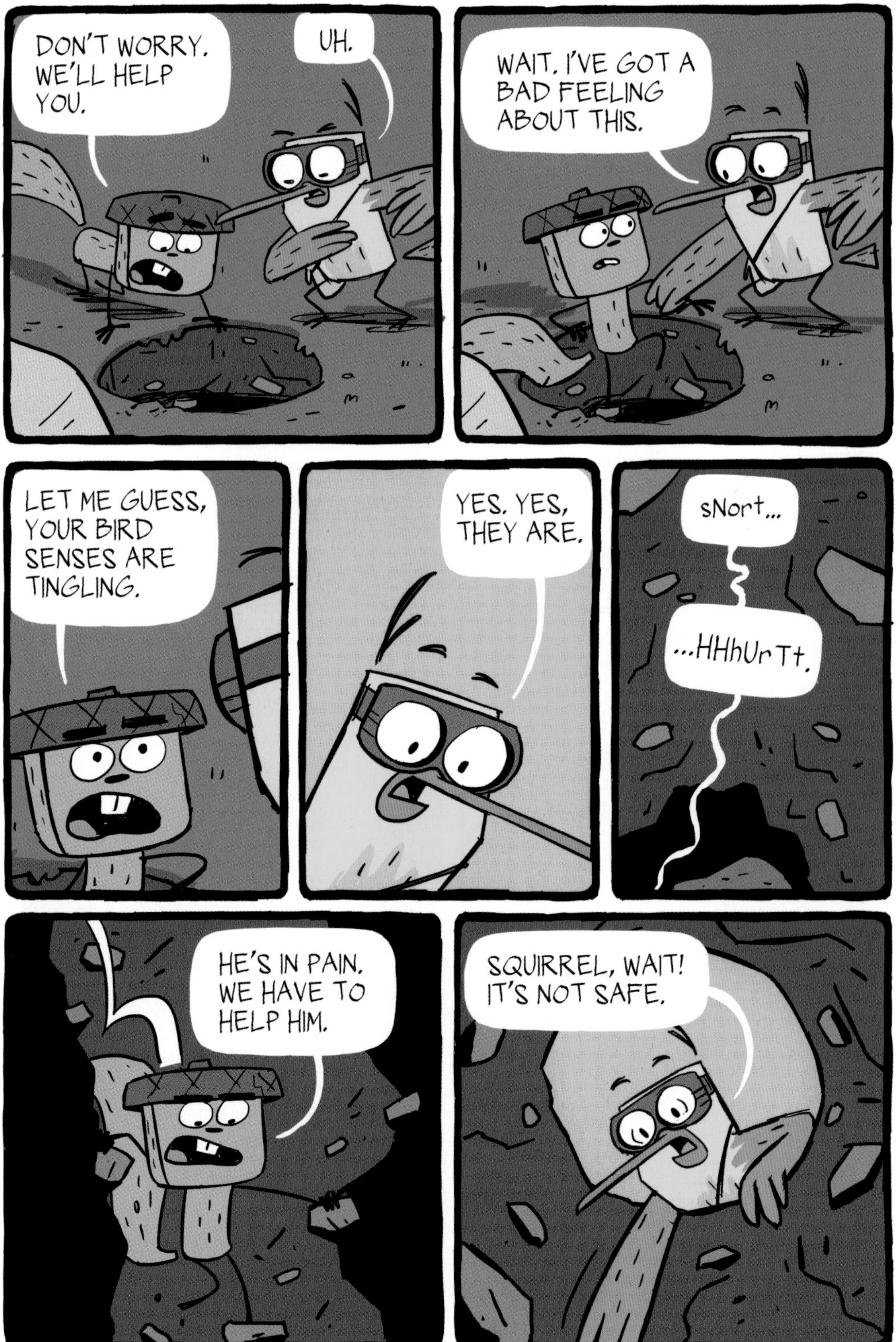
DON'T WORRY. WE'LL HELP YOU.
UH.
WAIT. I'VE GOT A BAD FEELING ABOUT THIS.
LET ME GUESS, YOUR BIRD SENSES ARE TINGLING.
YES. YES, THEY ARE.
sNort...
...HHhUrTt.
HE'S IN PAIN. WE HAVE TO HELP HIM.
SQUIRREL, WAIT! IT'S NOT SAFE.

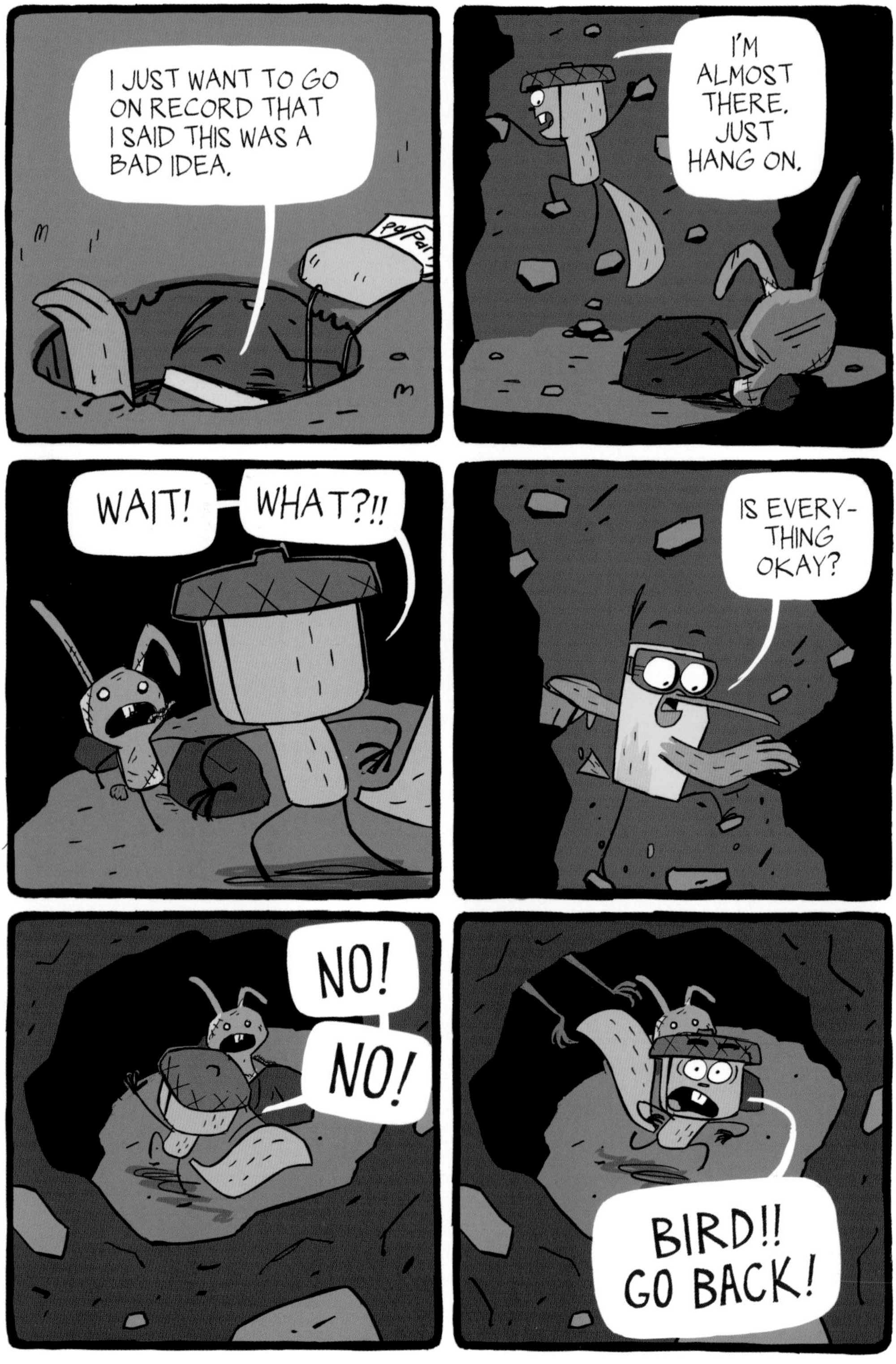
I JUST WANT TO GO ON RECORD THAT I SAID THIS WAS A BAD IDEA.
I'M ALMOST THERE. JUST HANG ON.
WAIT!
WHAT?!!
IS EVERY-THING OKAY?
NO!
NO!
BIRD!! GO BACK!

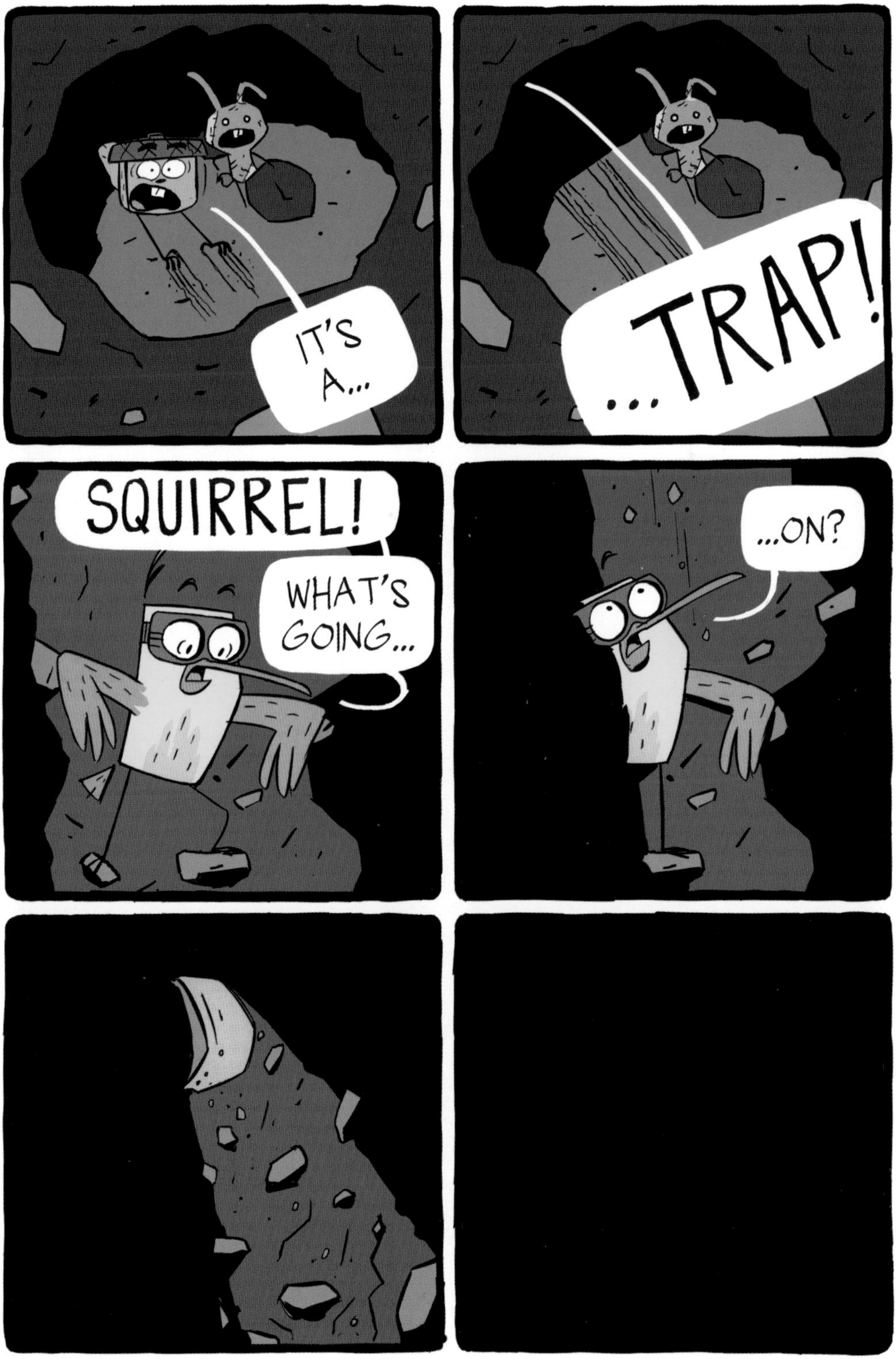
IT'S A...
...TRAP!
SQUIRREL!
WHAT'S GOING...
...ON?

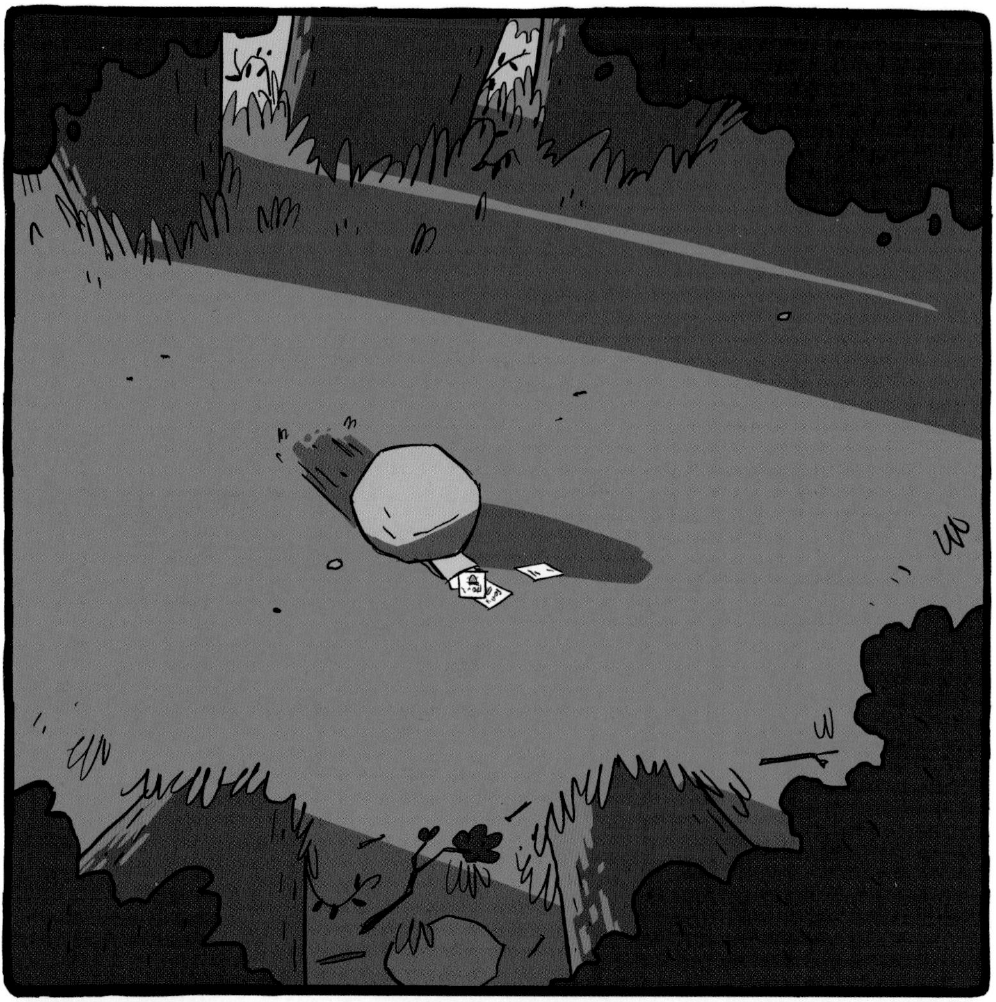

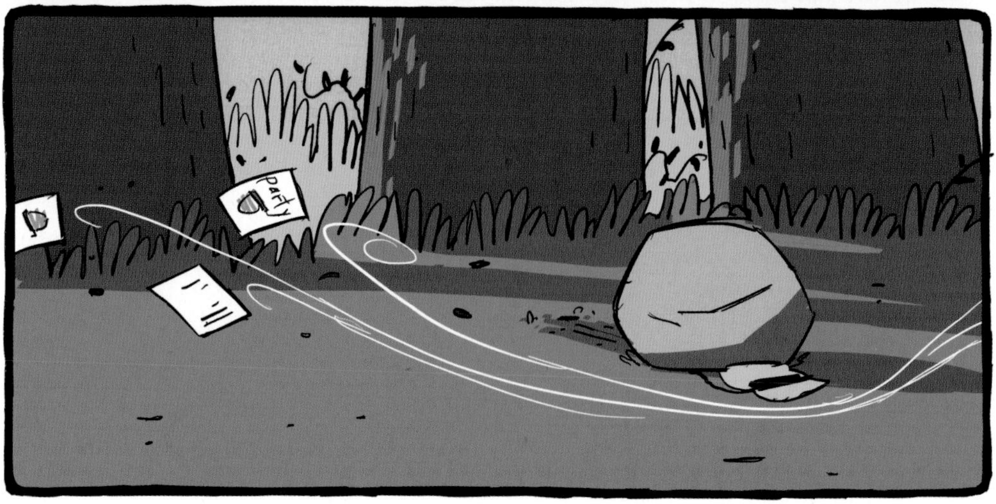
party

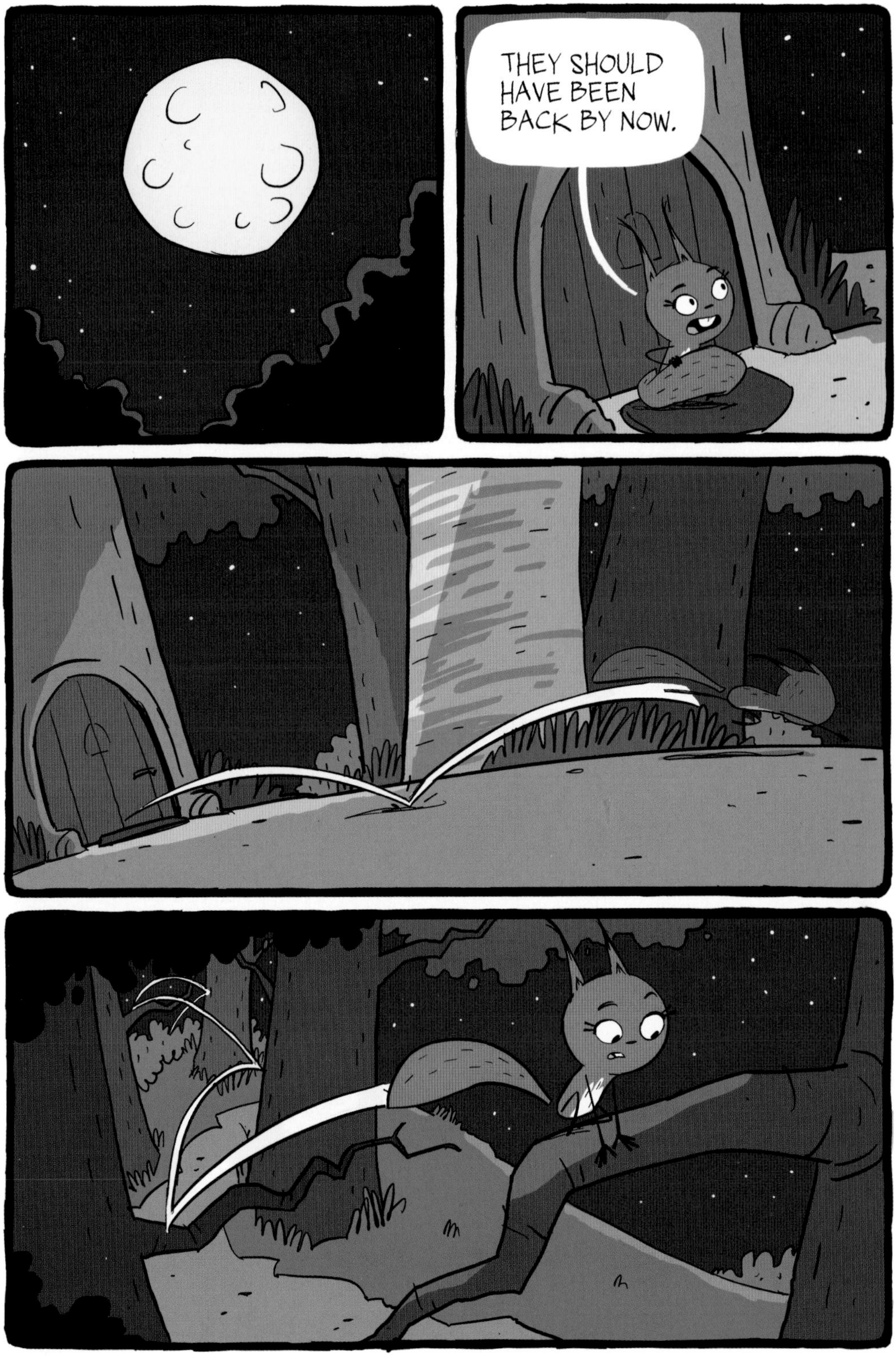
THEY SHOULD HAVE BEEN BACK BY NOW.

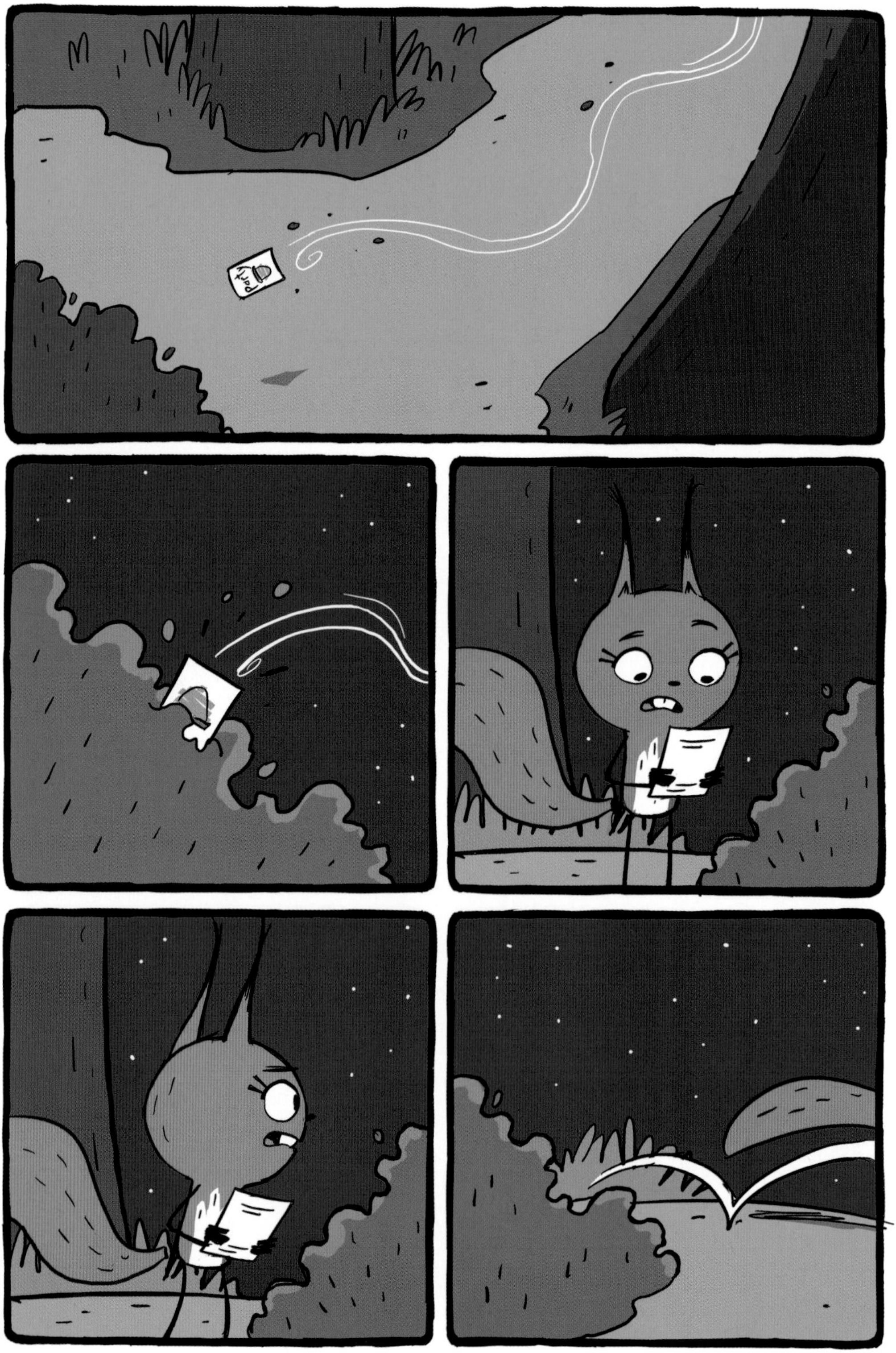
party

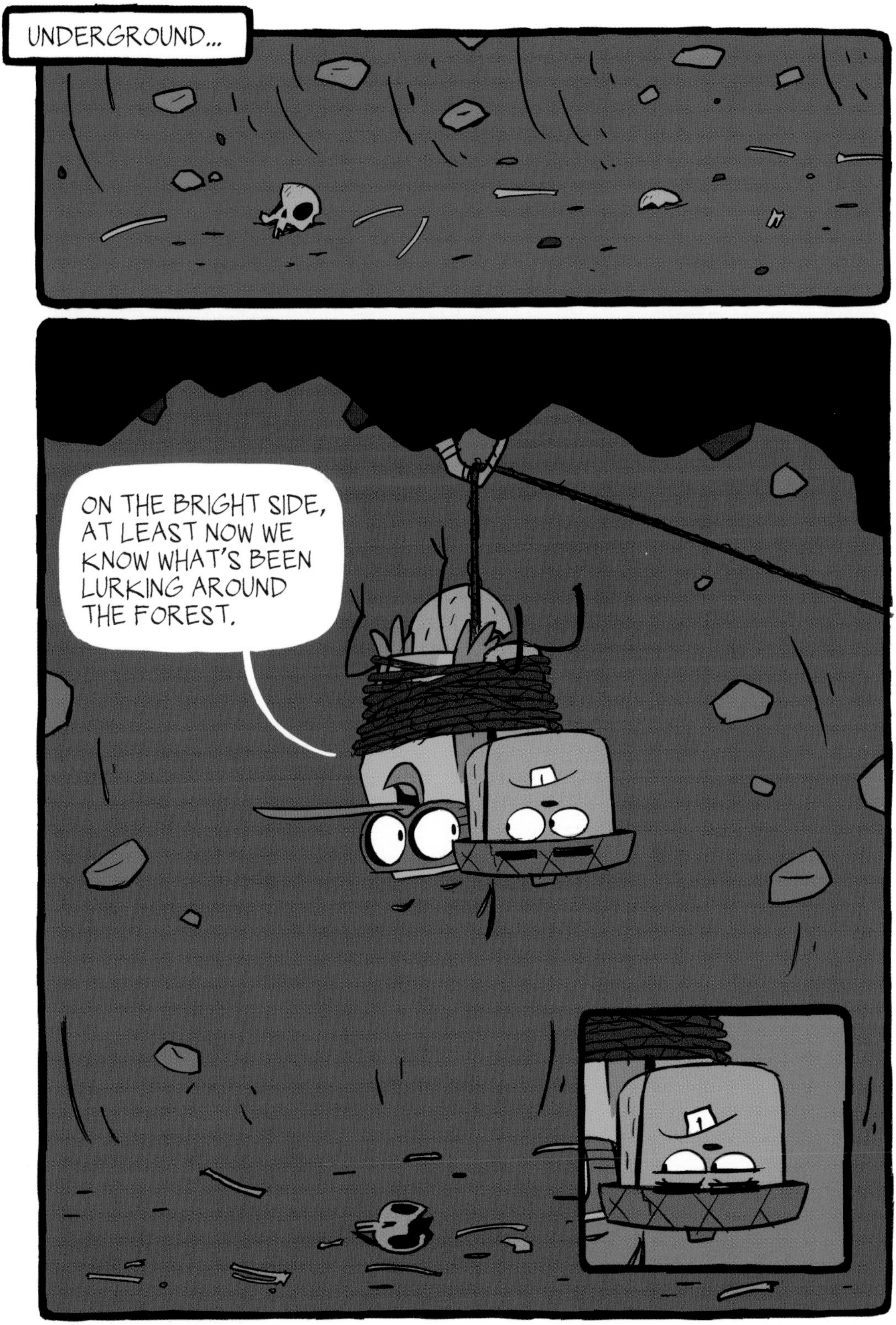
UNDERGROUND...
ON THE BRIGHT SIDE, AT LEAST NOW WE KNOW WHAT'S BEEN LURKING AROUND THE FOREST.

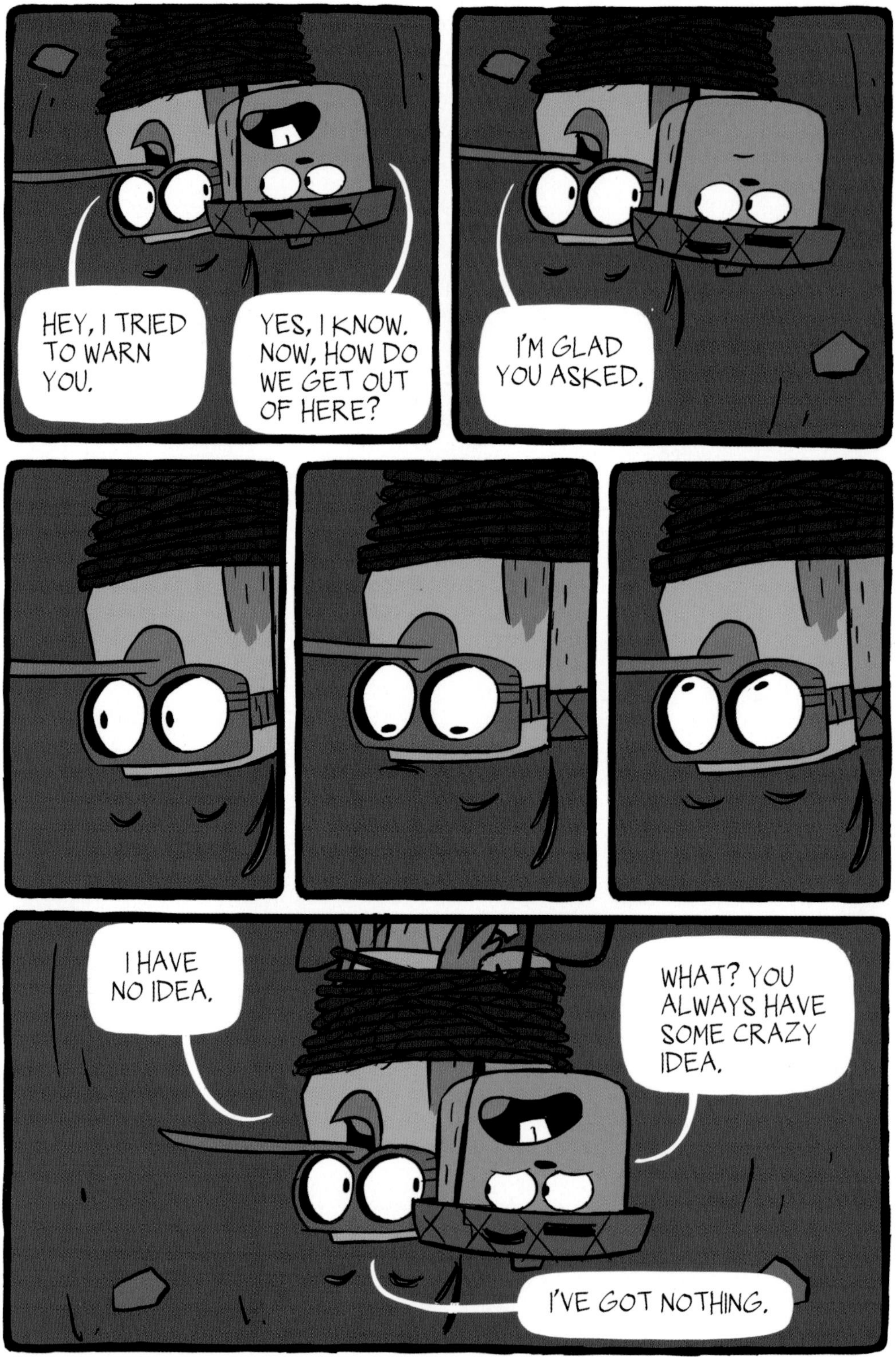
HEY, I TRIED TO WARN YOU.
YES, I KNOW. NOW, HOW DO WE GET OUT OF HERE?
I'M GLAD YOU ASKED.
I HAVE NO IDEA.
WHAT? YOU ALWAYS HAVE SOME CRAZY IDEA.
I'VE GOT NOTHING.

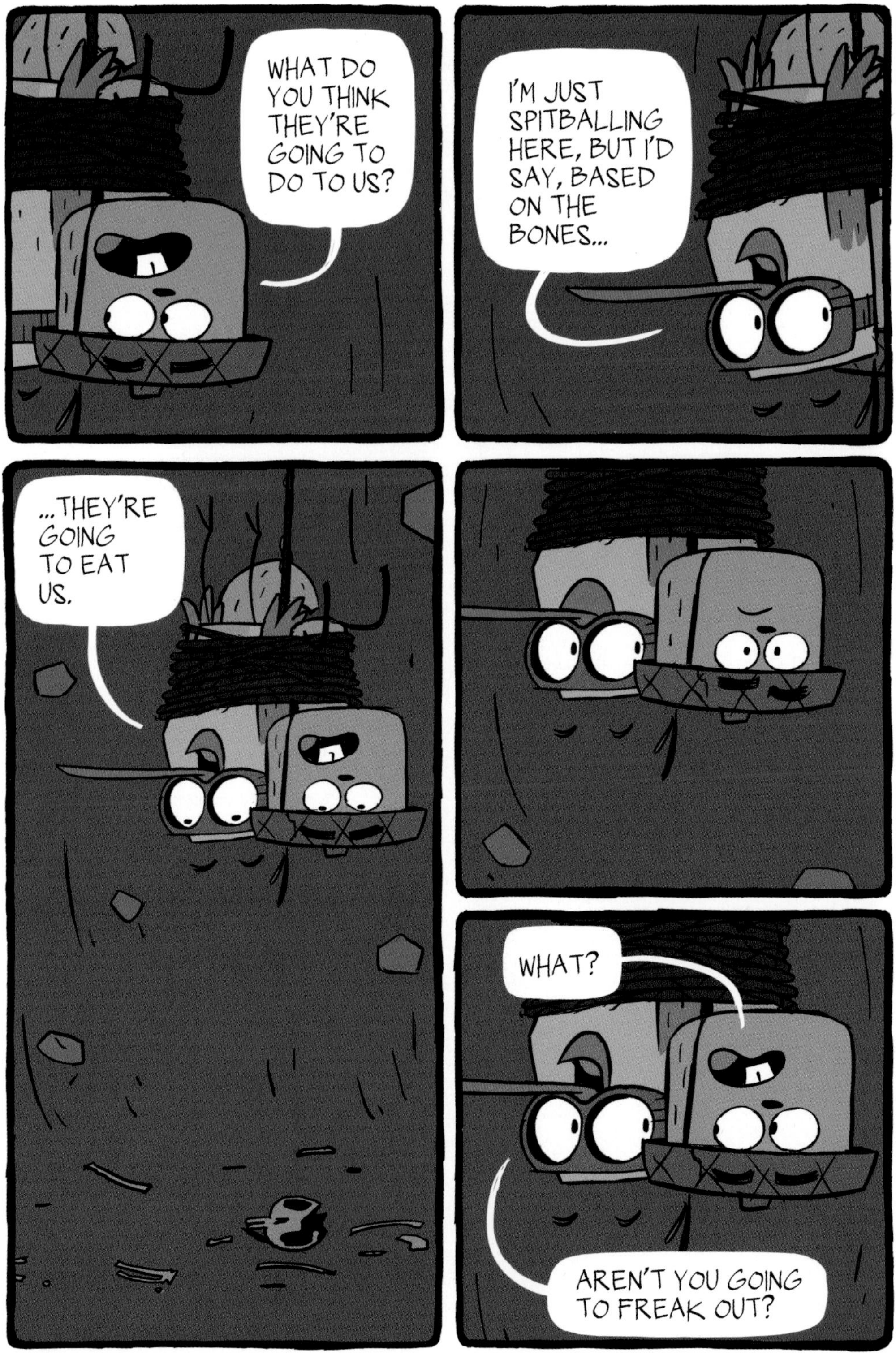

WHAT DO YOU THINK THEY'RE GOING TO DO TO US?
I'M JUST SPITBALLING HERE, BUT I'D SAY, BASED ON THE BONES...
...THEY'RE GOING TO EAT US.
WHAT?
AREN'T YOU GOING TO FREAK OUT?

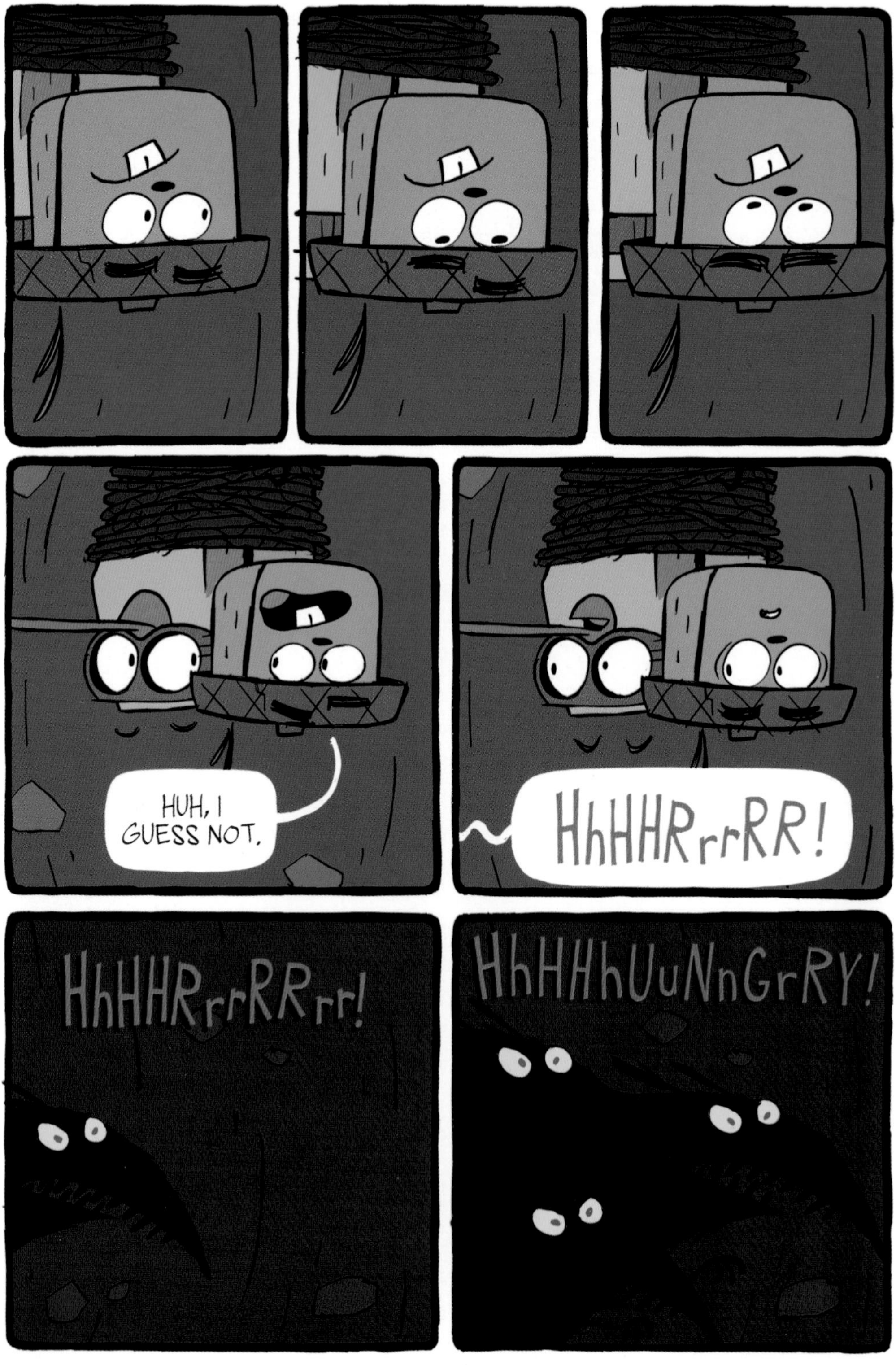
HUH, I GUESS NOT.
HhHHRrrRR!
HhHHRrrRRrr!
HhHHhUuNnGrRY!

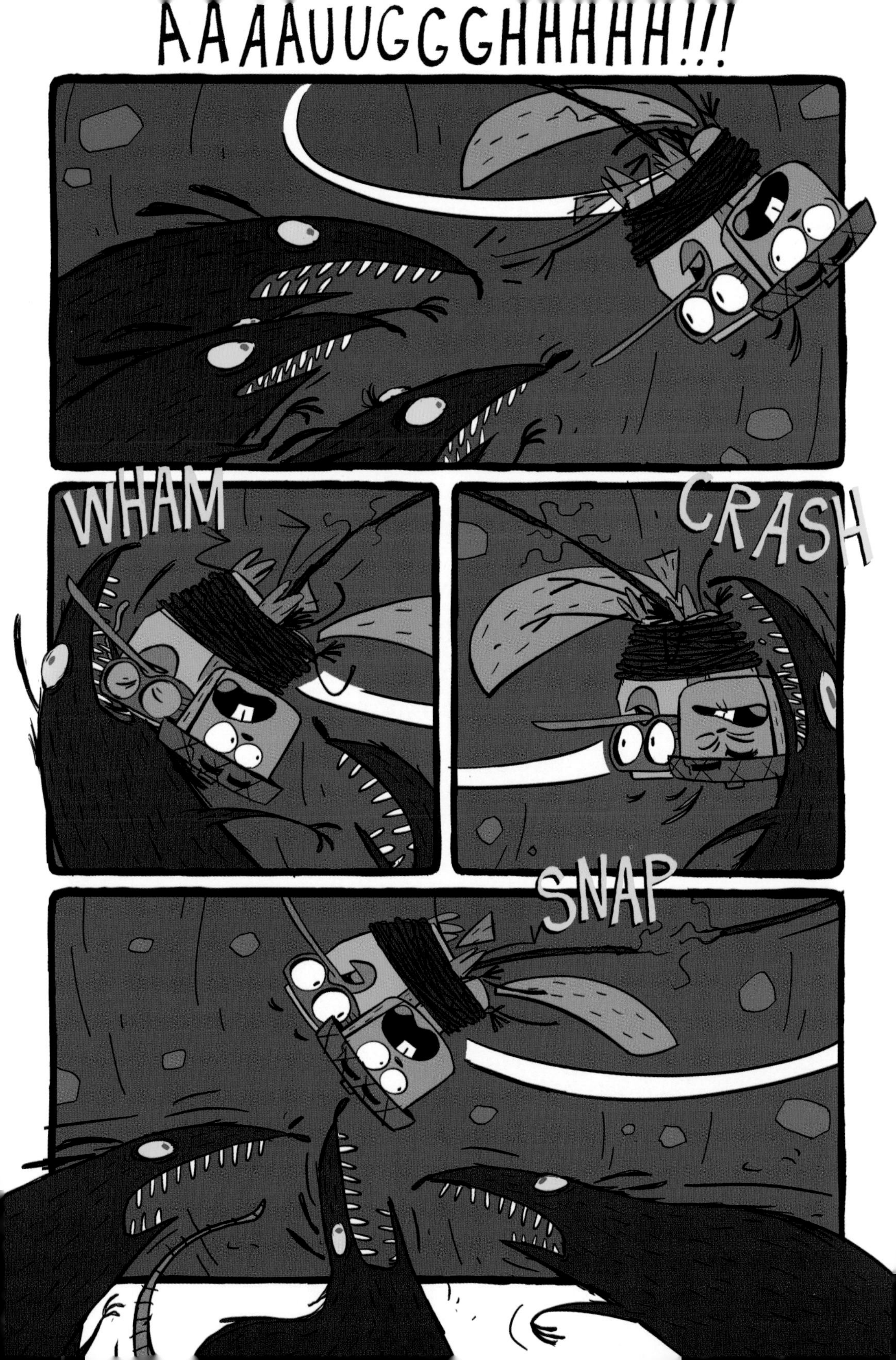
AAAAUUGGGHHHHH!!!
WHAM
CRASH
SNAP

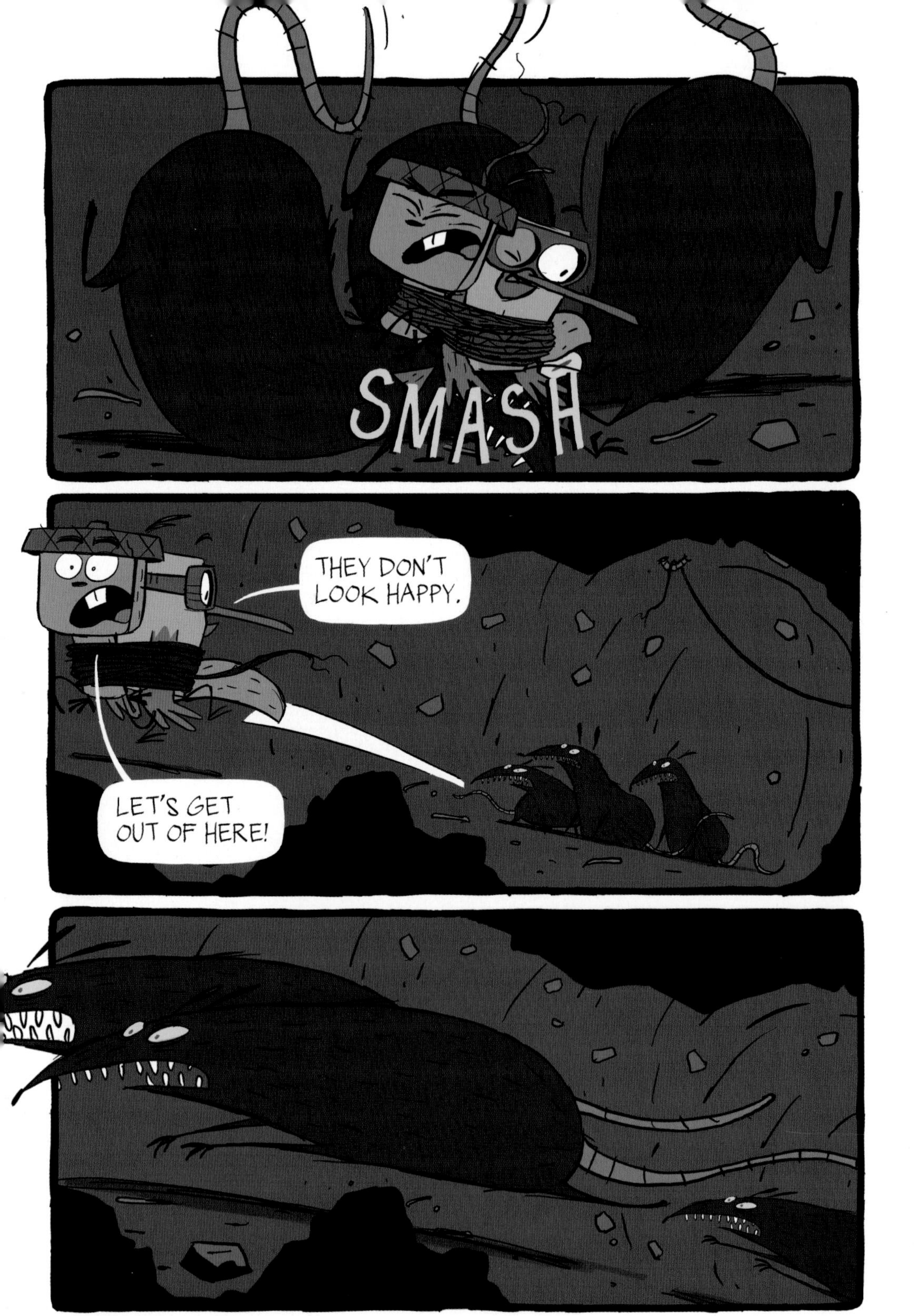
SMASH
THEY DON'T LOOK HAPPY.
LET'S GET OUT OF HERE!

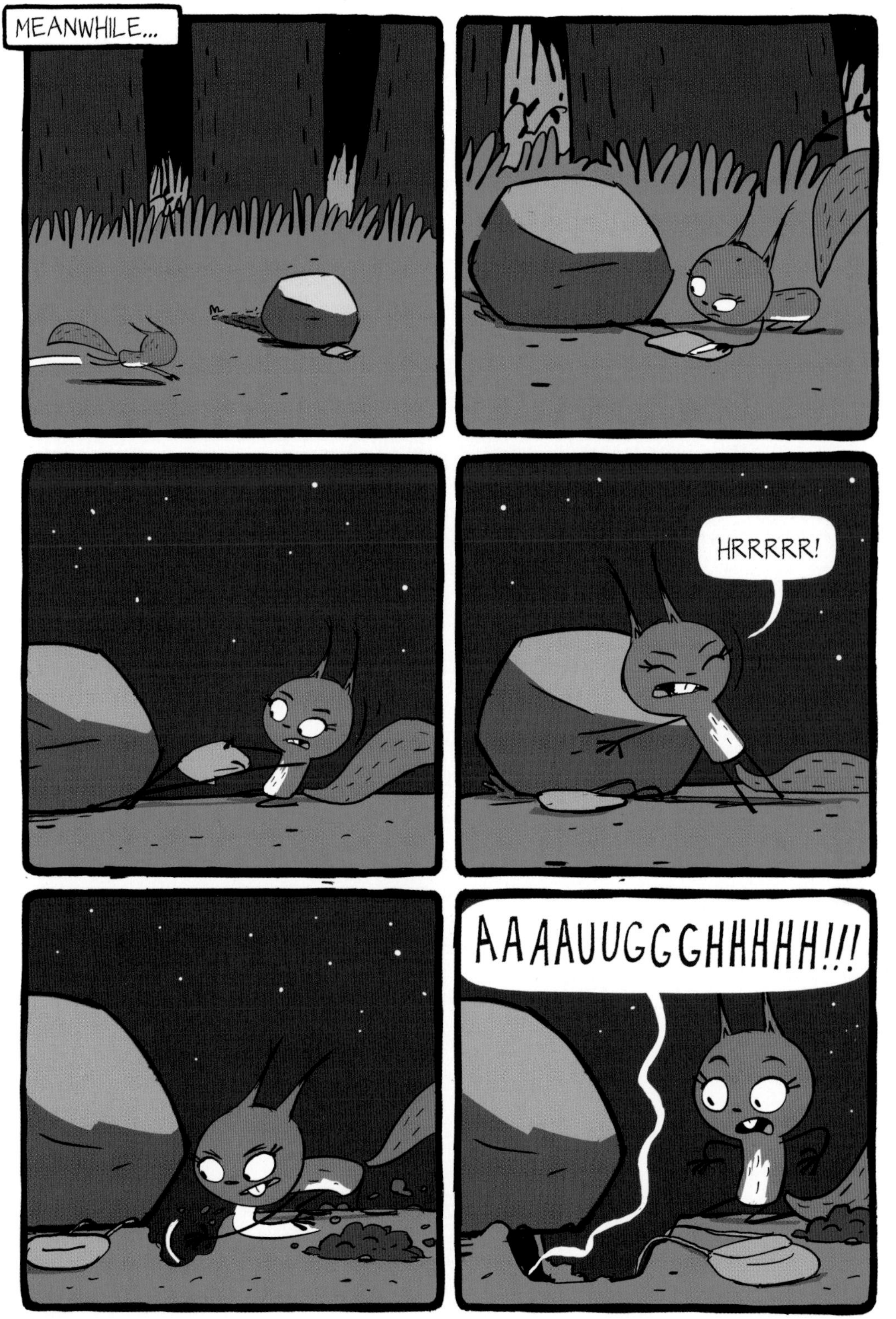
MEANWHILE...
HRRRRR!
AAAAUUGGHHHHH!!!

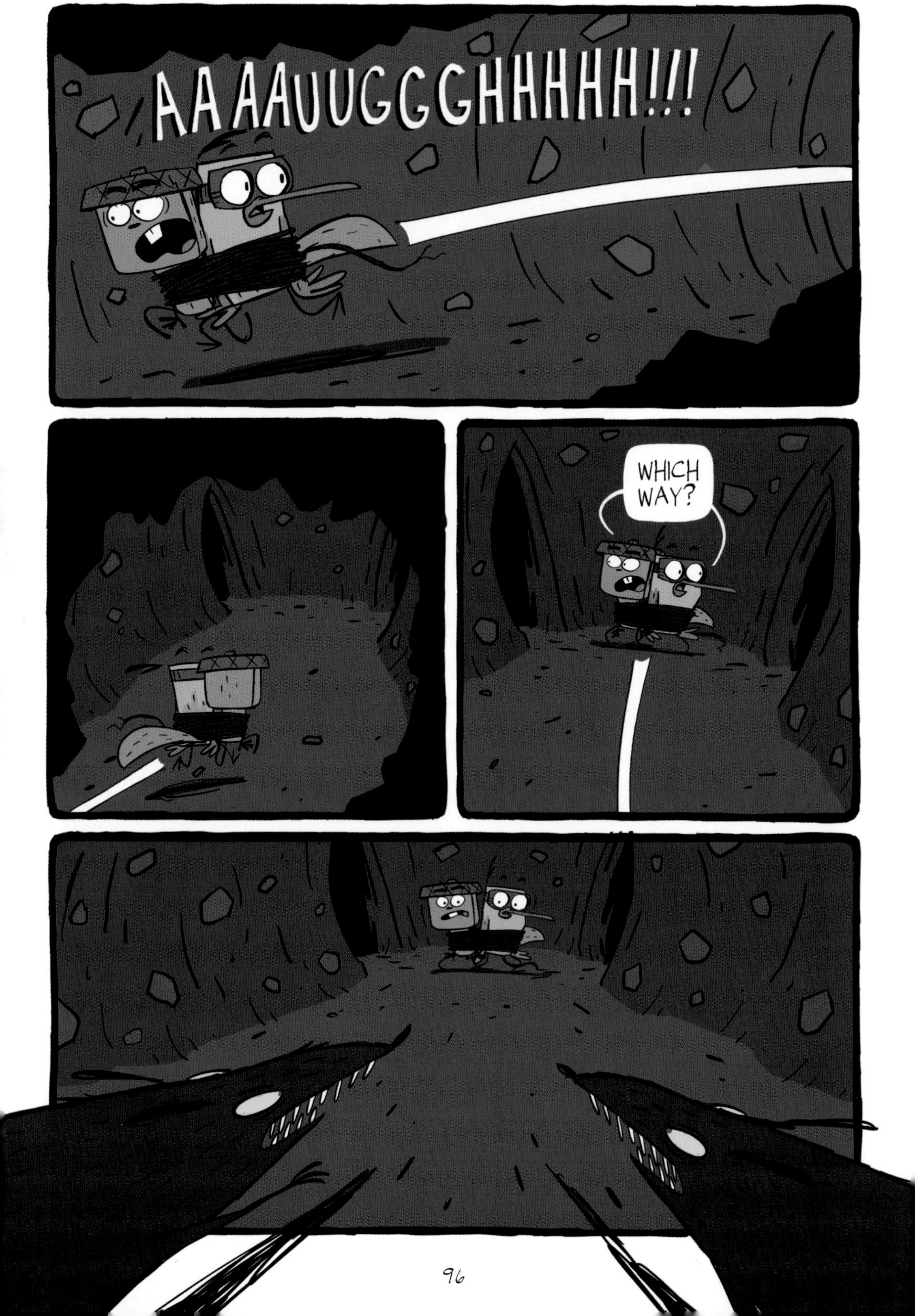
AAAAUUGGGHHHHH!!!
WHICH WAY?

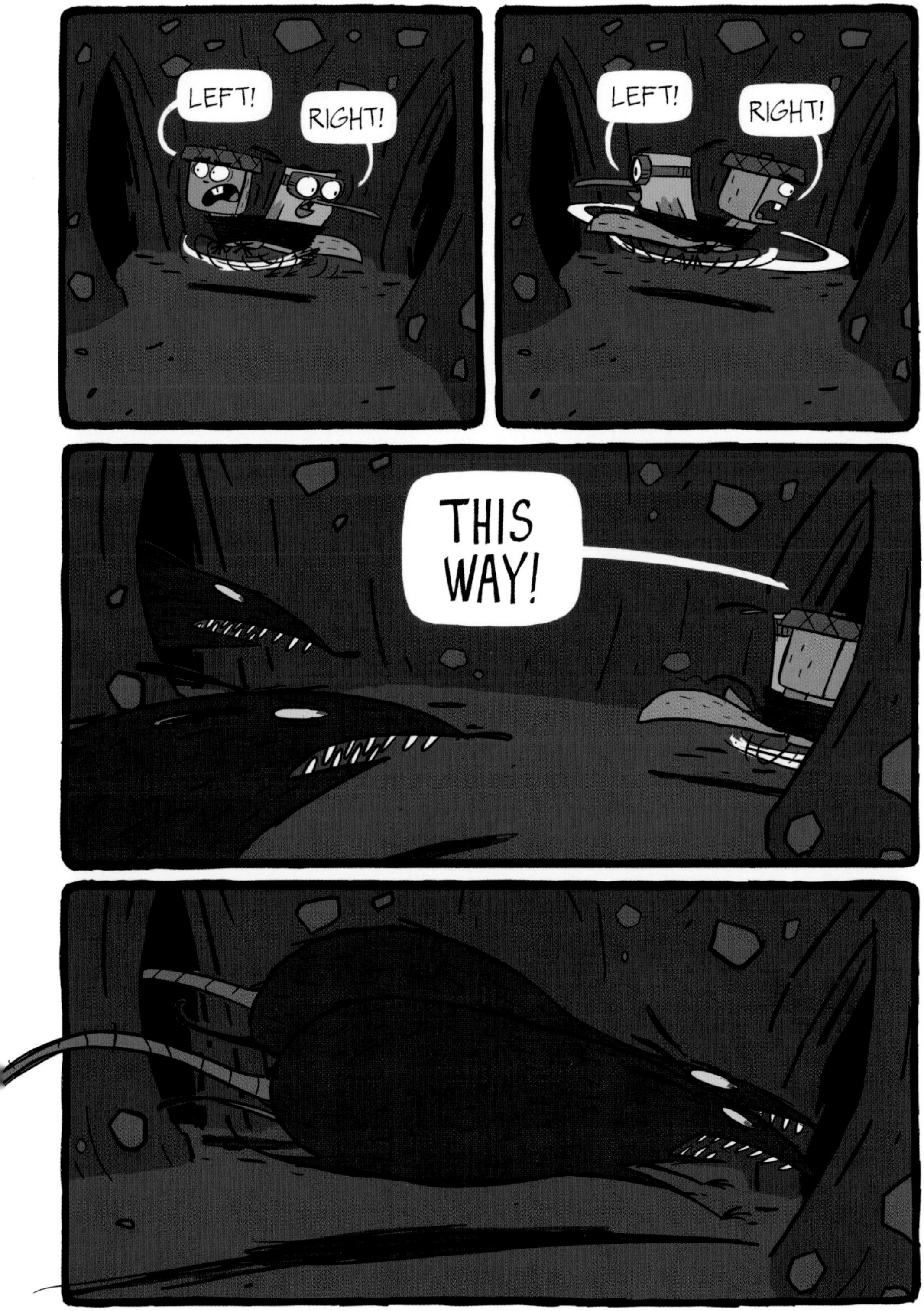
LEFT!
RIGHT!
LEFT!
RIGHT!
THIS WAY!

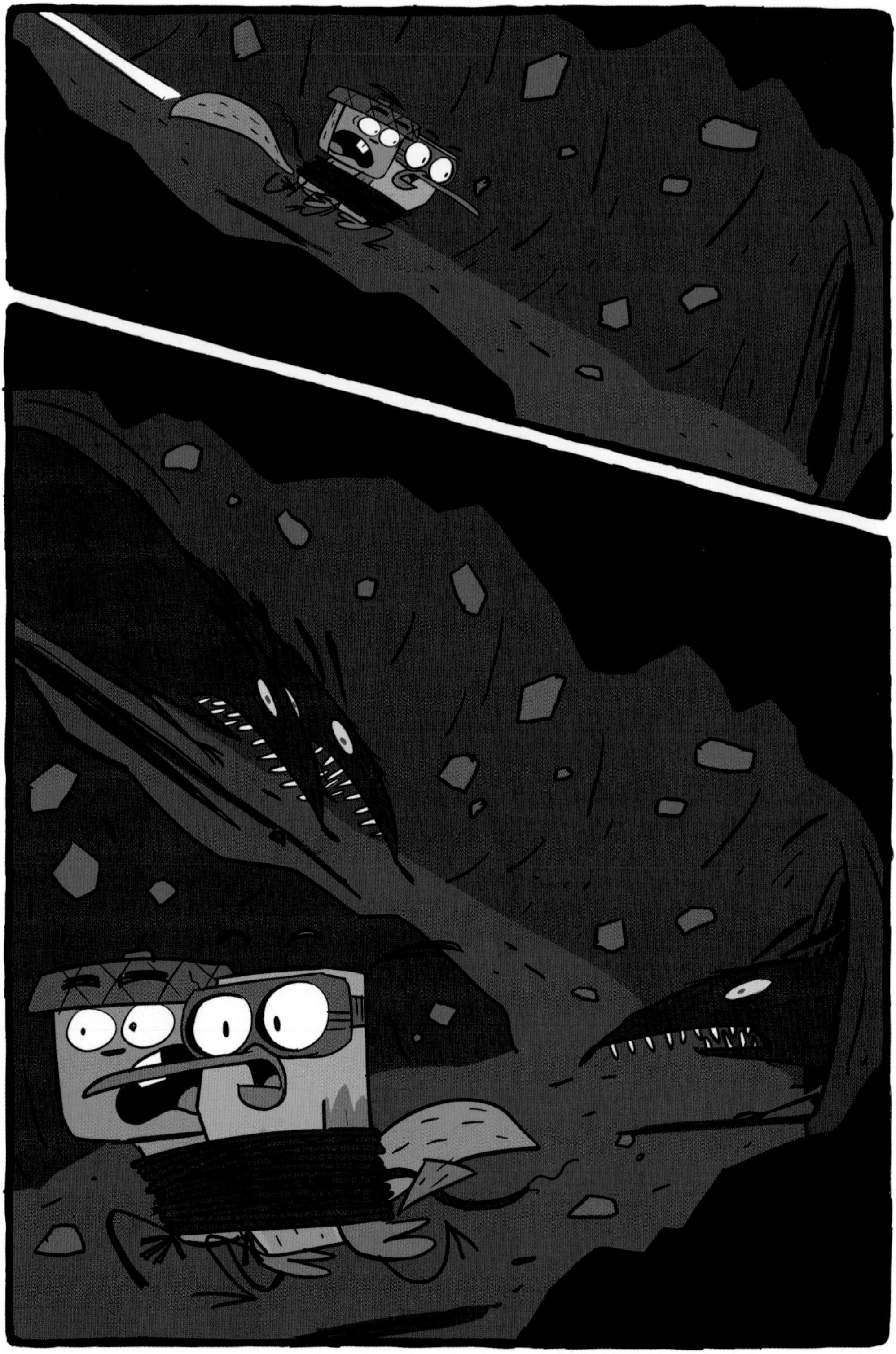

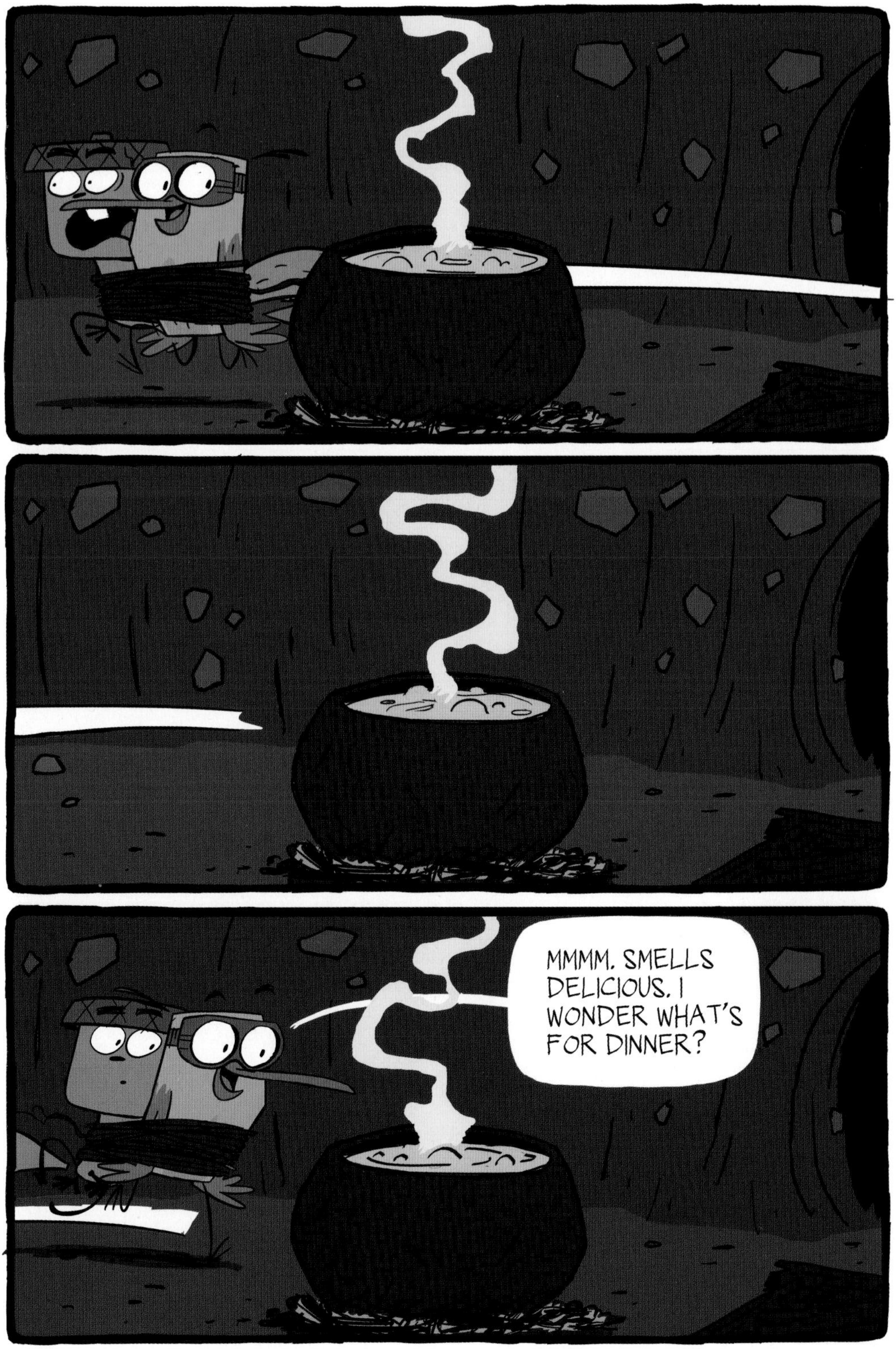
MMMM. SMELLS DELICIOUS. I WONDER WHAT'S FOR DINNER?

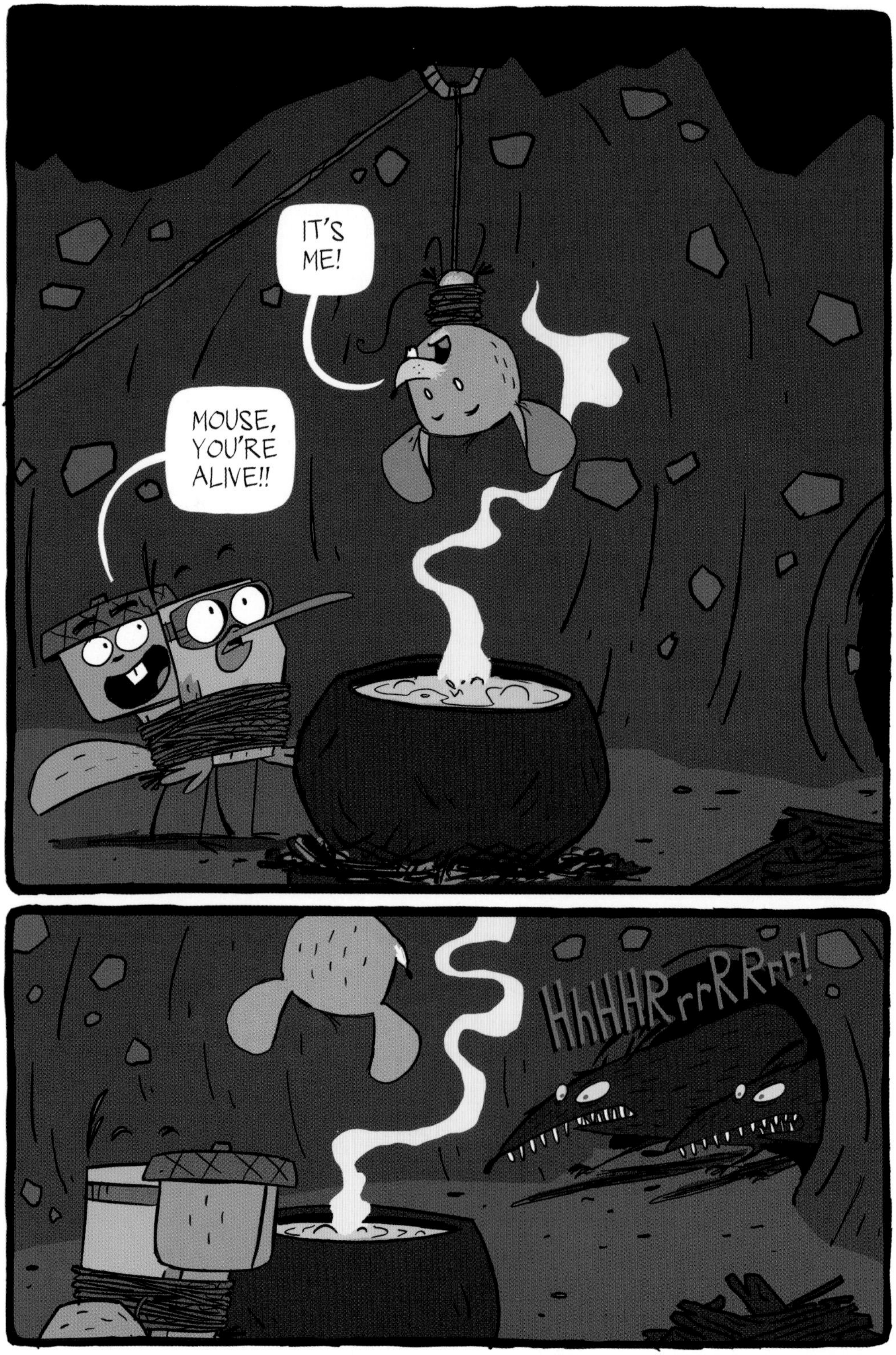

IT'S ME!
MOUSE, YOU'RE ALIVE!!
HhHHRrrRRrr!

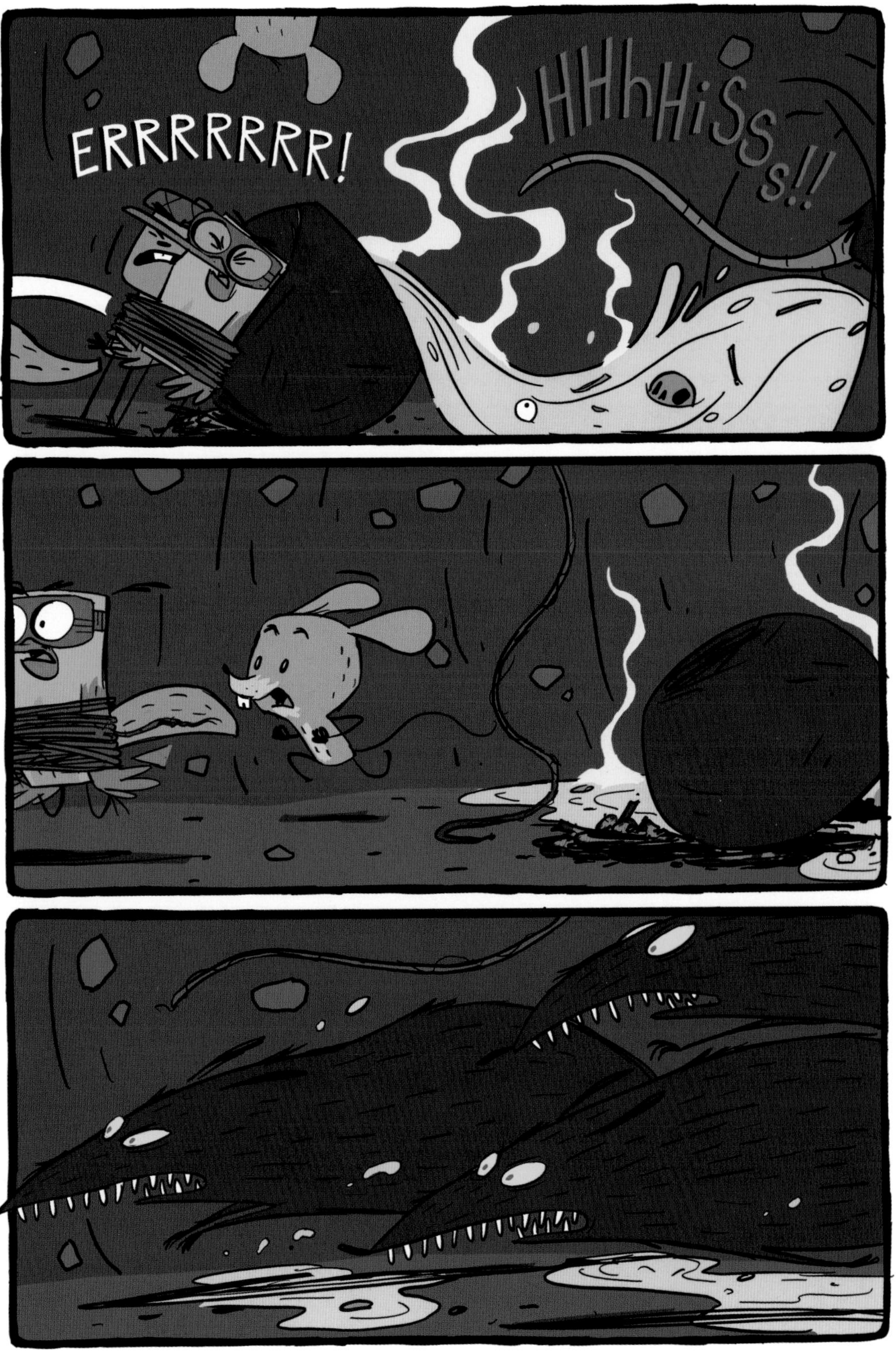
ERRRRRRRR!
HHHhHiSSs!!

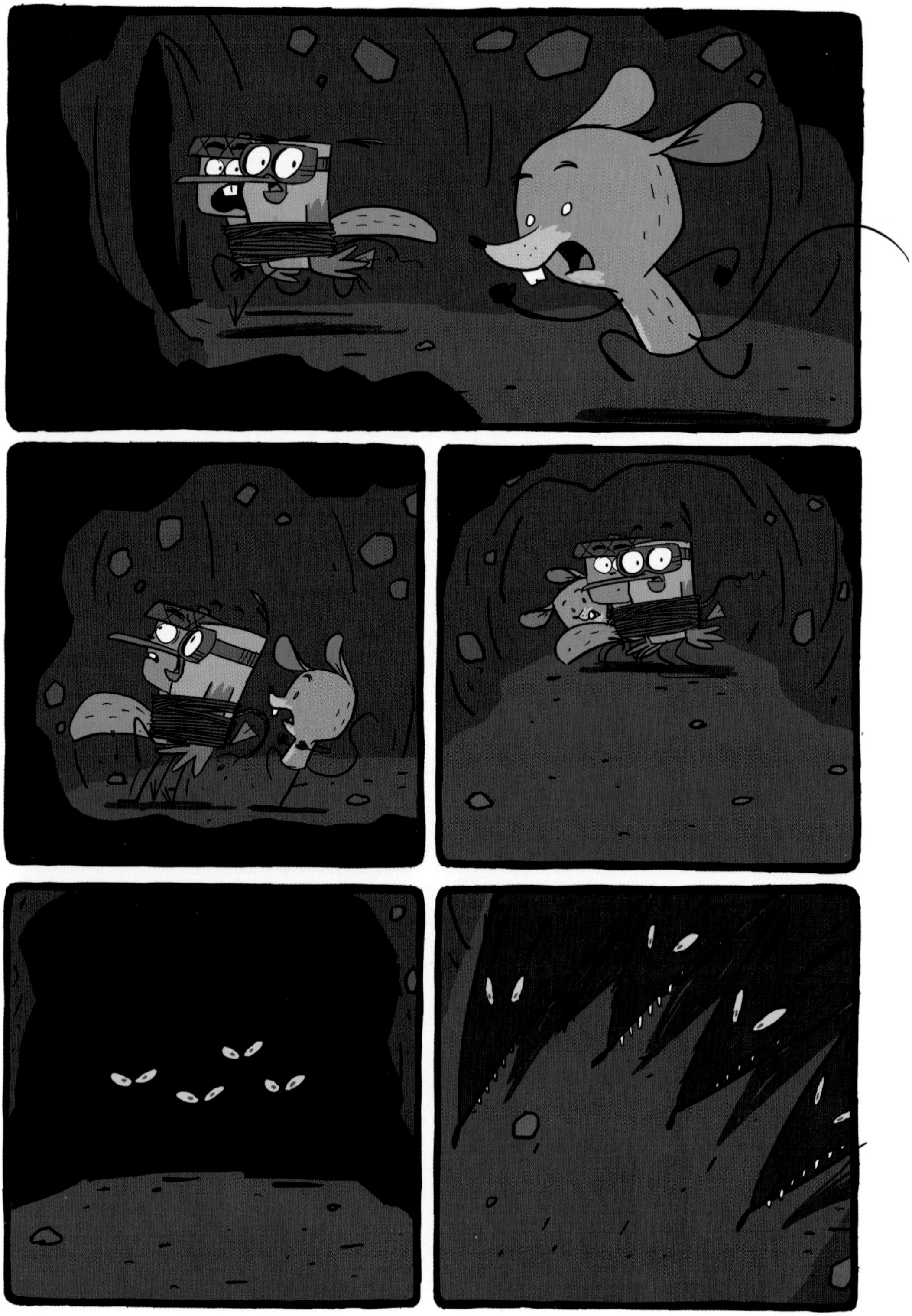

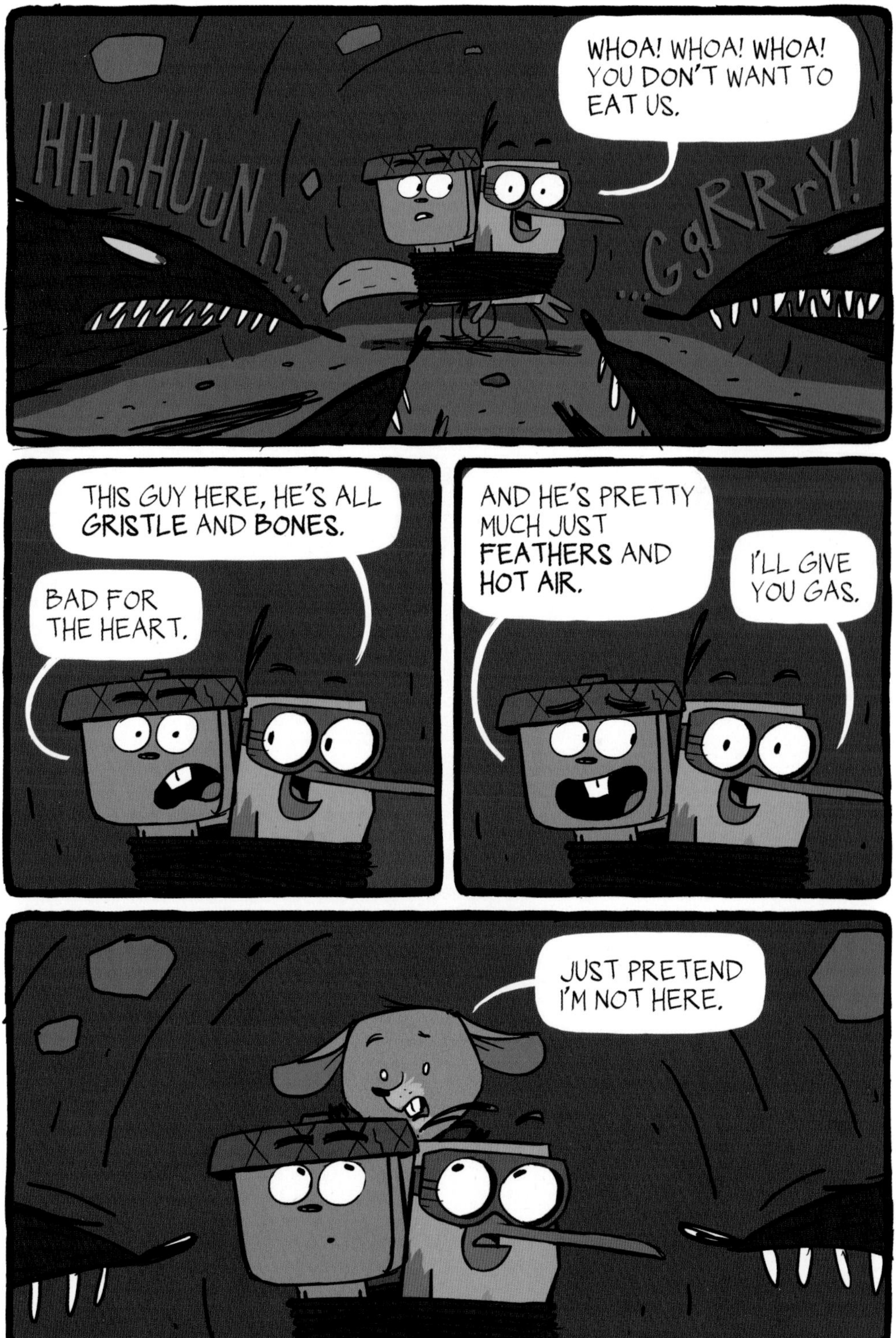
HHhHUuNn...
WHOA! WHOA! WHOA! YOU DON'T WANT TO EAT US.
...GgRRrY!
THIS GUY HERE, HE'S ALL GRISTLE AND BONES.
BAD FOR THE HEART.
AND HE'S PRETTY MUCH JUST FEATHERS AND HOT AIR.
I'LL GIVE YOU GAS.
JUST PRETEND I'M NOT HERE.

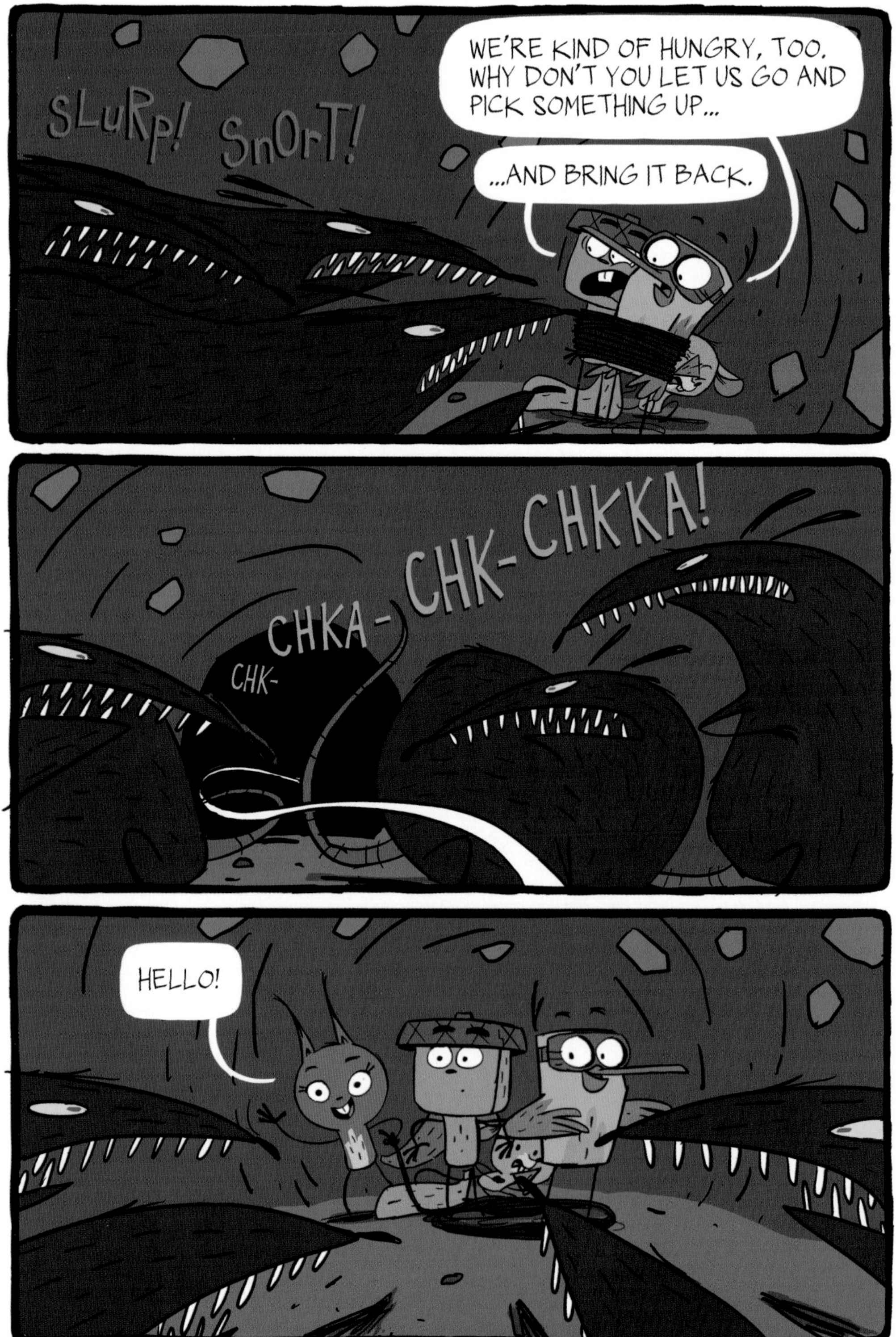
SLURP! SNORT!
WE'RE KIND OF HUNGRY, TOO. WHY DON'T YOU LET US GO AND PICK SOMETHING UP...
...AND BRING IT BACK.
CHK- CHKA- CHK- CHKKA!
HELLO!

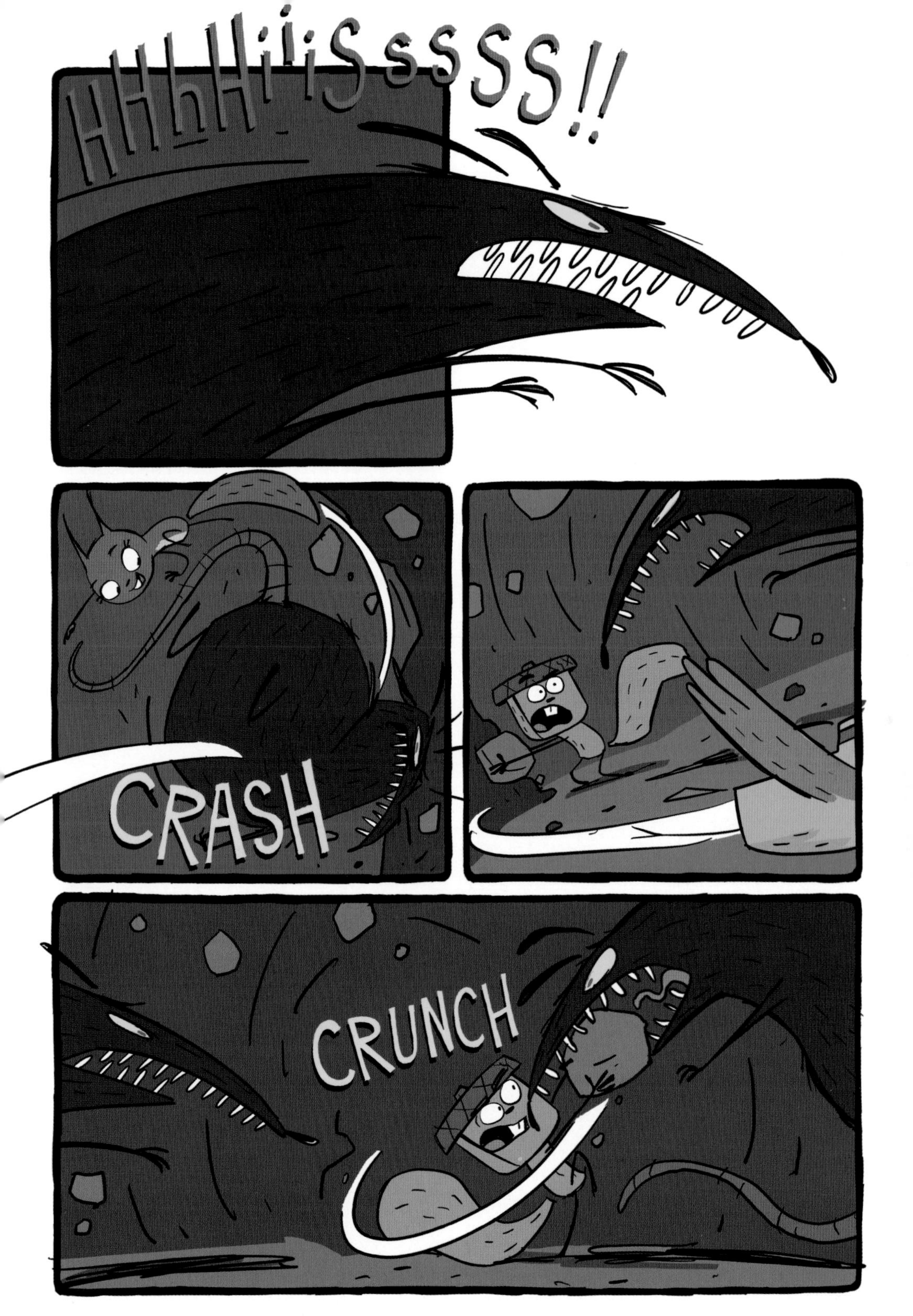
HHHHiiiSSSSSS!!
CRASH
CRUNCH

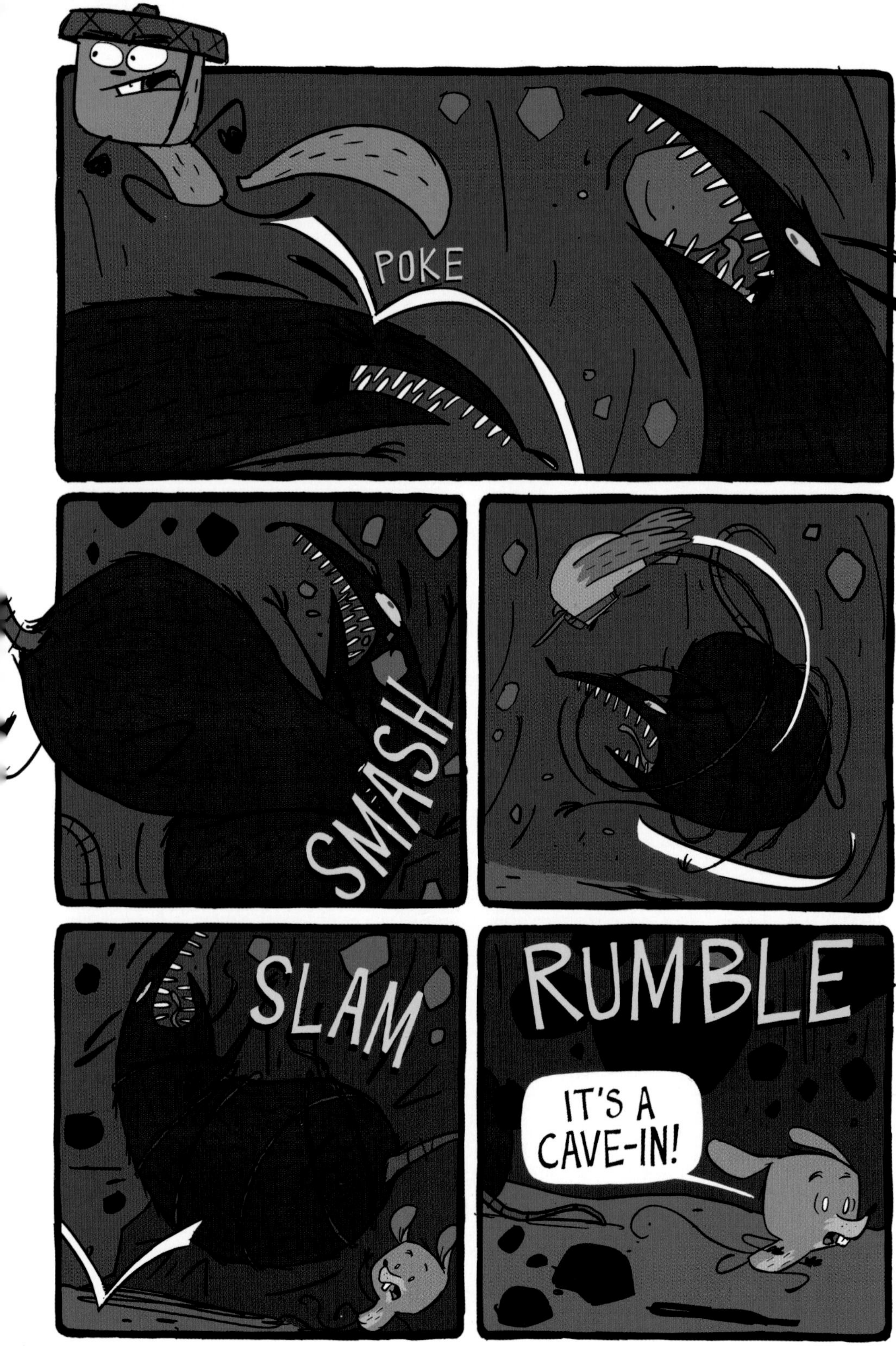
POKE
SMASH
SLAM
RUMBLE
IT'S A CAVE-IN!

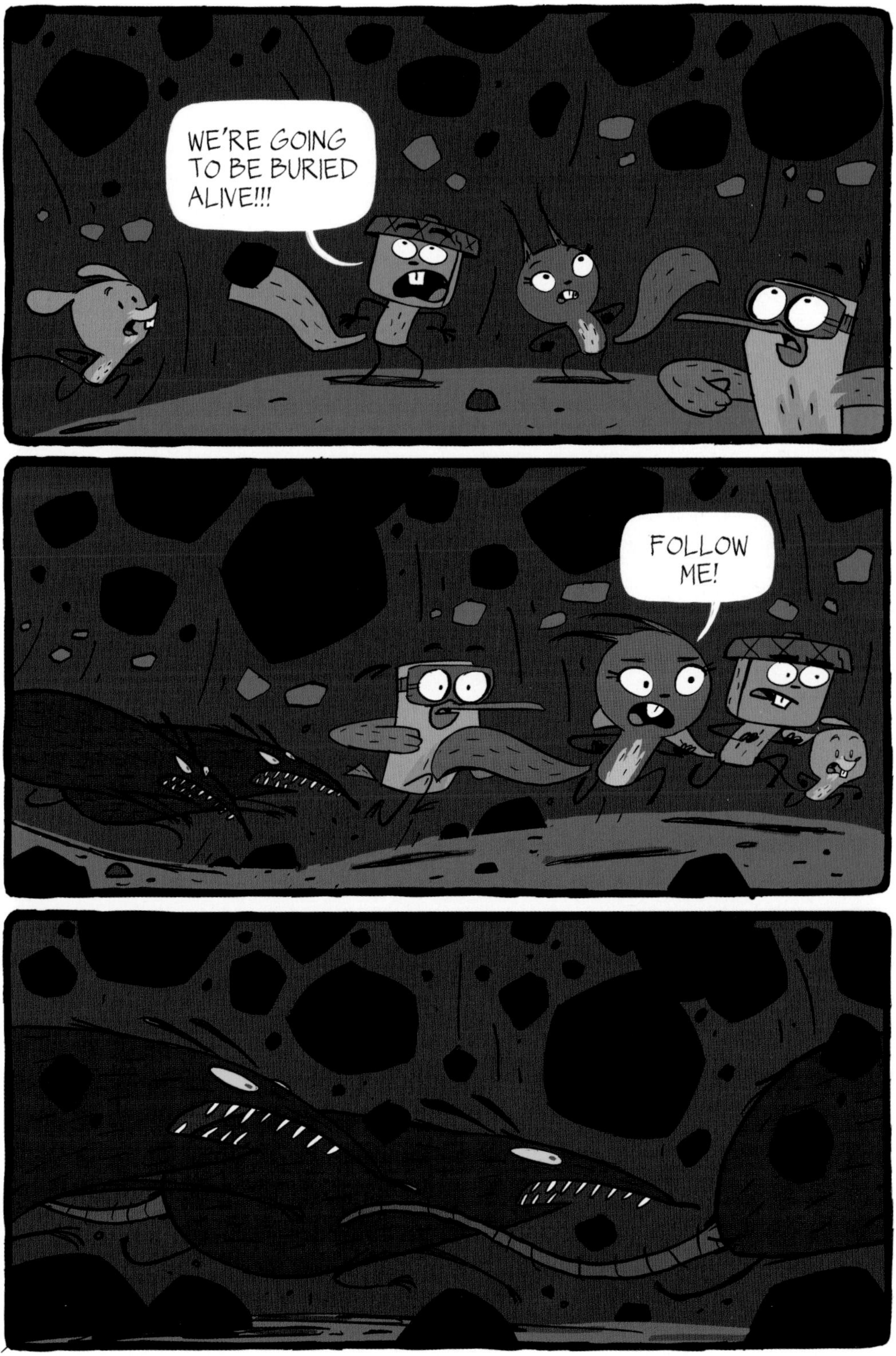
WE'RE GOING TO BE BURIED ALIVE!!!
FOLLOW ME!

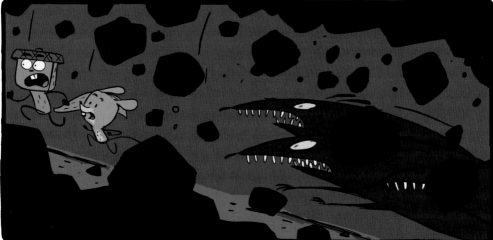

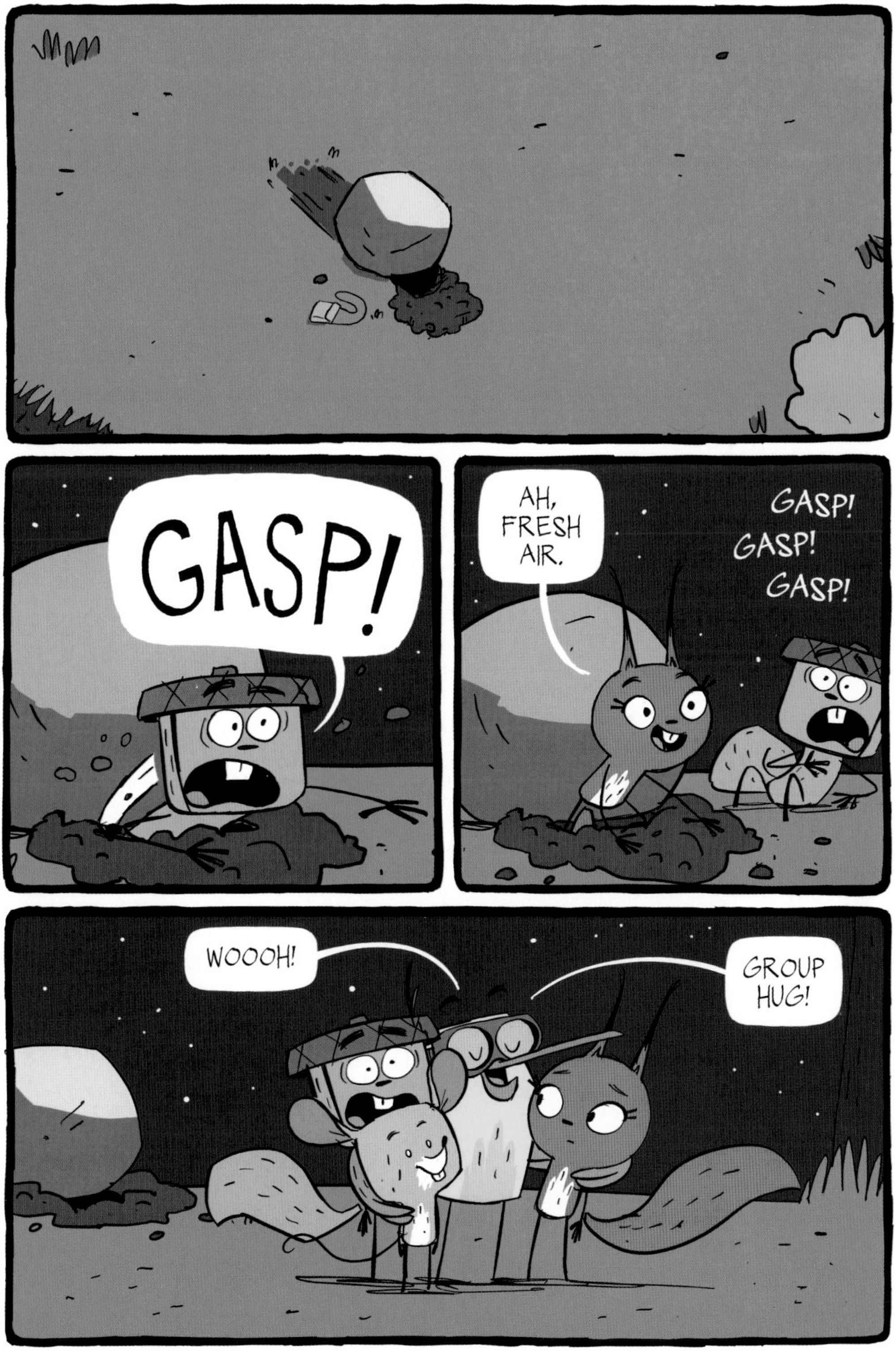
GASP!
AH, FRESH AIR.
GASP! GASP! GASP!
WOOOH!
GROUP HUG!

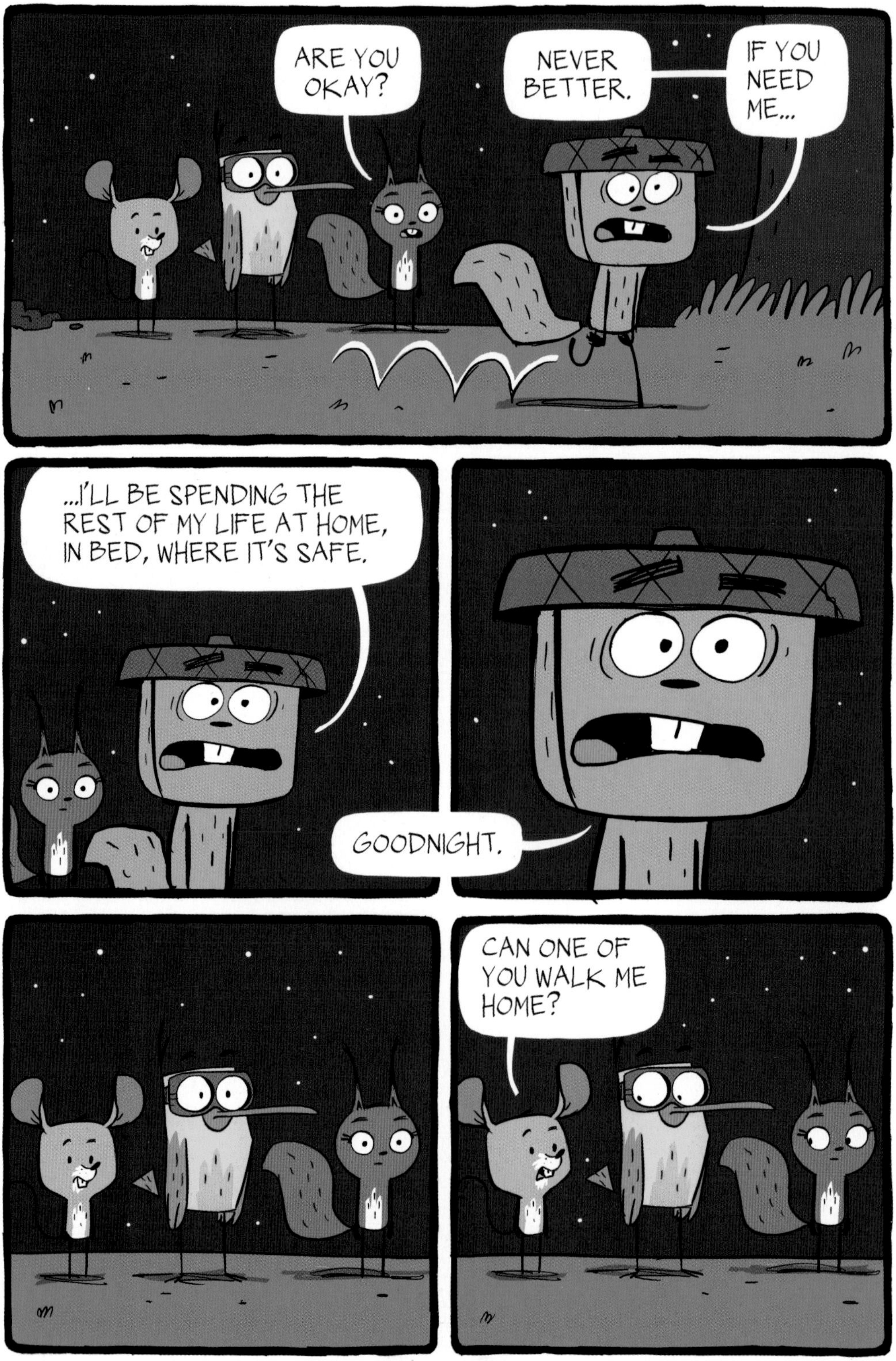
ARE YOU OKAY?
NEVER BETTER.
IF YOU NEED ME...
...I'LL BE SPENDING THE REST OF MY LIFE AT HOME, IN BED, WHERE IT'S SAFE.
GOODNIGHT.
CAN ONE OF YOU WALK ME HOME?

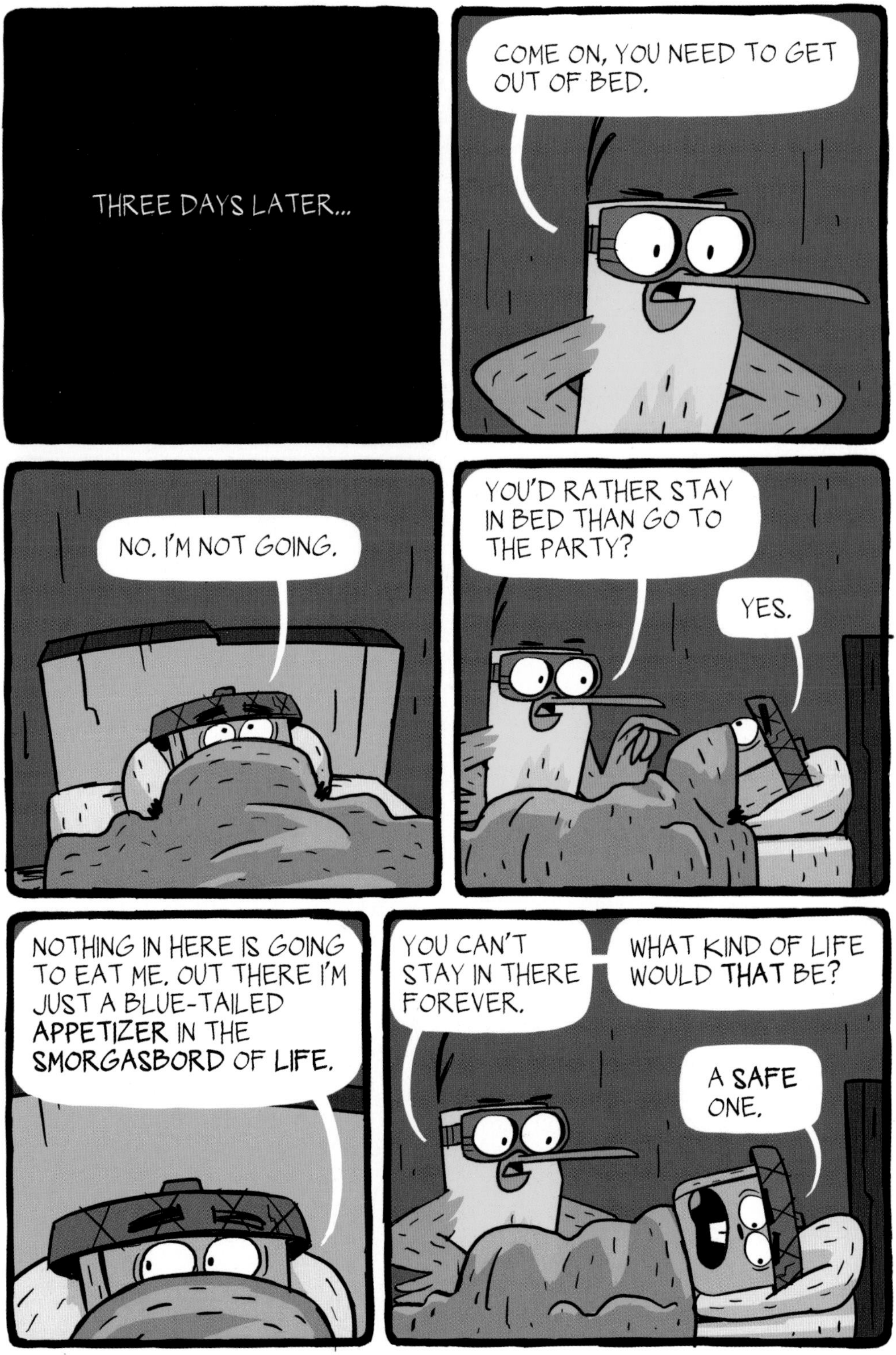
THREE DAYS LATER...
COME ON, YOU NEED TO GET OUT OF BED.
NO. I'M NOT GOING.
YOU'D RATHER STAY IN BED THAN GO TO THE PARTY?
YES.
NOTHING IN HERE IS GOING TO EAT ME. OUT THERE I'M JUST A BLUE-TAILED **APPETIZER** IN THE **SMORGASBORD** OF **LIFE**.
YOU CAN'T STAY IN THERE FOREVER.
WHAT KIND OF LIFE WOULD **THAT** BE?
A **SAFE** ONE.

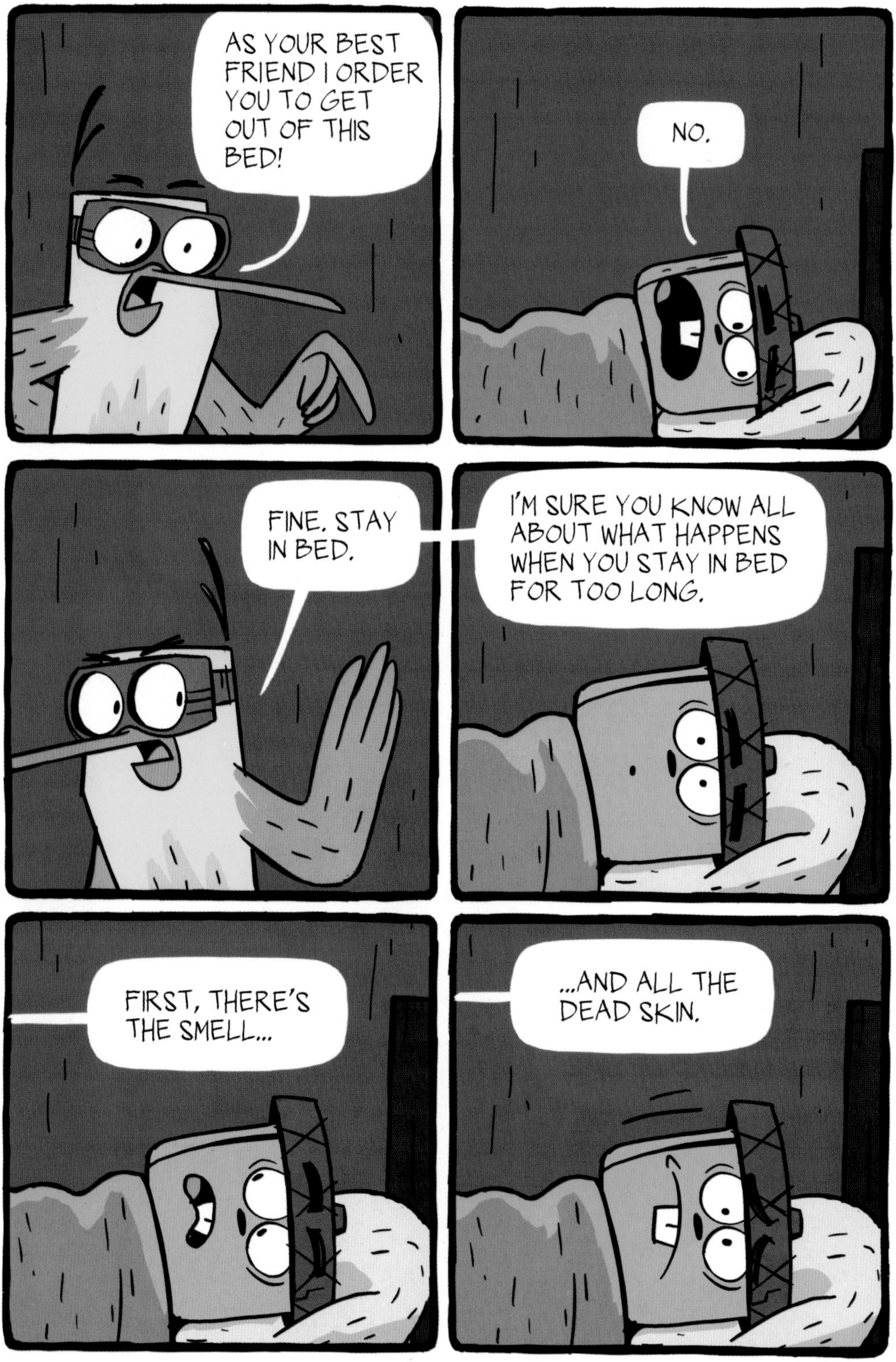
AS YOUR BEST FRIEND I ORDER YOU TO GET OUT OF THIS BED!
NO.
FINE. STAY IN BED.
I'M SURE YOU KNOW ALL ABOUT WHAT HAPPENS WHEN YOU STAY IN BED FOR TOO LONG.
FIRST, THERE'S THE SMELL...
...AND ALL THE DEAD SKIN.

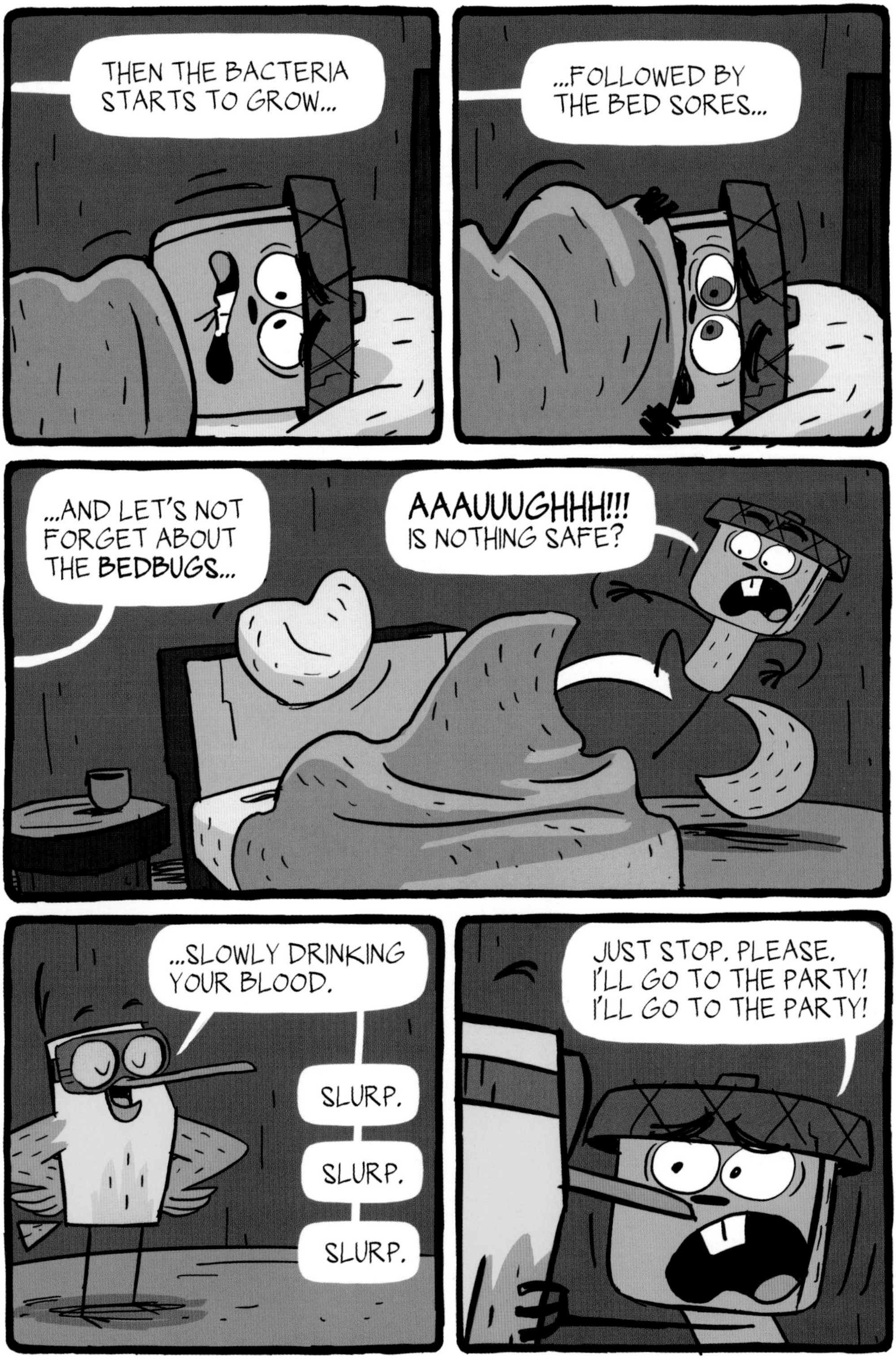
THEN THE BACTERIA STARTS TO GROW...
...FOLLOWED BY THE BED SORES...
...AND LET'S NOT FORGET ABOUT THE BEDBUGS...
AAAUUUGHHH!!! IS NOTHING SAFE?
...SLOWLY DRINKING YOUR BLOOD.
SLURP.
SLURP.
SLURP.
JUST STOP. PLEASE. I'LL GO TO THE PARTY! I'LL GO TO THE PARTY!

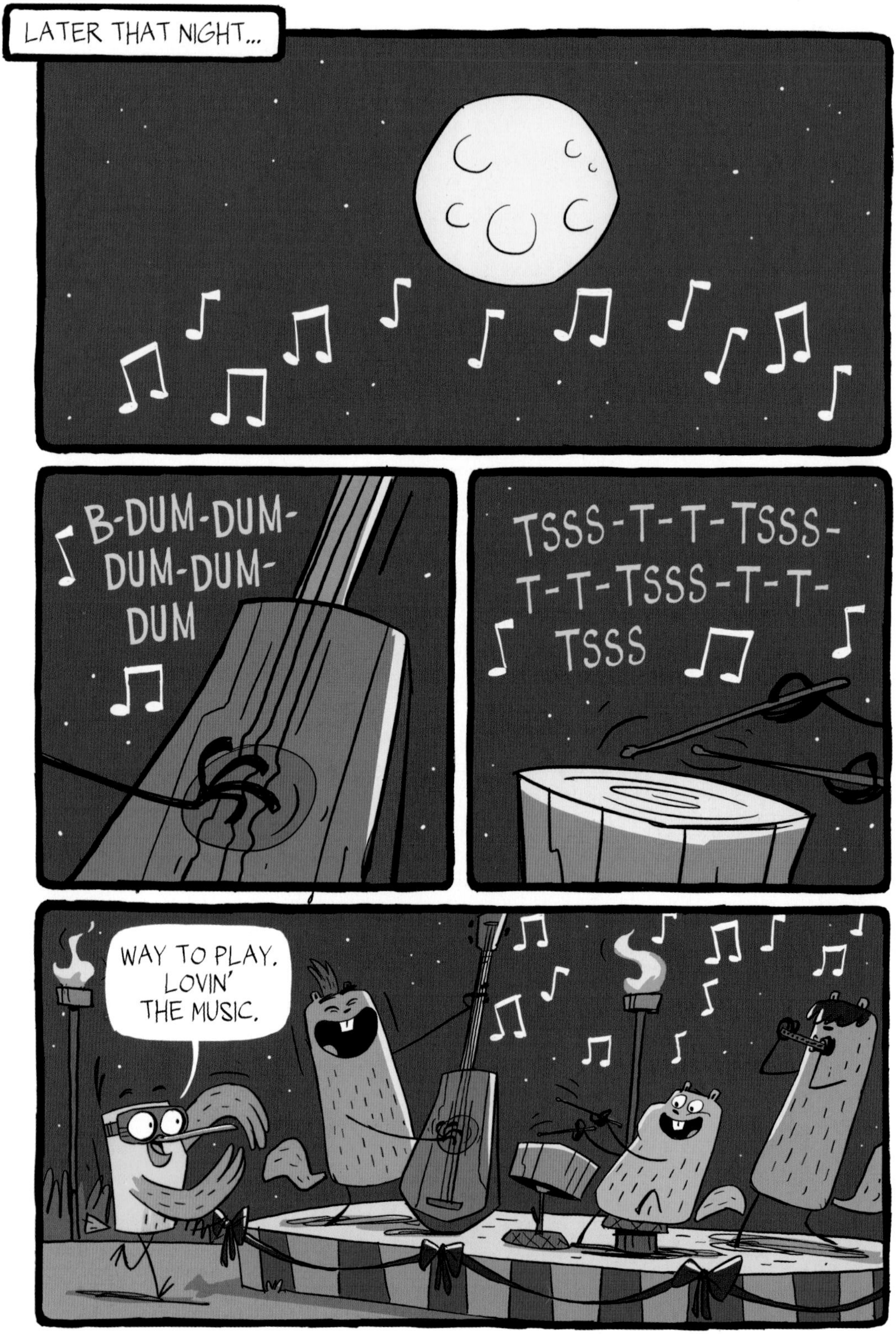
LATER THAT NIGHT...
B-DUM-DUM-DUM-DUM-DUM
TSSS-T-T-TSSS-T-T-TSSS-T-T-TSSS
WAY TO PLAY. LOVIN' THE MUSIC.

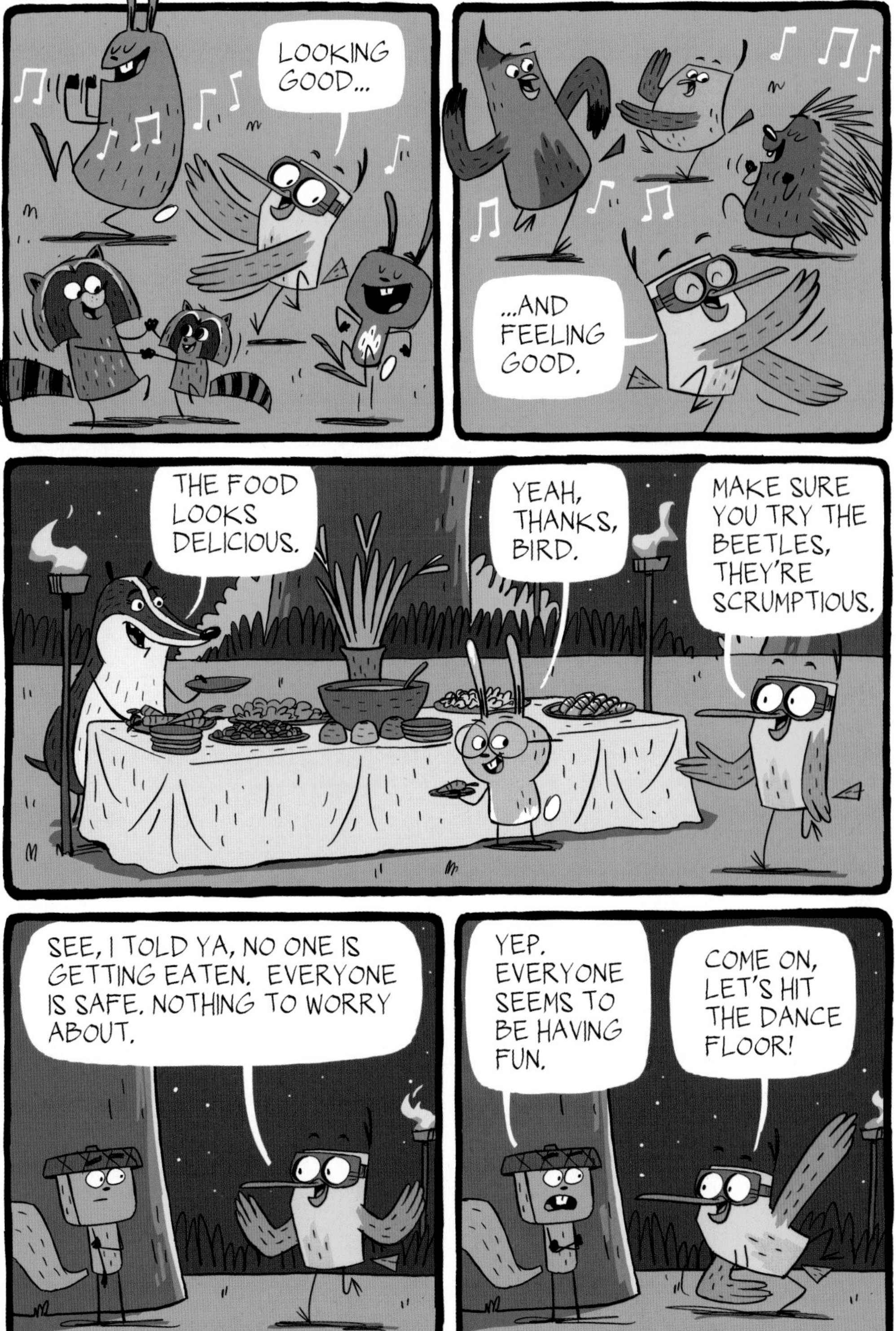

LOOKING GOOD...
...AND FEELING GOOD.
THE FOOD LOOKS DELICIOUS.
YEAH, THANKS, BIRD.
MAKE SURE YOU TRY THE BEETLES, THEY'RE SCRUMPTIOUS.
SEE, I TOLD YA, NO ONE IS GETTING EATEN. EVERYONE IS SAFE. NOTHING TO WORRY ABOUT.
YEP. EVERYONE SEEMS TO BE HAVING FUN.
COME ON, LET'S HIT THE DANCE FLOOR!

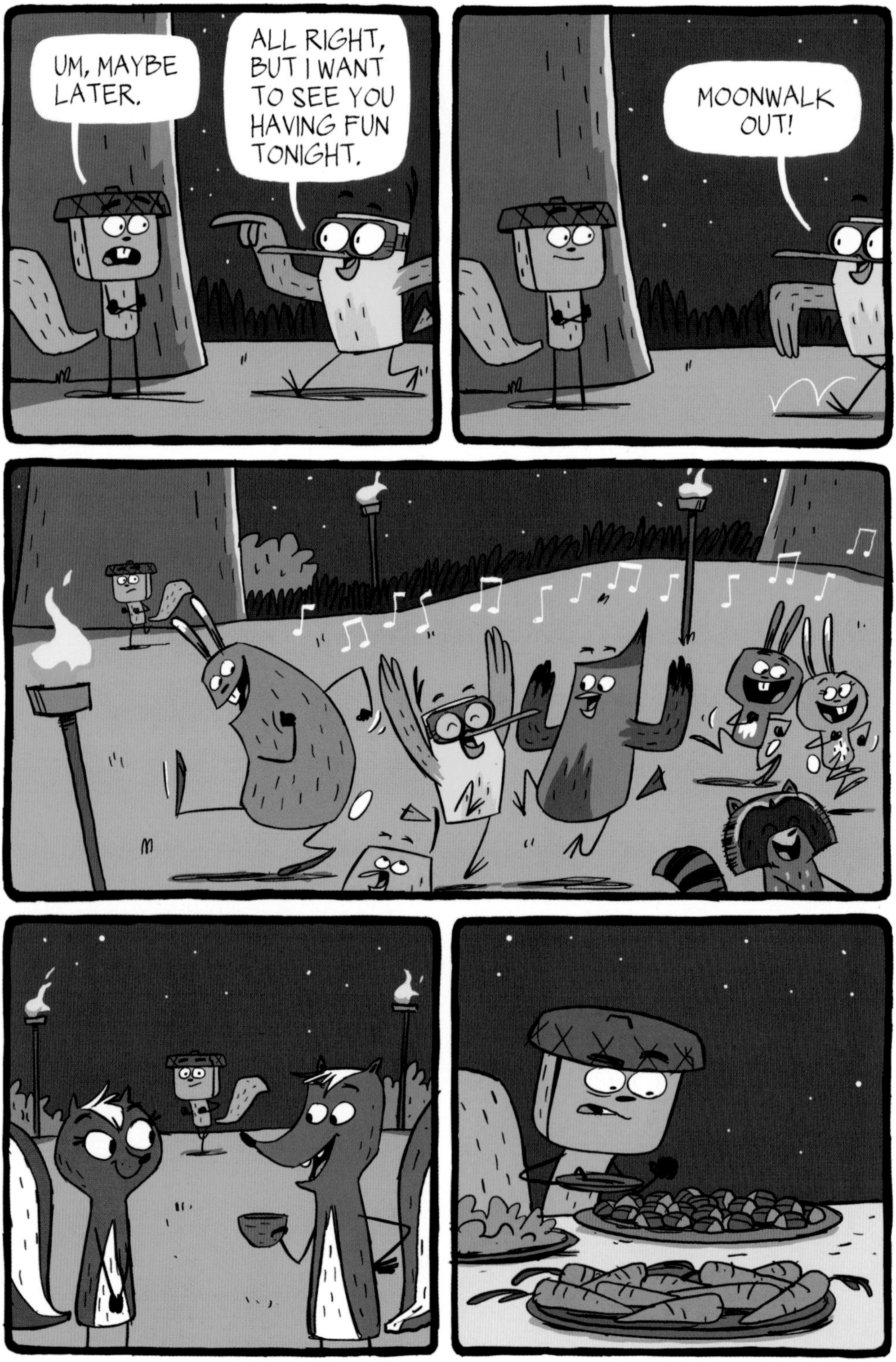
UM, MAYBE LATER.
ALL RIGHT, BUT I WANT TO SEE YOU HAVING FUN TONIGHT.
MOONWALK OUT!

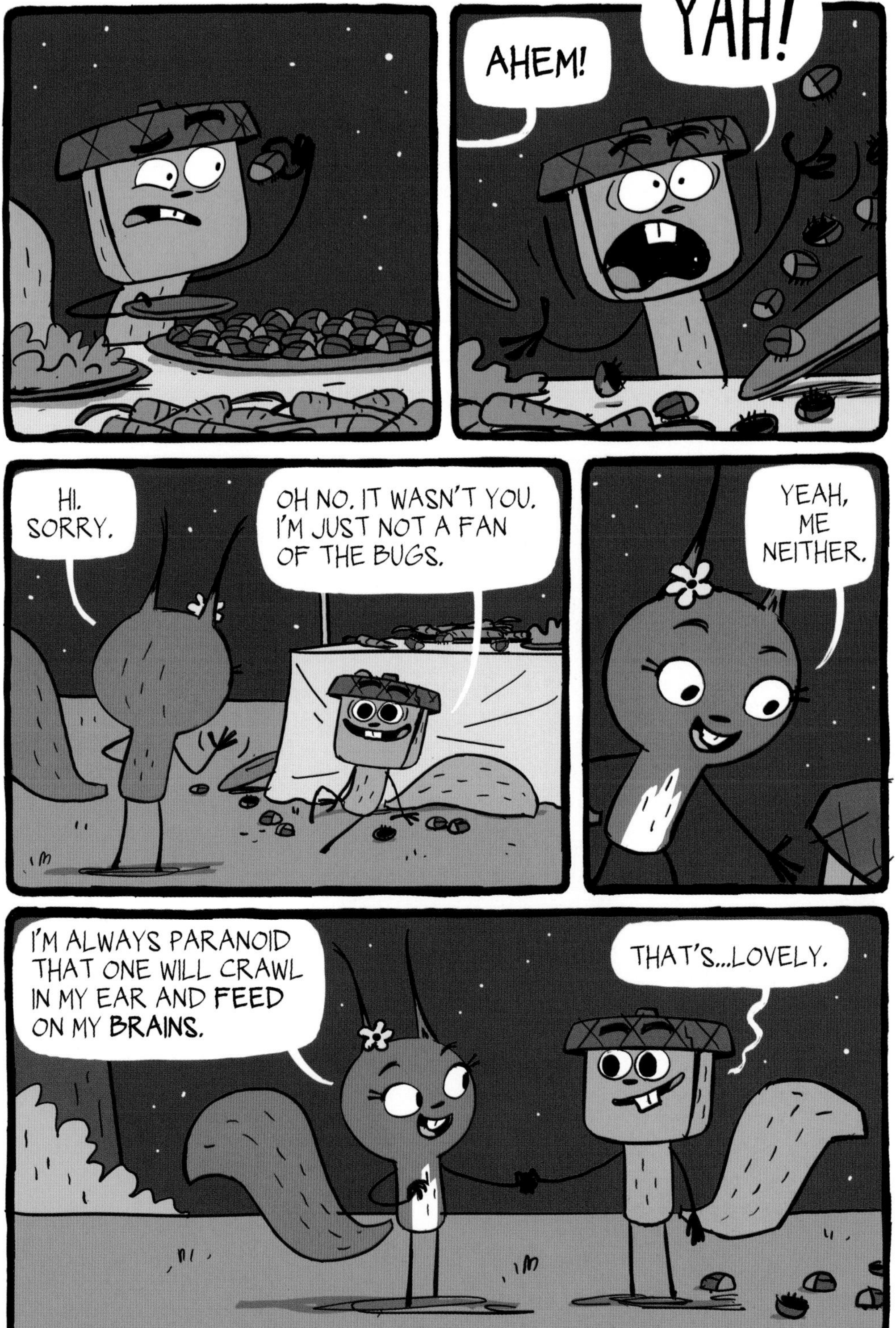
AHEM!
YAH!
HI. SORRY.
OH NO. IT WASN'T YOU. I'M JUST NOT A FAN OF THE BUGS.
YEAH, ME NEITHER.
I'M ALWAYS PARANOID THAT ONE WILL CRAWL IN MY EAR AND **FEED** ON MY **BRAINS**.
THAT'S...LOVELY.

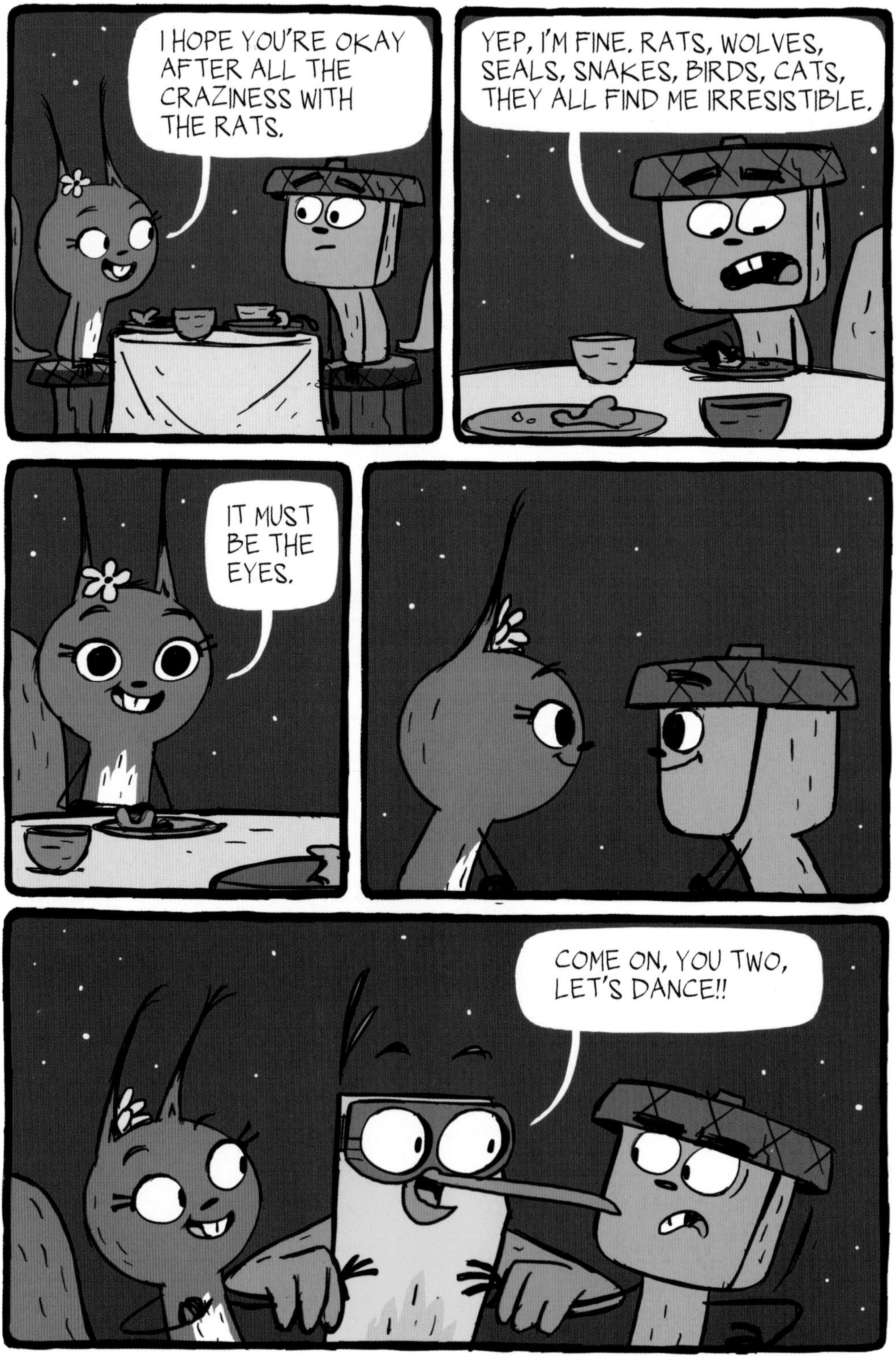
I HOPE YOU'RE OKAY AFTER ALL THE CRAZINESS WITH THE RATS.
YEP, I'M FINE. RATS, WOLVES, SEALS, SNAKES, BIRDS, CATS, THEY ALL FIND ME IRRESISTIBLE.
IT MUST BE THE EYES.
COME ON, YOU TWO, LET'S DANCE!!

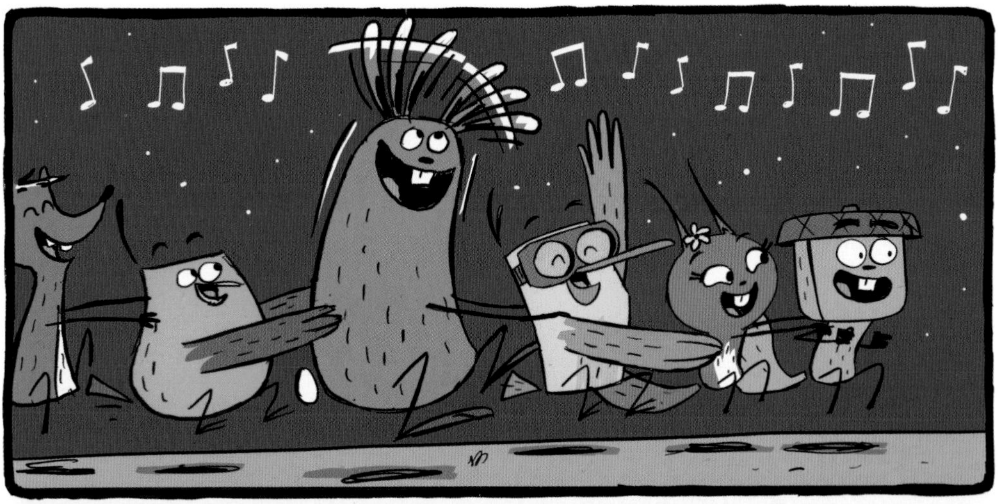

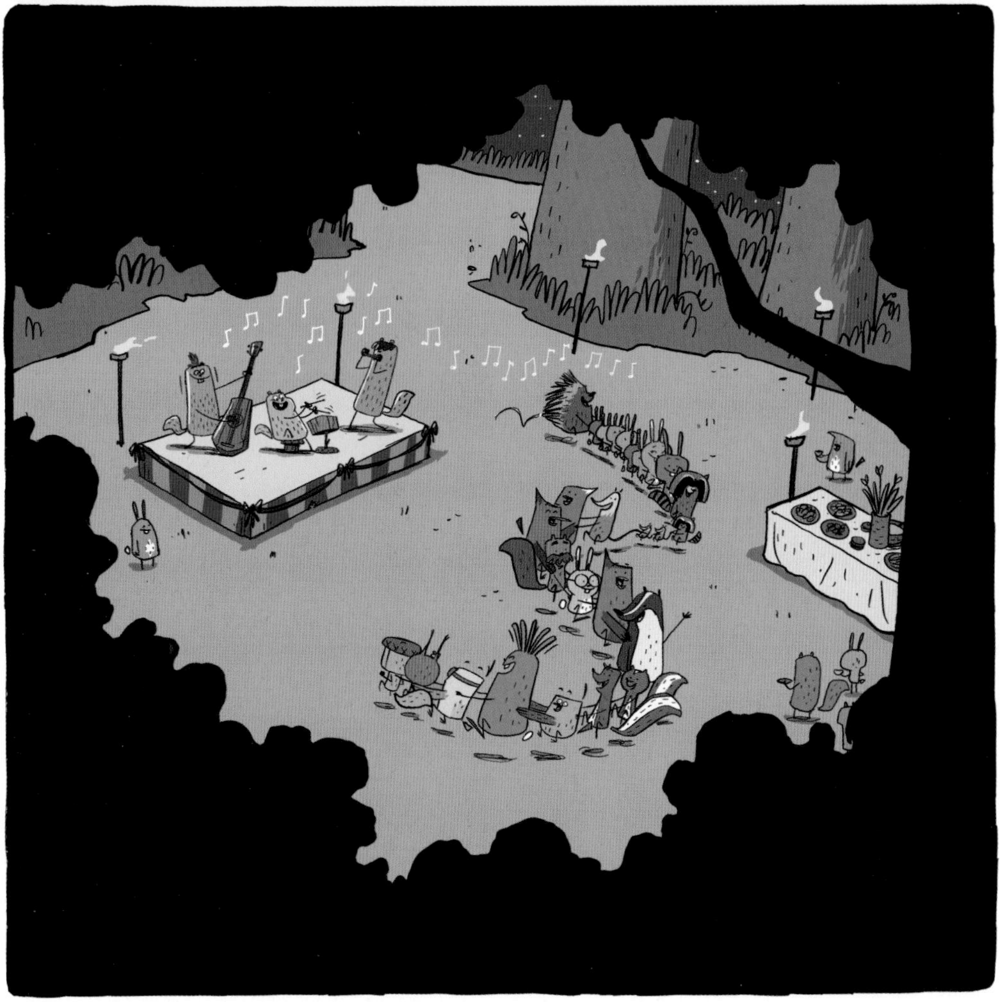

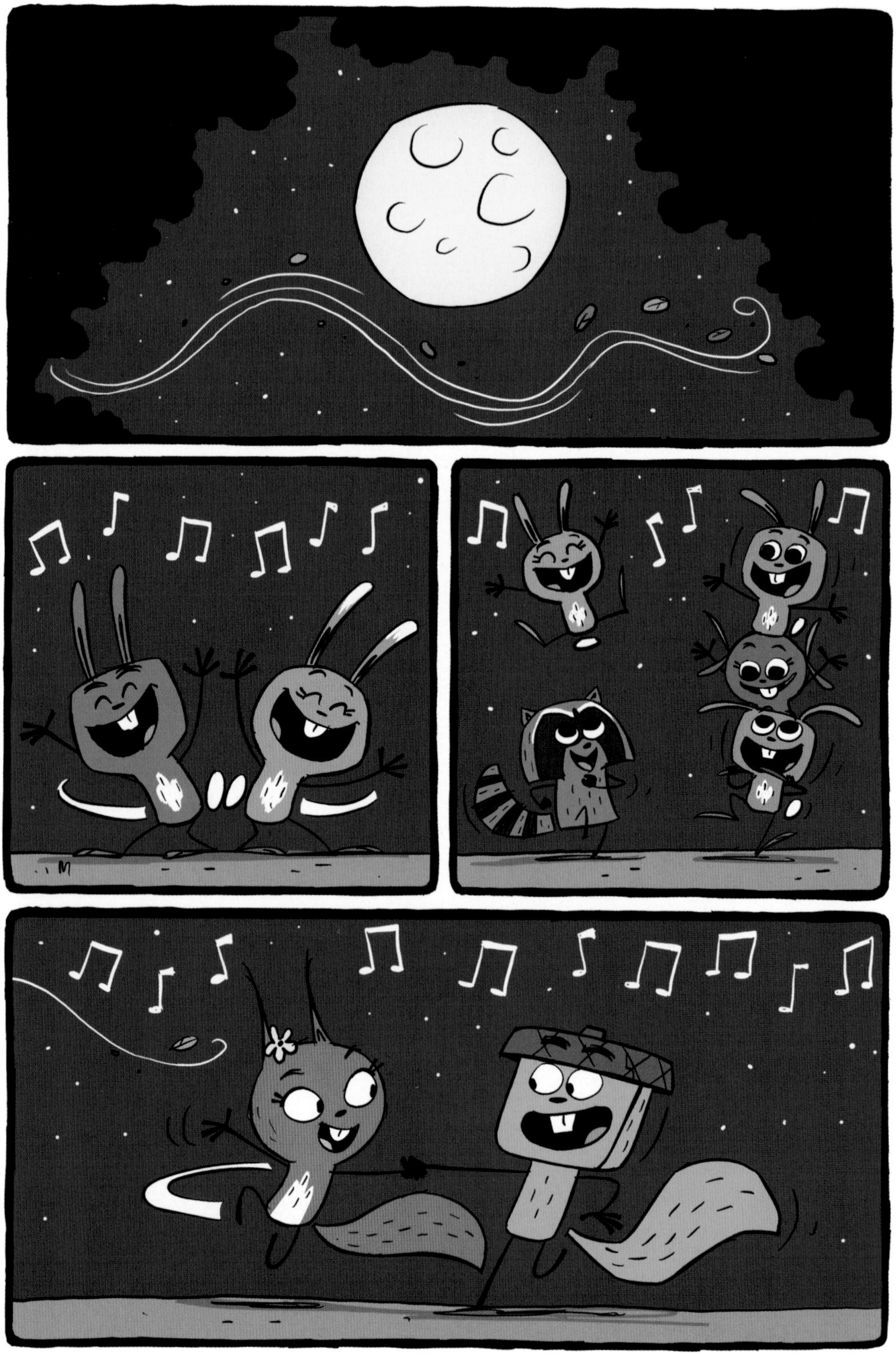

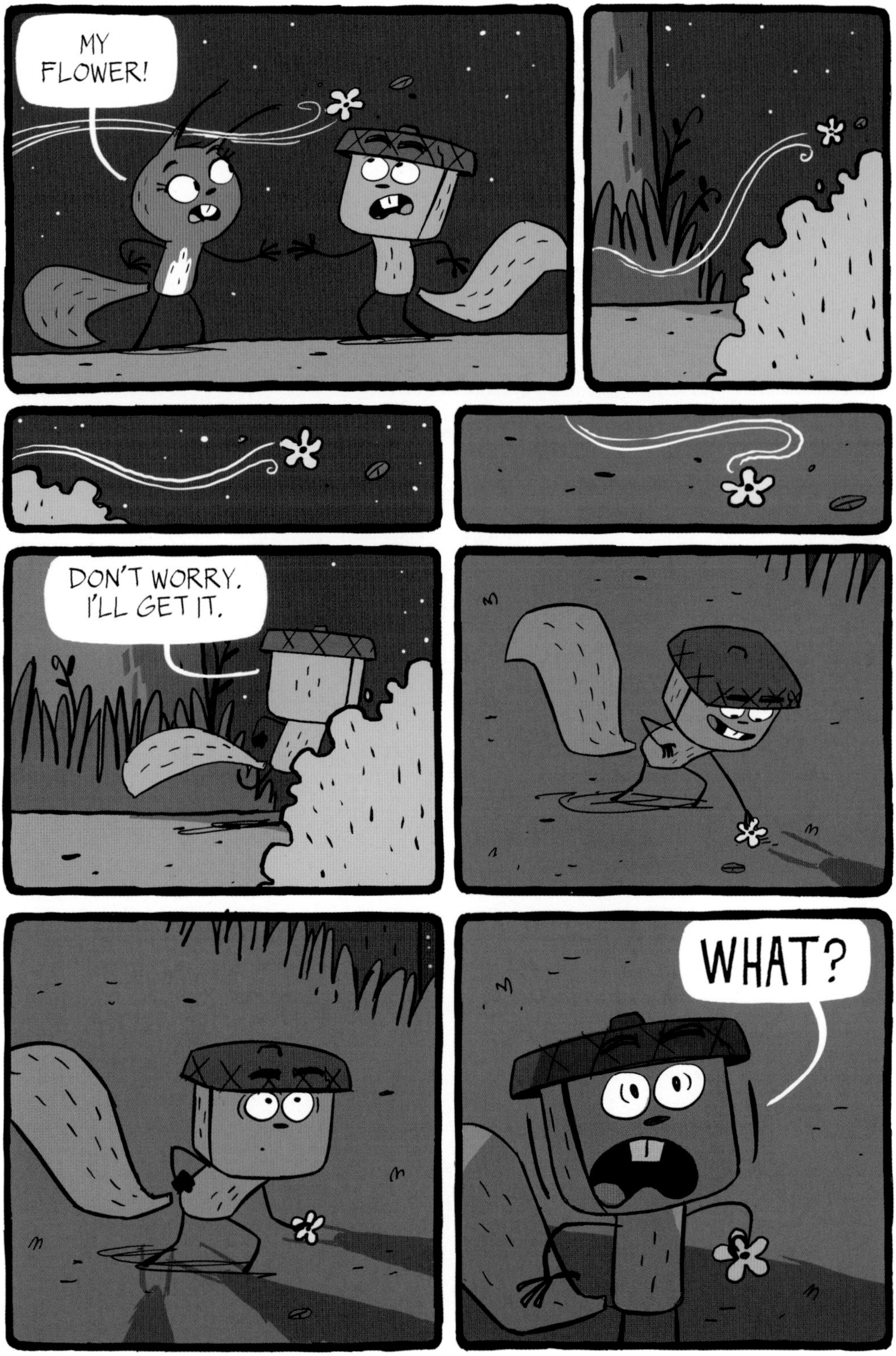
MY FLOWER!
DON'T WORRY. I'LL GET IT.
WHAT?

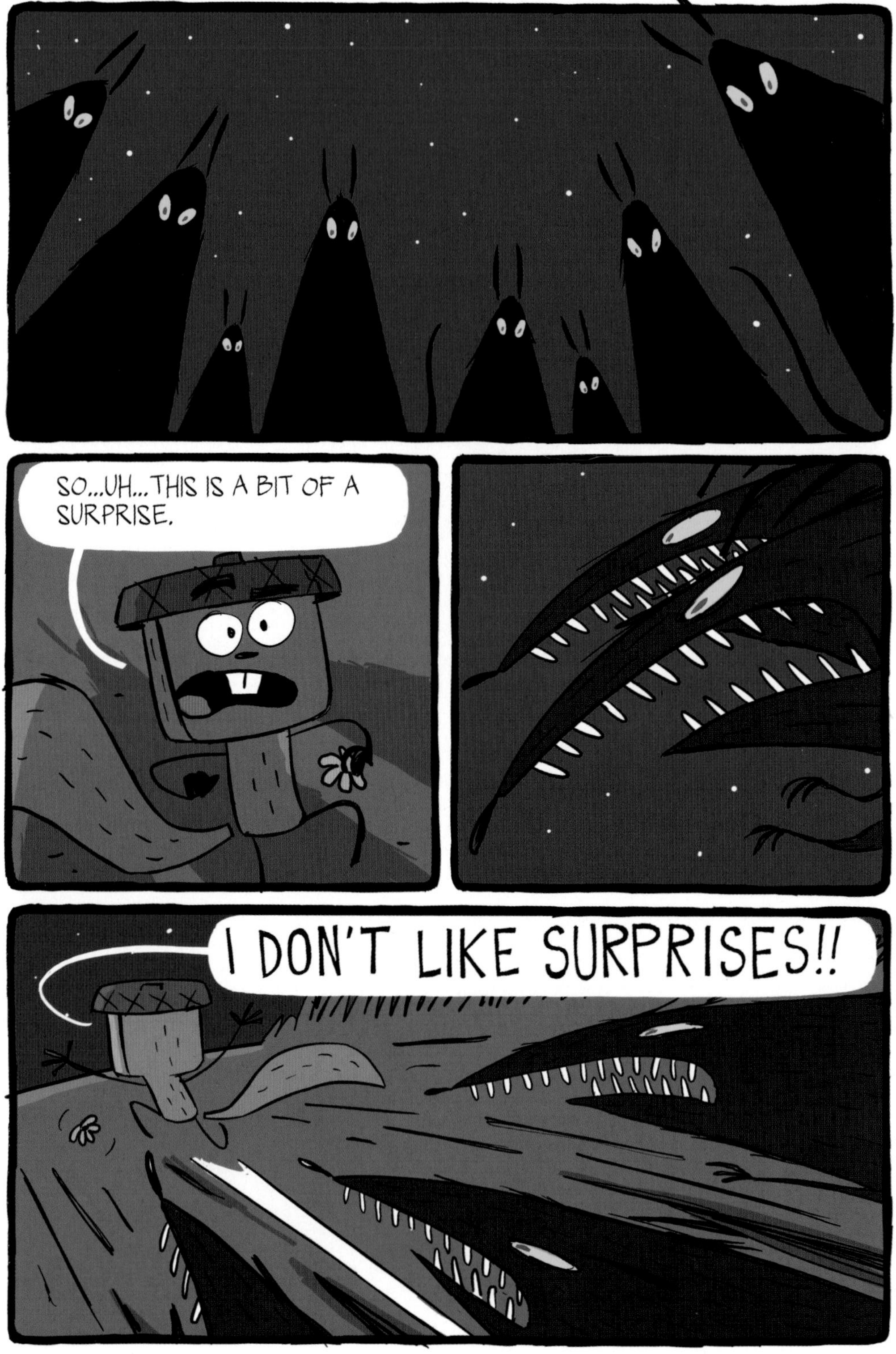
SO...UH...THIS IS A BIT OF A SURPRISE.
I DON'T LIKE SURPRISES!!

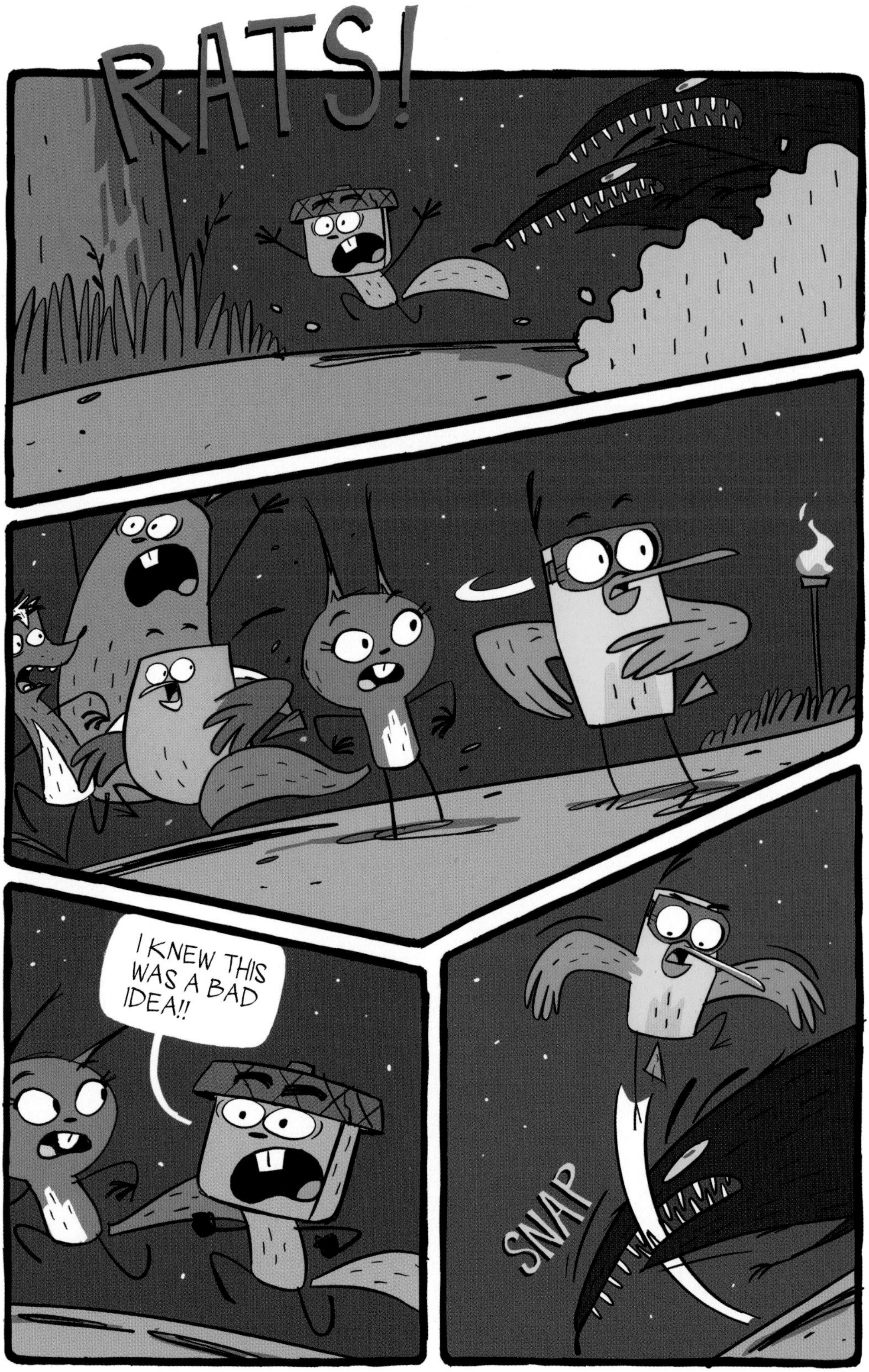
RATS!
I KNEW THIS WAS A BAD IDEA!!
SNAP

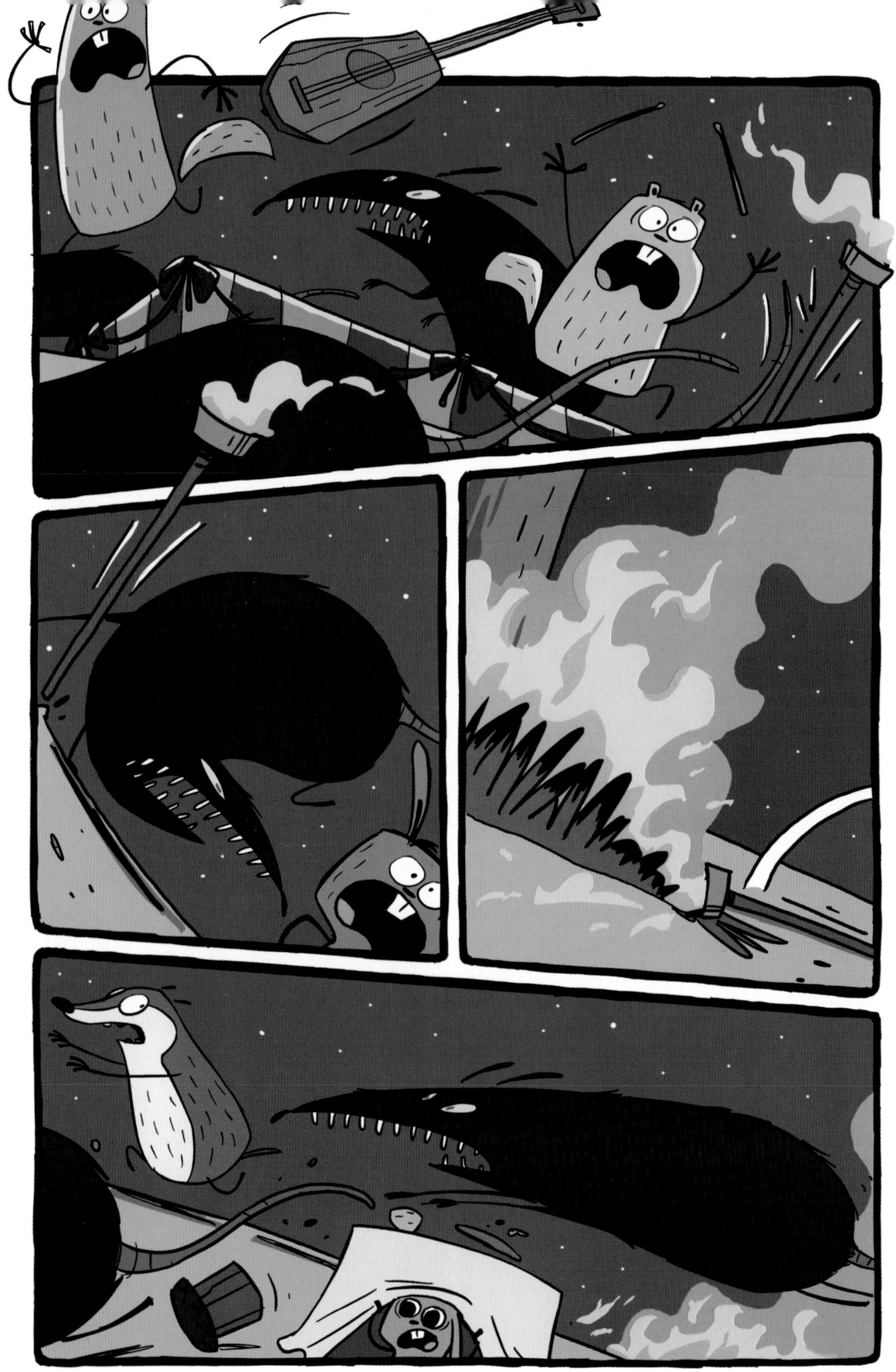

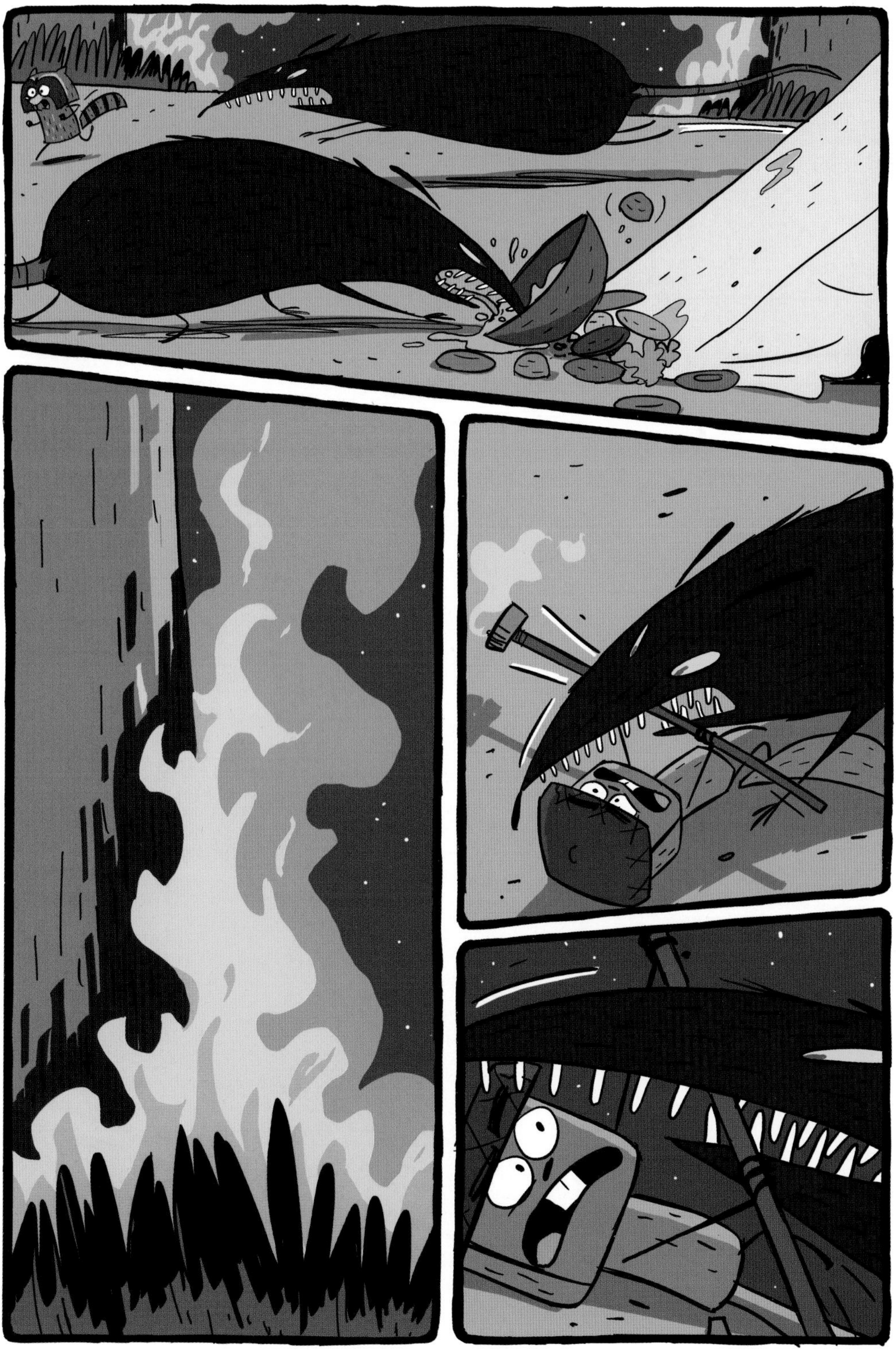

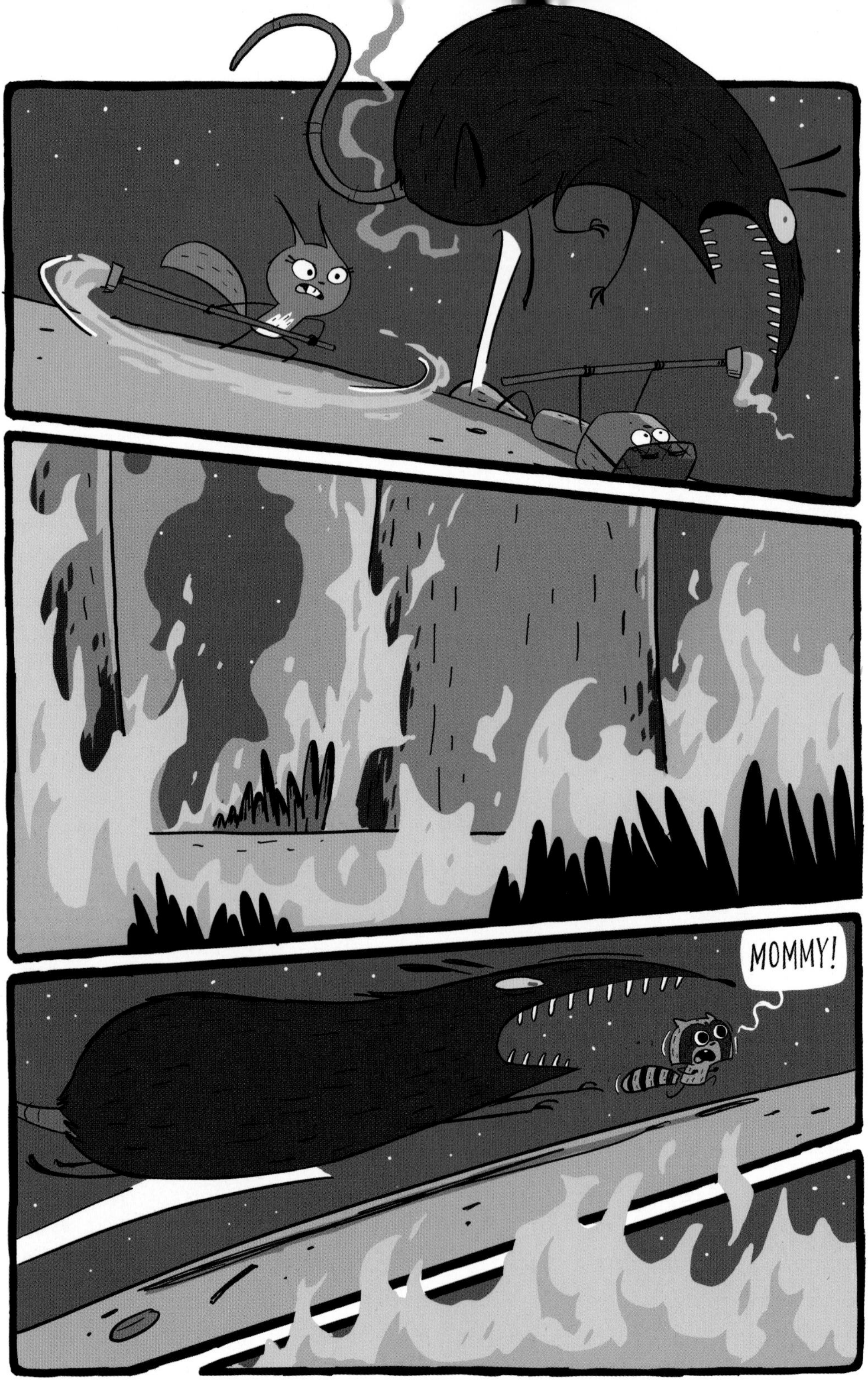
MOMMY!

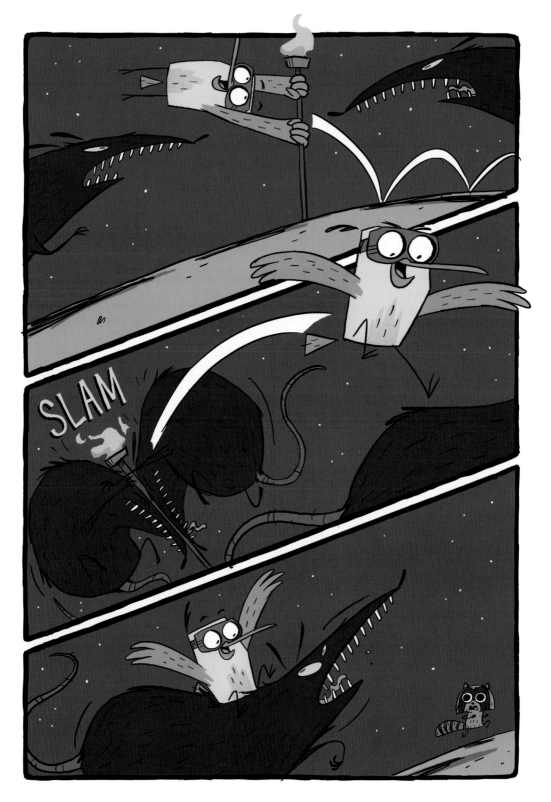

SLAM

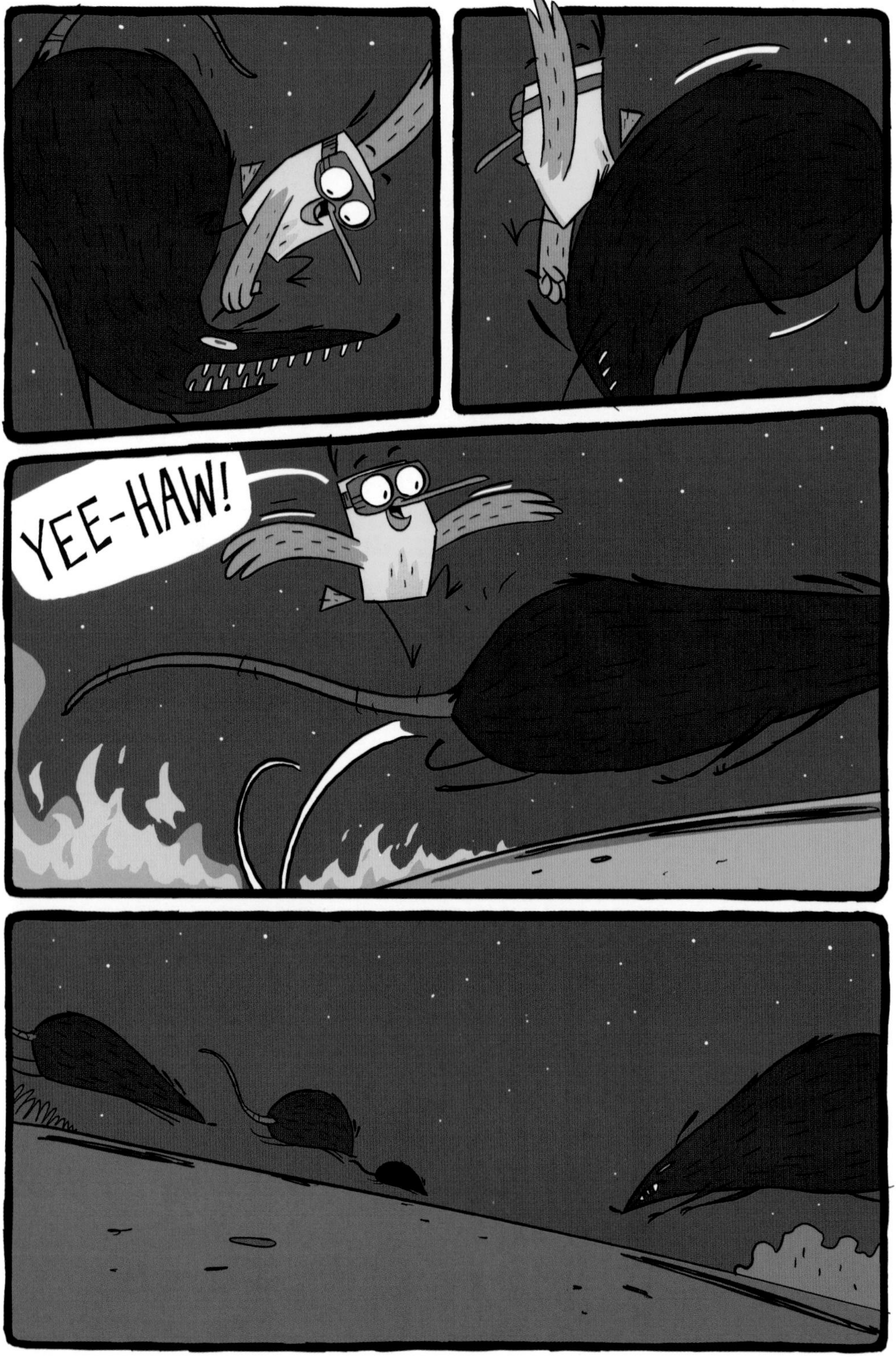
YEE-HAW!

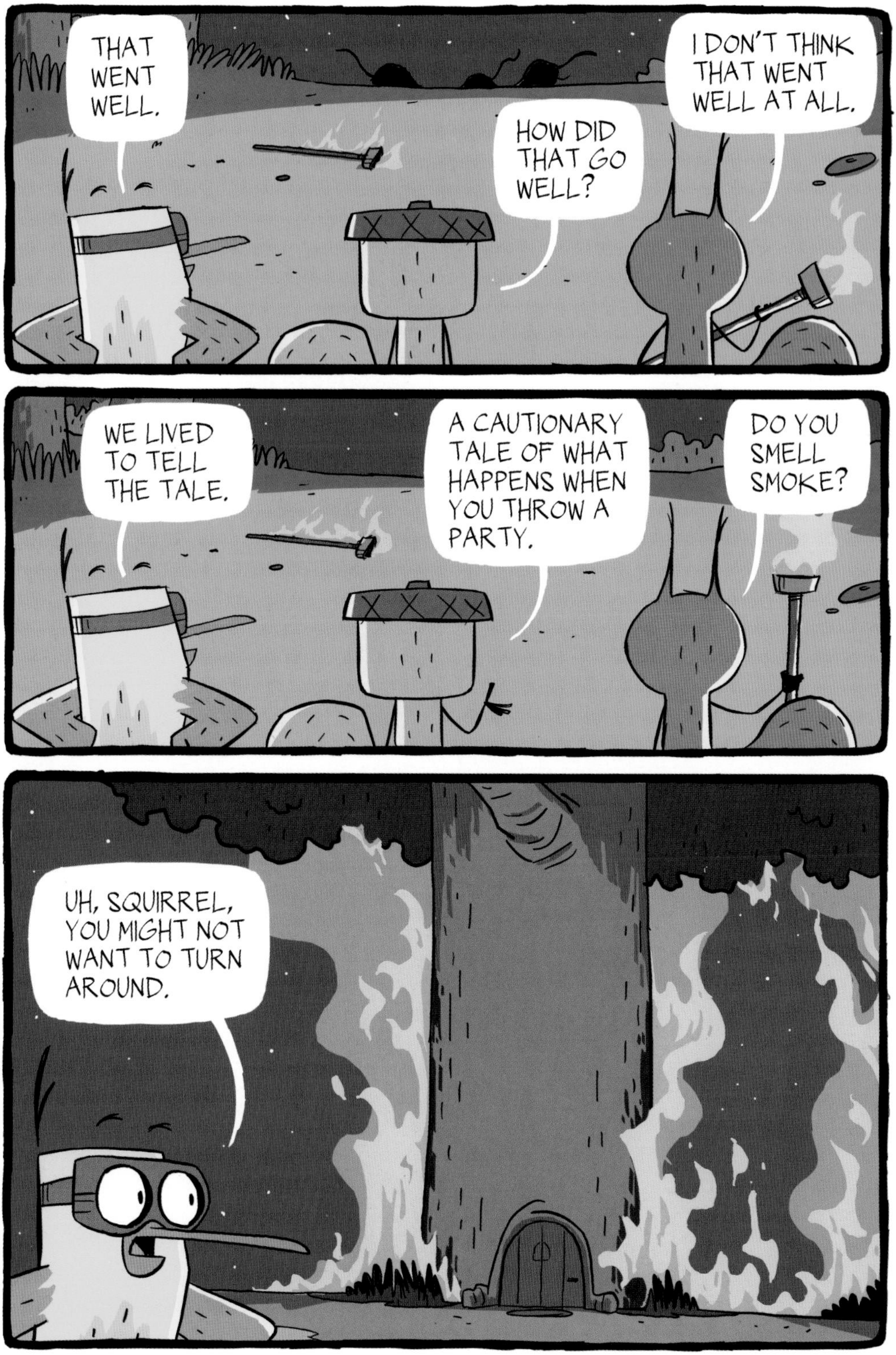
THAT WENT WELL.
HOW DID THAT GO WELL?
I DON'T THINK THAT WENT WELL AT ALL.
WE LIVED TO TELL THE TALE.
A CAUTIONARY TALE OF WHAT HAPPENS WHEN YOU THROW A PARTY.
DO YOU SMELL SMOKE?
UH, SQUIRREL, YOU MIGHT NOT WANT TO TURN AROUND.

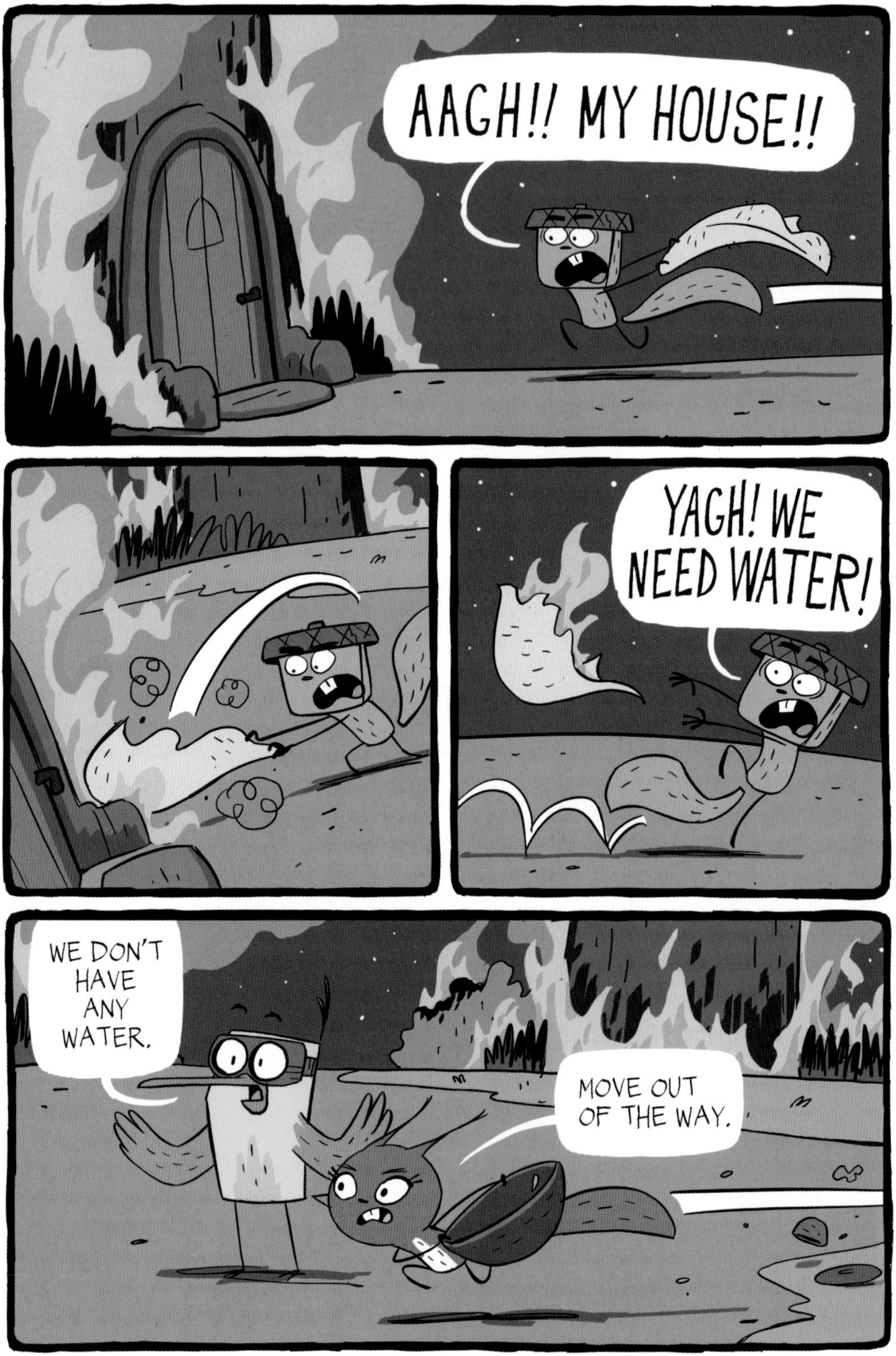
AAGH!! MY HOUSE!!
YAGH! WE NEED WATER!
WE DON'T HAVE ANY WATER.
MOVE OUT OF THE WAY.

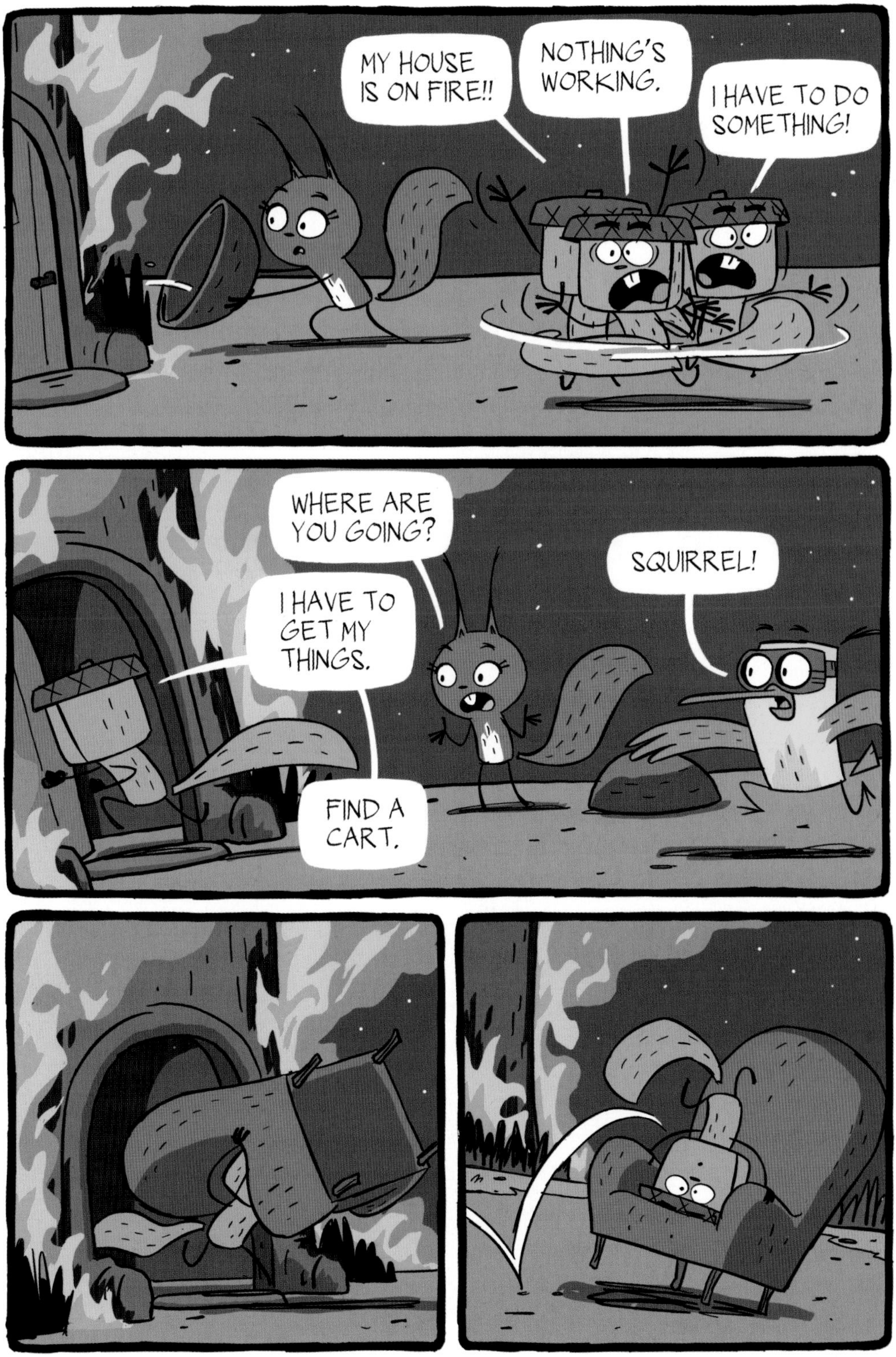
MY HOUSE IS ON FIRE!!
NOTHING'S WORKING.
I HAVE TO DO SOMETHING!
WHERE ARE YOU GOING?
I HAVE TO GET MY THINGS.
FIND A CART.
SQUIRREL!

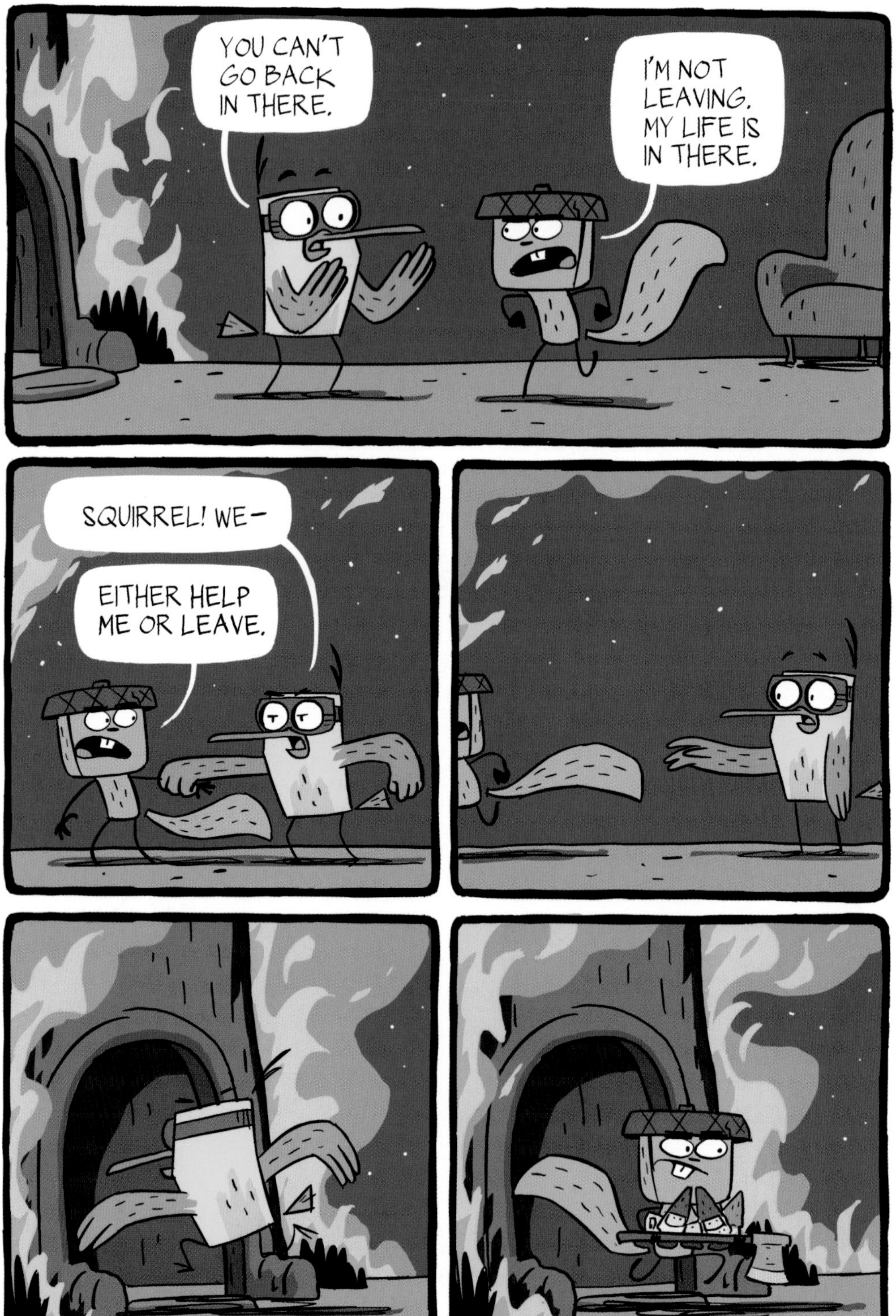
YOU CAN'T GO BACK IN THERE.
I'M NOT LEAVING. MY LIFE IS IN THERE.
SQUIRREL! WE–
EITHER HELP ME OR LEAVE.

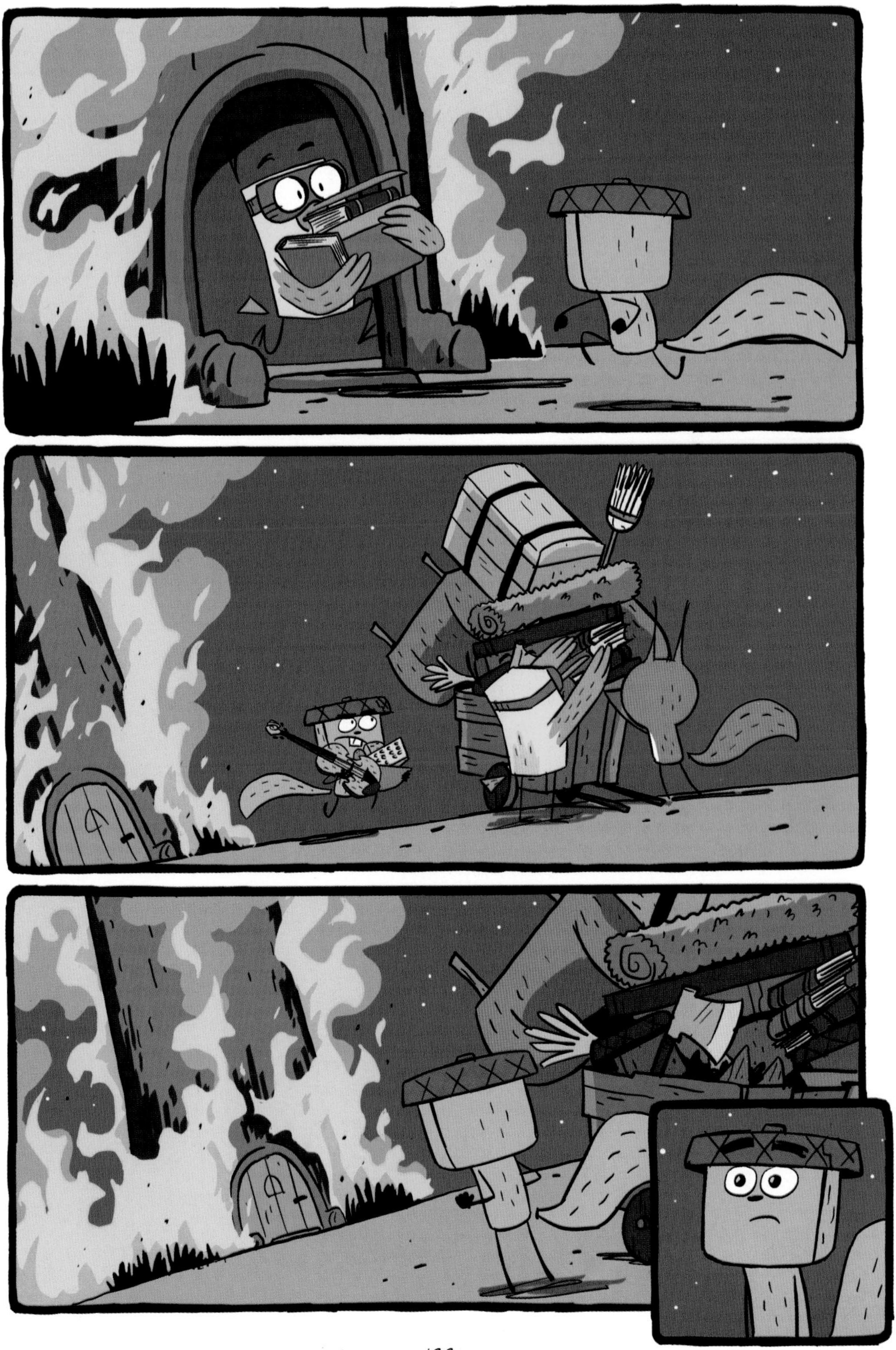

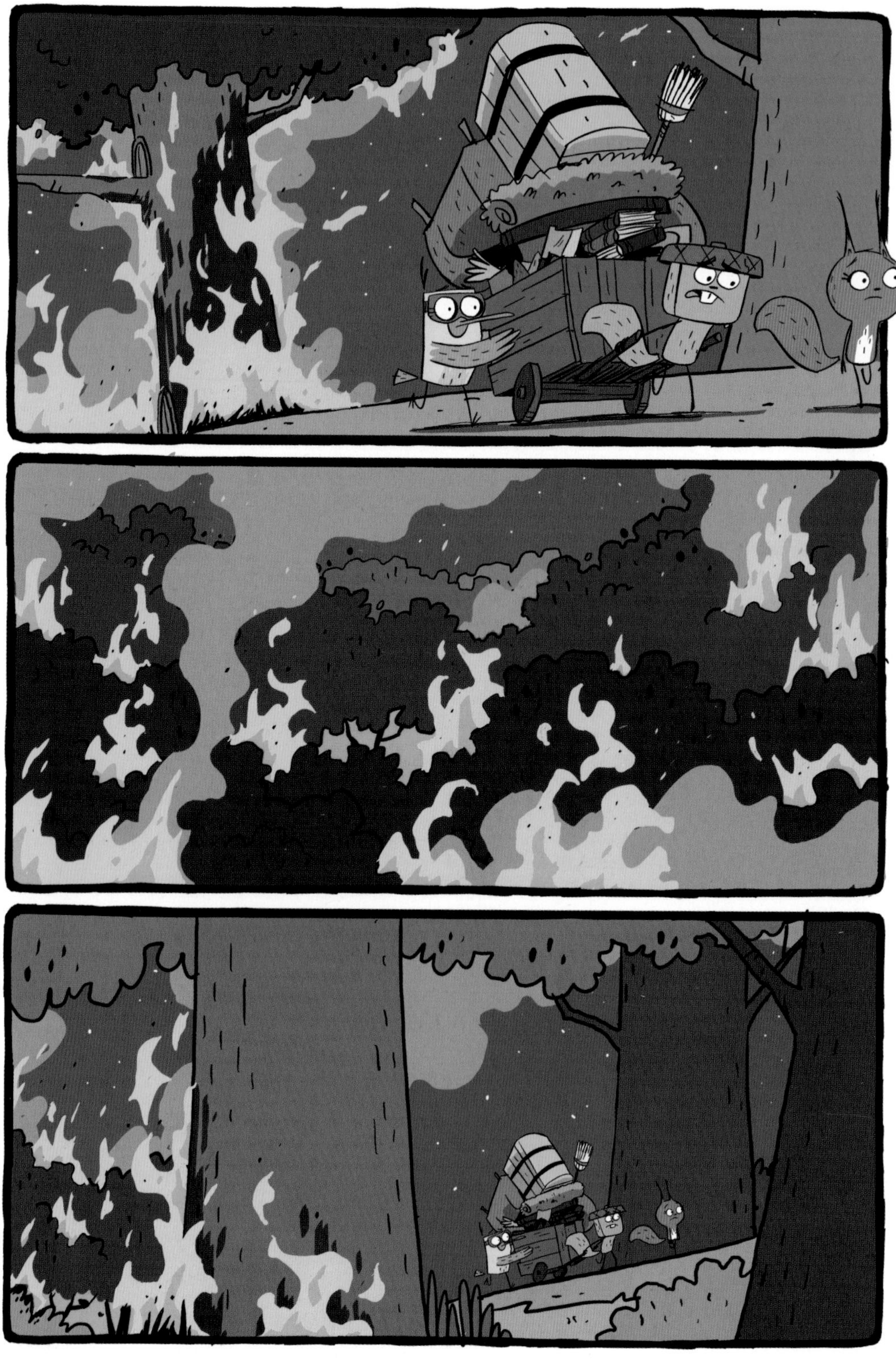

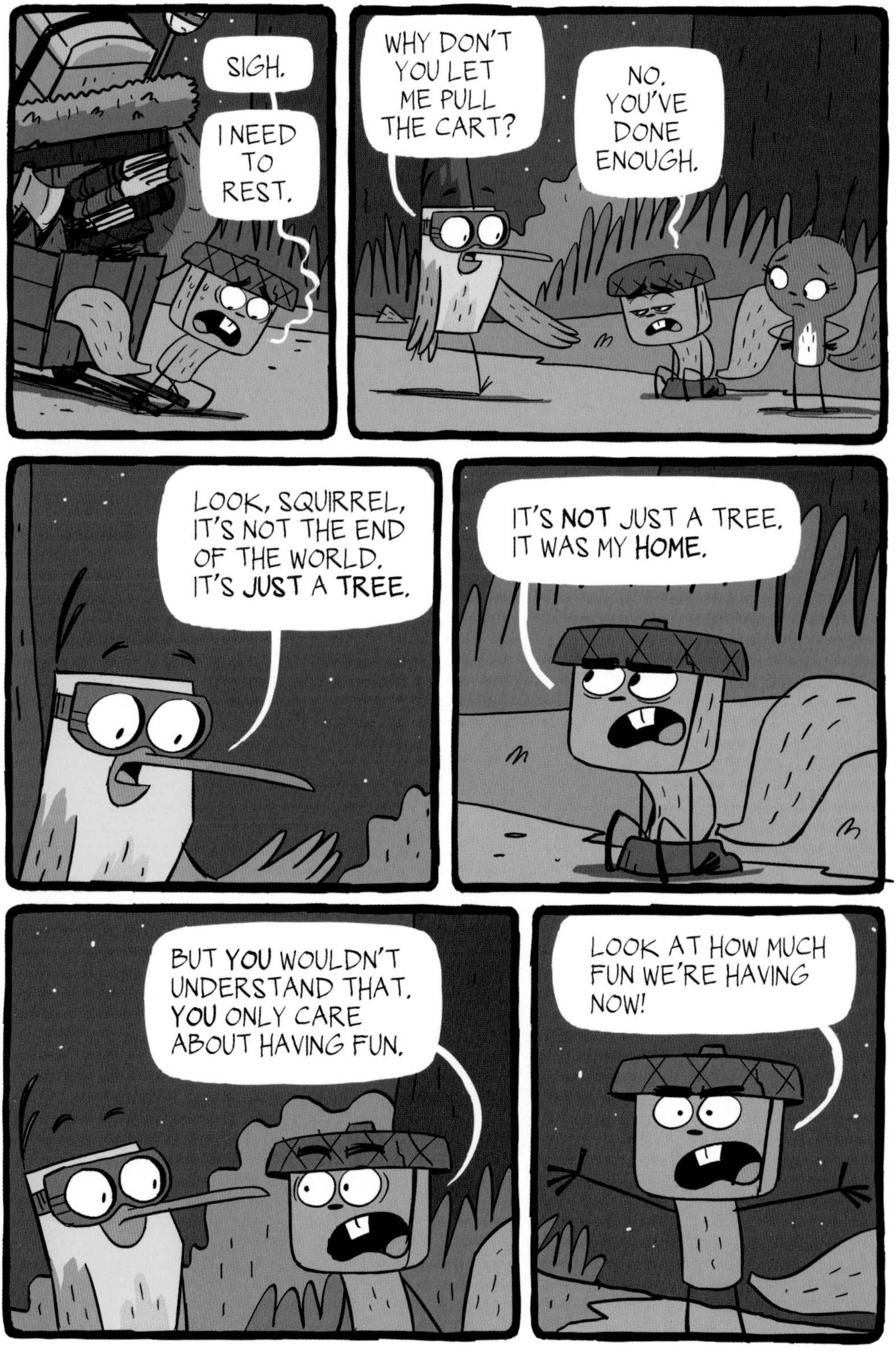
SIGH.
I NEED TO REST.
WHY DON'T YOU LET ME PULL THE CART?
NO. YOU'VE DONE ENOUGH.
LOOK, SQUIRREL, IT'S NOT THE END OF THE WORLD. IT'S JUST A TREE.
IT'S NOT JUST A TREE. IT WAS MY HOME.
BUT YOU WOULDN'T UNDERSTAND THAT. YOU ONLY CARE ABOUT HAVING FUN.
LOOK AT HOW MUCH FUN WE'RE HAVING NOW!

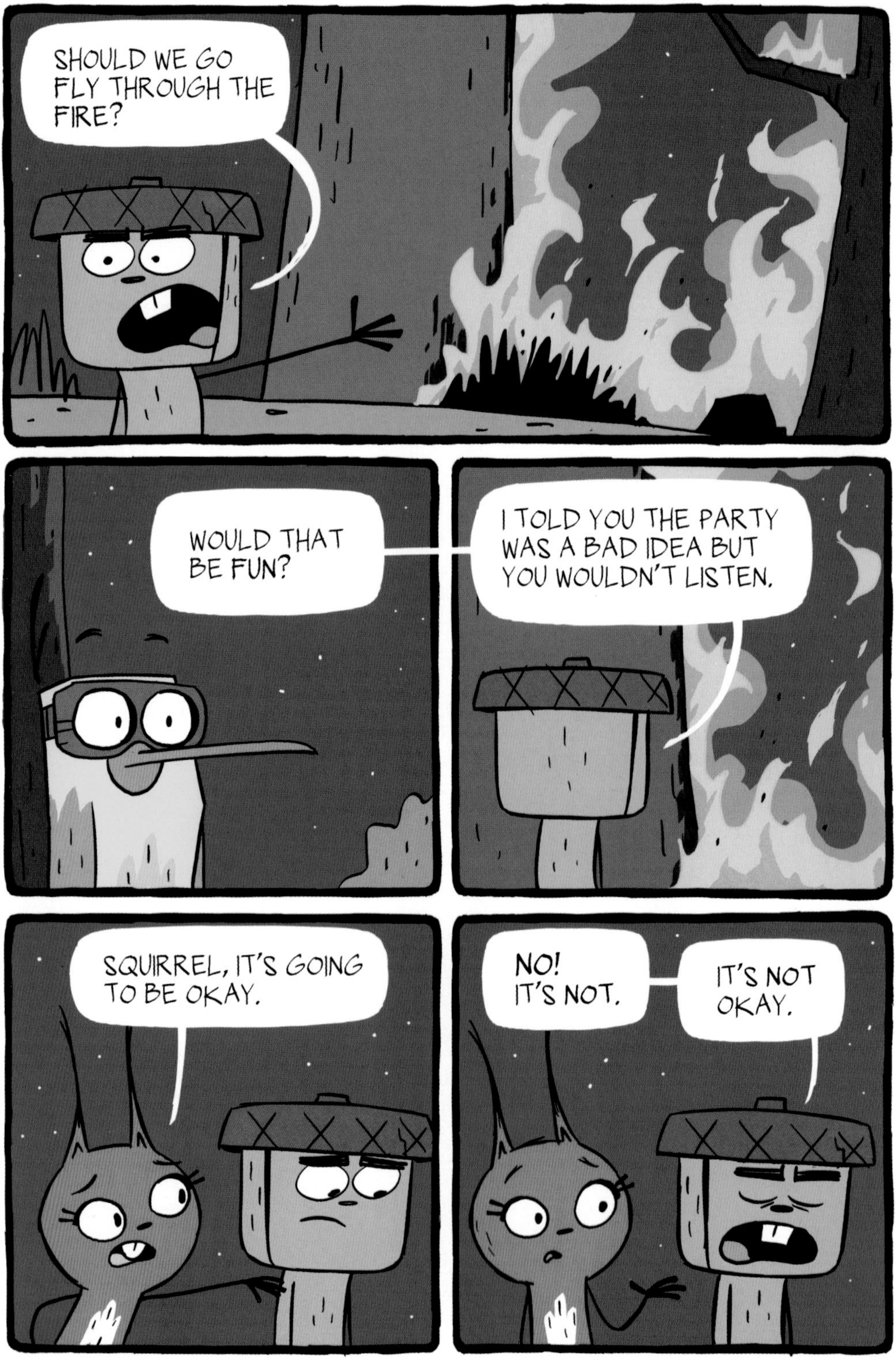
SHOULD WE GO FLY THROUGH THE FIRE?
WOULD THAT BE FUN?
I TOLD YOU THE PARTY WAS A BAD IDEA BUT YOU WOULDN'T LISTEN.
SQUIRREL, IT'S GOING TO BE OKAY.
NO! IT'S NOT.
IT'S NOT OKAY.

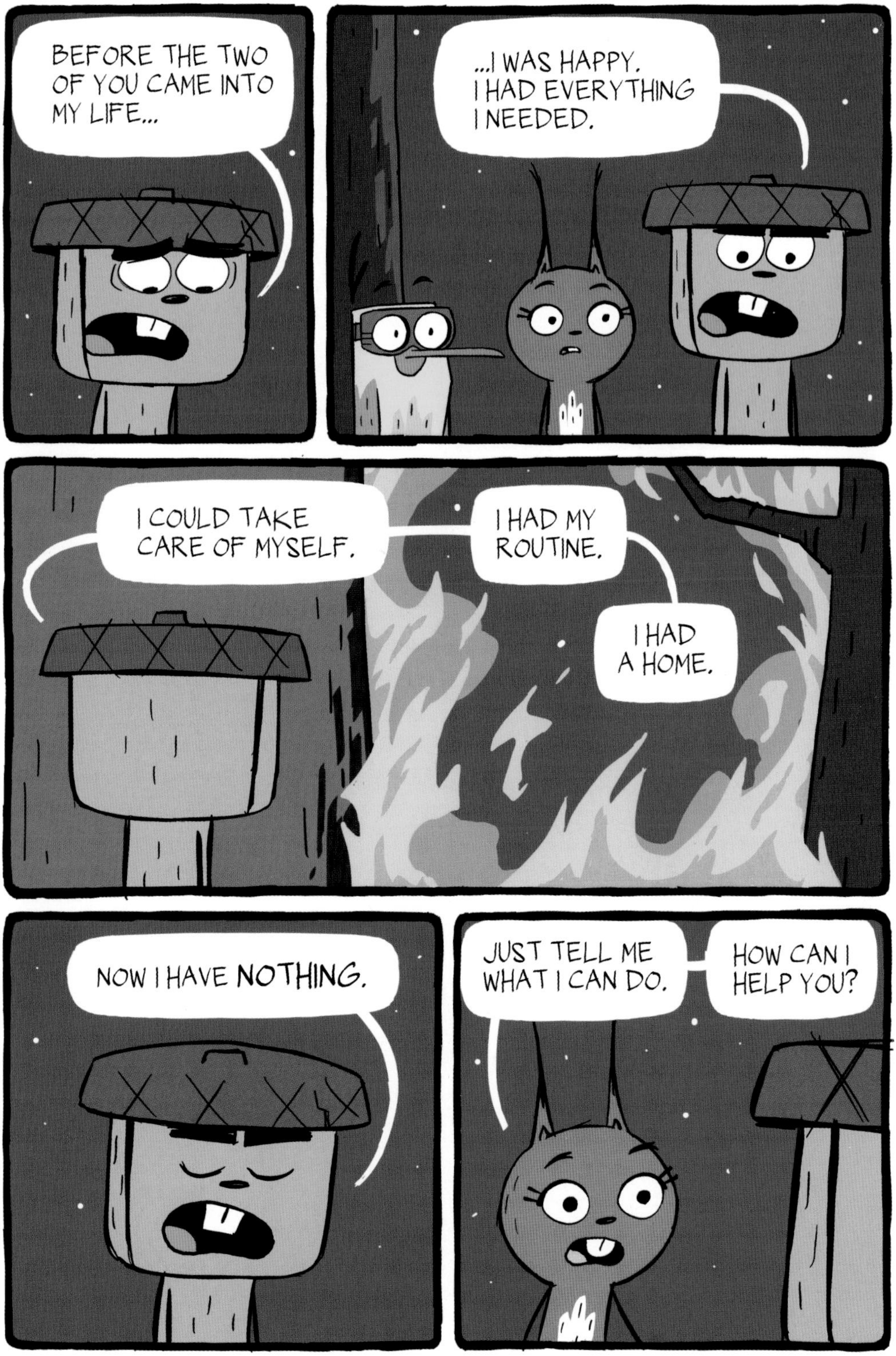
BEFORE THE TWO OF YOU CAME INTO MY LIFE...
...I WAS HAPPY. I HAD EVERYTHING I NEEDED.
I COULD TAKE CARE OF MYSELF.
I HAD MY ROUTINE.
I HAD A HOME.
NOW I HAVE NOTHING.
JUST TELL ME WHAT I CAN DO.
HOW CAN I HELP YOU?

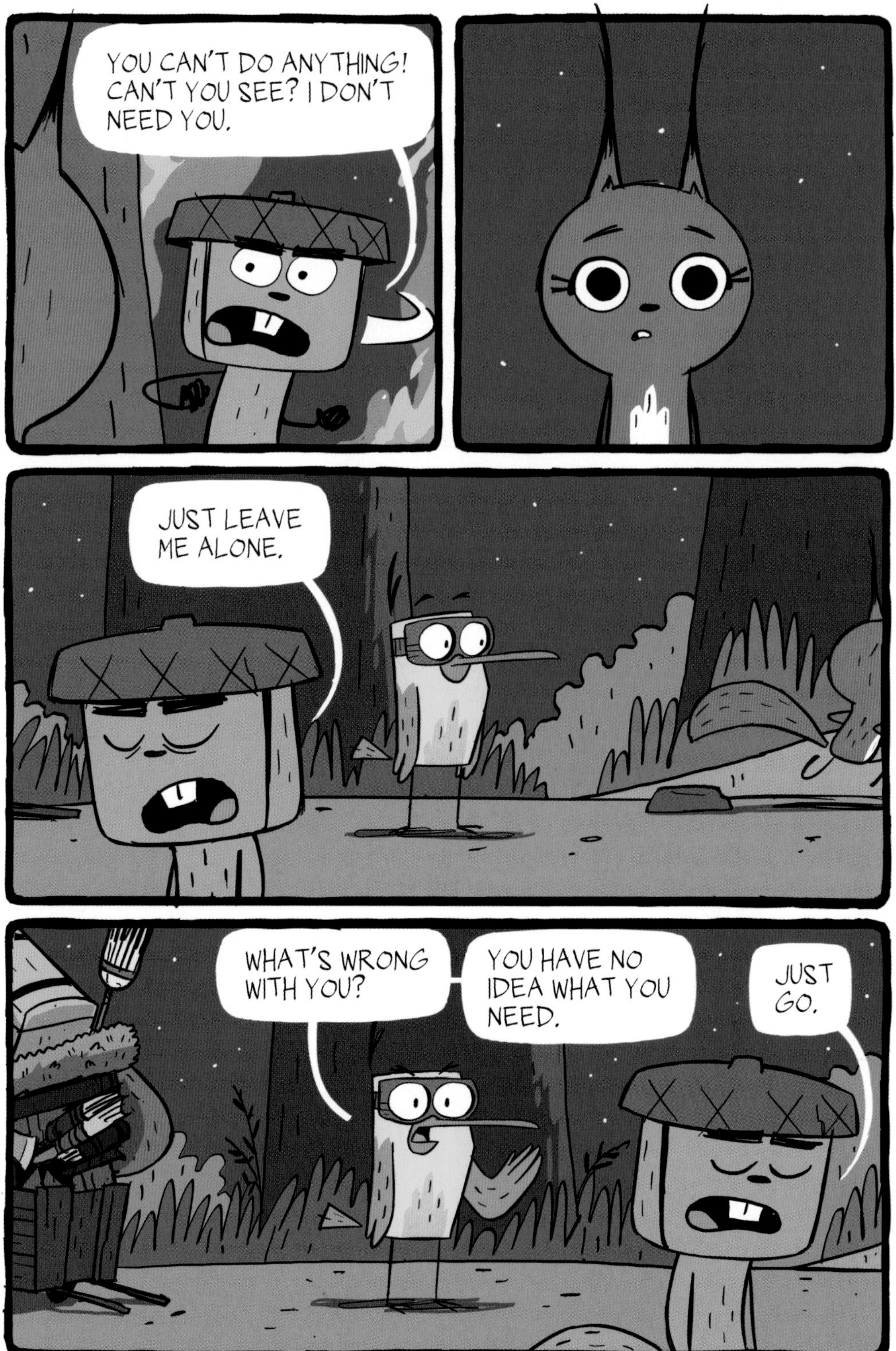
YOU CAN'T DO ANYTHING! CAN'T YOU SEE? I DON'T NEED YOU.
JUST LEAVE ME ALONE.
WHAT'S WRONG WITH YOU?
YOU HAVE NO IDEA WHAT YOU NEED.
JUST GO.

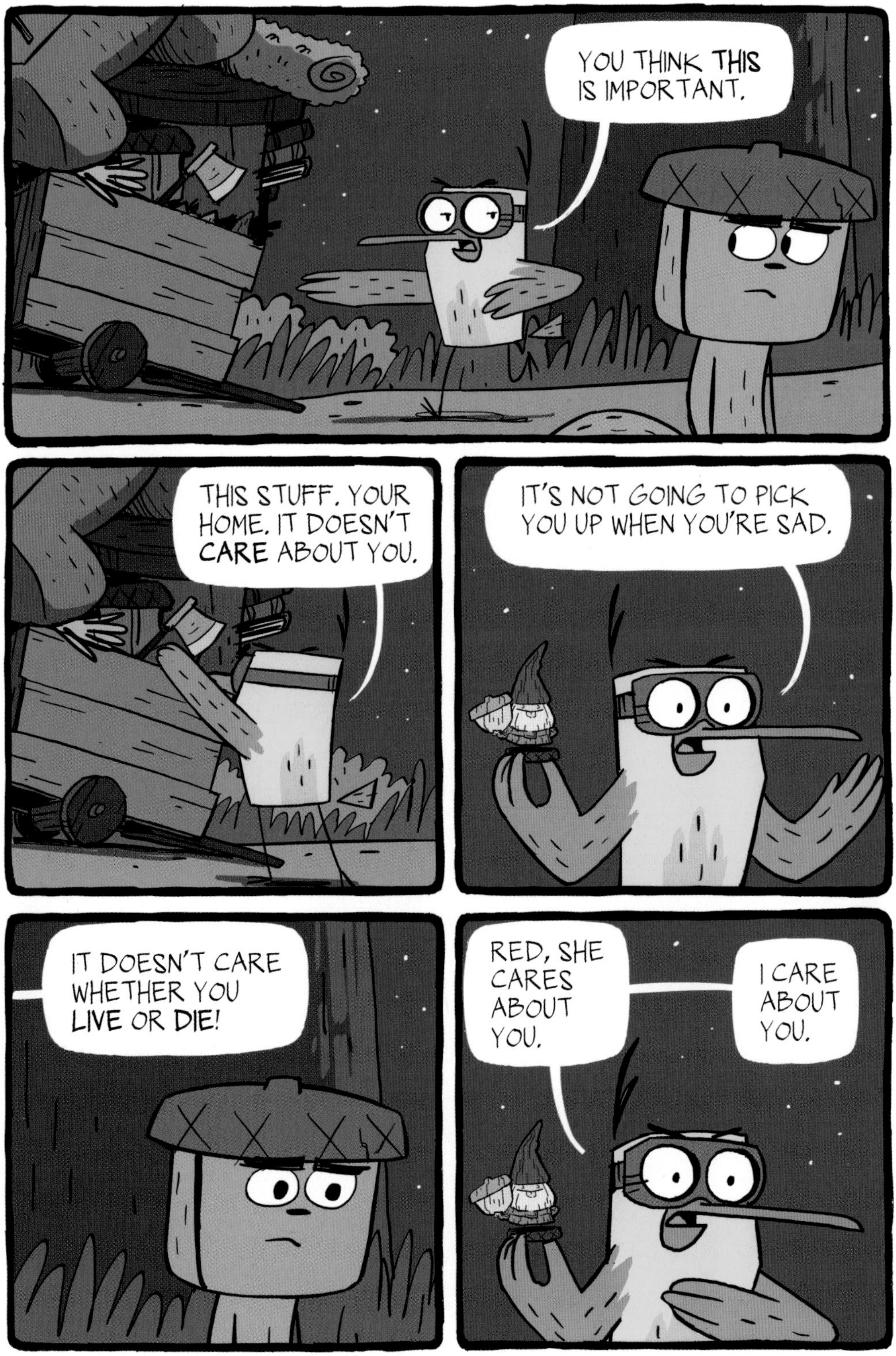
YOU THINK THIS IS IMPORTANT.
THIS STUFF. YOUR HOME. IT DOESN'T CARE ABOUT YOU.
IT'S NOT GOING TO PICK YOU UP WHEN YOU'RE SAD.
IT DOESN'T CARE WHETHER YOU LIVE OR DIE!
RED, SHE CARES ABOUT YOU.
I CARE ABOUT YOU.

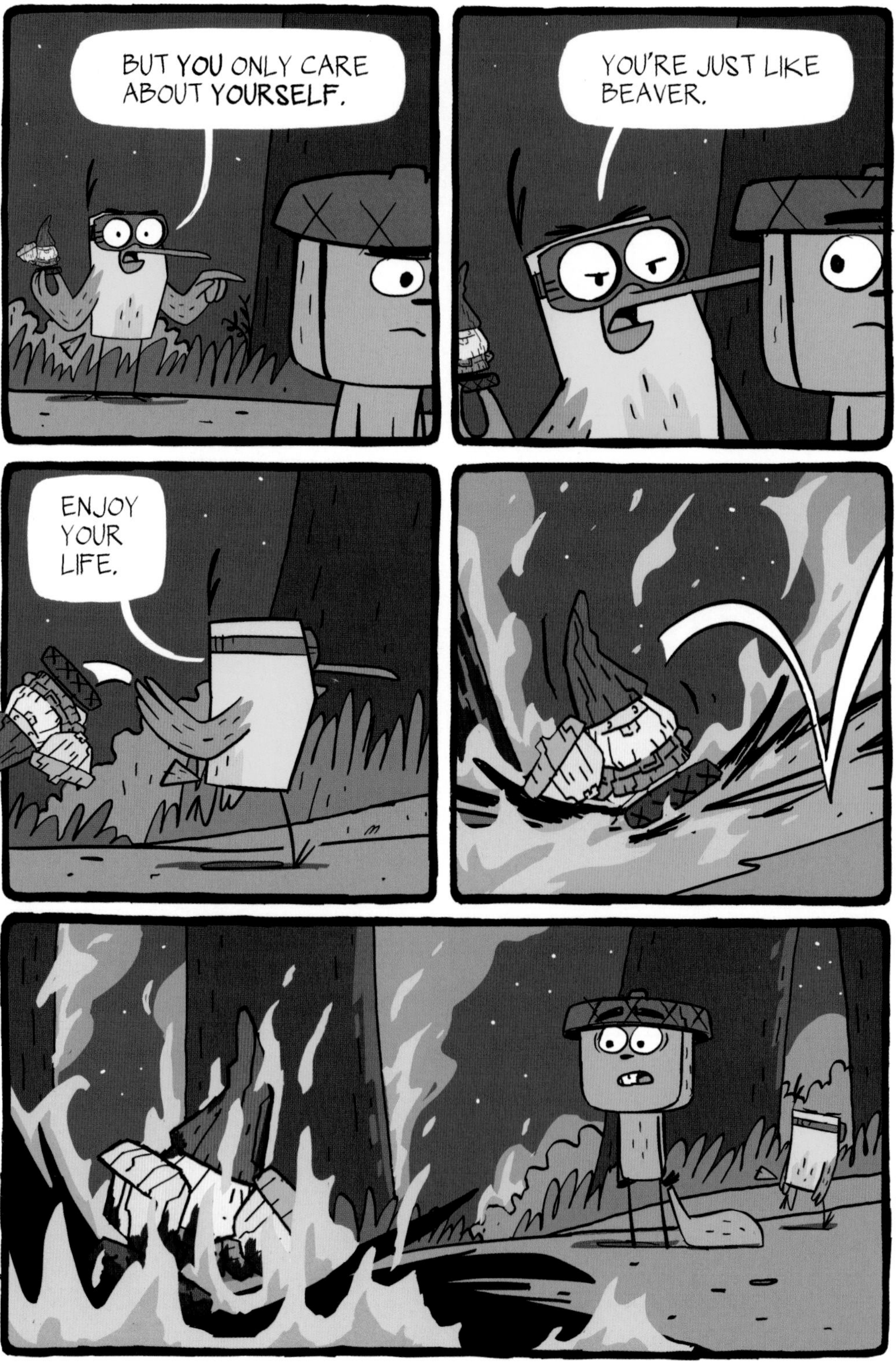
BUT YOU ONLY CARE ABOUT YOURSELF.
YOU'RE JUST LIKE BEAVER.
ENJOY YOUR LIFE.

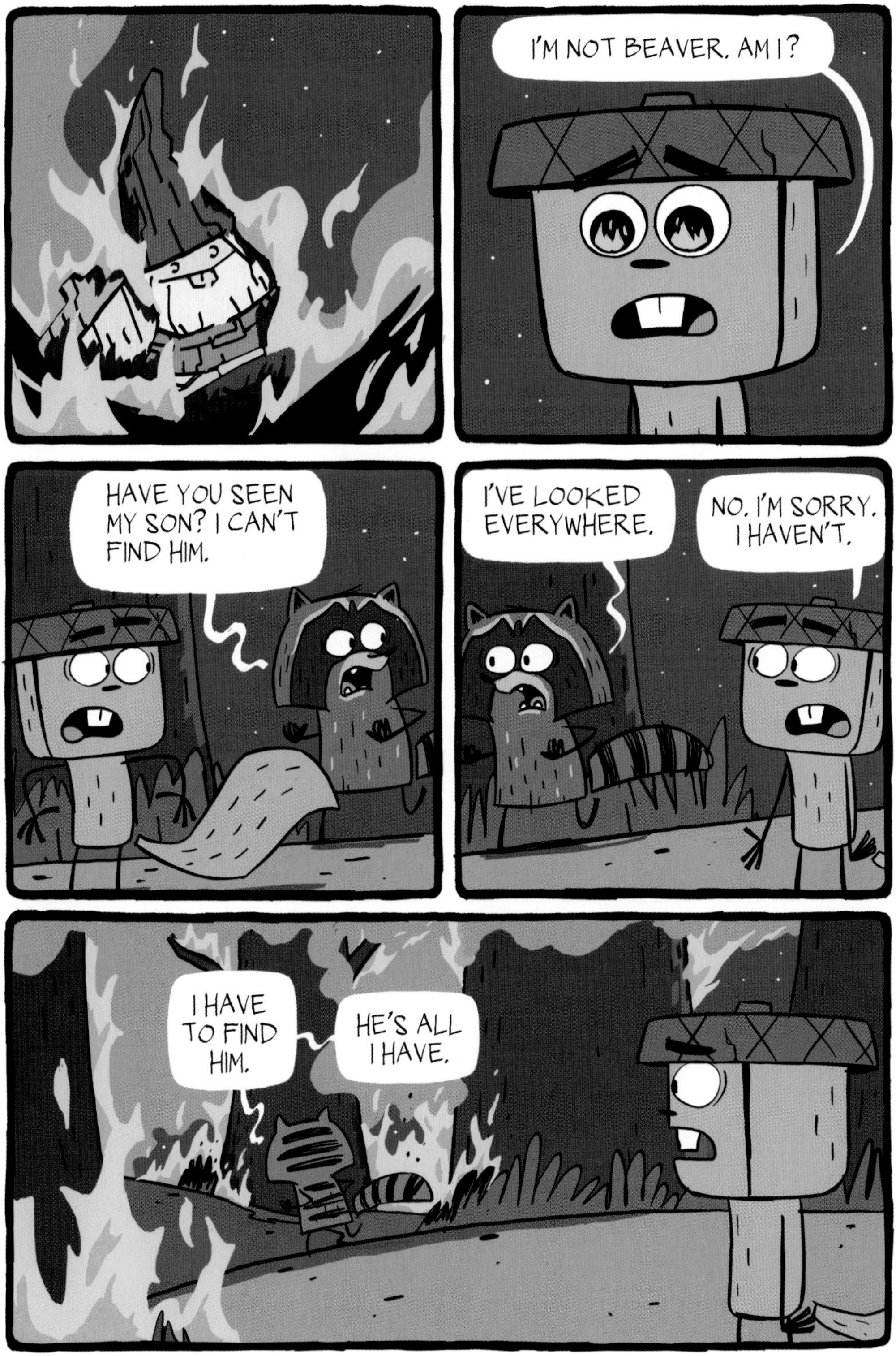
I'M NOT BEAVER. AM I?
HAVE YOU SEEN MY SON? I CAN'T FIND HIM.
I'VE LOOKED EVERYWHERE.
NO. I'M SORRY. I HAVEN'T.
I HAVE TO FIND HIM.
HE'S ALL I HAVE.

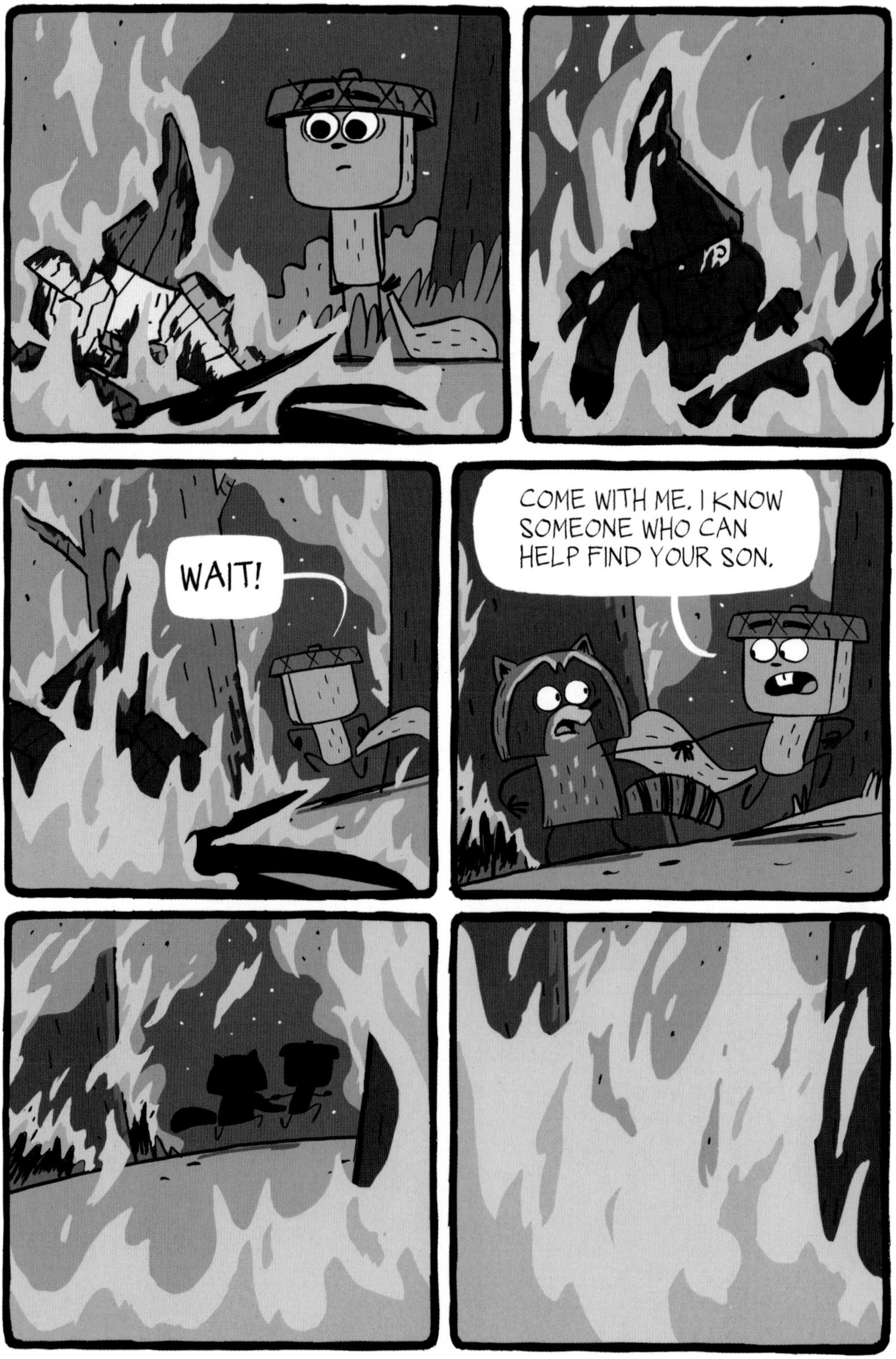
WAIT!
COME WITH ME. I KNOW SOMEONE WHO CAN HELP FIND YOUR SON.

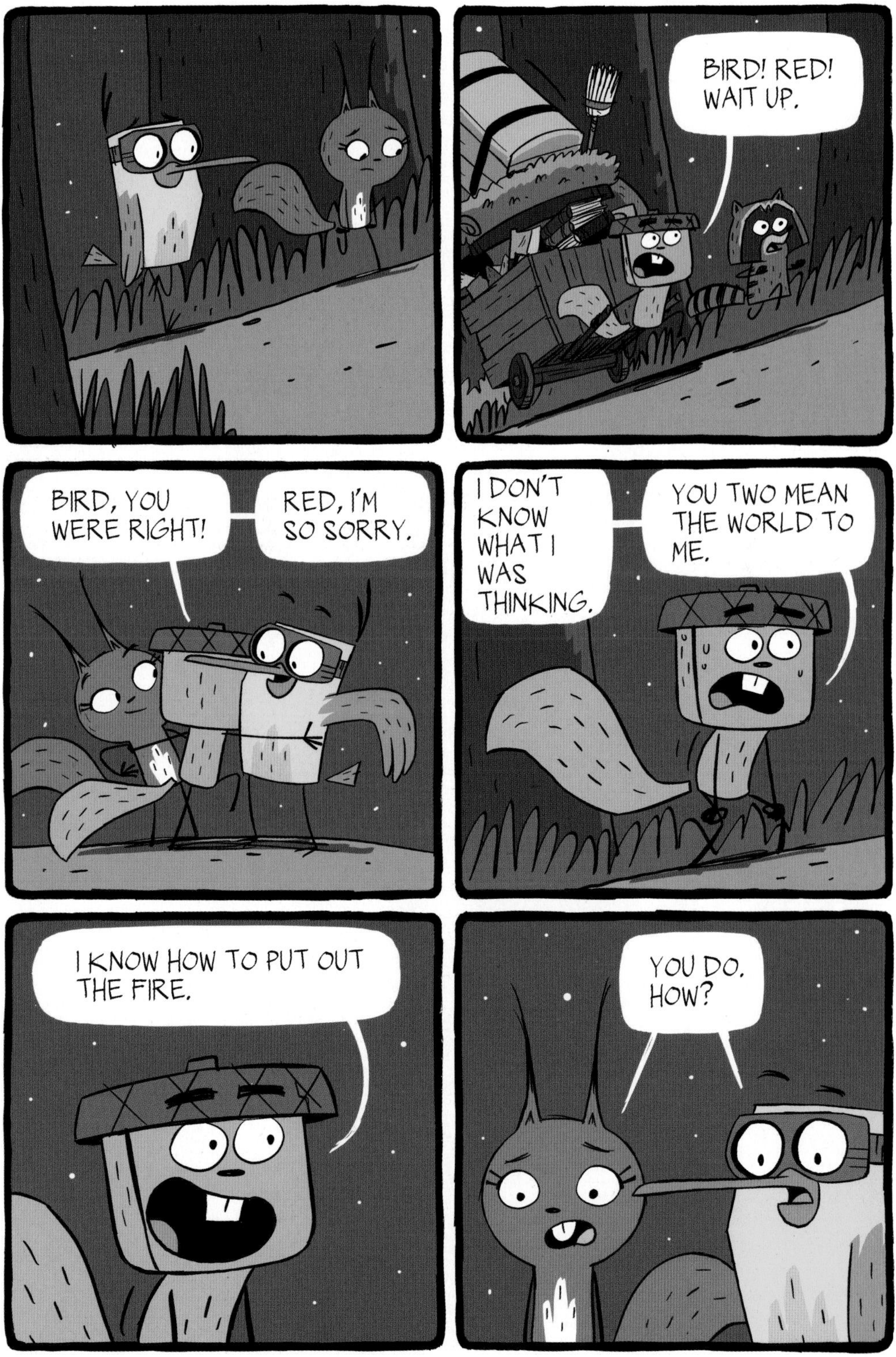
BIRD! RED! WAIT UP.
BIRD, YOU WERE RIGHT!
RED, I'M SO SORRY.
I DON'T KNOW WHAT I WAS THINKING.
YOU TWO MEAN THE WORLD TO ME.
I KNOW HOW TO PUT OUT THE FIRE.
YOU DO. HOW?

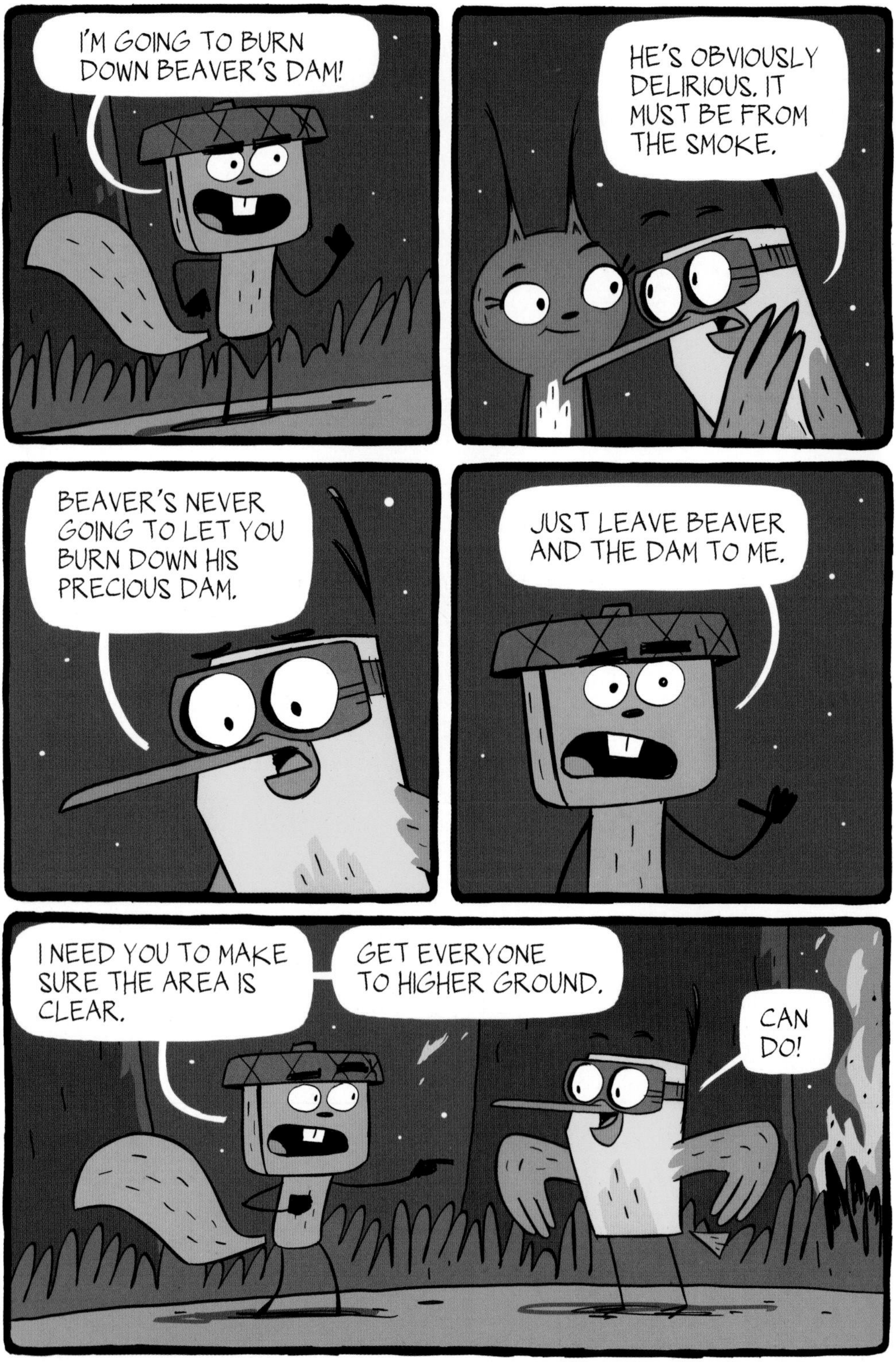
I'M GOING TO BURN DOWN BEAVER'S DAM!
HE'S OBVIOUSLY DELIRIOUS. IT MUST BE FROM THE SMOKE.
BEAVER'S NEVER GOING TO LET YOU BURN DOWN HIS PRECIOUS DAM.
JUST LEAVE BEAVER AND THE DAM TO ME.
I NEED YOU TO MAKE SURE THE AREA IS CLEAR.
GET EVERYONE TO HIGHER GROUND.
CAN DO!

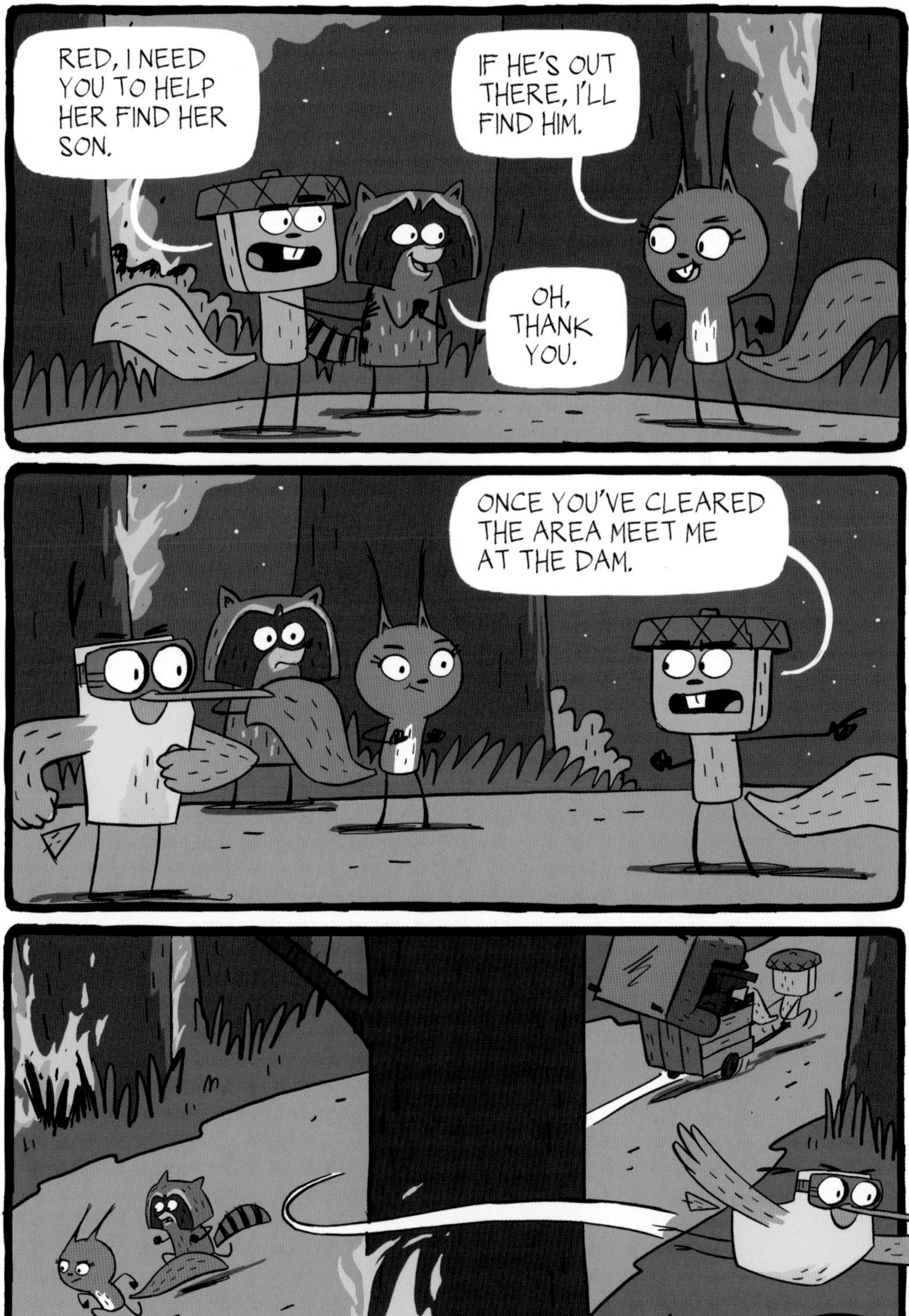
RED, I NEED YOU TO HELP HER FIND HER SON.
IF HE'S OUT THERE, I'LL FIND HIM.
OH, THANK YOU.
ONCE YOU'VE CLEARED THE AREA MEET ME AT THE DAM.

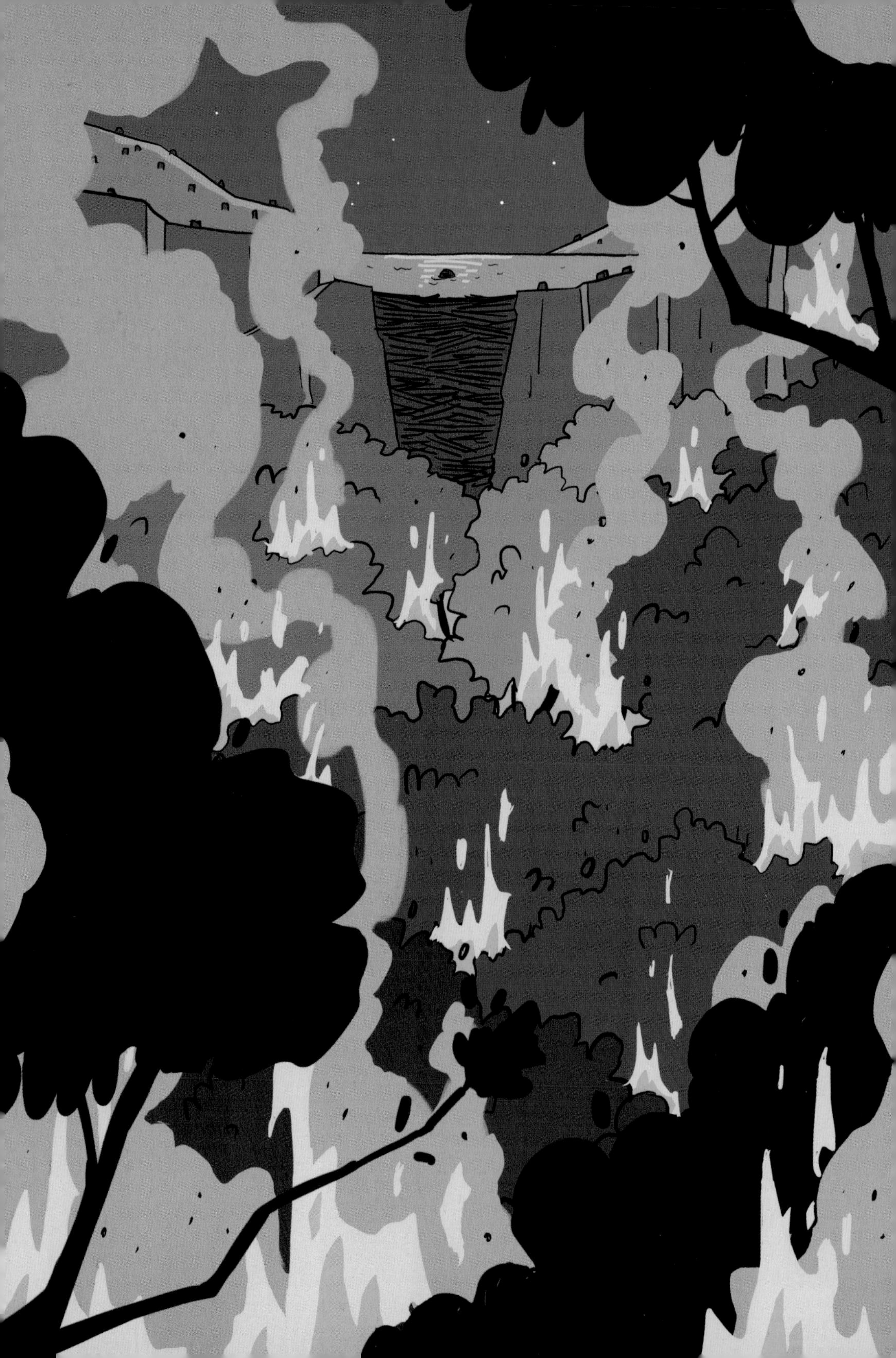

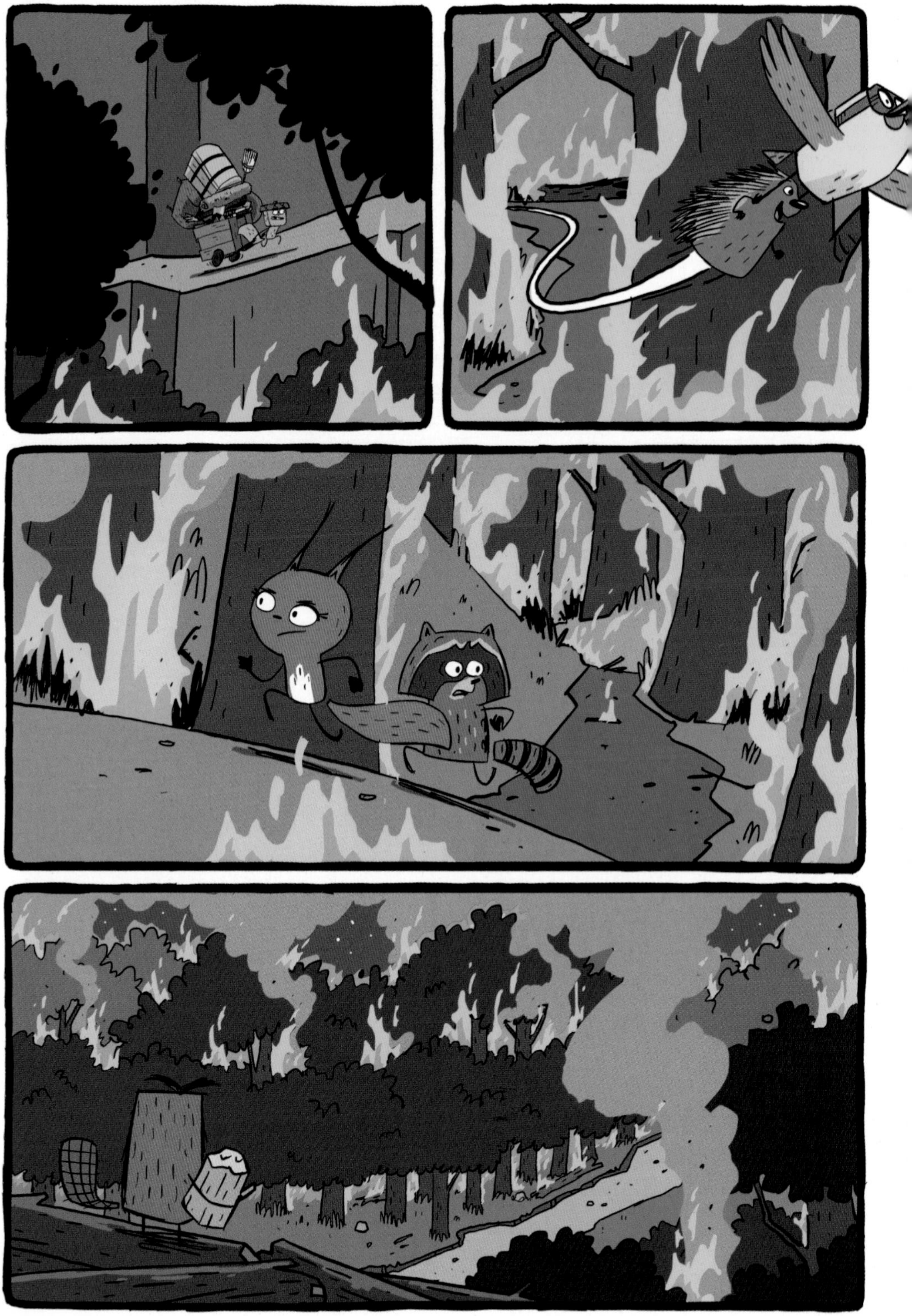

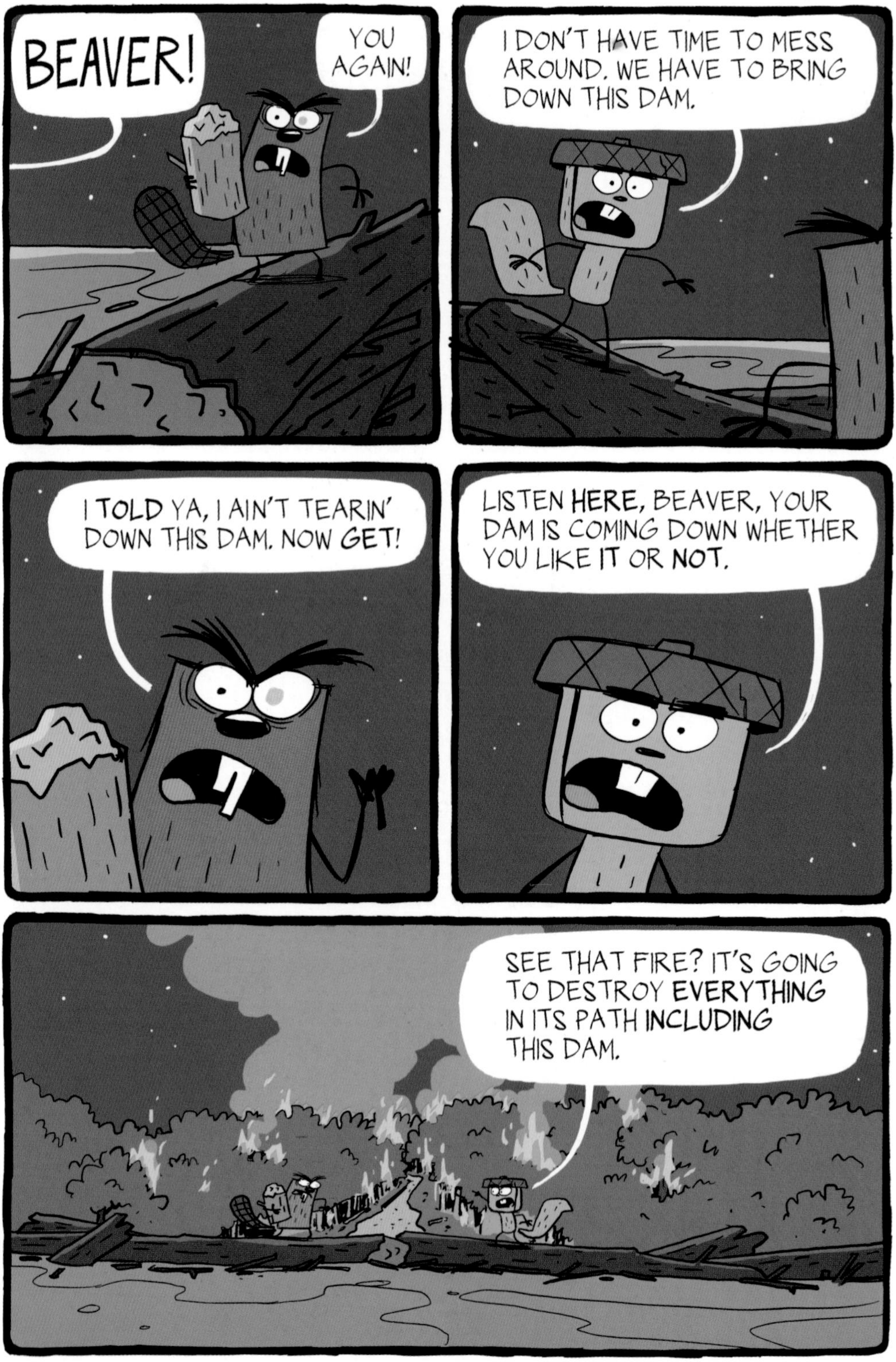
BEAVER!
YOU AGAIN!
I DON'T HAVE TIME TO MESS AROUND. WE HAVE TO BRING DOWN THIS DAM.
I TOLD YA, I AIN'T TEARIN' DOWN THIS DAM. NOW GET!
LISTEN HERE, BEAVER, YOUR DAM IS COMING DOWN WHETHER YOU LIKE IT OR NOT.
SEE THAT FIRE? IT'S GOING TO DESTROY EVERYTHING IN ITS PATH INCLUDING THIS DAM.

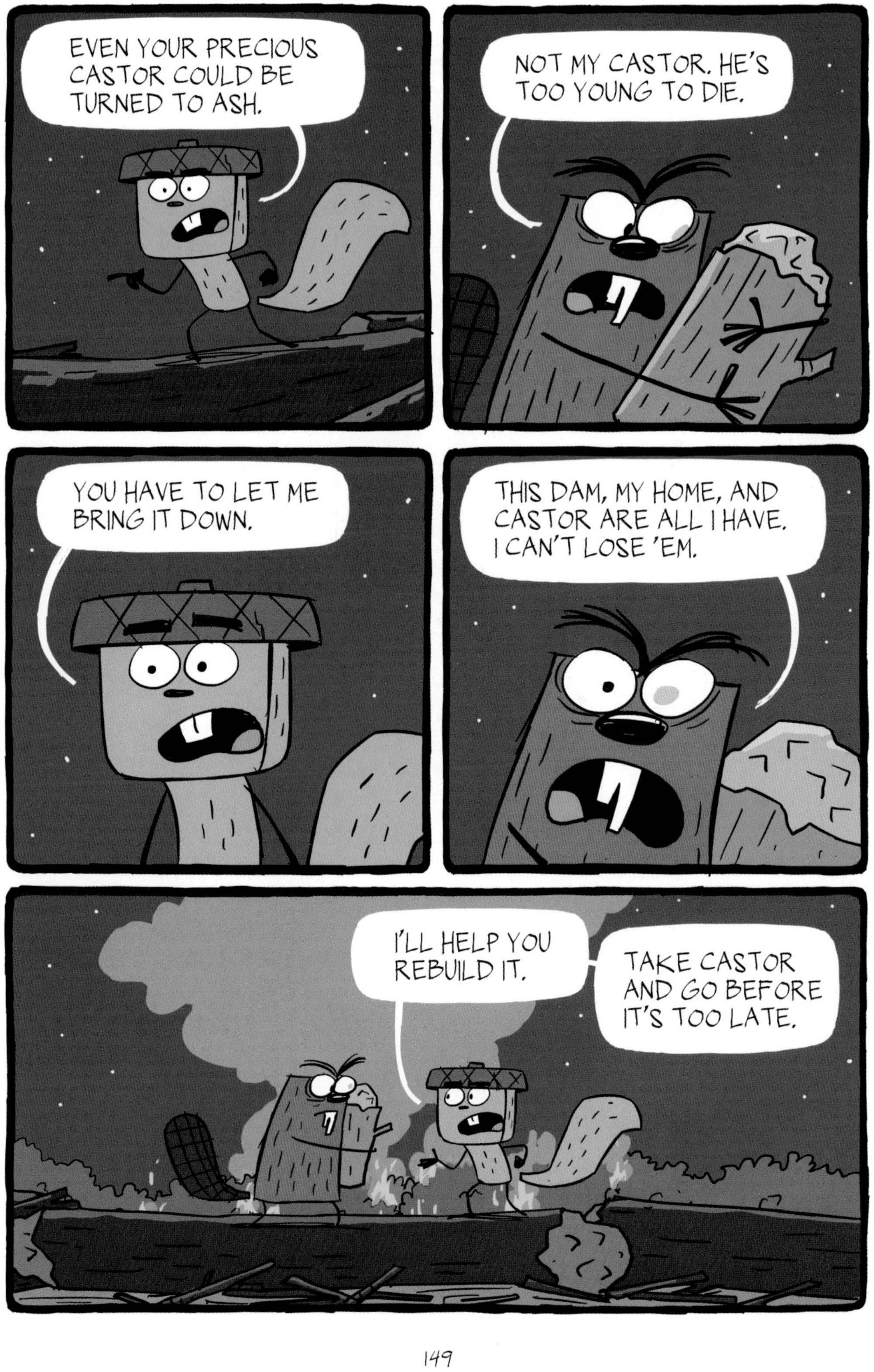
EVEN YOUR PRECIOUS CASTOR COULD BE TURNED TO ASH.
NOT MY CASTOR. HE'S TOO YOUNG TO DIE.
YOU HAVE TO LET ME BRING IT DOWN.
THIS DAM, MY HOME, AND CASTOR ARE ALL I HAVE. I CAN'T LOSE 'EM.
I'LL HELP YOU REBUILD IT.
TAKE CASTOR AND GO BEFORE IT'S TOO LATE.

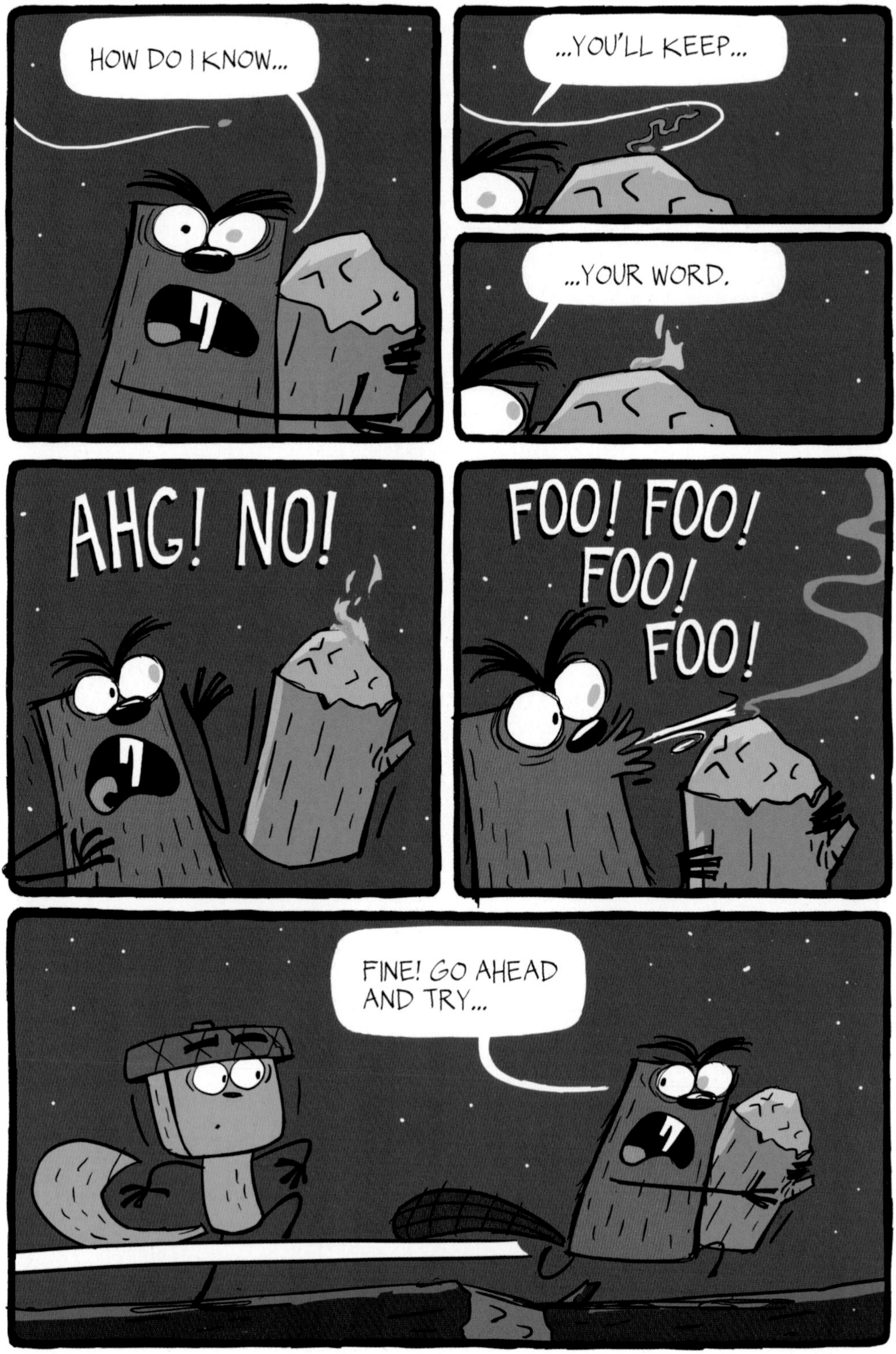
HOW DO I KNOW...
...YOU'LL KEEP...
...YOUR WORD.
AHG! NO!
FOO! FOO!
FOO!
FOO!
FINE! GO AHEAD
AND TRY...

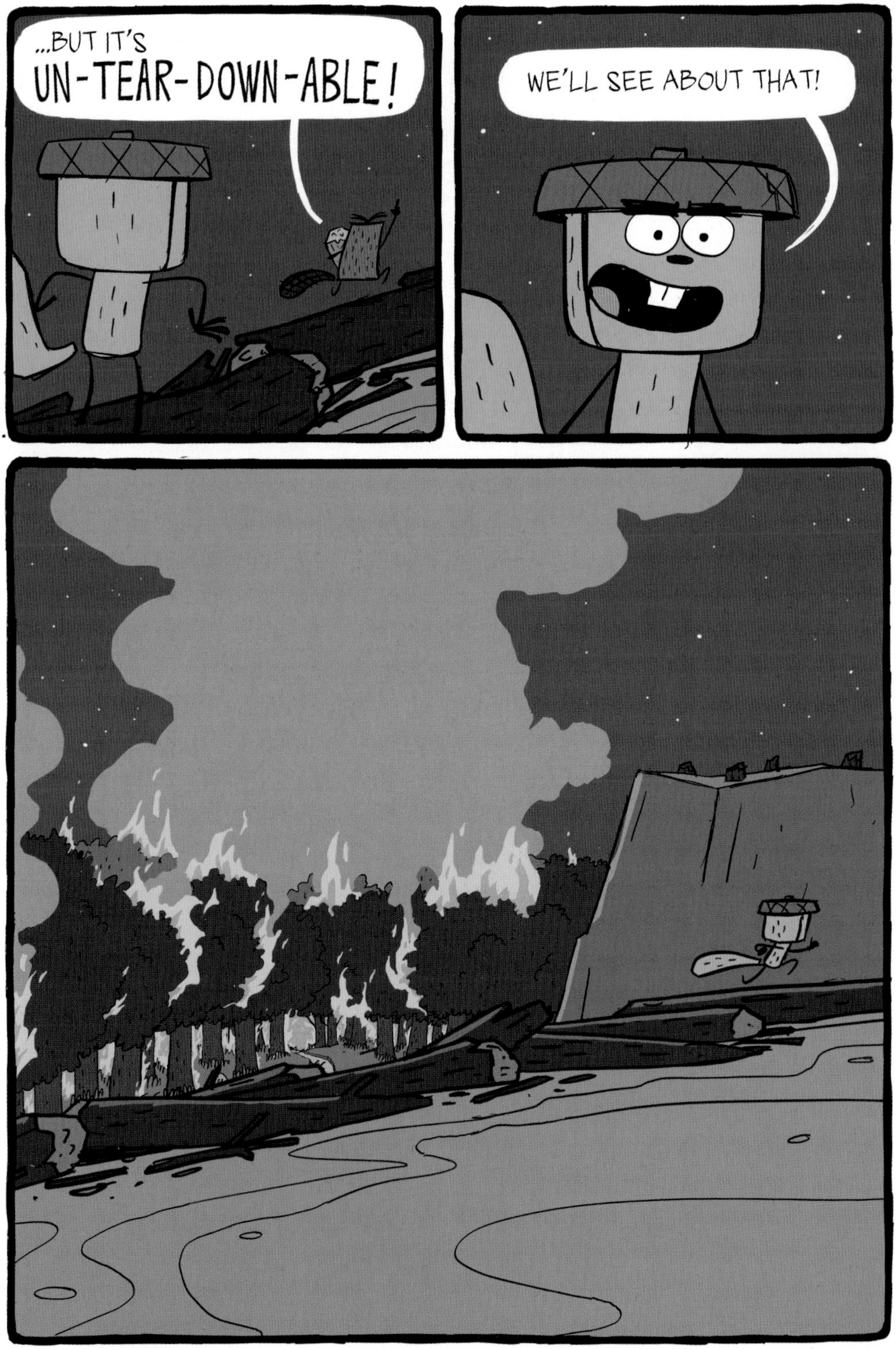
...BUT IT'S
UN-TEAR-DOWN-ABLE!
WE'LL SEE ABOUT THAT!

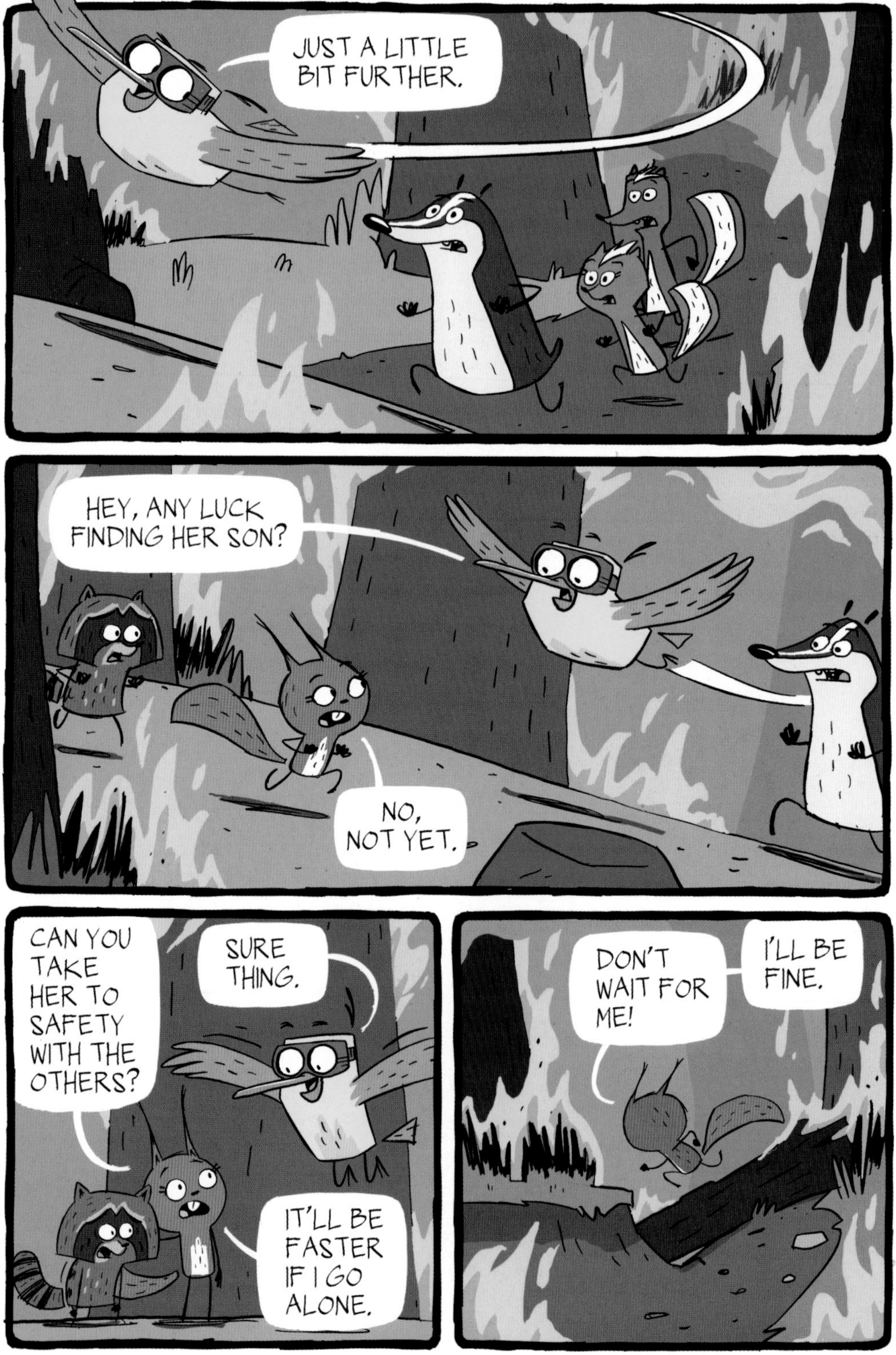
JUST A LITTLE BIT FURTHER.
HEY, ANY LUCK FINDING HER SON?
NO, NOT YET.
CAN YOU TAKE HER TO SAFETY WITH THE OTHERS?
SURE THING.
IT'LL BE FASTER IF I GO ALONE.
DON'T WAIT FOR ME!
I'LL BE FINE.

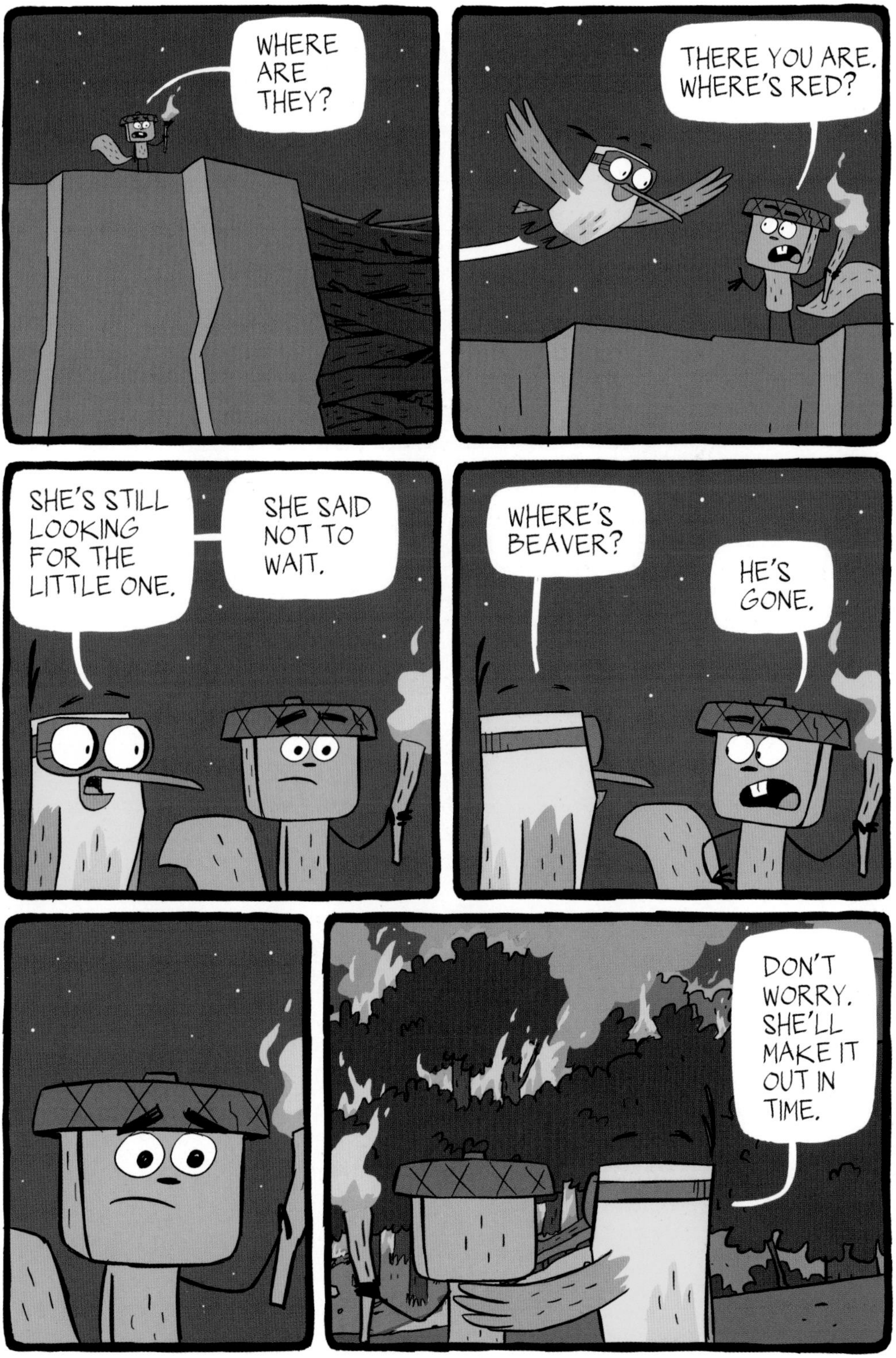
WHERE ARE THEY?
THERE YOU ARE. WHERE'S RED?
SHE'S STILL LOOKING FOR THE LITTLE ONE.
SHE SAID NOT TO WAIT.
WHERE'S BEAVER?
HE'S GONE.
DON'T WORRY. SHE'LL MAKE IT OUT IN TIME.

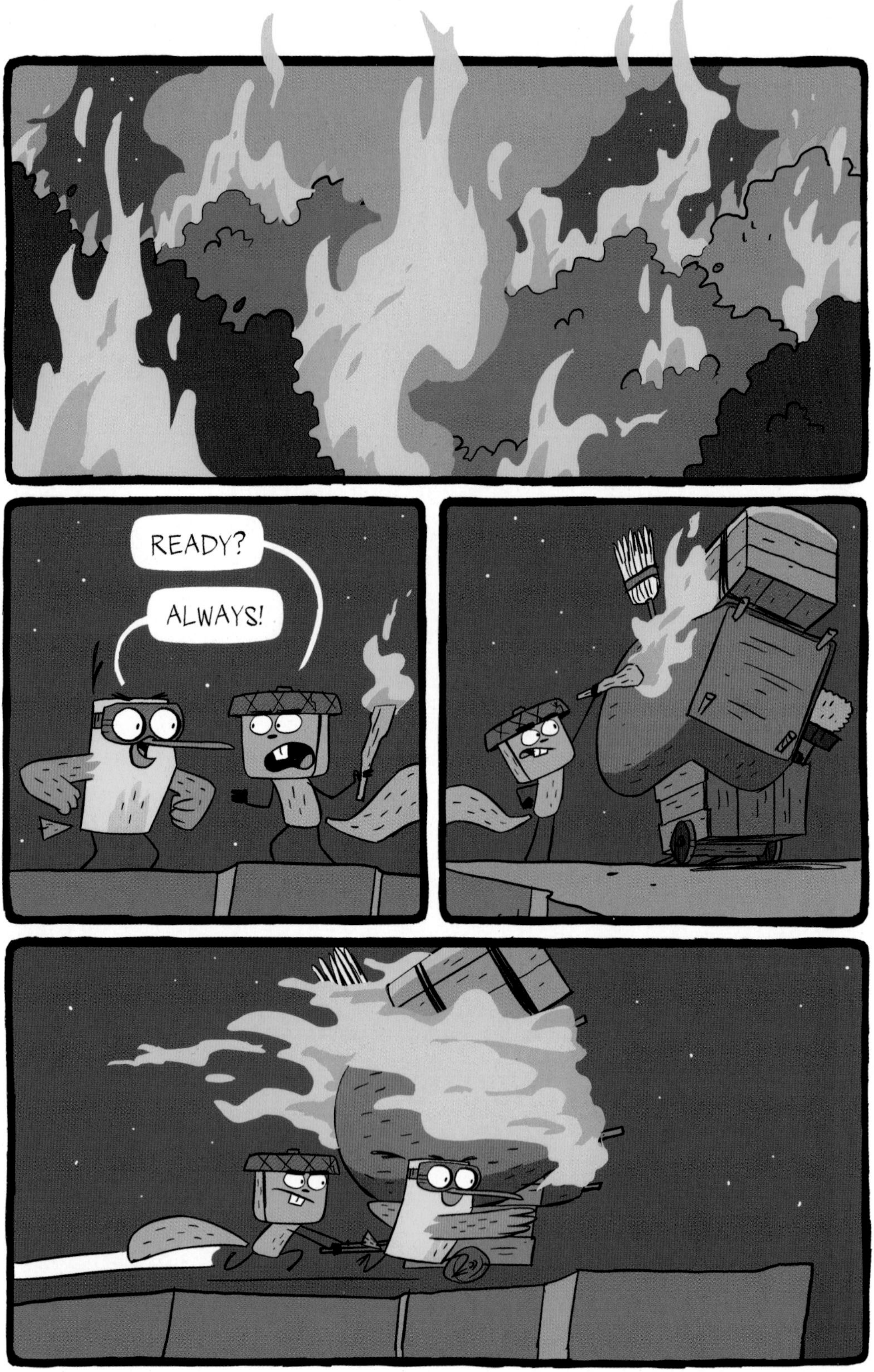
READY?
ALWAYS!

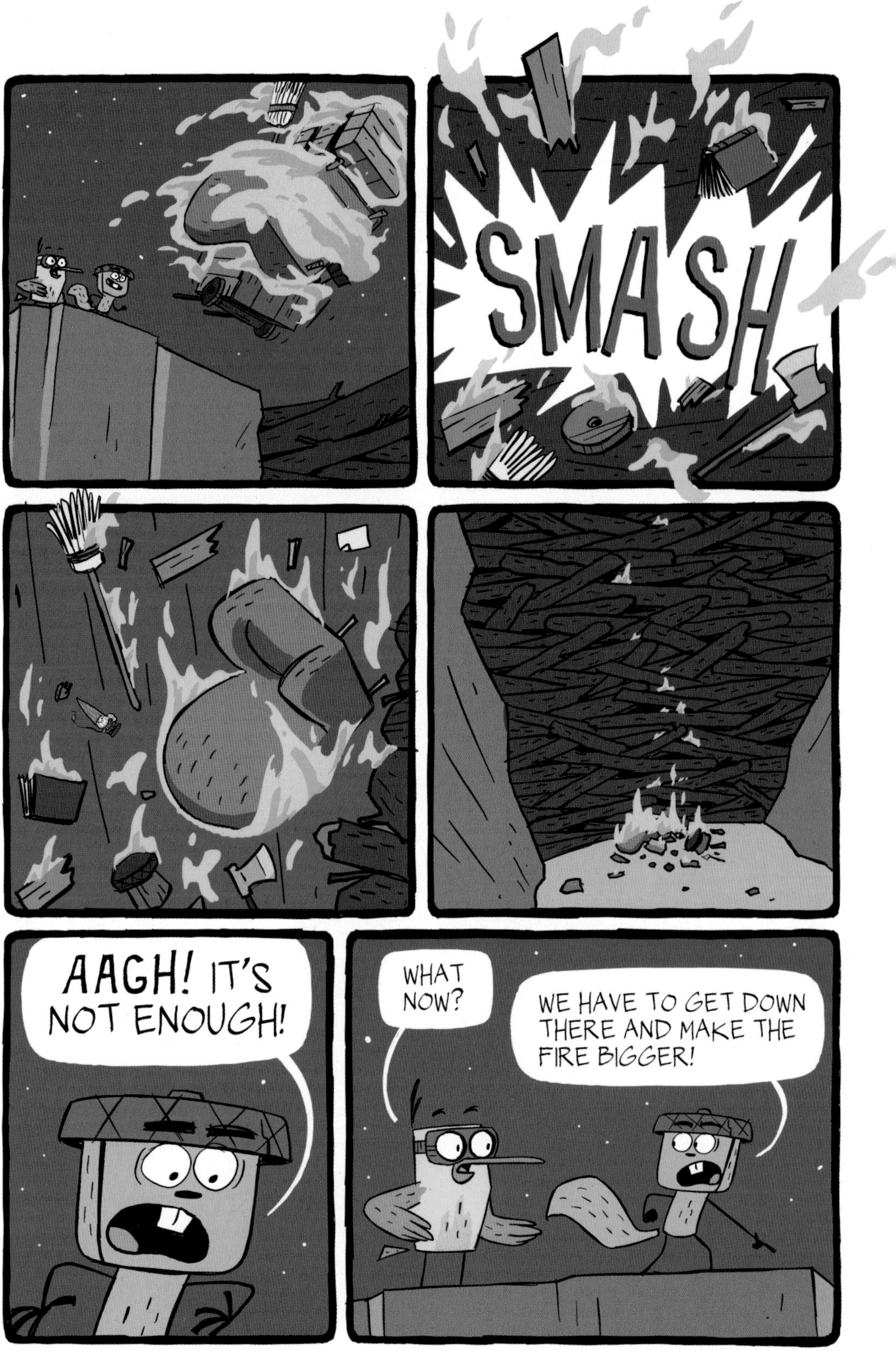
SMASH
AAGH! IT'S NOT ENOUGH!
WHAT NOW?
WE HAVE TO GET DOWN THERE AND MAKE THE FIRE BIGGER!

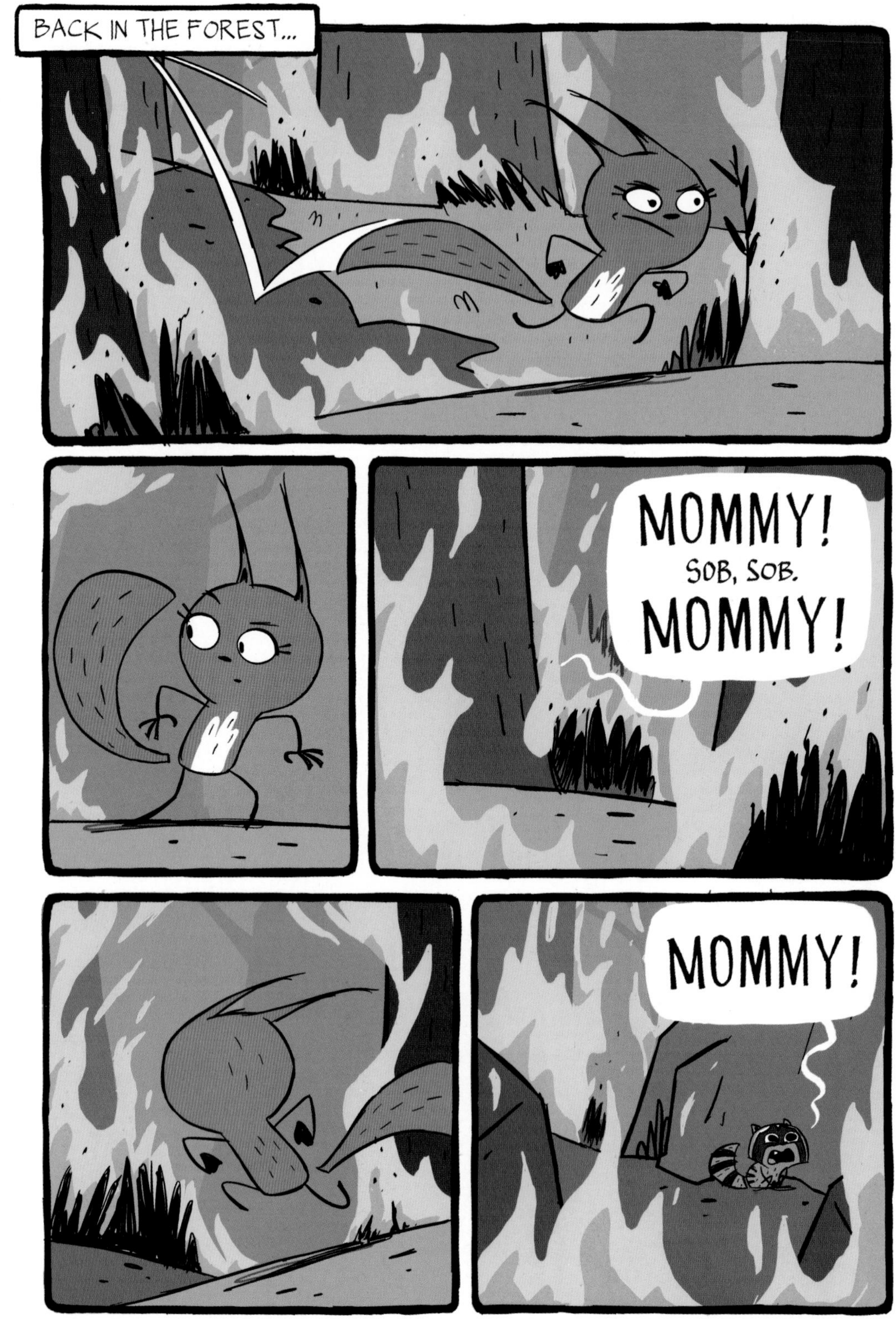
BACK IN THE FOREST...
MOMMY! SOB, SOB. MOMMY!
MOMMY!

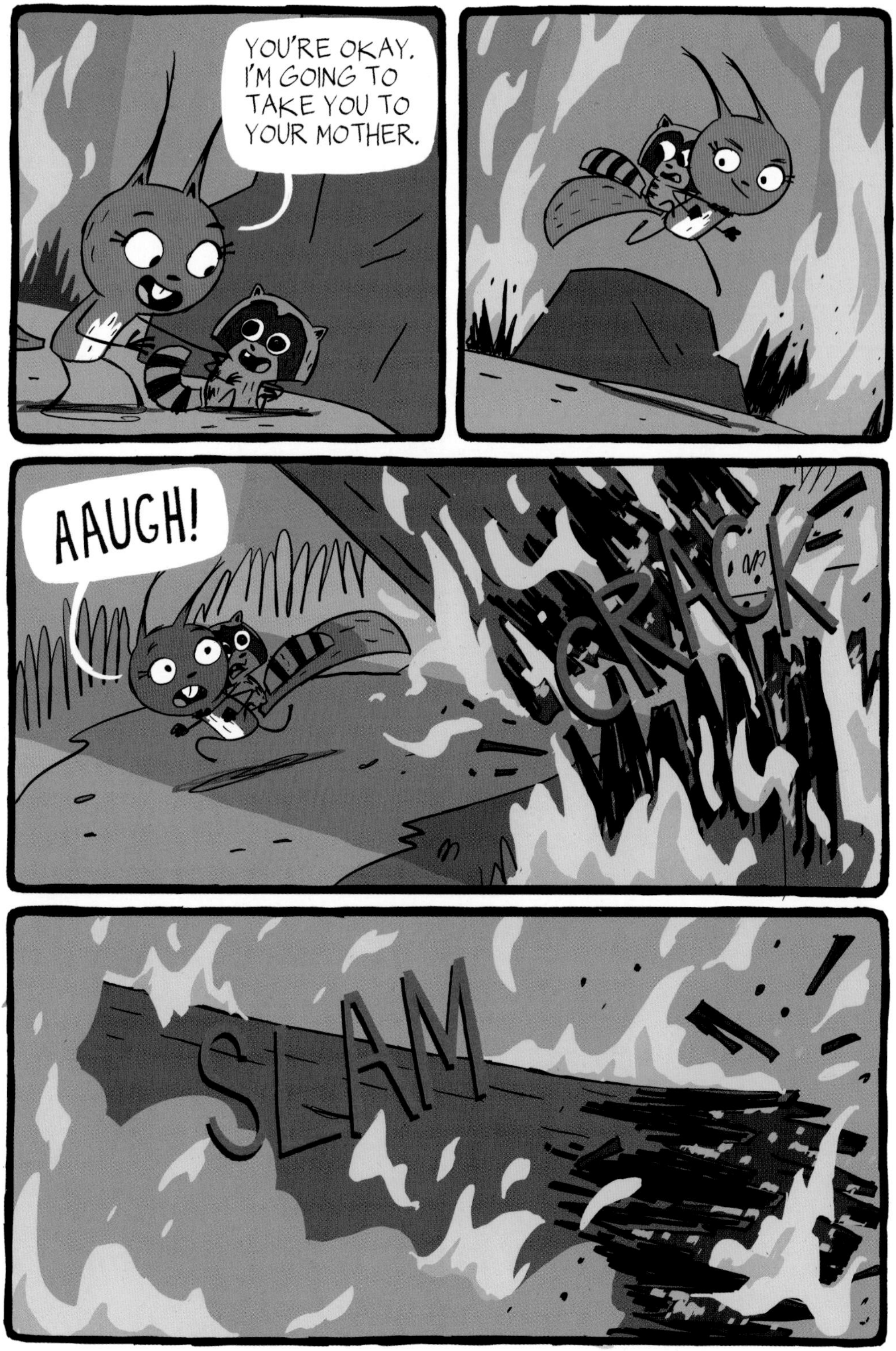
YOU'RE OKAY. I'M GOING TO TAKE YOU TO YOUR MOTHER.
AAUGH!
CRACK
SLAM

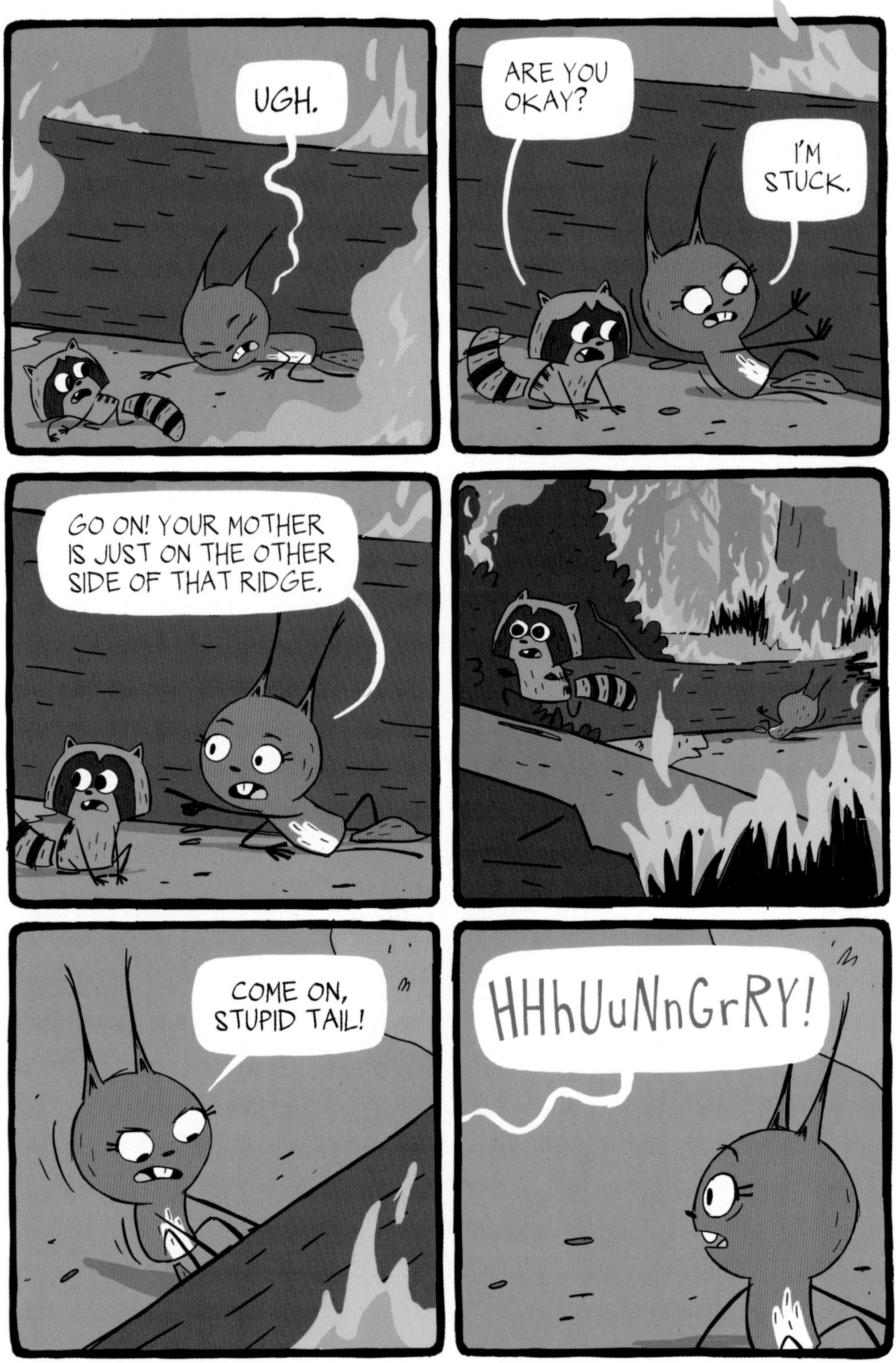
UGH.
ARE YOU OKAY?
I'M STUCK.
GO ON! YOUR MOTHER IS JUST ON THE OTHER SIDE OF THAT RIDGE.
COME ON, STUPID TAIL!
HHhUuNnGrRY!

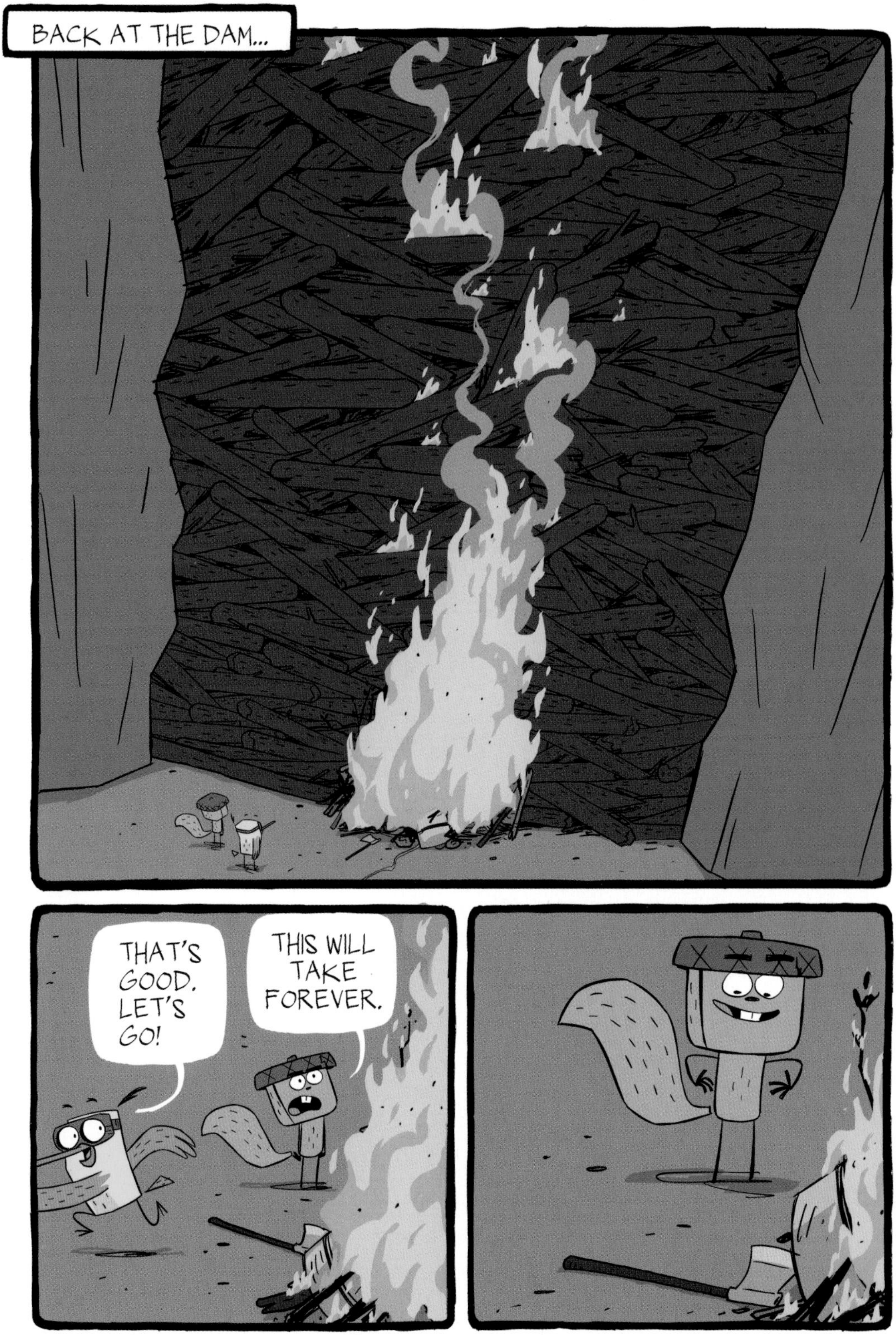
BACK AT THE DAM...
THAT'S GOOD. LET'S GO!
THIS WILL TAKE FOREVER.

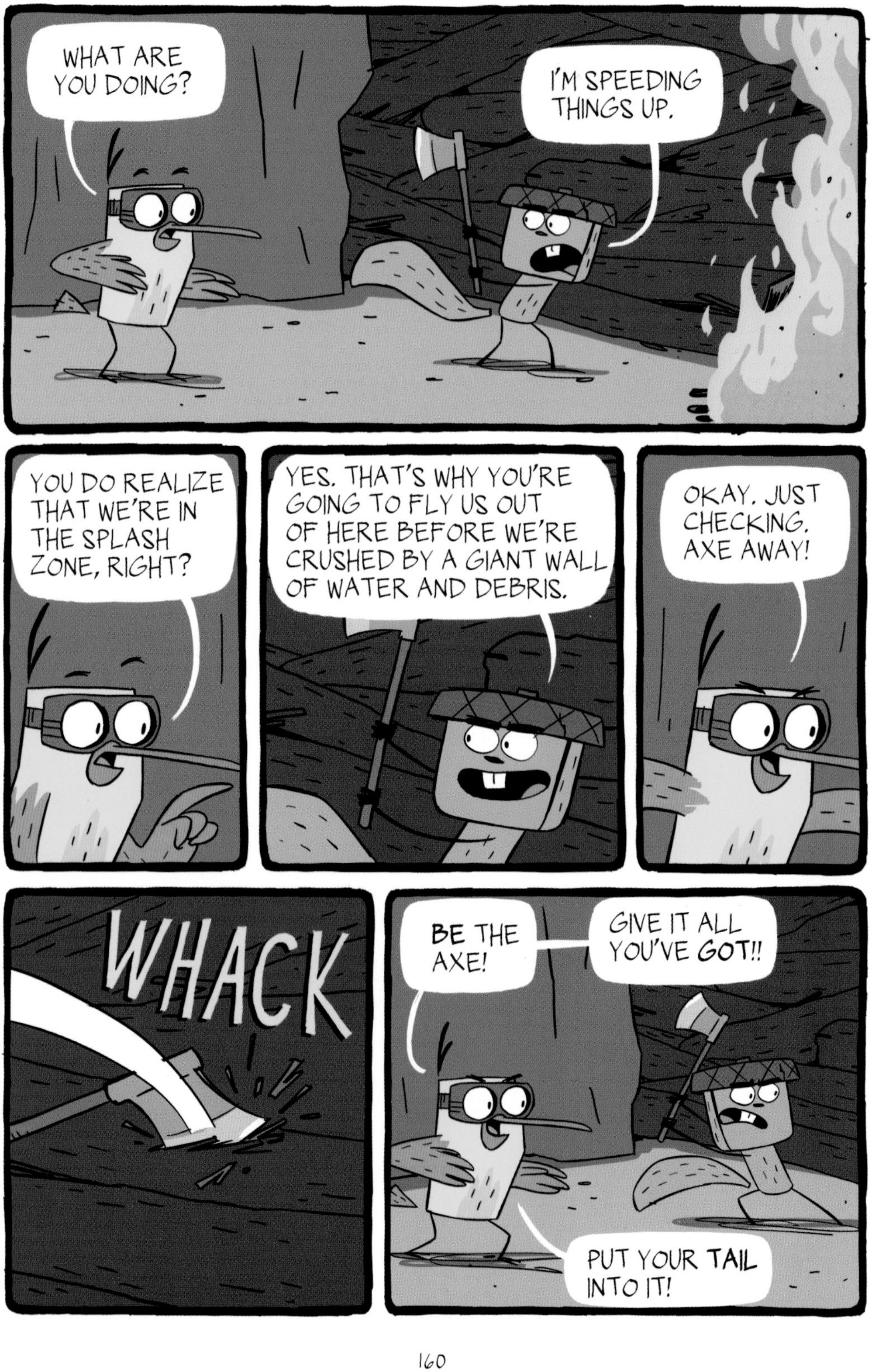
WHAT ARE YOU DOING?
I'M SPEEDING THINGS UP.
YOU DO REALIZE THAT WE'RE IN THE SPLASH ZONE, RIGHT?
YES. THAT'S WHY YOU'RE GOING TO FLY US OUT OF HERE BEFORE WE'RE CRUSHED BY A GIANT WALL OF WATER AND DEBRIS.
OKAY. JUST CHECKING. AXE AWAY!
WHACK
BE THE AXE!
GIVE IT ALL YOU'VE GOT!!
PUT YOUR TAIL INTO IT!

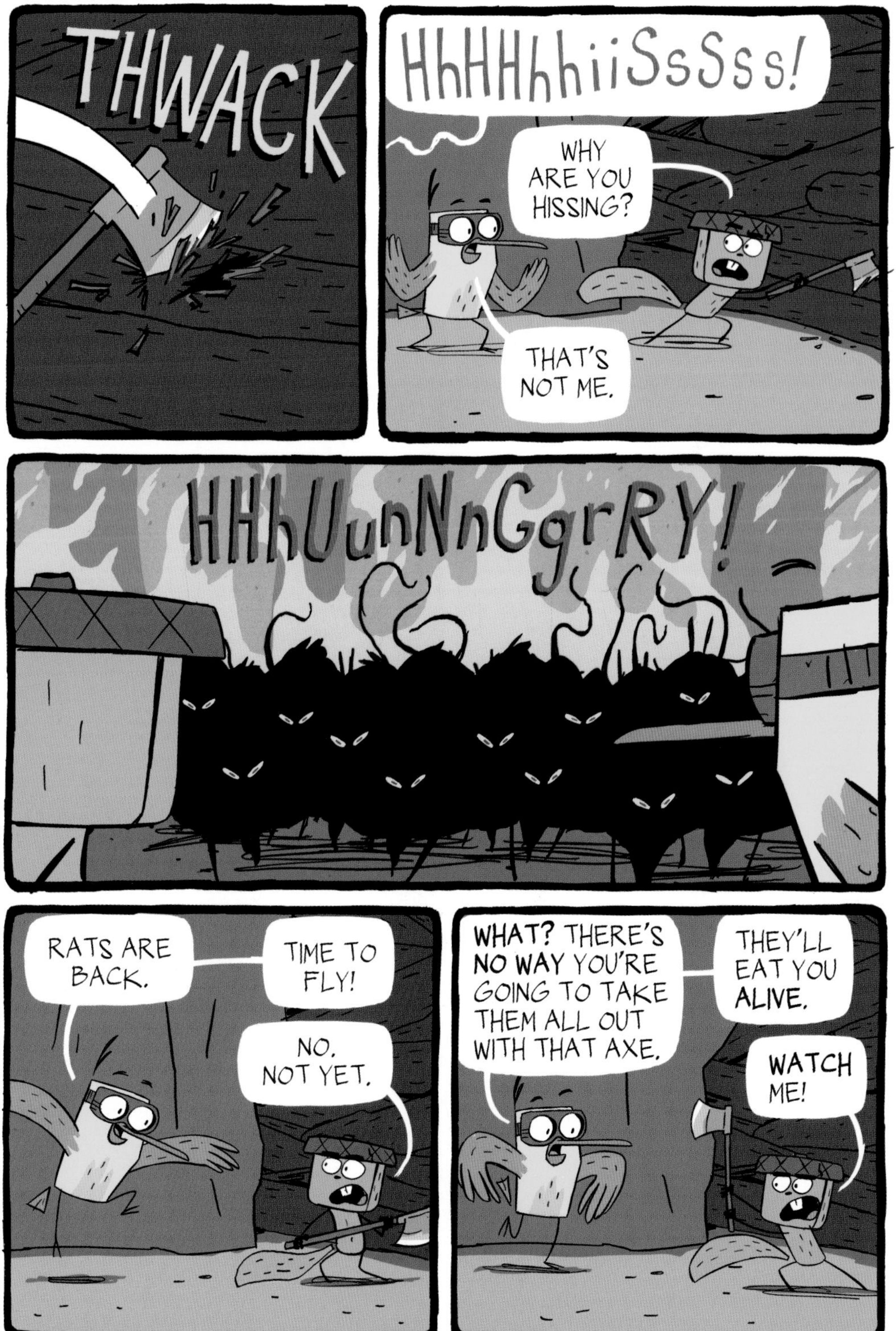
THWACK
HhHHhhiiSsSss!
WHY ARE YOU HISSING?
THAT'S NOT ME.
HHhUunNnGgrRY!
RATS ARE BACK.
TIME TO FLY!
NO. NOT YET.
WHAT? THERE'S NO WAY YOU'RE GOING TO TAKE THEM ALL OUT WITH THAT AXE.
THEY'LL EAT YOU ALIVE.
WATCH ME!

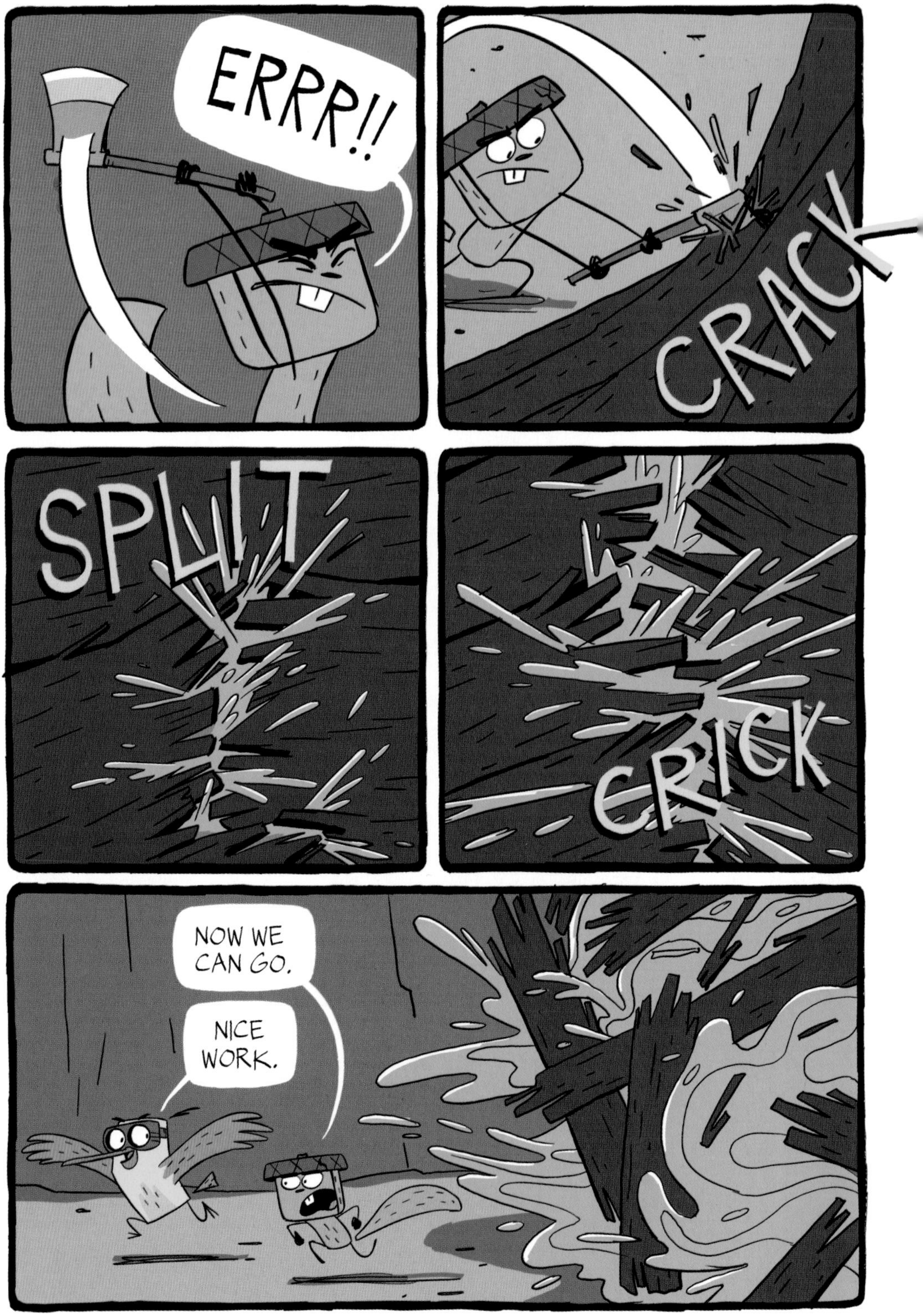
ERRR!!
CRACK
SPLIT
CRICK
NOW WE CAN GO.
NICE WORK.

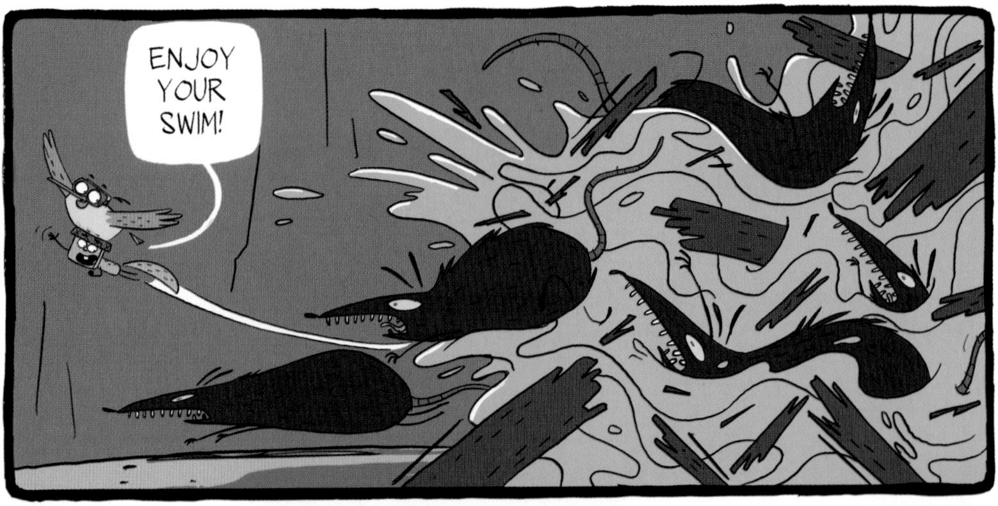
ENJOY YOUR SWIM!

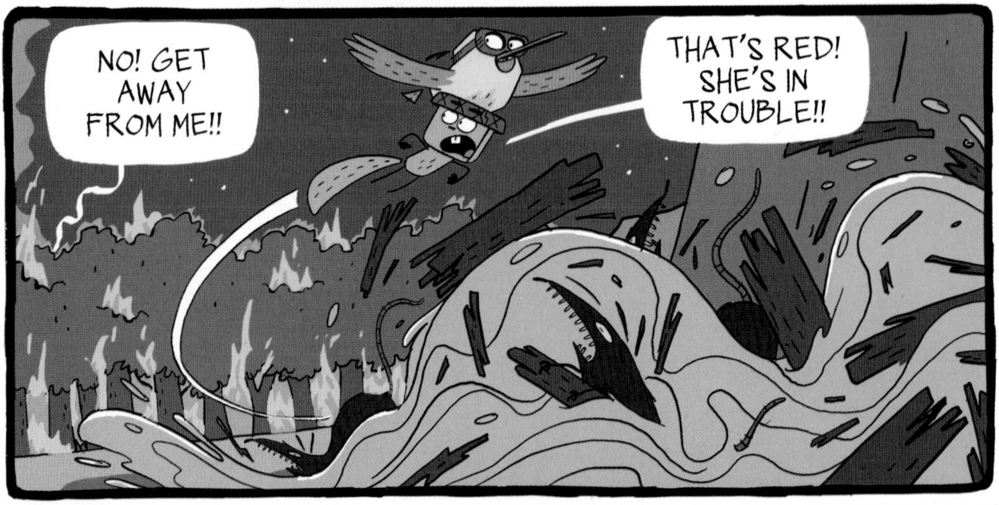
NO! GET AWAY FROM ME!!
THAT'S RED! SHE'S IN TROUBLE!!

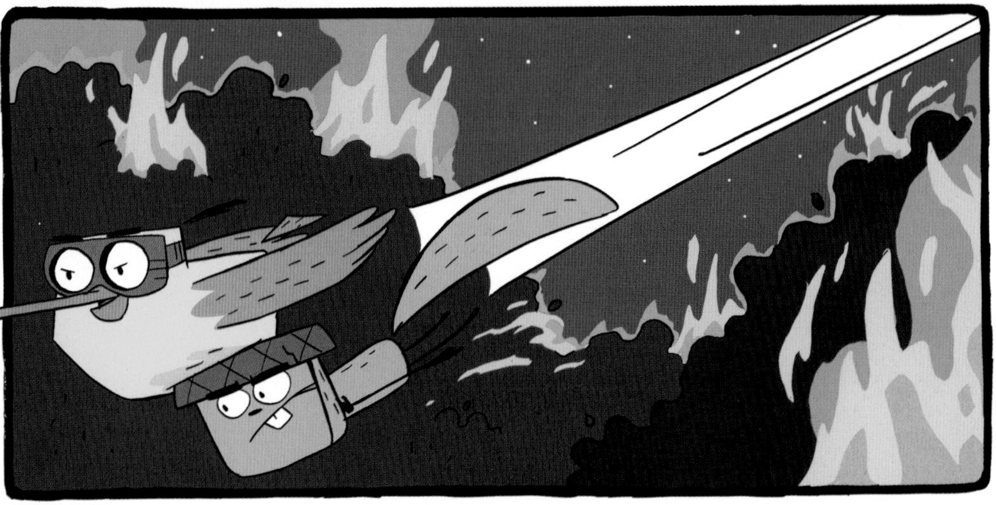

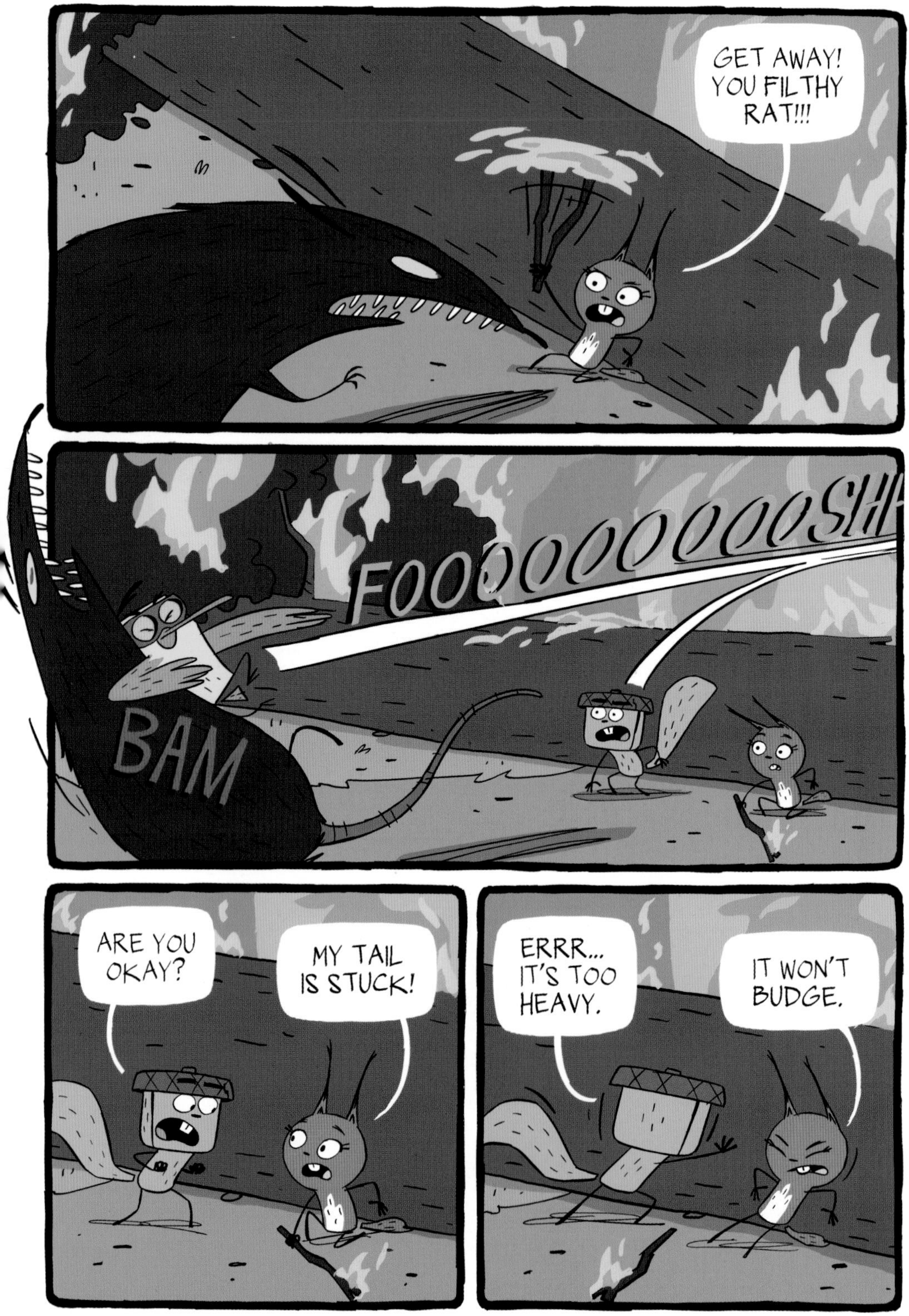
GET AWAY! YOU FILTHY RAT!!!
FOOOOOOOOOOOSHH
BAM
ARE YOU OKAY?
MY TAIL IS STUCK!
ERRR... IT'S TOO HEAVY.
IT WON'T BUDGE.

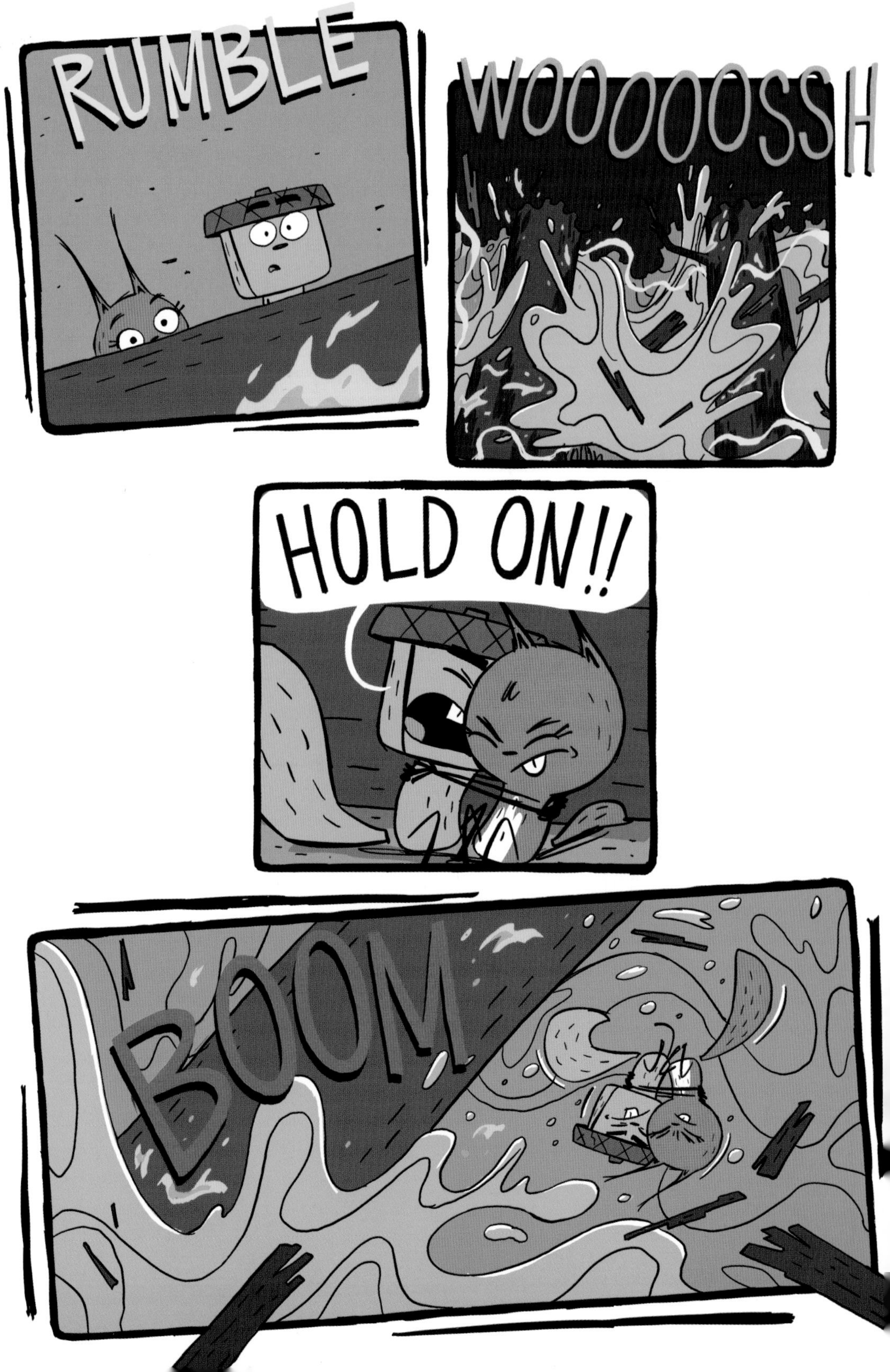
RUMBLE
WOOOOOOSSH
HOLD ON!!
BOOM

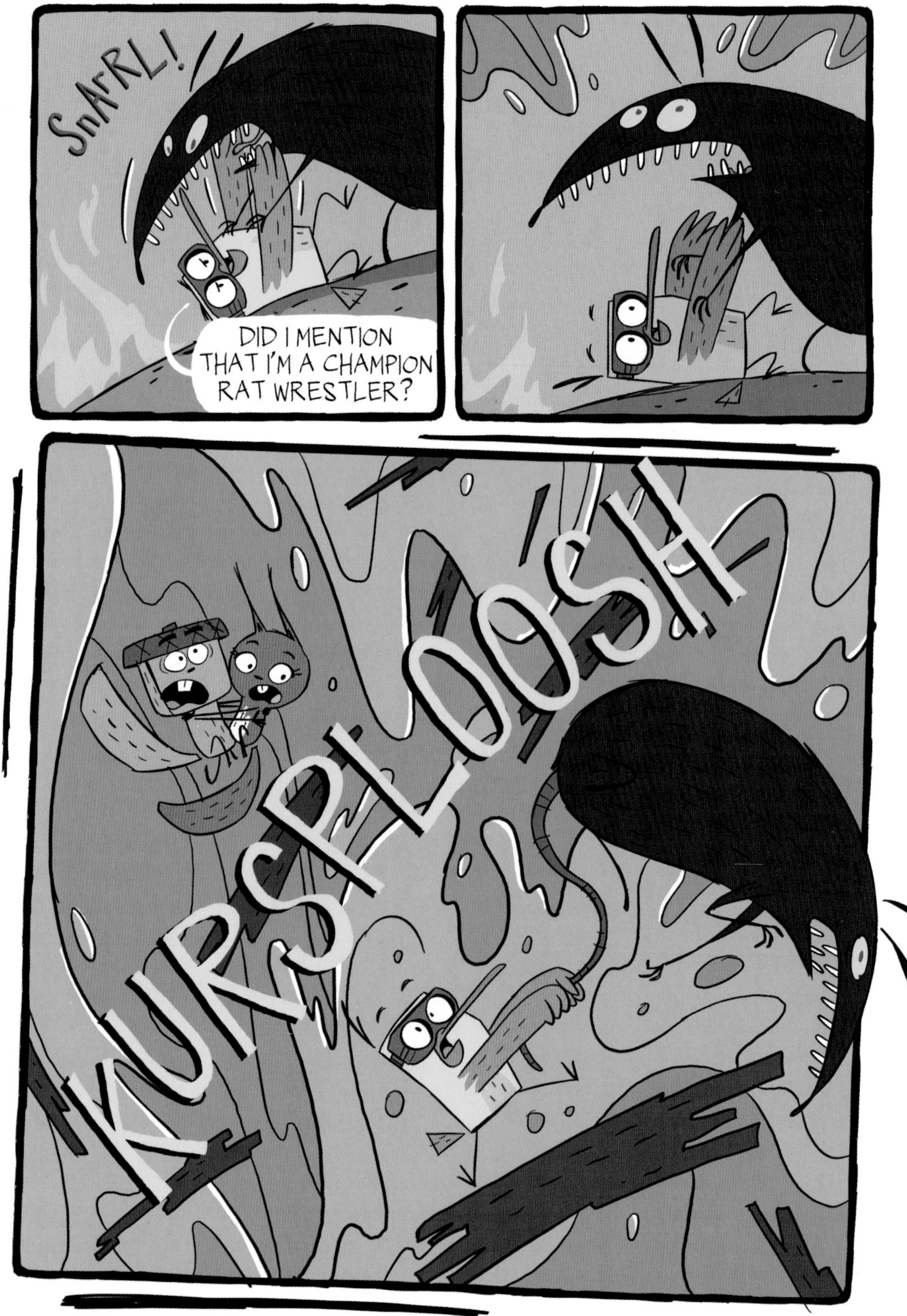
SNARL!
DID I MENTION THAT I'M A CHAMPION RAT WRESTLER?
KURSPLOOSH

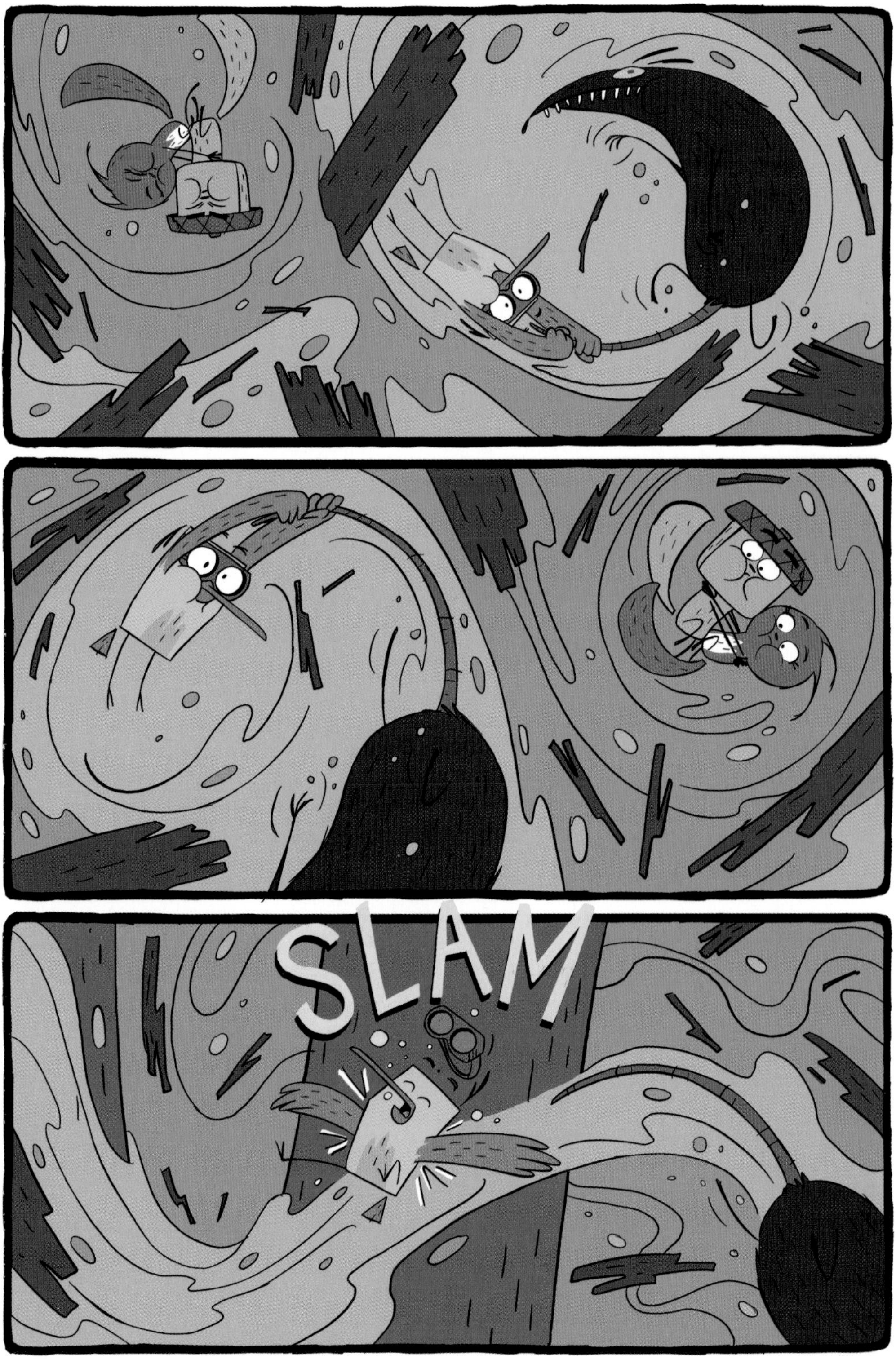
SLAM

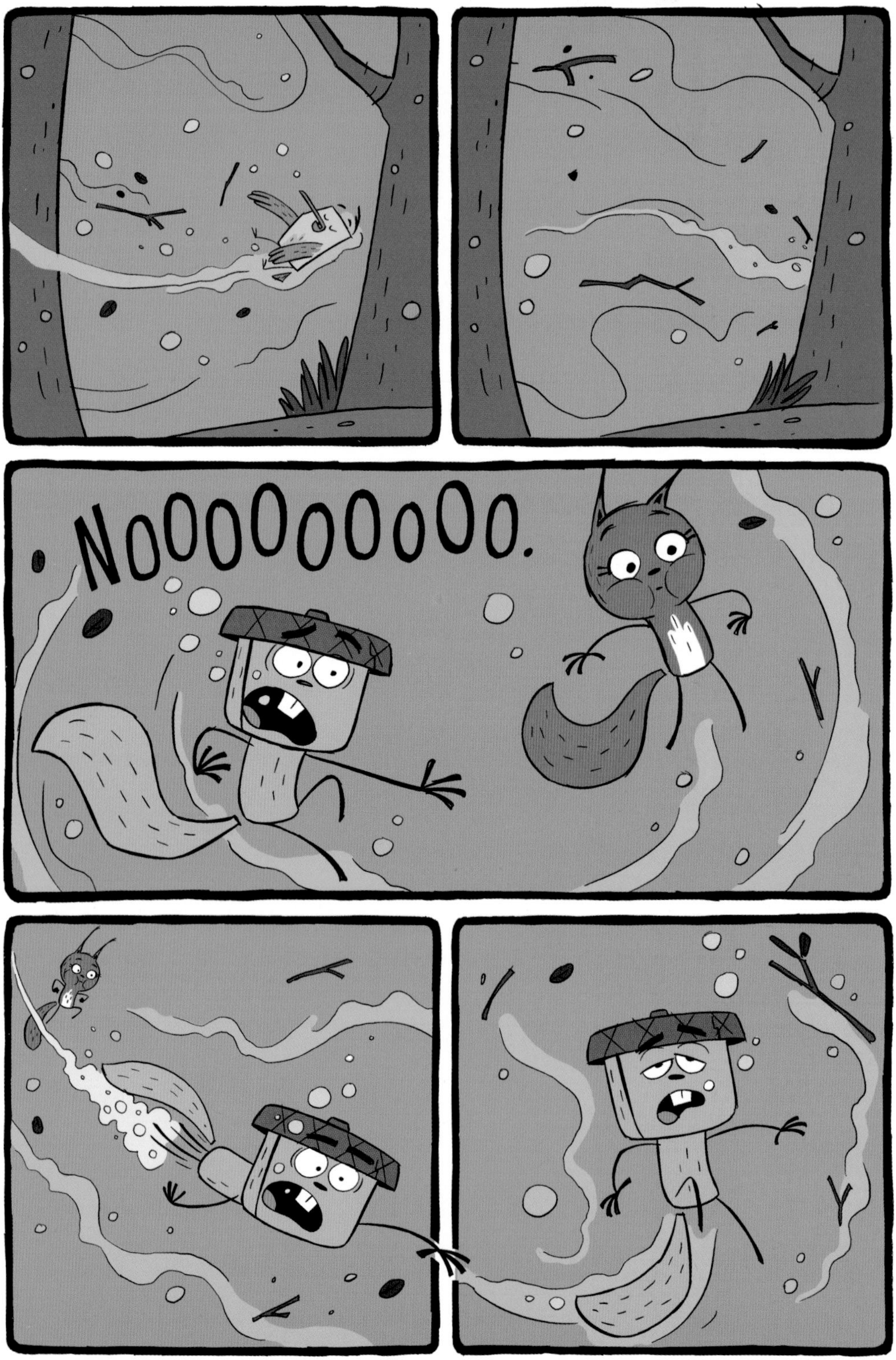
NOOOOOOOOO.

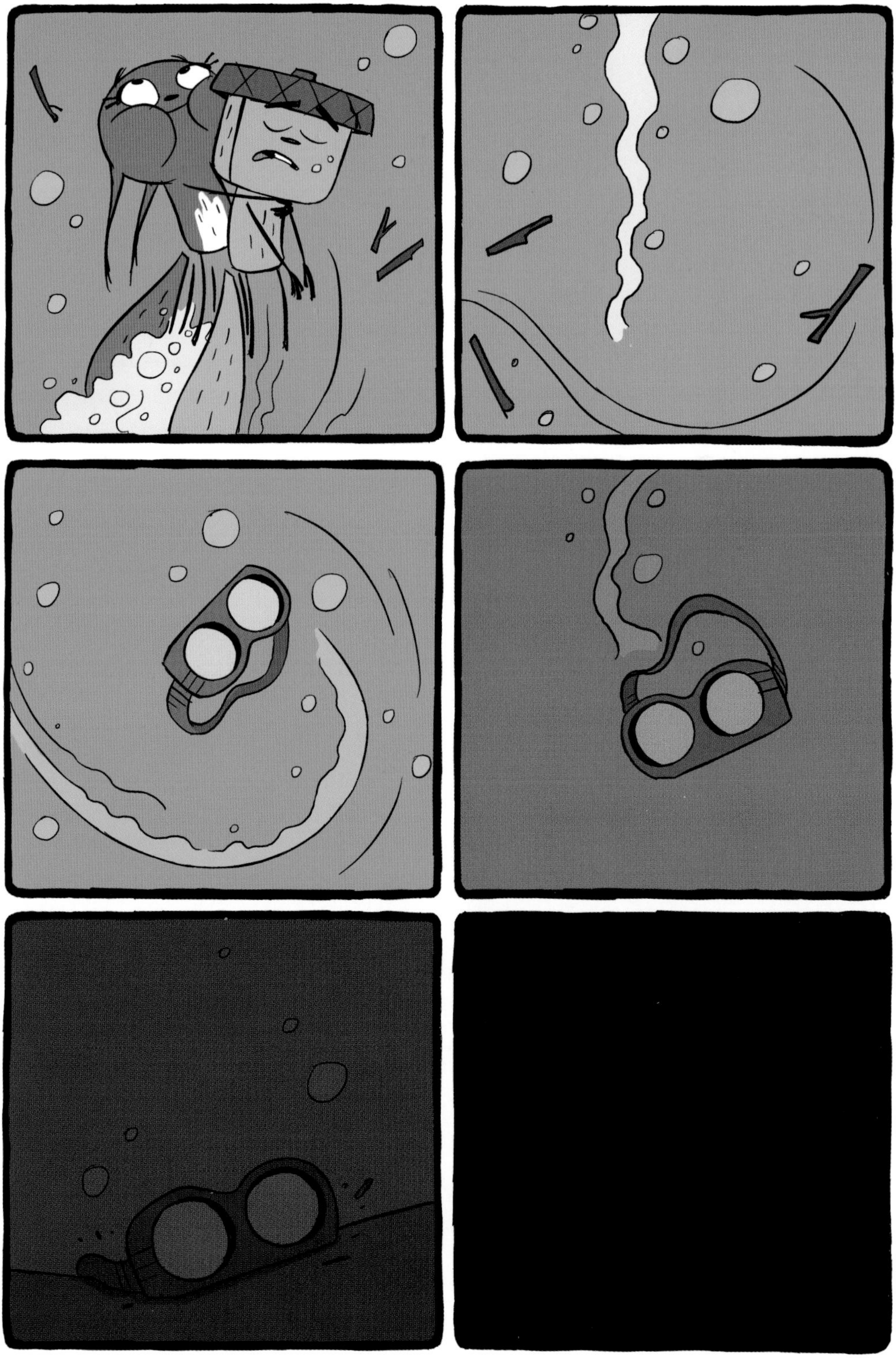

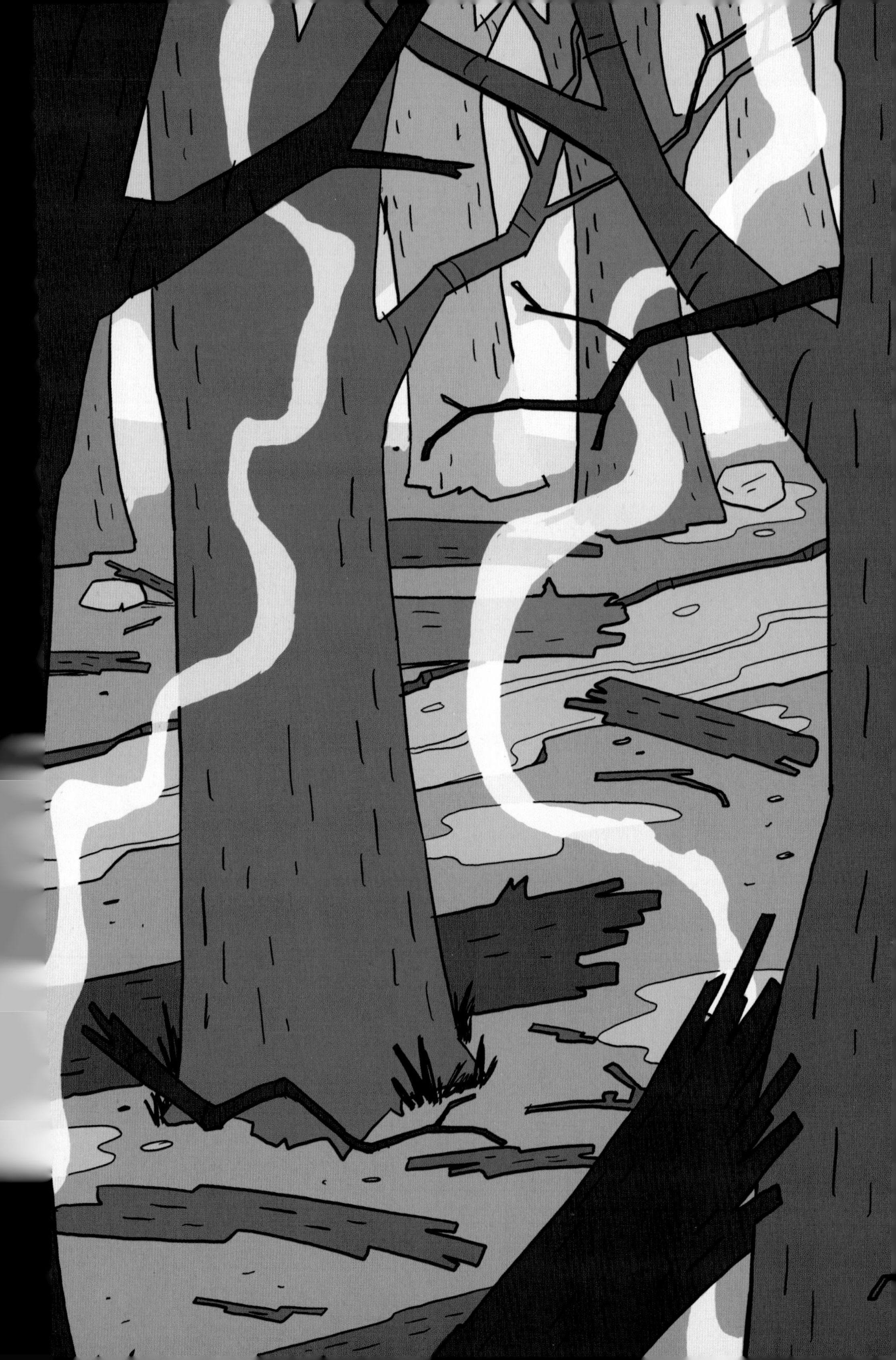

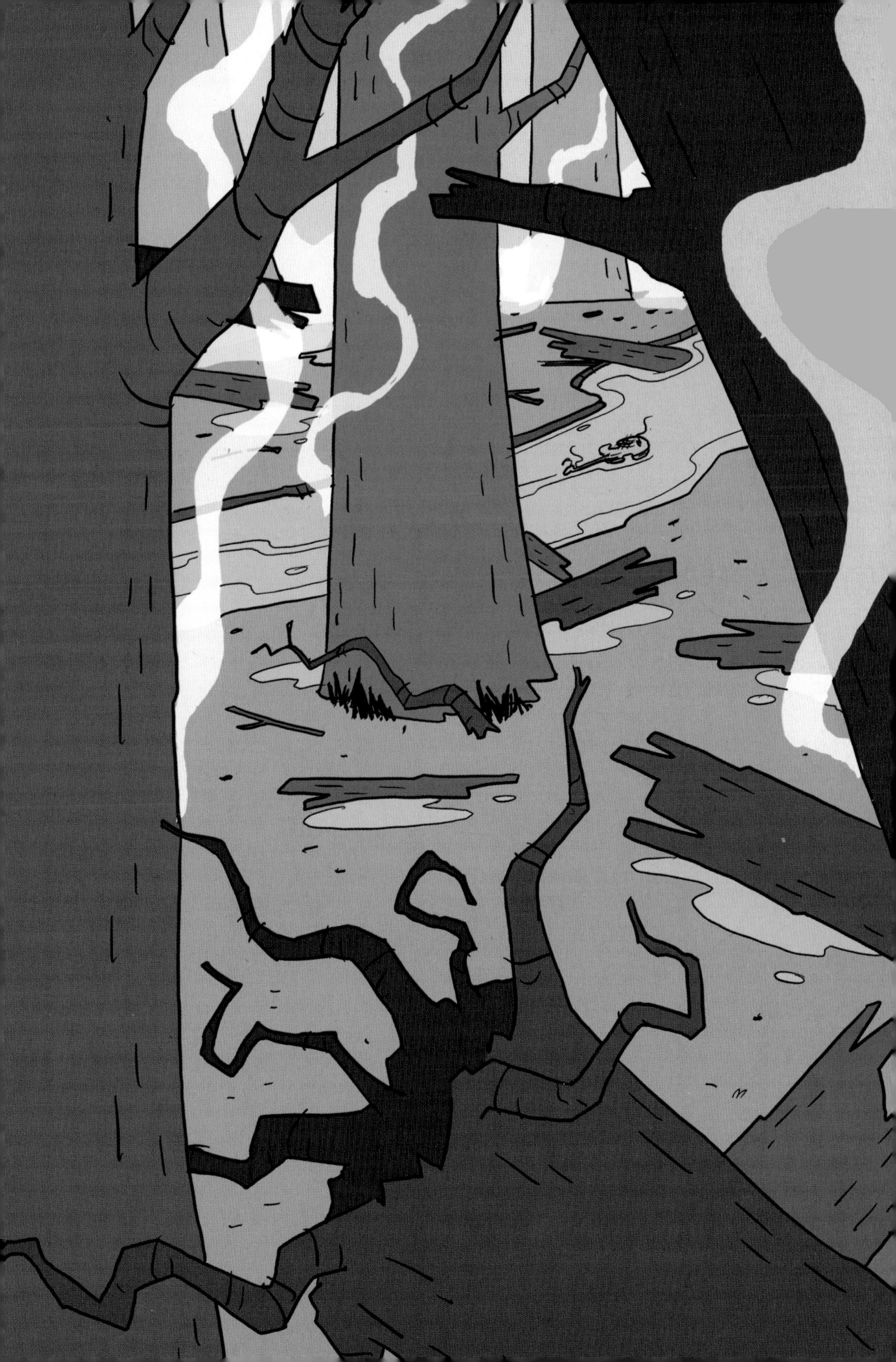

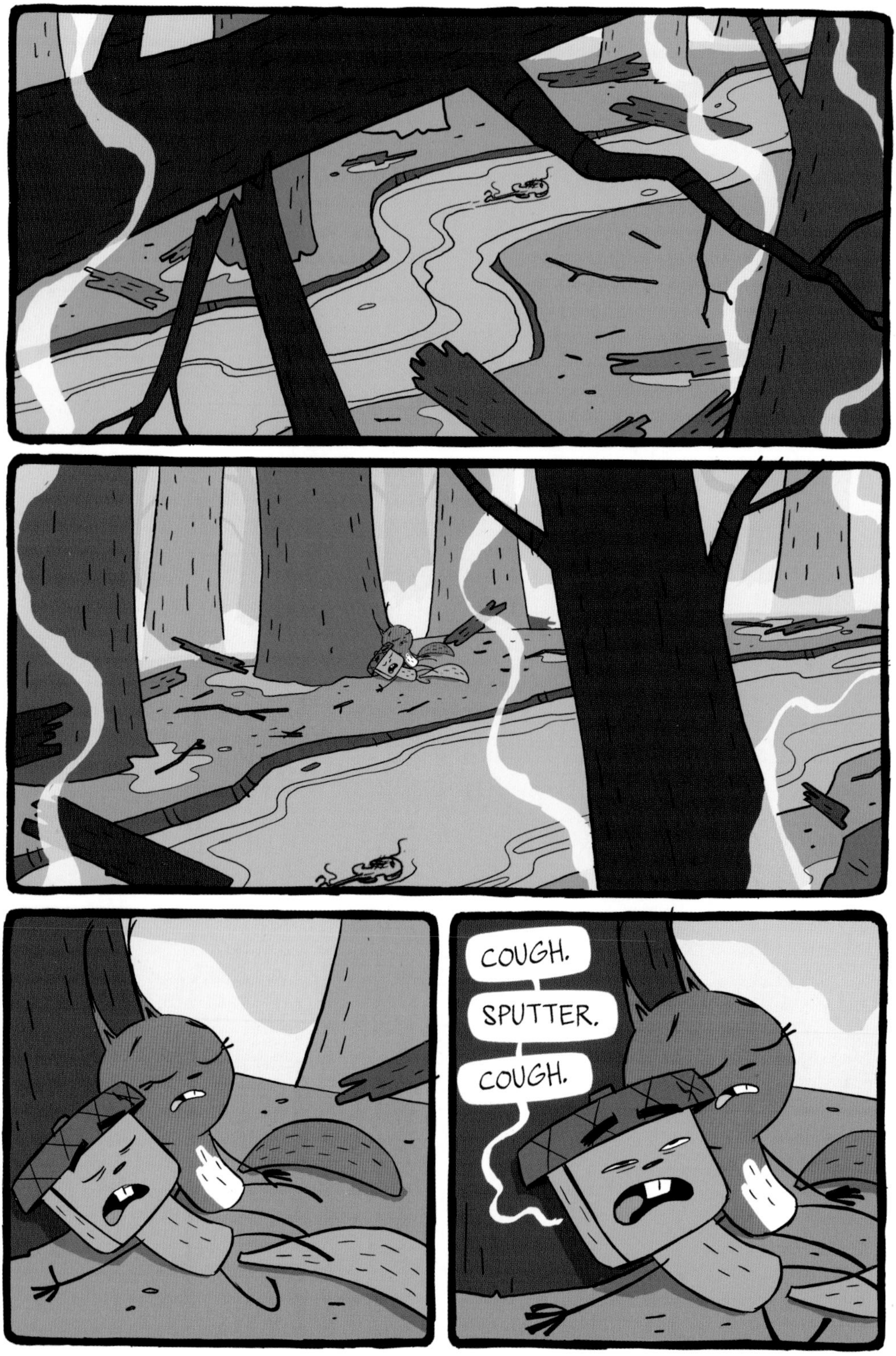
COUGH.
SPUTTER.
COUGH.

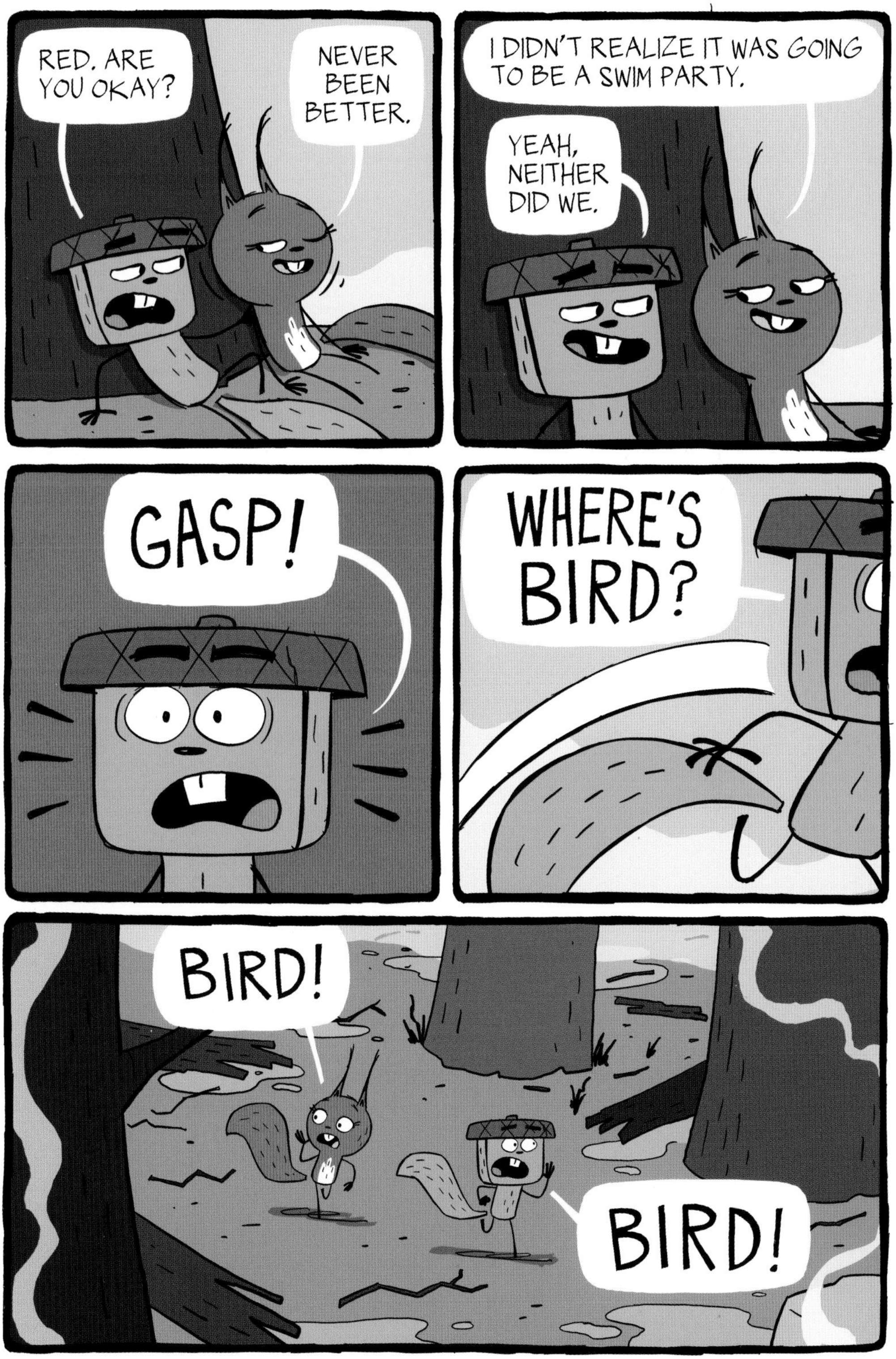
RED. ARE YOU OKAY?
NEVER BEEN BETTER.
I DIDN'T REALIZE IT WAS GOING TO BE A SWIM PARTY.
YEAH, NEITHER DID WE.
GASP!
WHERE'S BIRD?
BIRD!
BIRD!

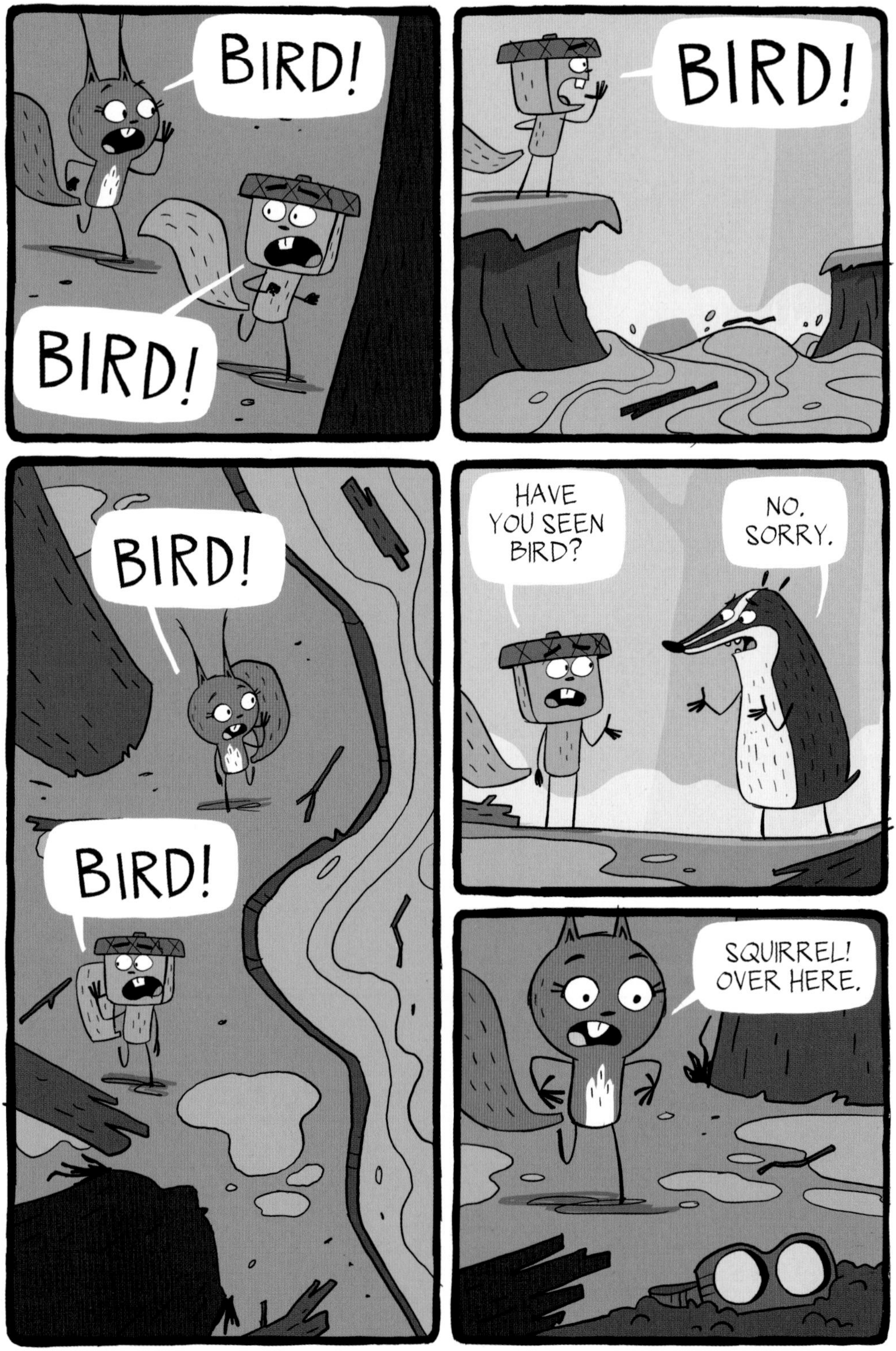
BIRD!
BIRD!
BIRD!
BIRD!
BIRD!
HAVE YOU SEEN BIRD?
NO. SORRY.
SQUIRREL! OVER HERE.

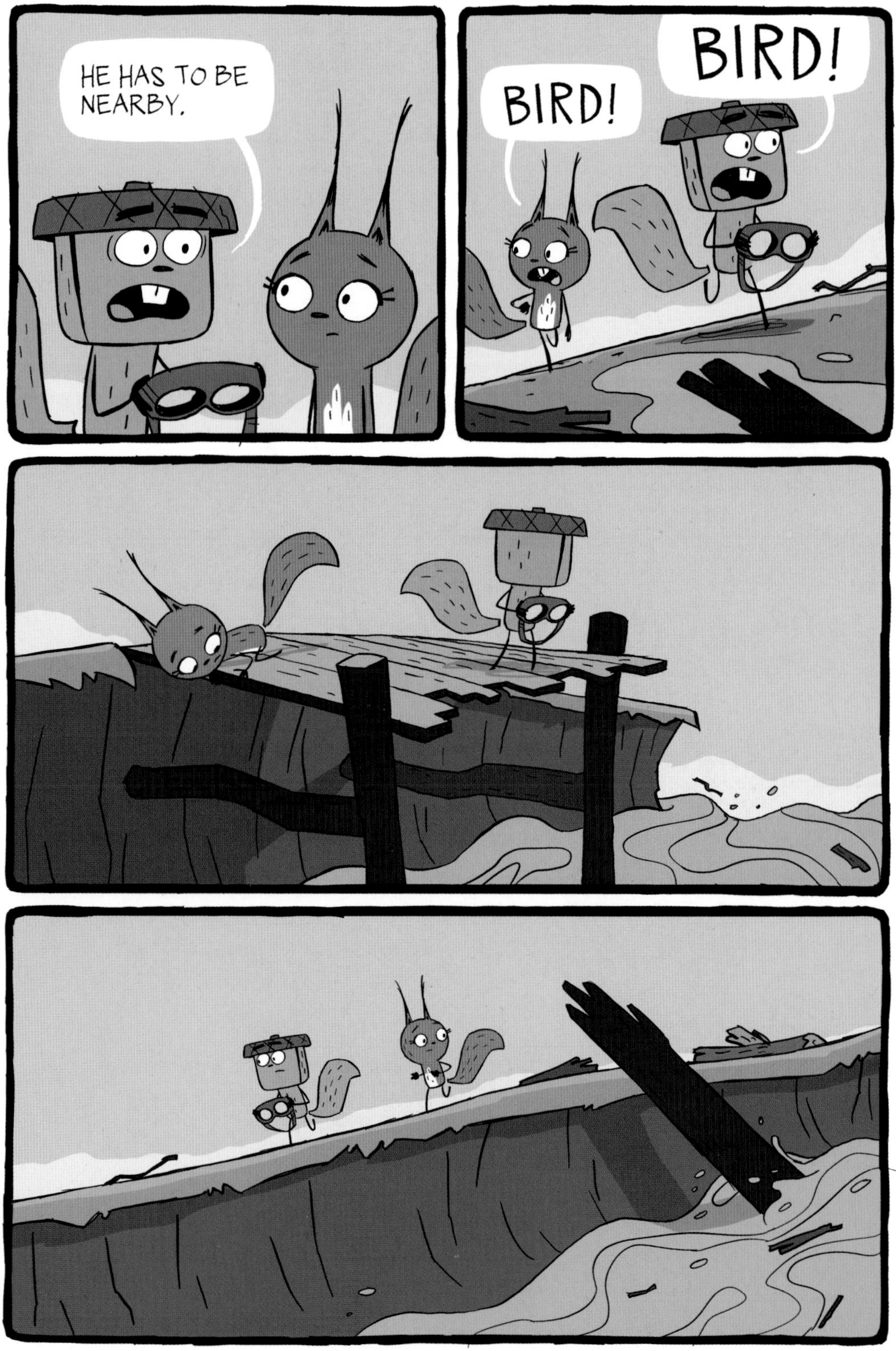
HE HAS TO BE NEARBY.
BIRD!
BIRD!

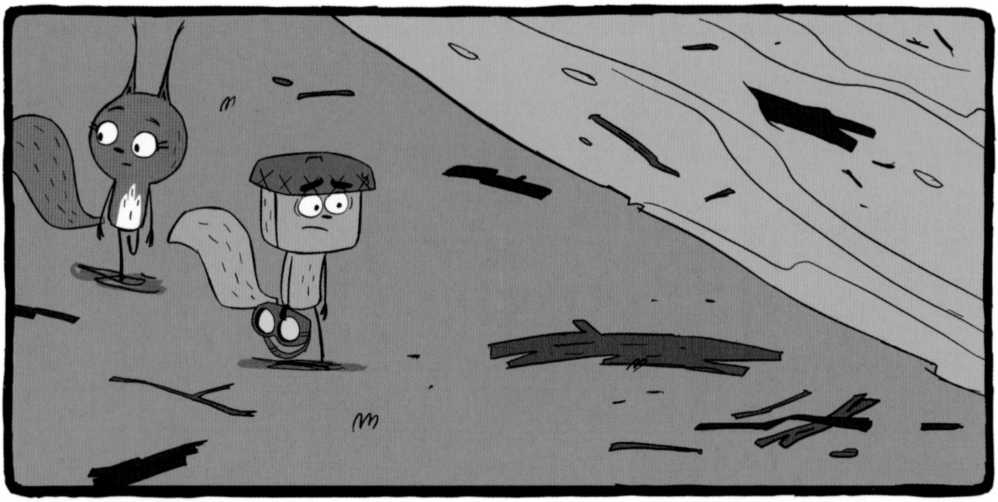

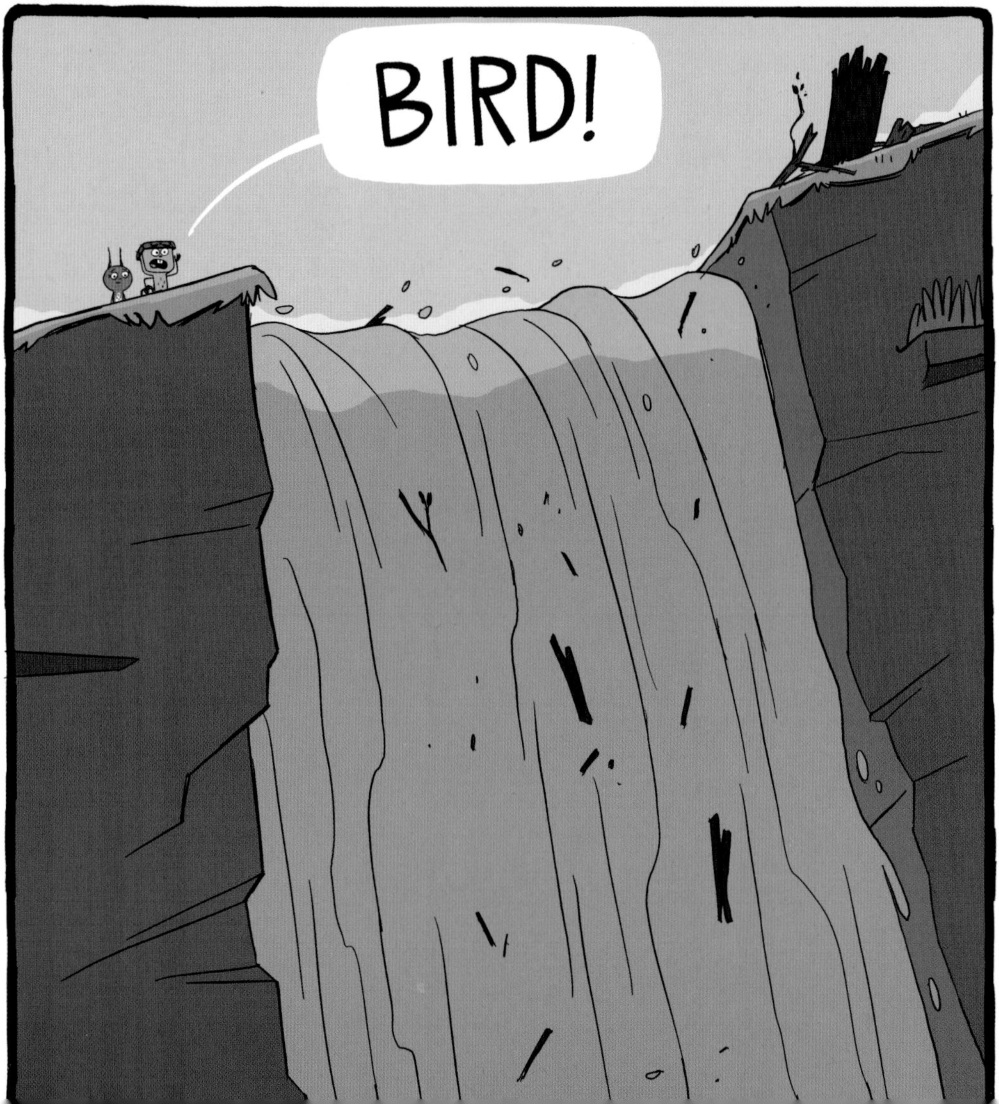
BIRD!

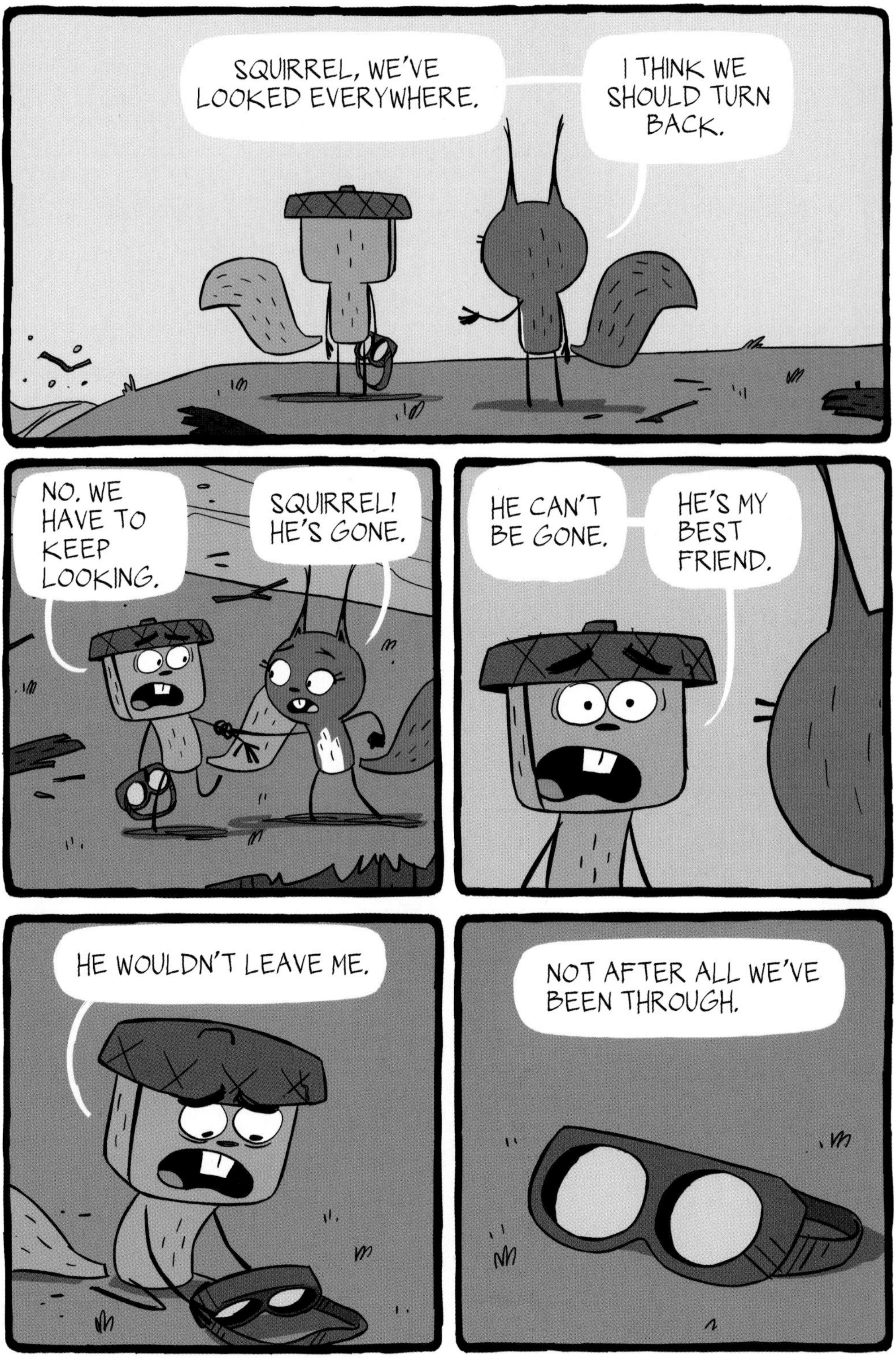
SQUIRREL, WE'VE LOOKED EVERYWHERE.
I THINK WE SHOULD TURN BACK.
NO. WE HAVE TO KEEP LOOKING.
SQUIRREL! HE'S GONE.
HE CAN'T BE GONE.
HE'S MY BEST FRIEND.
HE WOULDN'T LEAVE ME.
NOT AFTER ALL WE'VE BEEN THROUGH.

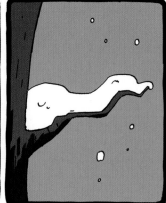

THREE SEASONS LATER...

ZOOOM

MORNING, BEE!

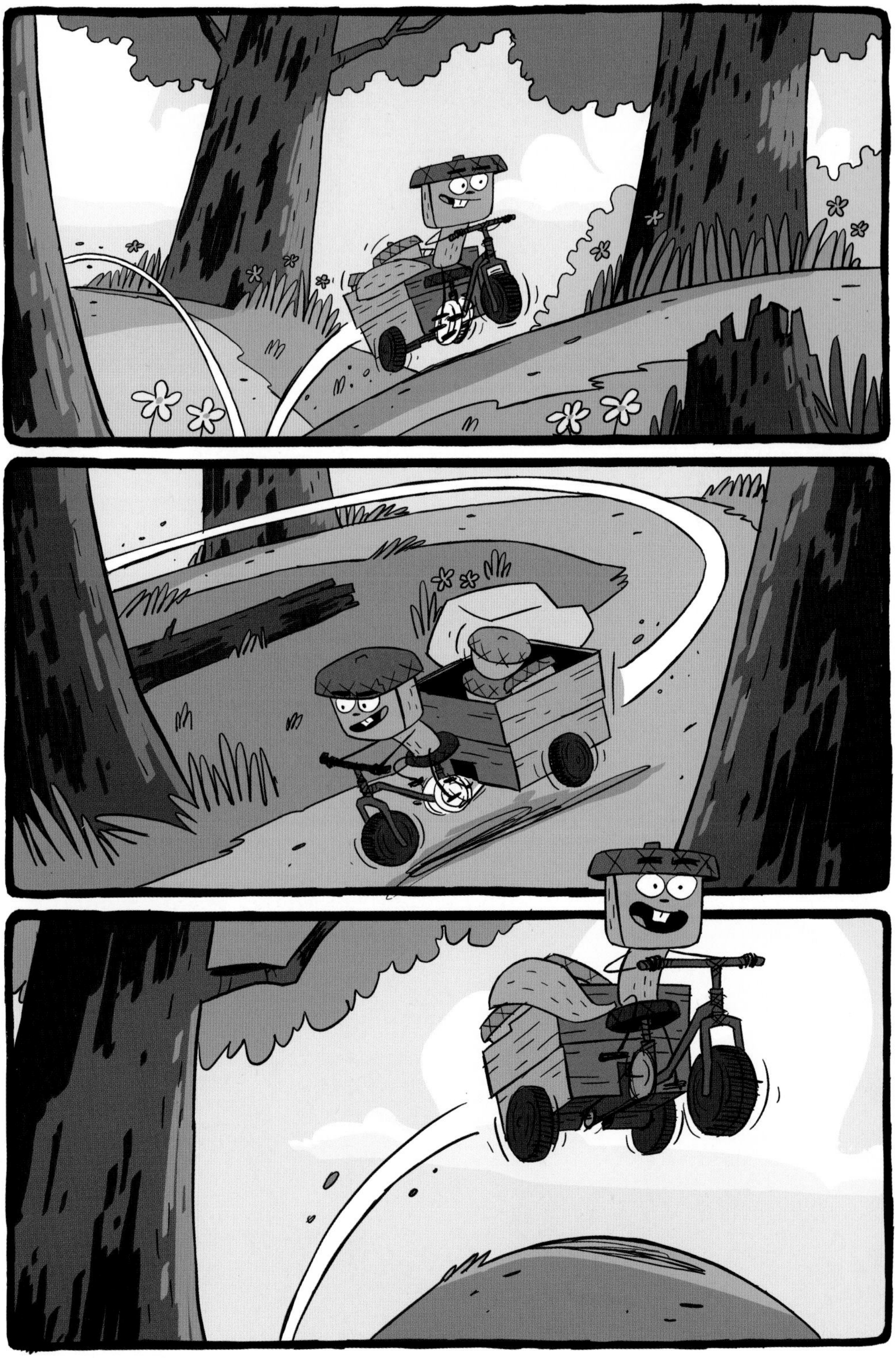

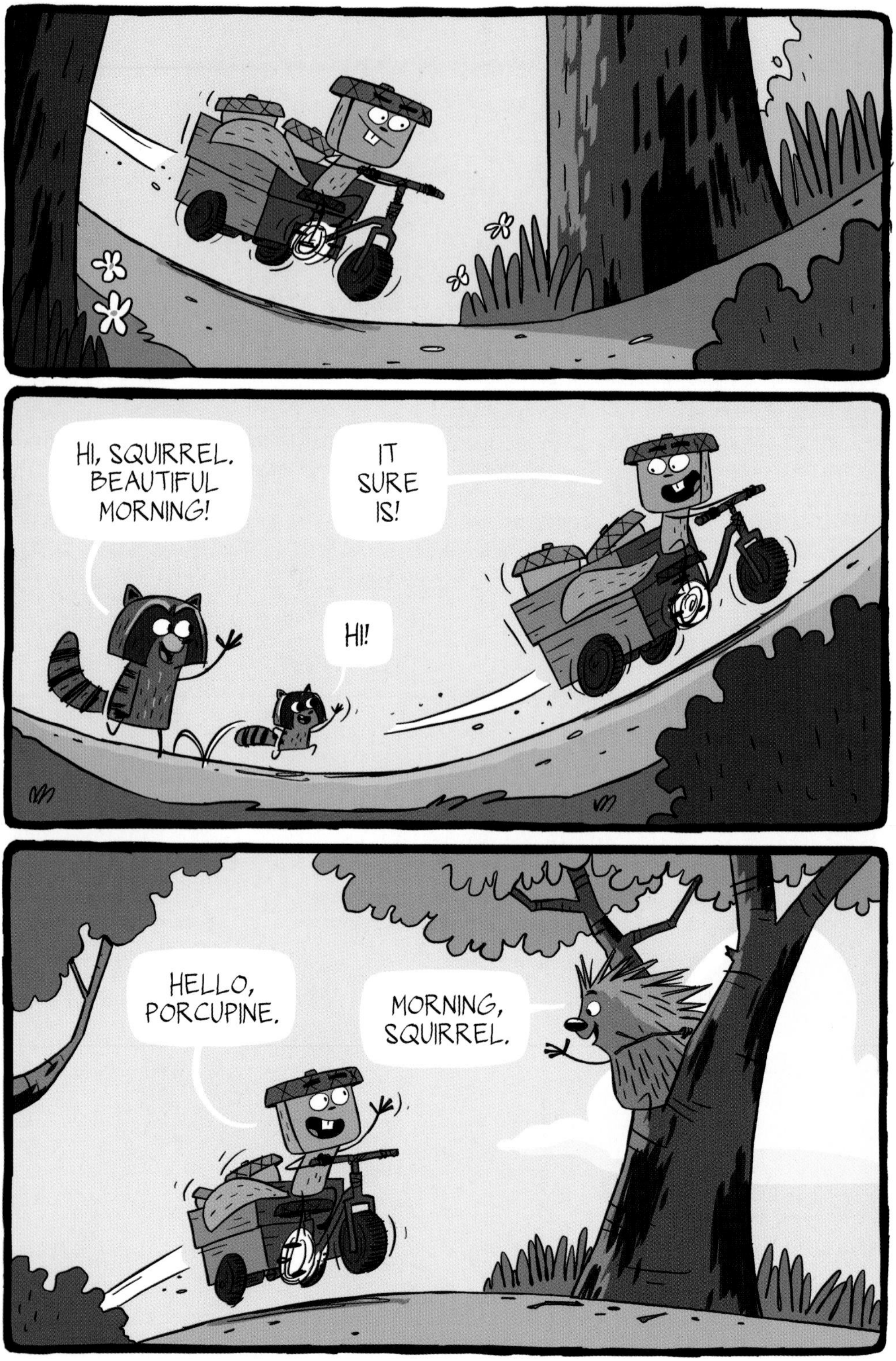
HI, SQUIRREL. BEAUTIFUL MORNING!
IT SURE IS!
HI!
HELLO, PORCUPINE.
MORNING, SQUIRREL.

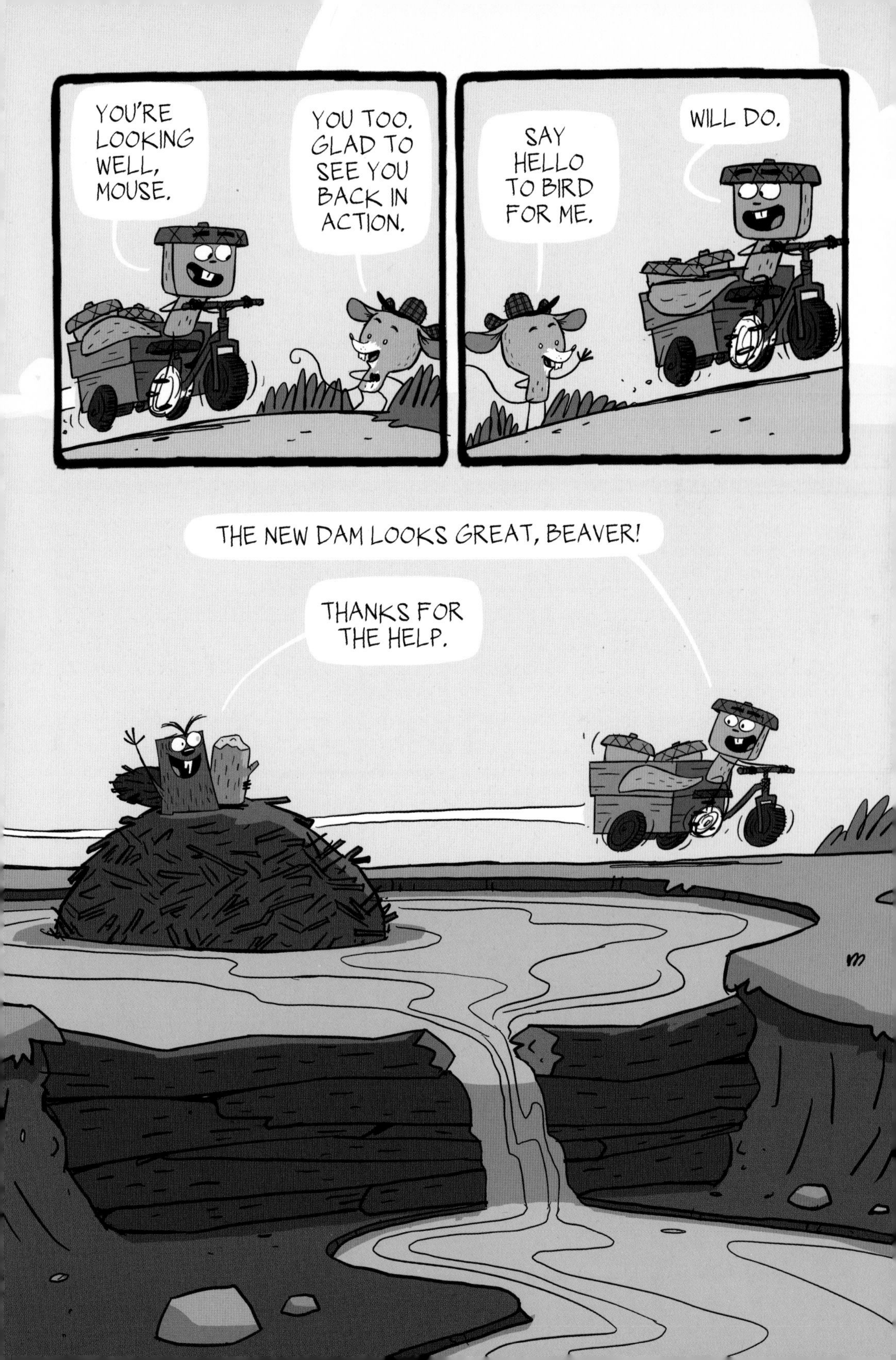
YOU'RE LOOKING WELL, MOUSE.
YOU TOO. GLAD TO SEE YOU BACK IN ACTION.
SAY HELLO TO BIRD FOR ME.
WILL DO.
THE NEW DAM LOOKS GREAT, BEAVER!
THANKS FOR THE HELP.

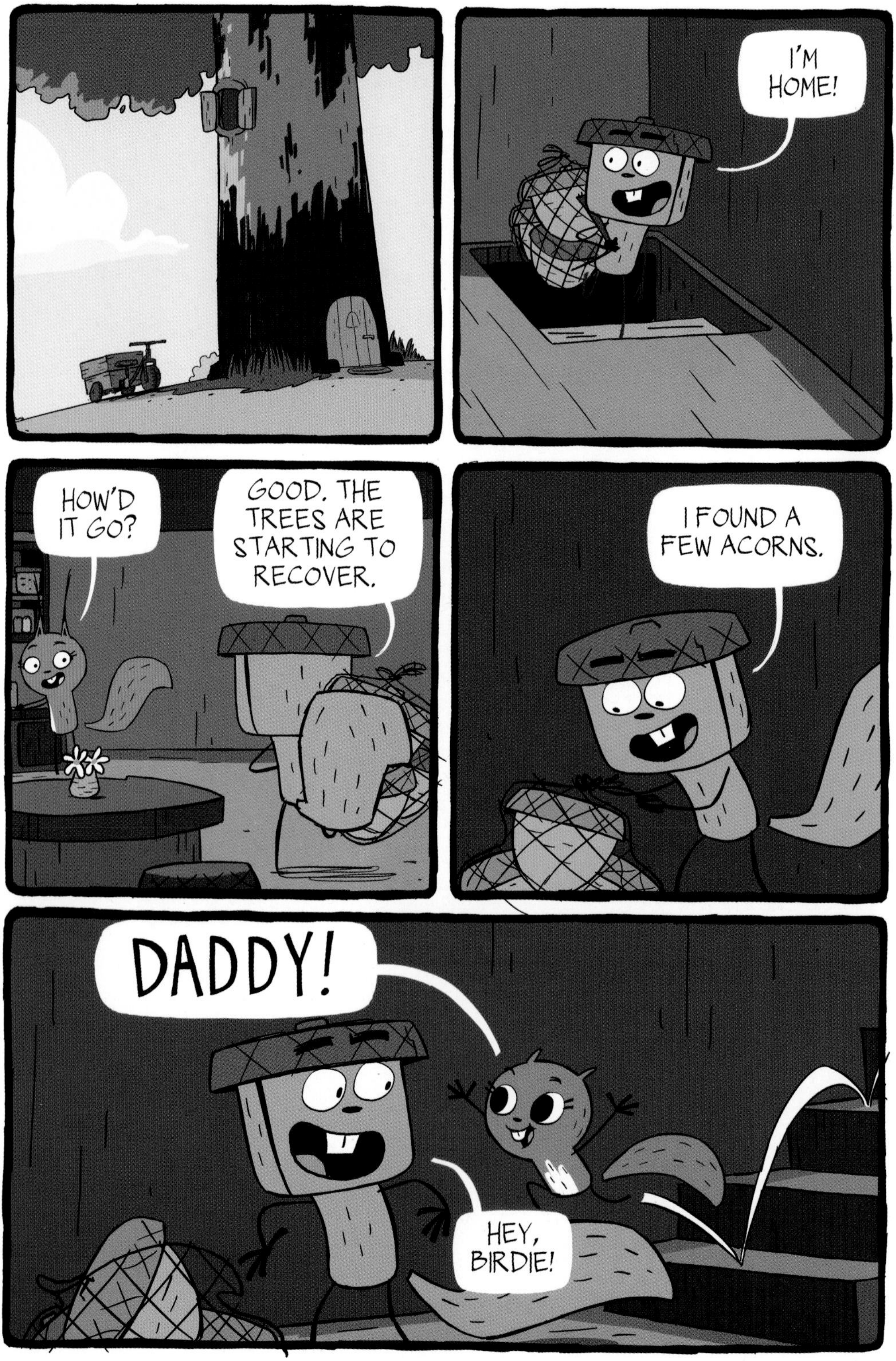
I'M HOME!
HOW'D IT GO?
GOOD. THE TREES ARE STARTING TO RECOVER.
I FOUND A FEW ACORNS.
DADDY!
HEY, BIRDIE!

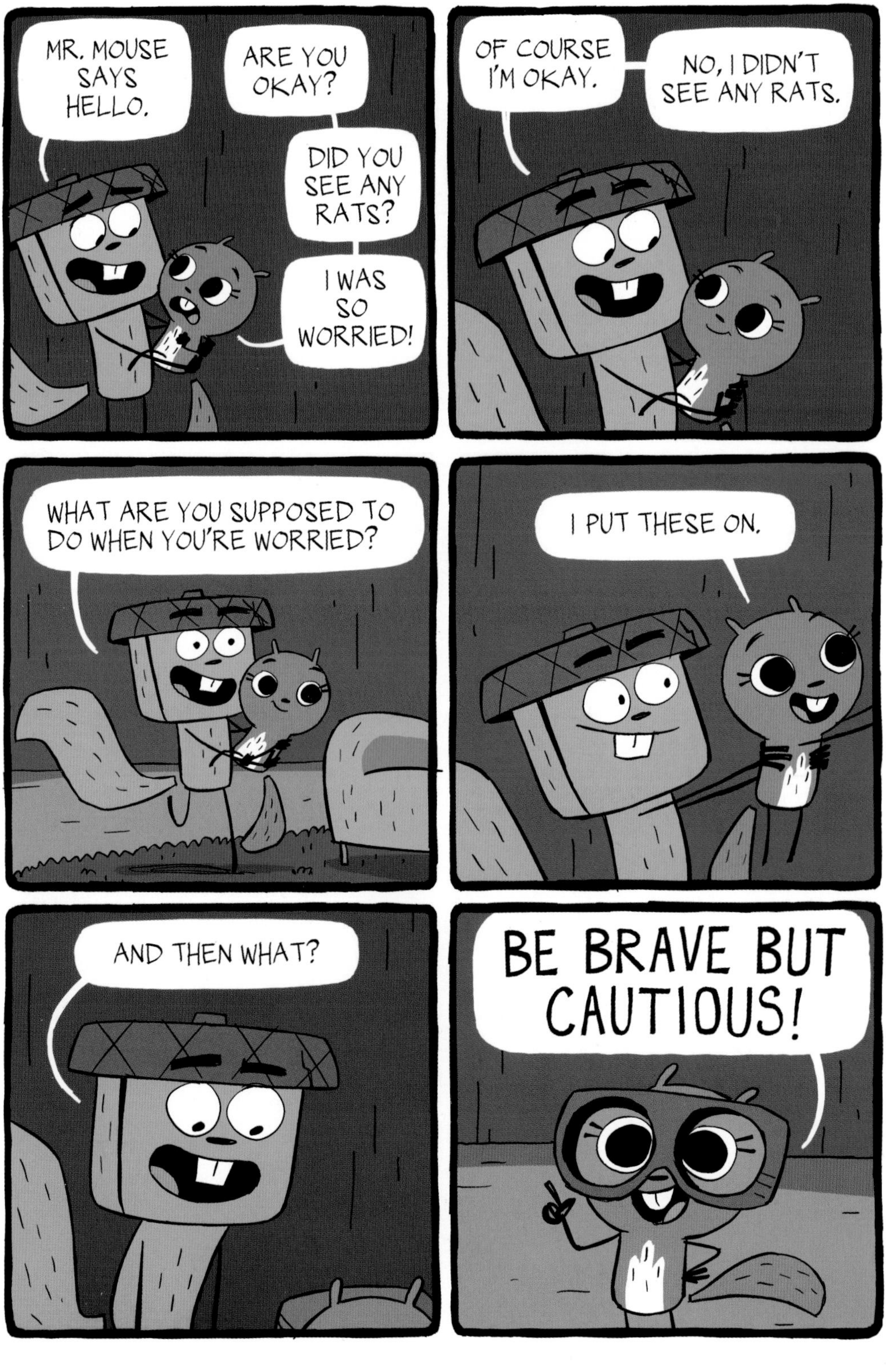
MR. MOUSE SAYS HELLO.
ARE YOU OKAY?
DID YOU SEE ANY RATS?
I WAS SO WORRIED!
OF COURSE I'M OKAY.
NO, I DIDN'T SEE ANY RATS.
WHAT ARE YOU SUPPOSED TO DO WHEN YOU'RE WORRIED?
I PUT THESE ON.
AND THEN WHAT?
BE BRAVE BUT CAUTIOUS!

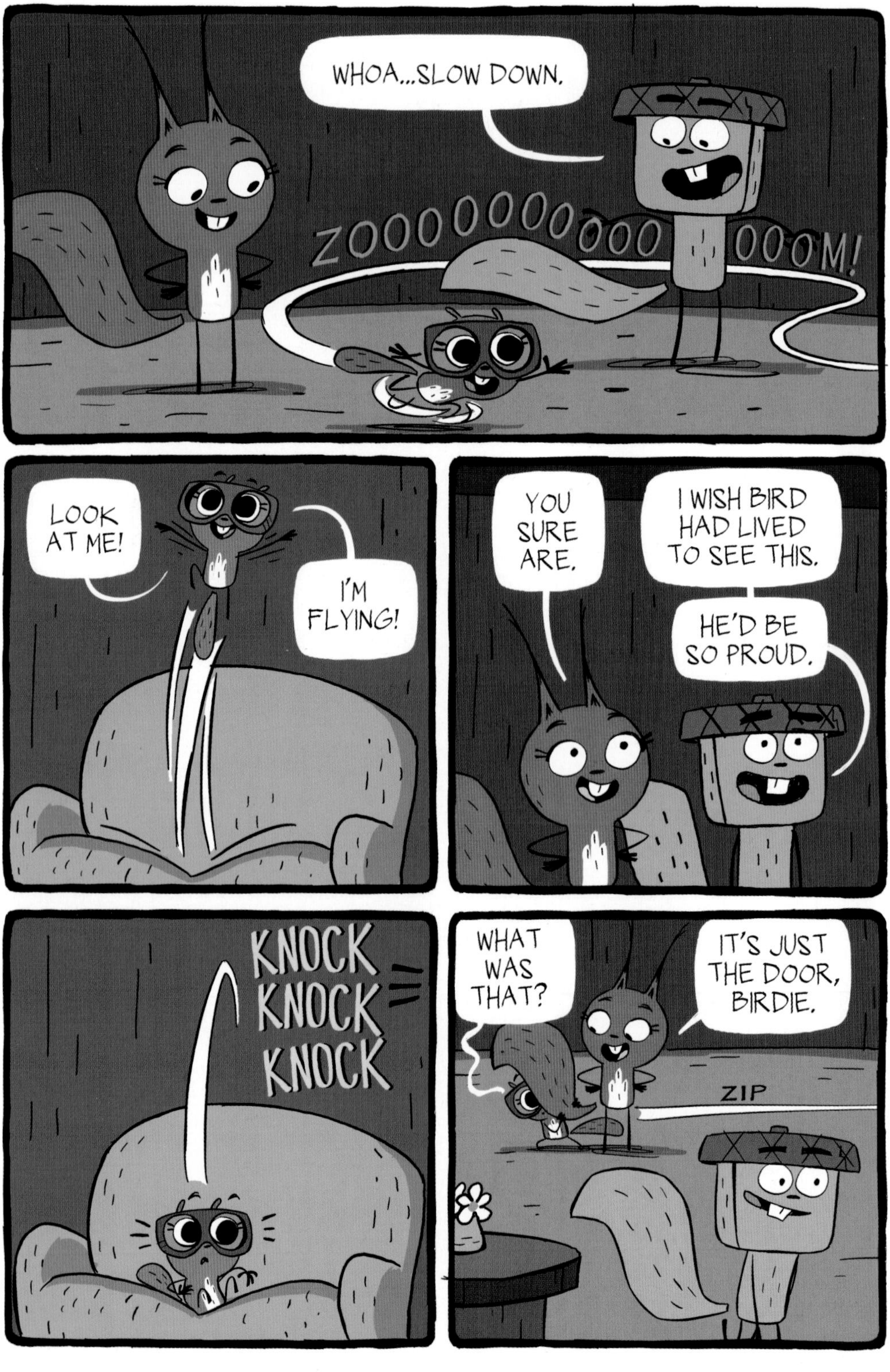
WHOA...SLOW DOWN.
ZOOOOOOOOOOOOOOOM!
LOOK AT ME!
I'M FLYING!
YOU SURE ARE.
I WISH BIRD HAD LIVED TO SEE THIS.
HE'D BE SO PROUD.
KNOCK KNOCK KNOCK
WHAT WAS THAT?
IT'S JUST THE DOOR, BIRDIE.
ZIP

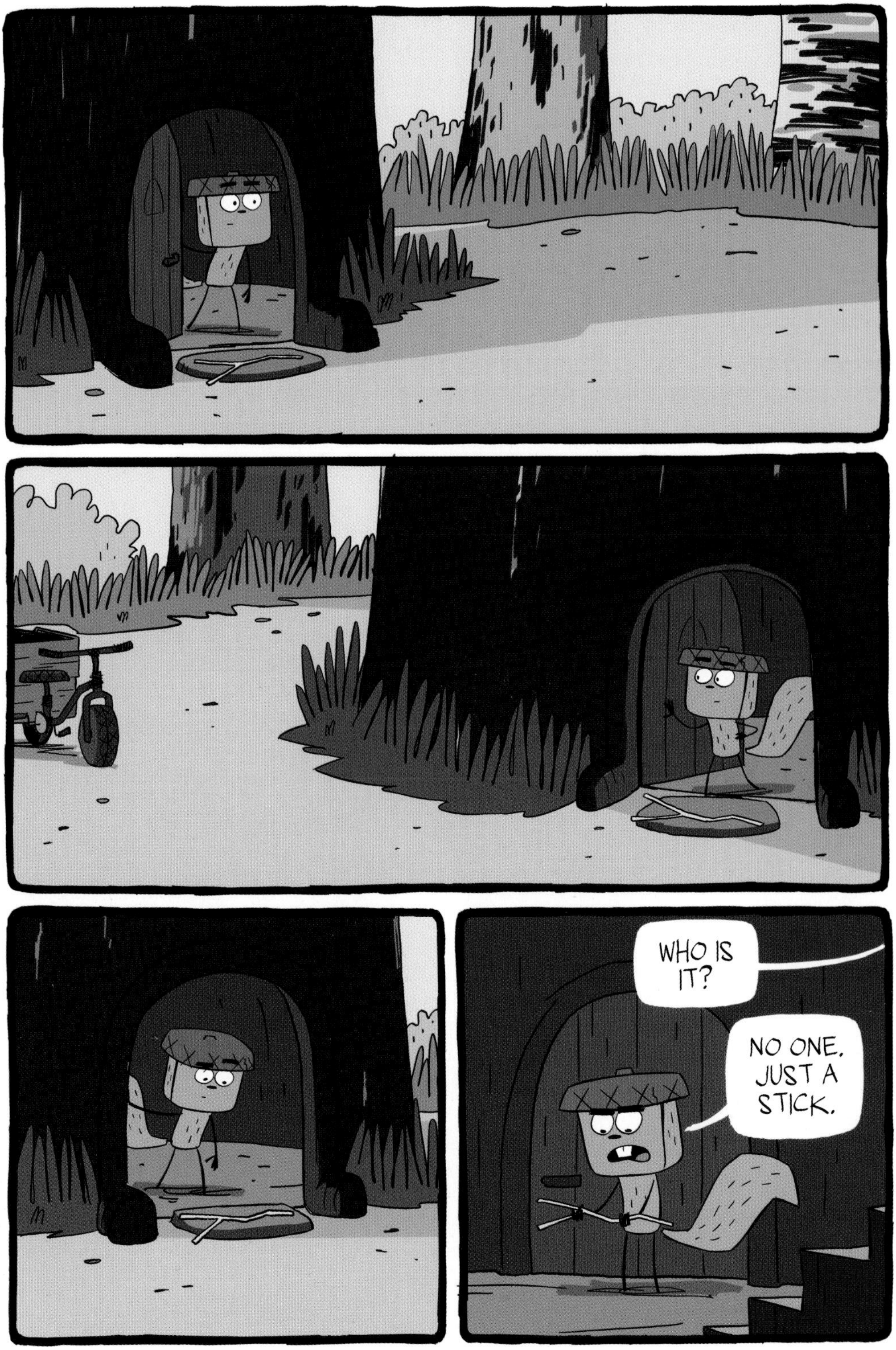
WHO IS IT?
NO ONE. JUST A STICK.

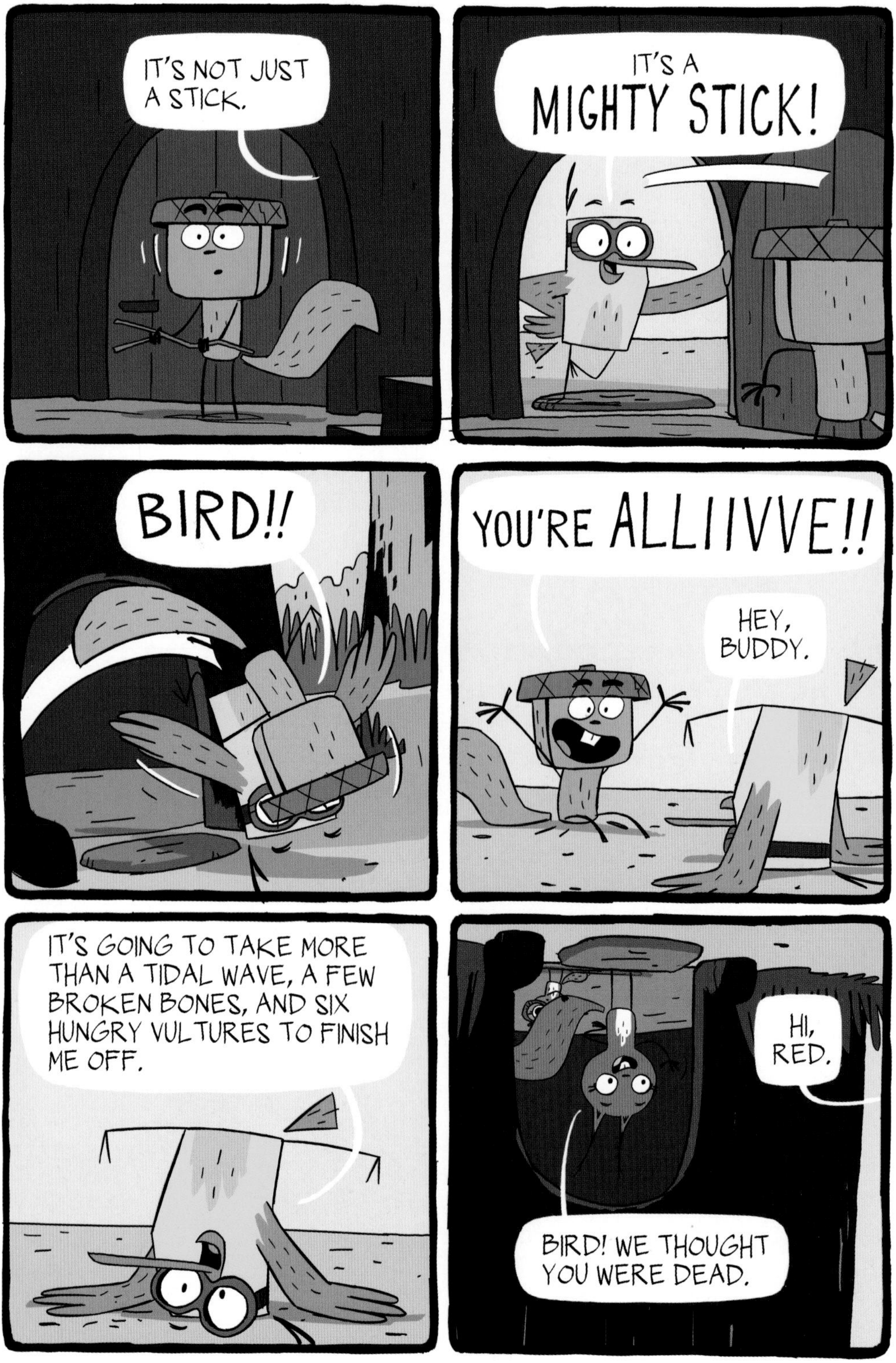
IT'S NOT JUST A STICK.
IT'S A MIGHTY STICK!
BIRD!!
YOU'RE ALLIIVVE!!
HEY, BUDDY.
IT'S GOING TO TAKE MORE THAN A TIDAL WAVE, A FEW BROKEN BONES, AND SIX HUNGRY VULTURES TO FINISH ME OFF.
BIRD! WE THOUGHT YOU WERE DEAD.
HI, RED.

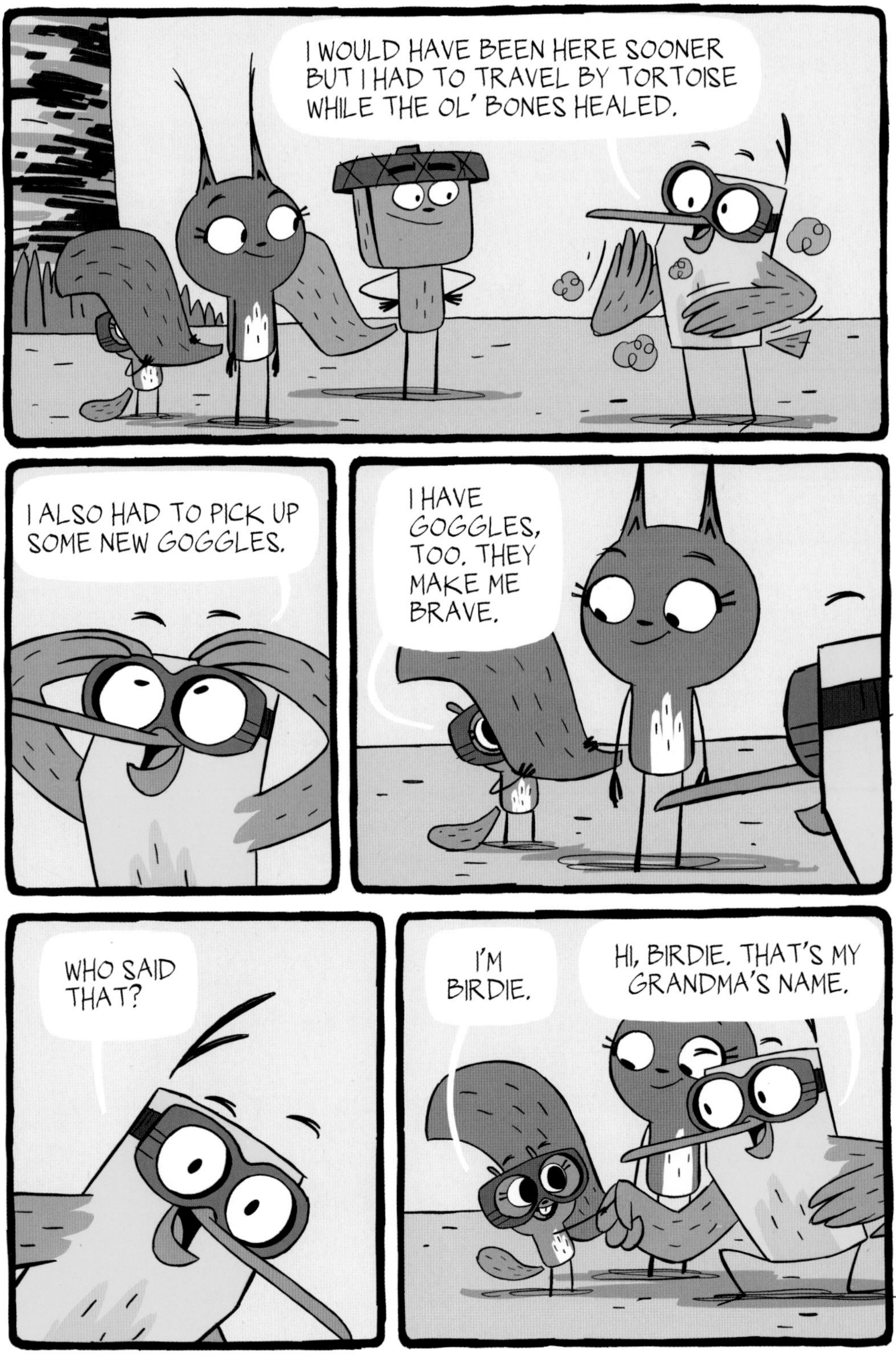
I WOULD HAVE BEEN HERE SOONER BUT I HAD TO TRAVEL BY TORTOISE WHILE THE OL' BONES HEALED.
I ALSO HAD TO PICK UP SOME NEW GOGGLES.
I HAVE GOGGLES, TOO. THEY MAKE ME BRAVE.
WHO SAID THAT?
I'M BIRDIE.
HI, BIRDIE. THAT'S MY GRANDMA'S NAME.

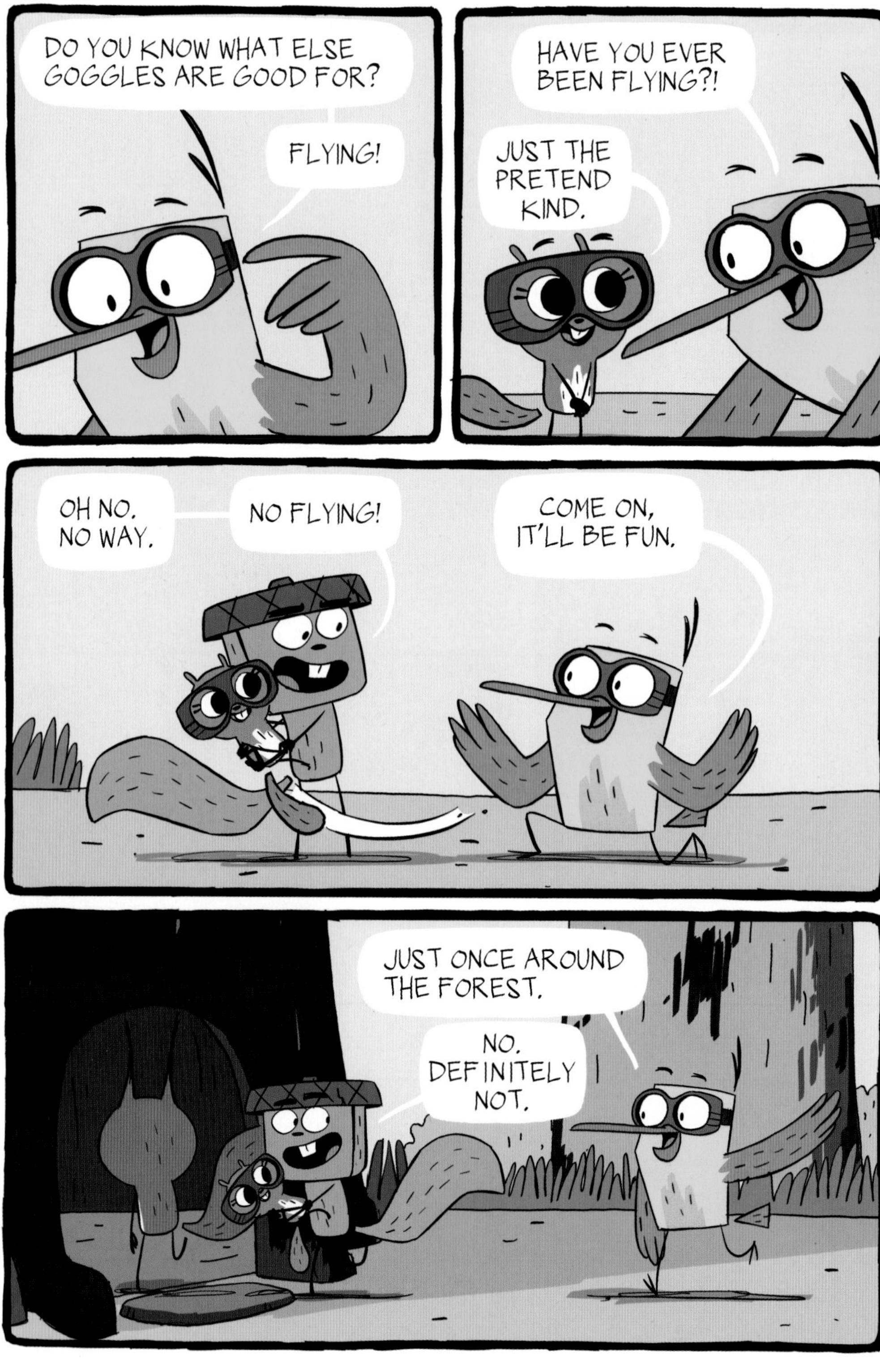
DO YOU KNOW WHAT ELSE GOGGLES ARE GOOD FOR?
FLYING!
HAVE YOU EVER BEEN FLYING?!
JUST THE PRETEND KIND.
OH NO. NO WAY.
NO FLYING!
COME ON, IT'LL BE FUN.
JUST ONCE AROUND THE FOREST.
NO. DEFINITELY NOT.

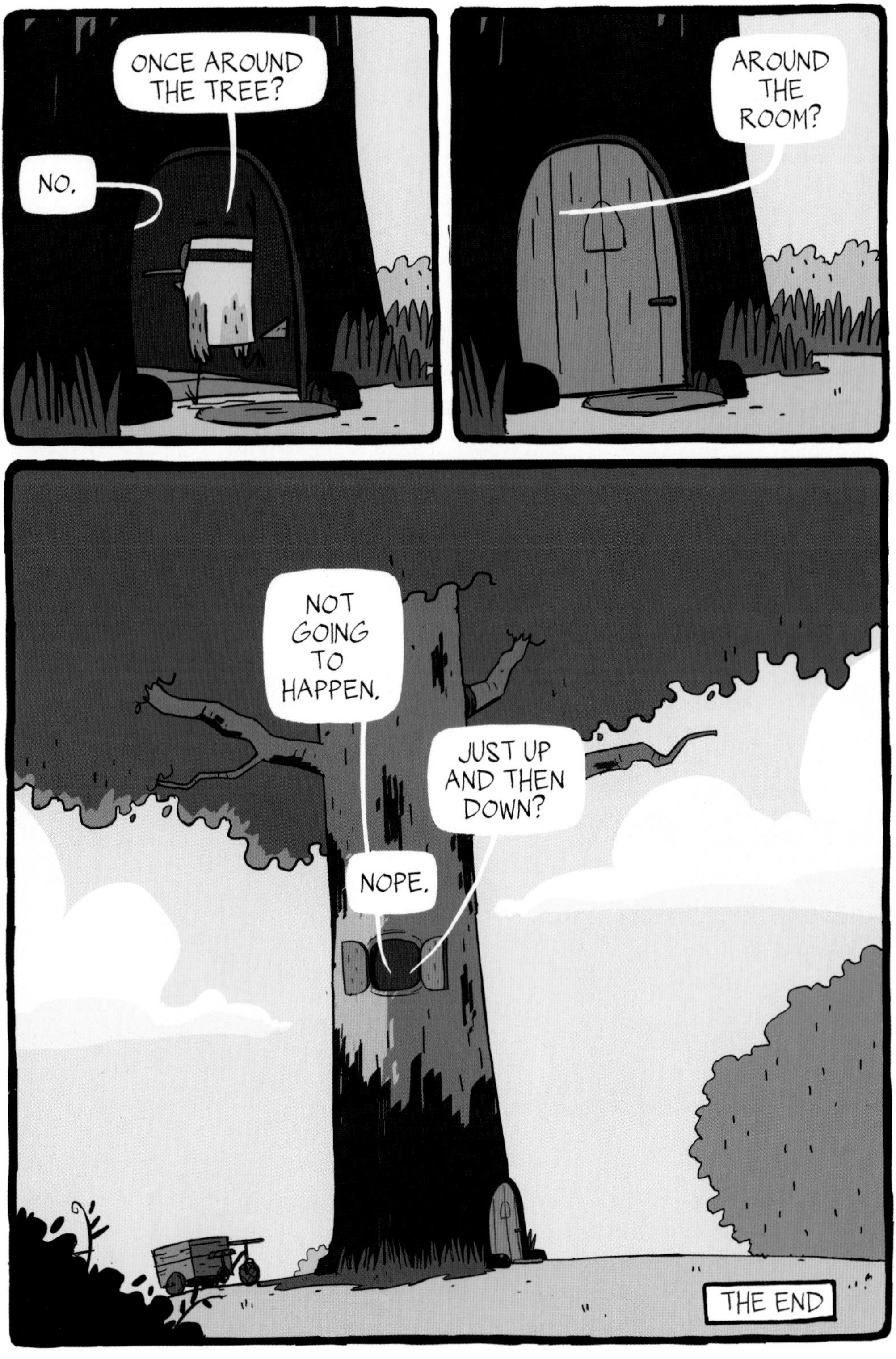
ONCE AROUND THE TREE?
NO.
AROUND THE ROOM?
NOT GOING TO HAPPEN.
JUST UP AND THEN DOWN?
NOPE.
THE END

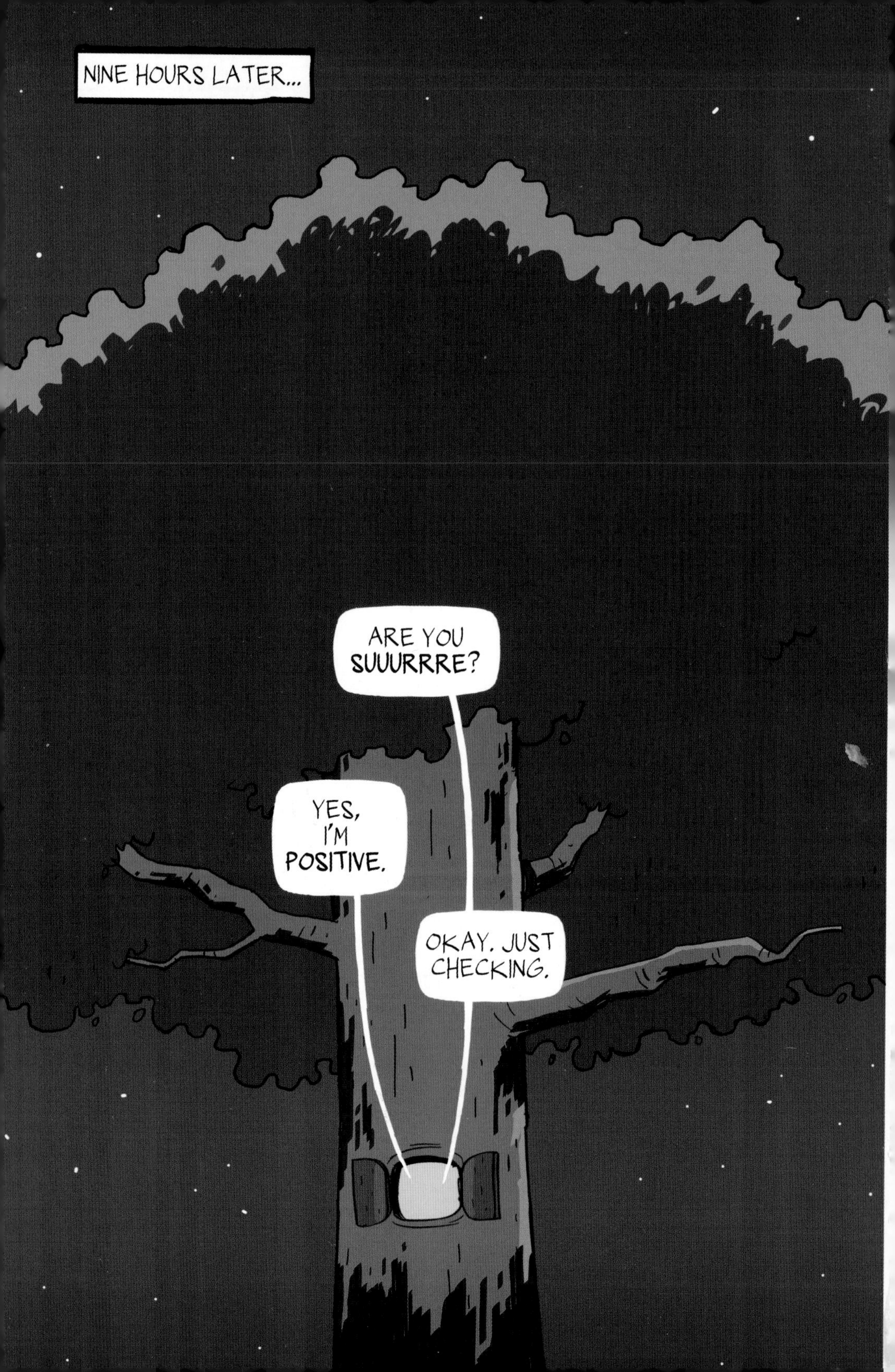
NINE HOURS LATER...
ARE YOU SUUURRRE?
YES, I'M POSITIVE.
OKAY. JUST CHECKING.